Major, Clarence.

rty bird blues.

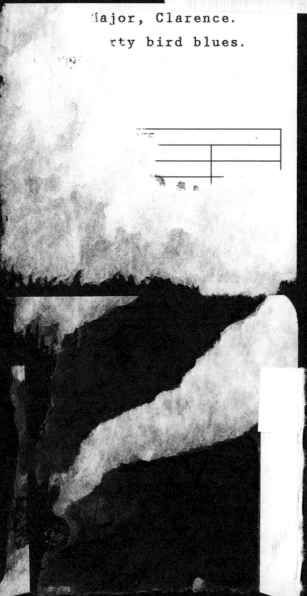

DIRTY

BIRD

BLUES

BY CLARENCE MAJOR

Dirty Bird Blues

Painted Turtle: Woman with Guitar

Such Was the Season

My Amputations

Emergency Exit

Reflex and Bone Structure

NO

All-Night Visitors

Fun & Games

Surfaces and Masks

Swallow the Lake

*Some Observations of a Stranger at Zuni in the
Latter Part of the Century*

Inside Diameter: The France Poems

The Syncopated Cakewalk

The Cotton Club

Private Line

Symptoms & Madness

Parking Lots

*The Dark and Feeling: Black American Writers
and Their Work*

*Calling the Wind: Twentieth Century African-American
Short Stories*

Dictionary of Afro-American Slang

Juba to Jive: A Dictionary of African-American Slang

The New Black Poetry

The Garden Thrives: Twentieth Century African-American Poetry

A NOVEL BY CLARENCE MAJOR

DIRTY BIRD BLUES

MERCURY HOUSE

SAN FRANCISCO

Published in the United States by Mercury House, San Francisco, California,
a nonprofit publishing company devoted to the free exchange of ideas and guided
by a dedication to literary values.

United States Constitution, First Amendment: Congress shall make no law
respecting an establishment of religion, or prohibiting the free exercise thereof; or
abridging the freedom of speech, or of the press; or the right of the people peaceably
to assemble, and to petition the Government for a redress of grievances.

Mercury House and colophon are registered trademarks of
Mercury House, Incorporated.

Design, typesetting in Adobe Sabon and Lithos, and crow motif
by Thomas Christensen.

Library of Congress Cataloging in Publication Data
Major, Clarence
Dirty bird blues : a novel / by Clarence Major. — 1st ed.
p.   cm.
ISBN 1-56279-083-8 (hardcover : alk. paper)
I. Title.
PS3563.A39D57   1996
813'.54—DC20   96-13310
CIP

5   4   3   2   1
FIRST EDITION

Endless thanks and love to you,
Duxie, all the way

and, Susan, thanks again and again
for not giving up, for having more faith
than I had, for the years—the long
time, like they say in the blues

and, Tom, thank you
for your vision

I love that woman,
I tell the world I do

—Traditional

"What I want to know is," he said,
"is you got the *dog?*"

—Ralph Ellison, *Invisible Man*

CHAPTER ONE

HE GOT THE WINDOW UP ABOUT twelve inches but it wouldn't move any more. Stuck. Then suddenly this big boom. And it came again real fast. A shotgun blast sho as hell. But he didn't feel anything. Then he thought, That nigger shooting at me. Preacher man shooting at somebody. Musta hit me too. Manfred felt something now. Can you beat that? Cleo in there and she let that nigger shoot me. Nigger done shot me.

Man couldn't feel much because he was still sailing high, the good liquor coating him from the hawk, the howling, now the gunshot wounds. Snow up-to-the-ass cold, colder than a witch's behind up here, cold as embalmed lovers still locked together, colder than Staggerlee's grin.

But he squatted there still trying to force the window, feeling so goddamned sick and drunk and mad at Cleo in there like that, his woman with his kid, in another man's home on Christmas Eve. Another man eating his jelly roll, another man grinding his coffee. My baby saying Daddy to nother man. Use that nigger to mop up a greasy floor, make that nigger think a mob of Georgia crackers lynching his ass, work my mojo on that nigger, pistol-whip that nigger till he bleed green pee. Make that nigger look like a pot of gumbo filé when I gets done with em.

Already Man was feeling these funny little prickly things mainly on the right side of his chest and across his stomach.

And he could hear her voice in there—Cleo screaming—that sharp, high sound of hers, and all this scuffling about.

Then just about that time he got his hand inside his shirt and felt this wet blood on his stomach. Blood serious shit. It talk to ya.

But he didn't get scared or anything, scared of dying, because he knew it wasn't all that serious, serious like a real heavy bullet, just these little buckshots. He knew buckshots from when he was little down South, shooting buckshots at rabbits.

And he thought, Sissy motherfucker shot me with buckshots. Felt like a whole lot of red ants stinging. Except even then, feeling the stinging, he didn't know for sure he was hit till he felt inside his shirt and touched his own blood.

Ain't no reason to fear dying—dying ain't nothing but sleeping without waking up. Because it was like the time he'd seen his own blood

1

coming out of him in his piss, that time, watching it going into the toilet, and his best friend with him, Solly, his buddy, saying, Fred you dying, you better get yoself to some kind of motherfucking hospital fo you drop dead out here on these goddamned streets.

But there wasn't anything to worry about and he was right and the blood-in-the-piss stopped in a few days and he never did have to go to a doctor. He thought: Heap of times thought I had to go to a doctor and didn't.

He yanked at the window. You can have the Chicago Monkey Man Blues and still be all right. You can be down and out like a yellow dog, at the end of the Yazoo Mississippi line and still feel like shouting, Jelly, jelly, mama, roll me some of yo good biscuits, let me hoe in yo cabbage patch. Took a lot to get a good man down. Good man gon keep on keeping on, ain't studying about giving up, no matter what. Death call a good man, good man say, Hold on Death, I be there directly but I'm fixing to do something else right now. Got to take care this little bit of business.

And he kept right on trying to get that motherfucking window open that Christmas Eve now because the man inside had shot him and he wanted to get to him more than ever. He'd break that preacher's head open. But he didn't have anything to break the glass with but his hand so he took off his jacket and wrapped it around his fist and pulled back and sent his fist into that glass like it was lightning striking, like the Chesapeake-Ohio shooting down the track.

Now the preacher started firing again. And this time he got Man in the chest again, this time more to the left. So Manfred stopped. Think, think man, think. Nigger's got a shotgun. You got nothing but yo fists. Wait till you can get him on your own terms. Take yo time. Wait. Don't get a hole shot in yo ticker or yo airbags. Don't argufy with the facts.

So he fell back away from the window, and resting his back against the steps going up to the next floor, he got back into his wool jacket and crawled down the fire escape. Wait to a better day. Lord, Lord. Wait till a better day. Time. Take yo time. And a song half-forming, or half-remembered—Little woman I just don't know why you treat me the way you do.

All right. Down in the alley he stopped, stooped over from the wind and buttoned his coat. A sprinkle of snow fell on him like quivering, weightless concrete. But he thought the liquor had him feeling warm—

> If I was a fish
> And the river was whiskey,
> I say, if I was a fish
> And the river was whiskey . . .

At least he didn't feel anything, but he knew he needed to get his ass to a hospital or somewhere, suddenly remembering one of last night's dreams about Madam Gazella Bellamy unzipping his pants, looking at it, saying, "You're a man now, boy," and the rest of it going to hell. Too young to die out here on these Chicago streets. And now the sharp memory of Madam Gazella rubbing Highest Quality Attraction Oil on her whores and sprinkling Jinx Removing Powder around their beds. He had to laugh. Lord, have mercy.

So he hit Sixty-third and ducked across under night lights, hoping like hell he wouldn't see anybody he knew, not even Solly. He heard the jukebox music coming from the Red Tiger and Ducky Wucky's, one stomping a Trixie Smith–type freight train beat, the other laying into a cool daddy jazz sound. Jazz was all right but he couldn't feel it like he could him some blues. And he was suddenly thinking about his *Sixty-Third Street Blues* song. Made up that summer, hearing the words. How'd it go? In rhythm to his walking—Up and down the main drag, the dope man hustles his bag. Up and down the main drag, the dope man hustles his bag.

> In any bar I can get a drink.
> In any bar I can get me a drink.
> The pretty womens they all give me a wink.
> Yeah, all the pretty womens they give me a wink.
>
> You can dance all night
> Till you think yo heart gon break.
> Dance all night long, dance, dance,
> Till you think yo heart gon break.
> You can wiggle all night like a snake.
> Yeah, you can wiggle all night just like a snake.

Yeah. Get anything you want on the strip, including a busted lip, yeah, if you ain't careful you get a busted lip. Got to boogie. Got to boogie hard. Nothing could stop him now. Like old folks said, like walking to Glory. Headed for that nigger hospital, Booker T. Washington Memorial, up on Stoney Island and Seventy-ninth where they say they had this Emergency Room. He'd never been in there but Cleo took the baby there all the time. Baby born at Cook County General. And he'd walked her to the door once. Running now through the snow, he felt like he'd been embalmed, weightless, without pain. Just like singing the blues. Lord, have mercy.

Along the way, he was hip to people staring at him. Three pretty

3

young women, strolling along with arms locked, started giggling. A man in a gray wool newsboy's cap and white spats carrying a cane passed him and turned up his nose. Two boys in his path fist-fighting with three or four other boys watching, calling out, "Duke him down, Jackie, duke him down," and "Get em in the mouth, Buddy, the mouth, Buddy." Scuffling, grunting, swinging arms, blood flying. Man had to make his way around cars to get past them. A guard, standing in a doorway eyeing him suspiciously, spoke. Man tried to grin as he nodded to an elderly woman in a heavy black coat walking by in the opposite direction carrying a big bag. Group of church sisters, heads covered with white cloths, marching toward the fighting boys calling out to them.

But there he was getting his shot-up ass into the black hospital that Christmas night, feeling just like a motherless child. In the doorway stood this woman leaning against the wall. Her nose bleeding. Two little scared boys about ten and twelve, her sons, he reckoned, holding her arms, pulling at her, trying to get her to go inside. And she's crying and just sobbing like somebody dying. Po woman. He felt sorry for her. He stopped and said to the tallest boy, "What wrong?" And the boy said his mama was hurt. What happened? His daddy went upside her head. Where was the daddy? The boys didn't know. Man took the lady's arm and tugged at it a little bit, "Miss, why don't you come on in and get yo-self took care of? Huh? Come on." And she looked up at him with a stream of snot hanging from her nose. Her eyes were swollen so bad they were closed nearly all the way. She was kind of peeking at him out of one small opening in the puff of the left one.

"What's that on your jacket?" said the tallest boy.

People were going and coming, just like shadows, up the walkway, down the walkway, under the canopy.

Man glanced at an old woman whose head was covered with the hood of a black raincoat as she came out of the hospital pushing a large baby carriage. In his glance his eye picked up a strange element. He looked again, this time at the baby carriage, and continued to gaze at it as it approached. When the carriage was in touching distance, he saw clearly that it contained another old—toothless, grinning—woman who looked just like the one doing the pushing. Seeing his confusion, she started cackling, then, speaking directly to him, said, "Everybody look that way when they see us. She my twin!"

"I said what's that on your jacket?"

"Huh?" He looked at the boy, then down at his jacket, at the blood stains. He had gotten a lot of it on the front of the jacket back there when he was buttoning up, got it on from his hands. Must have wiped his hands on the jacket. "I got hurt," he told the boy, shifting his eyes away.

But thinking, fuck, this kinda hurt ain't nothing. Got a big flock of hurts flying round in my head like them nervous starlings and just as noisy.

Then he saw the woman looking down at his blood. And between sobbings she said, "Ain't you something?"

"Come on. Come on, lady. Take her arm, boy." He touched her arm so she knew he wanted to help her.

◉

The jammed-packed waiting room smelled of vomit and piss. Turned his stomach. He kept getting up to go outside for a blast of fresh air. He wasn't hurt that bad so he could walk pretty good. He just felt some discomfort when he walked too fast. That was all. Shit, buckshots ain't nothing.

A brown-skinned nurse with unblinking eyes came to the waiting room carrying a clipboard. Said, "Anybody shot or cut deeper than an inch?"

The room was full. He expected many of them to raise their hands. But was surprised when he was the only one.

"Can you walk?" she said. She looked at him like he was a door or a wall. Nobody knows the shit I done seen. Lord knows.

He stood up. "Yeah." Nobody knows.

A youngster came into the room with a wheelchair.

The nurse turned to him and said, "That's all right. This one can walk."

The folk in the waiting room laughed. He wasn't sure what was funny. If he can walk he can dance, if he can dance he can sing and holler. Laugh, you fools.

"Come with me," the nurse said. Didn't crack a smile. All business.

Man followed her into a little shabby office off the waiting room.

A heavyset black policeman was there. "Sit down," the cop said. She sat next to the cop.

Man sat facing them. Both of them on the other side of this long table looking at him like he was a side a beef and they were trying to figure how to cut and preserve him.

"Who shot you and why?" the cop said.

He opened his mouth but the words weren't coming out. His story wasn't that easy, to just spill out like the cop wanted him to. Then Man didn't want to say anything to make it worse than it needed to be. So he lied, "I don't know. I was just walking down the street—" Walking down the street with the empty pocket blues, walking my blues away, singing a reel, a hungry, lowdown, made-up, sinful reel.

The cop, grim as old grits, pushed a sheet of paper across the table. "Fill out this form."

"You can write can't you?" said the nurse.

"I knows how to write." He didn't like the way she was looking at him.

"You need'n get huffy about it. Half the people coming through here can't." She kept looking at him like that, like she didn't like him. Then she said, "You got any insurance?"

He told her no, thinking, Ain't got a lot to carry, but one of these days, peoples, I'm telling you, I'm gon be gone. Lord, Lord.

"Another charity case. Please go ahead and fill out the form. In the blank where it asks for insurance write the letters *N O*."

Now she was making him real mad, thinking, If I ever get on my feet these people ain't gon treat me this way. Get my chance, get my chance. Rag, baby, rag. Sun's gon shine.

The policeman said, "When you come out of surgery there will be a couple of officers who will want to talk with you."

All right. He didn't say anything to this. He was writing his name. And he was thinking: I got to mend my ways. Lord knows. Get my chance and mend my ways. Get outta this city. Go to Omaha. Get these bloodhounds off my trail, wipe out my tracks. Be gone.

◉

Three hours later, after a doctor spent he didn't know how long picking the buckshots out of his chest, stomach, and thighs, he got himself up.

Another young brown-skinned woman with a big pretty smile said: "Where you going?" Liked her right off. Country girl. You could tell by the sweet music in her accent. Hear ya knocking, daddy.

"Home," he told her. He was sitting up on one of those examination tables and she was standing right there wrapping bandages around his chest.

"You don't think I'm gon stay here, do you? I could die in this place," he told her, grinning. He got like that sometime. Stubborn as a mule. It was his nature. Just natural, natural for him, like singing the natural story of what happened to him.

He sang—

> This morning, this morning,
> Gon find me a lucky rabbit foot.
> This morning, this morning,
> Gon find me that rabbit foot.
> I jes got to change my luck, baby,
> Got to get me some love and loot.

6

The young woman started grinning, probably taking him to be some kind of clown. But that was all right. Probably rather see peoples grin than not. He kept right on—

> My baby she so mean,
> She makes me wants to scream.
> Yeah, my baby so mean,
> She makes me wants to scream.
> She hitched me to a mule wagon,
> She drove me night and day.

He too now was grinning, liking the sound of his own voice, his words tumbling like snowflakes up a string of lakes. And the nurse kept wrapping.

> Gots to change my luck, baby.
> Sho gots to change my luck.
> Gave that woman all I had to give.
> Gave her all I had to give.
> Needs myself a lucky rabbit foot.
> Cause I gots no mo to give.
> Sho ain't gots no mo to give.

She was smiling as she wrapped up his chest. "You sing real nice. Got a nice voice."

"Thank you, ma'am," he said with irony in his voice, but feeling at the same time like he might as well be nice. Nobody knows, not even the early rider, not even C. C. Rider. Might as well. Who can tell?

"You could be a real singer."

"I is a real singer."

"I mean, you could make a living doing it."

"That what I been trying to do."

"It must be hard."

"Yeah, but ain't nothing gon stop me."

She finished wrapping him and clucked like a hen who'd just dug up a worm big as a snake. Standing there with her hands on her hips. "All right, if you think you strong enough. Lord knows they ain't got no beds to spare. Unless you got insurance. You got insurance?"

"Do I looks like I got insurance? I already told them back there in the office." Was she trying to make him eat his shame and choke on it too?

"That's what I thought. Who shot you?"

"My wife boyfriend, a preacher." Who you think: the Grand Dragon?

She didn't say anything, just looked at him with that look he knew, a look that said, "Don't shit me, man," but then something came over her and she looked like she believed him. And she said, "You trying to tell me a preacher come in your home and shot you over your own wife?"

He laughed. "Naw. Not like that . . ."

"You know they already reported this to the police. You going to have to talk to some officers out there in the lobby before you leave."

"I know. But I ain't pressing no charges so why I gots to talk to them?"

"Because that's the law. They waiting to see you now."

Walking down the hallway with the nurse at his side, he hummed to himself. He did that. That was him. Not ready to say, Hush, somebody's calling me. When he didn't have an instrument to say what he had to say, he said what he needed to say, talking to himself, keeping himself company, especially when things got bad, humming now the Leadbelly song about hanging crepe on the door, like when somebody died. And he remembered it something like this—

I may not be dead, but I ain't coming back here no mo.

He walked out into the waiting room and the lady with the bleeding nose was still there. Now there was this man standing over her. He was pulling at her arm, trying to make her stand up. People all around were ignoring them, or pretending to. Man looked around for the cops. They were coming in through the front door.

Without thinking about it, he walked over to the man pulling at the woman's arm.

"What you doing?" he asked the man.

"What's it to you?"

"Ain't this woman here to see a doctor? She hurt. What you trying to do to her?"

"Listen," he said, "this ain't none of your goddamned business."

The woman said, "He's just trying to get me back outside so he hit me again."

That was all Man needed to hear.

By then the nurse was bringing the coppers over, two of them. Man knew them by sight and reputation. One had the face of a bullfrog and the other a lizard. They were Sixty-third Street headbeaters, Saturday night gorillas with billysticks. They used to drive a paddy wagon, park in front of a joint, bust in, and arrest everybody in sight. Beat heads on the way. That was their style. Now they walked the sidewalk and beat heads.

"Okay, Big Boy," Bullfrog said. "What's going on here?"

"This man is bothering this woman," Man said.

Lizard took his arm. He had this shit-eating grin. Believe it, Man knew what that meant. "But that ain't none of your business, now is it, Big Boy? Come on. We want to talk with you outside in the car."

He looked at the pleading woman. In a odd way she reminded him of his mother. And how many times had he seen his sad mother weeping, making desperate animal sounds, after falling under Quincy's back-handed blows? In the dusty shadow of his father's red rage and his mother's deafening screams he'd tremble and cringe, feeling as though a circle of rose thorns was embedded in his stomach, feeling all torn up inside. Chairs, tables, dishes, glasses broke when Quincy's fists were flying up against Charity's head. At such times Charity would cry out for help and his older brother, Bill, a long-legged teenager, would get the old man from behind with a hammerlock while Man, no taller than Quincy's belt-line, pounded at his drunk father's thighs.

Now the woman in the waiting room had that pleading look that Charity used to get, and it caused Man to feel those rosebush thorns in the stomach again, as Lizard pulled him away toward the door.

JUST OUTSIDE THE HOSPITAL THEY grabbed him. Took him by surprise. All of a sudden they put the handcuffs on him. Kept knocking and pushing him in the back all the way to the car.

CHAPTER TWO

"Hey! Why for you gots to put cuffs on me? I ain't done nothing."

"Shut up," said Lizard and pushed him harder.

Bullfrog said to him, "Where you from—down South somewhere? You talk like one of them backwoodsy niggers fresh outta the sticks."

Lizard chuckled himself silly for a minute.

Bullfrog opened the back door and Lizard gave Man another push from behind. Sent all kinds of pain racing up through his chest. He fell face down on the back seat. "Damn, man. Watch it," he said. "You don't have to treat me like that. I ain't done nothing."

"Nobody's ever done anything wrong, Big Boy."

Lizard got in on one side of him and Bullfrog on the other. He could see their faces from the hospital entryway lights.

"Now, you say somebody you don't even know shot you. Right?" This was Lizard.

"That right."

Then out of nowhere, like lightning, Lizard punched him hard in the stomach. Electric waves, like you see in the comic books, from out in space, went all through him. He thought he was going to pass out. The cop punched him again.

Man started crying. He couldn't help it. The pain got him so good. He wet a tiny bit in his pants.

Lizard said, "I'm gonna keep right on until you tell us what happened, Big Boy. Far as I'm concerned your stomach is my punching bag."

Bullfrog got out and got in the front at the wheel.

Lizard said to him, "We going for a little ride, Manfred. You gonna tell us a story. All about what happened. You going to make your story real sweet too, or else—"

He was sick, not from the buckshots, but from the pain of the punching, from tiredness and hunger, from no sleep, and the whiskey was wearing off and he had a bad headache and a raw stomach. He was fit to die.

As they headed south he said, "All right. I know him when I see him but I never met him."

Lizard said, "We got this little report tonight, Big Boy. Reverend Eddie Bedford phoned in saying somebody—he thinks it was you—tried to break into his home by way of the fire escape."

All right. They had him. "I wont going to hurt him. Just wanted to talk to them both, to my wife and him. Try to reason with them. I missed her. Christmas Eve and everything. I was feeling lonely. Just got a little too tight. I know I shoulda not done it."

"Your wife is living with this Reverend Bedford?"

"My wife and baby."

Lizard didn't say anything to that.

"Well, looks like you in luck, Big Boy. The reverend don't want to press charges," Lizard said.

"Yeah," Bullfrog said. "But we just might press charges ourself. Teach you a lesson."

Man knew their reputation for beating niggers. And he was too tired and sick for a beating. A beating might have killed him that night. And that's all these two niggers were good for, beating other niggers. Word was they had beat at least a hundred niggers to death and nobody did anything about it. Courts didn't care. A nigger was just a nigger and a dead nigger was only another dead nigger.

Over his shoulder, Bullfrog said, "Maybe we ought to see if we can't get the reverend to press charges. Huh?"

"That's a good idea. Go on, drive by there."

The cops drove him to Reverend Bedford's building, on Sixty-first, and Lizard got out and walked up the walkway with that strut like he thought he was God's last gift to the earth. Some kind of rooster hell on two legs. Bullfrog stayed with Man in the car.

He lighted himself a cigar and blew the smoke in Man's face. Man loved cigars himself but this time the smoke was making him sick because he was so hungry and thirsty.

Little while later Lizard came down and said, "Looks like your luck still holding out, Big Boy."

He got in and Bullfrog drove on through the dark cold night.

At a stoplight, Lizard said to Bullfrog, "What you think we ought to do with this nigger, Gene?"

"Drop him in the lake."

They were moving south through Washington Park.

"Naw. His body might stink up the water. Then nobody could use the beaches anymore."

They came out of the park and drove slowly over to Drexel and on

11

down Drexel. Somewhere in the Hyde Park section Bullfrog turned and drove over to Stoney Island and back north toward Sixty-third.

At the corner of Sixty-third and Stoney, under the El tracks, they stopped. Lizard said, "All right, Big Boy. You on your own. If we get any more trouble out of you, I'm gonna personally put a bullet through your head. Right there." He pressed his index finger against Man's forehead. "Is that clear?"

Man didn't say anything. Lizard unlocked the handcuffs and Man rubbed his thick wrists.

"I said is that clear?"

"Yeah."

"Okay. Thatta boy. All right. Out!"

AS MAN WALKED THROUGH THE COLD
snow-packed streets, he felt like crying **CHAPTER**
again. Hands in pockets, in the right he felt **THREE**
the folded letter from his sister, a small token of
security, a comfort. On the phone she sounded so
sophisticated, so different from the down-home big sis he remembered.
Sure didn't grow up to be like mama. Mama, mama. Always trying to
keep him out of trouble. But he just had something in him that wanted to
go. Singing was his way of talking out this furious, crazy thing in him
that made him glide, leap, holler, and scream as if over treetops without
even moving. But it made him look like a bad nigger to white folks. He
knew that. Mercy, mercy. And it made colored folks worry about him or
laugh at him. Double mercy. It was why his wife left him. It wasn't always good for him. He knew it then, he knew it now.

Then he started remembering Cleo. Loved that woman as much as life
itself. Her leaving hit him hard, though he tried to pretend it had no ef-
fect. But now he was trying to be sure about the things that led up to her
going. Why he hadn't seen the signs. He knew now he was just too blind,
too stuck on himself, too much in his own desire, his music. Too much
diddy wa diddy.

She started going to church more and more. He asked, "Why you
going to church so much?" "Because it makes me happy," she said.
"Besides, Fred, you're never here. You're always out with Solly somewhere drinking." "That's not true," he said. "It is true. Since the baby
was born you stay out all the time." She got him there. The crying got on
his nerves. He didn't say anything. "You just scared I'm going to ask you
to change her diaper." "That ain't true. Looka here, I change her diaper
this morning." Cleo laughed, "So, you changed the baby's diaper this
morning. Big deal. One time you changed the baby's diaper, one time in
one whole week." "Last week too." "So? You changed her diaper one
time last week. Big, big deal." Cleo had this real sweet disposition, you
see. Calm-like. She couldn't stay mad at him for long, but she wouldn't
take any shit. She would laugh and all but she was serious. And she kept
right on going to that screaming-and-shouting church. Got so she was
wrapping the baby up every afternoon going off to the church—First
Christ Baptist Church at Fifty-eighth and Indiana Avenue. In the beginning she used to try to get him to come with her. Then one time, he

remembered, he said, "Okay. Listen here. I'm going with you." She gave him this look as if to say: You speaking some kind of foreign language? Didn't know what it meant then. But now he knew she didn't want him to come, not that night. She was gone a long time. Her excuse for staying so long at church was she was helping the sisters with the bookkeeping and one thing and another.

After a while he let it go. Gave him more time by himself. Didn't have to hear her nagging him about drinking. Could practice his singing, play his harmonica, or fool around with the sax. Sit in the chair and blow. Or go out to Jackson Park and blow to the sky. Blow up a breeze. Walk around and blow. His sax had this real pretty sound, tenor. Mellow and sweet. He could make that Stadler talk back to him like they were in love. He could do that. Wasn't far anyway, just to walk over there with his sax. Got so he liked it, her at church all the time, the baby out of the house too. No crying. No noise. Solly would stop by and he and Solly would get a taste and try out a number. Maybe he'd sing one of his own songs, something he'd just written the night before, and Solly would pick it out, give it a melody, with his guitar. And Solly was a natural born straight musician. Play anything, pick anything, mandolin even. Could make a violin come all over itself, he played it so sweet. Couldn't anybody touch Solly. Man himself was pretty good with instruments too, but he was nowhere near that good. Cain't nobody touch Solly no kind of way.

That's how Man got sort of relaxed with Cleo gone so much. How she got away without him even noticing it. Because he trusted her. Thought she and he were so tight nothing could come between them. After she left he told himself he had too much confidence in people. What he tried not to tell himself was how much in love with her he still was. He had to keep reminding himself that people weren't going to do right half the time. He thought about that old saying: "Nobody loves me but my momma, and she might be jiving too."

◉

That was one terrible night, walking to his little old kitchenette in a block between Sixty-third and Sixty-second. The El train rumbled by overhead. He looked up. It was all lighted up and empty except for one old white man in a felt hat and a gray overcoat.

Christmas Eve! Shot and then beat up by the police. And then just him alone, on the snow-packed sidewalk, walking in the cold night. Nobody else out, as the sun was coming up, just a tiny bit of it, along the top rim of the buildings, touching the tips. Couldn't see much sky. Just a hint of sun through the thick clouds and it made him feel sorrowful and all he wanted was his harmonica or his sax, and a place to sit down, the side of a bed, their bed, Cleo's and his, and blow a little bit, comfort himself, and sing to himself, sing his feelings, sing even if he had to whisper to himself to keep from waking up the neighbors. Humming, blue as a man can be, so low down I can hear ants sneezing and coughing way down under the snow and the sidewalk.

> Little old George Washington, he cut down trees.
> Little George, he cut down some trees.
> Now, elephants, they gots four knees.
> Yes, Lord knows elephants have gots four knees.
> Big ole Santa Claus, he got him some bags.
> Yeah, that ole Santa got them big ole bags.
> And look at me out here all alone and in my rags.
> Yeah, I'm out here freezing all alone and in my rags.

First thing he did was go to the little sink for a glass of water. Filled the fruit jar full at the tap, and resting against the sink, drank it down in one long, slow swallow. The building was still quiet, holiday morning quiet. When the people left for their slaves on any regular day, you could hear this clumping down the steps past his and Cleo's kitchenette, which was on the first floor at the bottom of the stairway. Just a one-bedroom apartment, a kitchenette they called it. He and Cleo and the kid hardly had room to turn around in. But now he had his mind on one thing: his Stadler under the bed.

First time he ever blew it in public, before a bunch of people, was at the Regal, winter 1947. They, a bunch of them, local musicians, were sometimes getting these little gigs through a South Side booking agency. This agency hired them to warm up for stars coming through. With this particular agency you didn't have to belong to the Musicians Union or anything. The guy who ran the outfit was a crook who ended up in prison. But somebody like Man could pick up a few dollars this way while it lasted. They'd be allowed to do what they do for about twenty minutes. All right. His first time was to warm up for Billie Holiday. She was a solo act then. Man and she were shooting the shit backstage before he went out. She was real nice people, in his opinion, down to earth. He fastened the catch at the back of her gown for her. It wasn't any big deal but he was proud of doing that cause he thought she was a great lady and people weren't respecting her like they should. He remembered she gave him a cigarette and although he didn't care that much about cigarettes, he smoked it for her. Hanging around long enough, he, Billie, and some of the boys from the band ended up going to this after-hours joint down on Twenty-ninth near State Street. Partied till the crack of day. Joint ran by an old man named Poppa Blake. Blake had that thirty-years-of-hard-liquor look but that nigger loved him some blues—dipper-mouth blues, gutbucket, nasty Lucille Bogan blues, red-light-district blues, cathouse blues, jump-back-in-the alley blues.

Man got down on one knee, pulled the case out by the handle, and sat on the side of the bed with it resting on his lap. Just the touch of it made him feel better. The room was still kind of dark but he could see the saxophone. Daylight was coming in around the sides of the shade so he saw pretty well. Didn't need any electric light. Grew up in the country—except for those two years with Aunt Ida and Uncle Sam in Atlanta when he was ten to twelve. In the country never had no electric lights. Took a long time to get used to electric lights. Kerosene light. Miss the smell. You could understand Leadbelly in prison complaining about the electric lights: "Lord, I been down yonder where the lights burn all night long." Burned because the guards wanted to see what all the cons were doing in the dark, wanted to make sure they were sleeping and not thinking about escaping.

Sitting there, Man opened the case and took up the reed, put the case on the bed, and stuck the reed in his mouth, wet it, and put it on. Used the harmonica or the sax to say what he couldn't find words to say. But singing was best when he knew what to sing. Time, take yo time. Somebody upstairs flushed a toilet. Time, take you good time. He put the reed on the mouthpiece, placing it on the flat side and turning it a little so it was just a tiny bit below the tip. Took just two fingers to tighten up the screws, feeling for them, testing them, so natural it was like getting up in the night to pee, you just find your way to the bathroom, if you're not drunk or something, in which case you might piss on the floor. He'd done that too. Didn't put the strap around his neck. Just lifted that reed to his mouth, holding the sax just a little to the right of his right thigh. Straightened his back up, tired as he was. He felt his feet flat on the floor, real solid-like. Toes still cold though inside the shoes. But he didn't pay them no mind. He had forgotten his pain and even the bandages around his chest and stomach till he took a deep breath and felt them pulling at him. Forgot Cleo too. Forgot that sissy preacher she was with. His sax was a tenor so he thought of her as female and he handled her gently, like he'd handle a woman, his right hand going back down by his thigh, holding her softly. He took a deep breath, filling his lungs, then placed the tip of his tongue on the end of the reed. Strong underbite, too. Tongue stiff as a middle finger pushing against the reed. His left hand near the palm keys. All this natural as scratching his own ass. His fingertips lightly finding the six natural keys, just lightly, slowly then quickly. And he was still holding in his wind. Ready. Feeling alive for the first time since way back there before he jumped from the ground in the alley, grabbing that fire escape, lifting himself up, feeling nothing but this siren in his head. Then he let loose, forcing all his wind into the sax, and his fingers knew what to do at the same time. Eyes closed, his whole self turned down to the pinpoint of that mouthpiece. A streak of sound strong as the old Southern Line booming under the yellow moon all night long heading up North. And he blew his heart out, fingers jumping and dancing everywhichawhere—getting that real nice high tone. Time, baby. He was doing this little number he wrote by himself, you know, just a little sad sweet thing he liked to play when he was kind of down like this and needed a liftup, thing with no name, but with words he heard in his mind. The sax was saying what he was saying—

> I may be up to my neck in trouble,
> Hoodooed at the door of my own wake.
> I say I'm up to my neck in deep trouble,
> Hoodooed at the door to my own wake.
> But Lord knows I ain't gon let these blues
> Take me down to that ice cold lake.
> No, no, not to that ice cold lake.
> Rock ain't gon be my pillow,
> Cold ground ain't gon be my bed.
> Cold ground won't be this black man's bed.
> No, sir, rock ain't gon be my pillow.
> I may be up to my neck in trouble,
> I say I may be up to my neck in trouble,
> But I ain't gon follow, and I sho ain't gon be led.

He kept saying these words into the sax, making the sax say them. It was real nice. Then he got tired of his own song and went into the first few riffs of *Feeling Lowdown*, hearing in his head Big Bill Broonzy singing it with that little edge of humor to his voice like he could do. And Man bore down hard.

And not two minutes into it, then this goddamned loud banging on his door, door shaking nearly off the hinges. Man got up, still blowing, and walked over to the door. Just for a minute, just one minute was all, he couldn't help cutting loose. He'd lost himself and his self-control. But just the taste brought him back to himself. Baby please don't go. He opened the door and there in his doorway, big as an ape, stood the building manager in his robe with his nappy hair standing everywhichaway on his head looking evil as the devil. And Man held the sax down to his side and just gave the devil this big pretty smile and said, "Good morning Mister Johnson. Didn't mean to disturb you, sir."

After Johnson left and he was sitting on the side of his bed brooding, he once again remembered his sister's letter. He dug in his jacket pocket and found it, unfolded the thing and took it over by the light.

November 12, 1949

Dear Freddy:

I'm writing again so soon just so you'll know how serious I am about trying to get you to come out here. Lyle, the boys, and I would love to have you stay with us until you get on your feet. I know how important to you your music is. I haven't forgotten. (Smile.) I know you'd do real well here. And there is a popular place right in North Omaha called the Palace where they have a band on the weekends. The owner, she is always looking for new people to sing or play. And there are many places in other towns around here, colored places, where they always needing people, mostly on weekends. If you did some singing on the weekends that would leave you free to find a regular job for the weekdays, and there's lots of work out here right now, in the factories, and construction work too. But the main thing you would give yourself is a chance. It's not good for anybody to be alone when a marriage ends. The last time we talked on the phone you sounded so depressed I got really worried. Lyle and I—and the boys too—would be so happy to see you after all this time. Like I told you on the phone, we got the extra room upstairs and it's yours anytime you want to come. We all love you very much. Let me know soon what you're planning to do.

> *Your big sister*
> *Love always,*
> *Debbie*

In his sleep Man heard Mama singing *Leaning on the Everlasting Arms*, then somehow she turned into Aunt Ida, still singing that song, bent over a washing tub. But that was Mama, not Aunt Ida. Aunt Ida ran an elevator in a big building up on Piedmont Street. She didn't wash white folk's clothes. Then the next door lady came in and said to Aunt Ida: "Ida, you too nice to yo man. Every smart woman gots to have herself a back-door man, girl, somebody who can creep for her." And Aunt Ida said to the woman: "Sissy, you go on and live your life like you want to. Let me live mine, honey." And Aunt Ida turned to him at the door watching. She said, "Man, ain't you spose to be heading out to school? It's late." And he grabbed up his satchel and turned to leave. He looked back and said, "Aunt Ida, I love you." She said back: "I love you too, baby boy." And he thought, Mama never told me she loved me like that. Outside going down the steps he started crying, crying for himself. Then at the bottom of the steps a bully snatched off his cap and tossed it back across the ground. Man wasn't about to go back and pick it up. The bully was going to pick it up himself. He just didn't know it yet. The bully thought he was the baddest. He just didn't know about Man. And when Man started kicking his ass all these people came around looking. And there was Aunt Ida coming through the crowd. Then she was pulling at him, trying to pull him off the bully. She got him off, holding him by the collar. Then she said: "When somebody mistreat you, Man, you got a right to be sad. Sing about it, boy. It's like turning the other cheek. That's the Lord's way. But you disnounce violence. You hear me?"

He is in the back seat of a police car except it's not a police car. It's one of those little red cars the fire chief rides around in. Has a four-inch-tall silver ash tree on the tip of the hood. But mainly what he can see is the back of the fire chief's head. To the fire chief he says, "Where you taking me?" and the fire chief says, "I'm not a fire chief." "But where you taking me?" the dreamer say. "I'm taking you where you asked me to take you," says the driver. Out the window the dreamer can see storm-buzzards begging on the street corners, jitterbuggers bopping along looking for that next chickenbone special. This must be Chicago but it looks like Atlanna. Or is it N'Orleans? Death, in a long white gown, stands at the curb waiting to cross. A black dog stands beside him. Schoolgirls skipping and brooming along eating nickynacks. His eyes feel sore but he can't rub them. He realizes now that his hands are tied behind his back. Something on the seat beside him catches his eye. It's a dead bat. And beside the bat is a wren's nest, no doubt snatched down from some tree. More confused than ever, he looks again out the window. A whistling wind seems to have come in from somewhere, pushing things along the sidewalk: a wooden leg, an empty plastic purse, a dog collar, a sheet of newspaper. A big butter-and-egg man moving along in his struggle buggy. Bound to be headed for Diddy-Wah-Diddy. West Hell. Zar. Once again the dreamer tries to get some information from the driver. Says: "I may have stumbled but I didn't fall yet. Stop acting like a swamp boss and tell me where you taking me." Driver doesn't seem to know diddly. The driver says: "Take it easy greasy." The dreamer says: "Yo talk is slick as greased lightning." The driver says: "All right, all right, if you can't remember:

You asked me to take you to church." "Church?" he says, trying to shout but it comes out a whisper. And at this point the driver says: "And here we are. Here's the church." And he pulls the fire chief's car over to the curb and parks. The dreamer looks into the driver's face for the first time when he helps him from the back seat and unlocks the handcuffs. The man has a moon face with the eyes of a rat. "Right this way," says the rat man. But who is he? He leads the dreamer along a narrow path to the red entrance door of a grand white structure that looks like a church. A black man who is dressed like a bishop in black comes to the door. The driver says, "Here he is." And hands the dreamer over to the bishop. In the arched hallway, the bishop takes him firmly by the arm and leads him across the green-and-yellow marble floor into the big cold church with its high ceilings and delicate railings, ornate iron-framed stained glass windows, carved moldings. The dreamer is led up to the altar where candles are burning and on through a small doorway into a back room. But the room itself is by no means small. Although the ceiling is low, it's a great room. The floor is covered with a blue-and-red Chinese carpet. The dreamer sees three plush red silk–covered chairs, one by the door where they stand, and the other two on either side of a huge bed. He sees himself reflected in a nearby free-standing mirror trimmed in gold. And there is an ancient cherry wood bed complete with a white silk canopy against the far wall. The bishop holds his hand out toward the bed and says, "I believe this is what you wanted to see, isn't it?" And the dreamer gazes steadily at the bed. At first it's not clear what he sees. Then it hits him: Cleo's creamy light brown backside, the cheeks of her ass moving in a rhythmic up-and-down motion. God! A big man is beneath her. Looks like she is riding high up on somebody six-months-in-front-and-nine-months-behind. So to speak. But this isn't funny. The dreamer wants to laugh and cry at the same time. But all he can do is whisper, "Oh, God!"

HE MUST HAVE SLEPT DEAD FOR SIX
hours, at least. In the dream he woke up on
he was trying to clean the blood from his
jacket but it wouldn't come off.

Sitting up, he swung his feet to the floor. Still in
his underwear, he was cold and thirsty. The room was chilly.

He felt more pain sitting up than he did lying down. But he was going
to pay it no mind. He needed a drink. And he didn't have but about a
dollar and thirty cents. He got his good clean jacket out of the closet, the
one with the red turned-up collar. Put it on. Got it for three dollars at
Salvation Army store up on Sixty-third next door to Sid Feinstein's
Pawnshop. They had good clothes in there because they picked up things
from rich white folks out in places like Wilmette, Wheaton, and Elgin.

The bloody jacket was on the floor by his ratty armchair. Under the
sink he found one of those big supermarket paper sacks. He opened it,
sat it on the floor. Took the coat and rolled it tight as it'd go then stuffed
it in the bag.

He got himself a jar of water at the tap and drank it down in one swallow, shivering, his teeth chattering.

He smelled under his arms. Funky. His mouth tasted like dogshit. Cold
as it was, he knew he needed a bath. But the water never got really hot,
just sort of warm, if you ran it a long, long time. And if you ran it a long,
long time Mister Johnson came knocking on the door saying what's the
matter, your water faucet stuck on *on*.

Man turned the water on in the tub and let it run till it started getting
warm then he put the stopper in and let it go on running. Fuck Mister
Johnson. This wasn't his building anyway. He was just some Uncle Tom
nigger for some white slumlord who probably lived out in Wilmette
somewhere. When it was nearly full Man stuck his finger in to test it. Just
lukewarm.

He couldn't stand being nasty, smelling bad. Took off his clothes and
got in. It felt cold to the touch but he forced himself and stood on his
knees so he wouldn't get his bandages wet—but they got wet anyway.
Then he took up the little piece of soap he had left of the bar he bought
two weeks ago.

Closed his eyes. Remembered how Aunt Ida used to wash his back.
Himself sitting in the bathtub. He'd never seen a bathtub before he had

21

to go stay with her and Uncle Sam in Atlanta. In Lexington they took their baths in a big washtub, same kind Mama used to wash clothes in. Just sat in there and when it came time to get their hair rinsed somebody dumped a bucket of water over their heads. But this was a cityfied true bathtub. Aunt Ida washing his back was one of the first great pleasures of life. He felt special, like somebody loved him. He'd left home because he and his daddy couldn't get along. Actually, they sent him to live with Aunt Ida, Mama's older and only sister. Aunt Ida was the first grown-up to treat him like he was a human being. She talked with him about all kinds of things. He remembered sitting at the kitchen table with her when Uncle Sam was at work or gone out barrelhousing. She'd fix Man a cup of something, apple cider maybe. Tea sometimes. And she'd put her dimpled elbows on the table and smile across at him and say something like, "When you grow up, Freddy, you be good to your wife." And he remembered thinking: I didn't even know I was gon grow up, let lone have a wife. Aunt Ida was the first grown-up to talk straight with him about sex, too. She caught him spying on her through the bathroom keyhole. She came out and said, "Freddy, I knowed you was there peeping. Now, listen, if you so curious about what a woman's body look like let me show you a picture." She took down this big encyclopedia-type book she kept up on a little shelf with the Bible and a cookbook and she put it on the kitchen table and opened it and kept turning the pages till she come to this drawing. "See here, Freddy," she said, "It say, 'The Human Female Body.' This here is what a woman look like. These here is her breasts she nurse the baby with. This is her pee-pee hole. Babies come out there too." Then she said, "It's not polite to peep through a keyhole when somebody in the bathroom. Now promise me you won't never do it again." He felt so shamed he couldn't look at her. But he promised. She kissed his head and hugged him. Said: "Don't be sad. It was just natural curiosity." He didn't know what that meant but it sounded all right. At least he wasn't going to hell for his sin. He loved Mama but he never liked her much. Aunt Ida he loved and liked.

The only thing she ever did that bothered him happened when he was twelve with not much time left to be with them. There was talk of sending him back to Lexington because Aunt Ida had asthma and was sick with other kinds of things, female troubles they called it, and couldn't take care of him much anymore. She used to bribe him. That's what he didn't like. She'd say, "If you scrub the floor, Freddy, I'll make sure you gets some valuable things of mine when I die." He didn't mind so much scrubbing the floor but he didn't like the way she was trying to get him to do it. And he told her. Told her he didn't want nothing from her. But she still went on saying things like that. He reckoned she thought she was being nice to him. But Sunday his daddy, Quincy, came down from Lexington on the bus and took him back. Seemed like not long after that Aunt Ida died from asthma. They said she couldn't breathe anymore. And for years he remembered trying to figure how somebody just stopped breathing. And she never did leave him nothing. He didn't think there was anything to leave. Never expected it. Didn't want nothing from her but her love. And that was gone.

Anyway, he finished his bath and got out, dried on the only towel of the three they had that Cleo hadn't taken.

He put on some clean underwear, his pants, and a clean shirt, put on his shoes, put on his jacket, and picked up the bag with the bloody jacket. Figured he'd just drop it in the trash can out by the side of the house.

When he got out there he saw the overflowing can, with garbage stacked on the ground around it. And a rat shot down alongside the building as he walked back there. He thought, well, he wouldn't add to the mess. He'd just take the jacket and drop it in one of those street cans somewhere or maybe somebody else's can if he could find one not too full.

On the way up to Sixty-third he kept glancing to the side of each building but the only cans he saw were full or behind locked gates.

At the corner of Sixty-third there was a city can. He took the top off but the damned thing was full, full of all kinds of junk—soft drink bottles, a canvas shoe, a snuff can, a rotten comic book, a bunch of crumbled-up cork, an empty paint can, the leg of a child's rocker, half a doll's head, candy wrappers, greasy wax paper, a barbecue box, a brassiere. He sat the bag on top anyway and started pushing down, forcing it in.

In mid-motion he felt somebody touch him on the shoulder. His body gave an involuntary jerk then he turned around. It was Lizard, grinning. "What you doing, Big Boy? Can't stay out of trouble?"

Man stood there with his mouth open. Said, "I didn't think putting something in a garbage can was gainst the law."

"What I say is against the law is against the law. These city cans ain't for you to bring your garbage from home. I should run you in for this."

Man took the bag out and held it at his side.

"Okay. Once again, luck is with you. But you gonna keep trying me until your ass will be mine."

Walking away, Man headed west. Thinking: That's what you think.

He heard Lizard call after him, "Merry Christmas, Big Boy. Try to stay out of trouble."

He had forgotten it was Christmas Day.

Looking back at Lizard, Man saw the police car at the curb parked in front of a closed liquor store. Which reminded him how badly he needed a drink. Lizard's buddy Bullfrog was sitting at the wheel. He waved to Man and smiled.

◉

Man stopped at a greasy spoon called Aunt Sally's Cafe on Sixty-third near South Parkway. The place smelled of stale bacon grease and mildew. The waitress said Merry Christmas to him and he said it back. He set the bag on the floor beside him at the counter, ordered a bowl of bean soup, and started eating without thinking about it or tasting it. Folks up and down the counter talking policy on Christmas Day. The whole cafe talking policy. An old man with ears like a rabbit's next to him was grumping at the old woman sitting at the counter beside him. He told her if he'd followed his own mind he'd have bet on Four-Eleven-Forty-four and not on her Seven-Eleven-Twenty-two. The waitress said she hit the numbers for two hundred dollars last year playing her dream from the dream book.

Man finished his soup, paid, and started out. The old man called him back. "Son, you forgot yo bag." Man shrugged, picked it up, and walked back into the cold, blinding, daylight.

He started walking, thinking he'd save his money and put it toward a taste later on. It was around noon and cold. Not many people out. He kept walking.

But he got tired, the pain in his thighs and chest started talking to him so he waved down a jitney, crawled in, set his bag on the floor beside him, thinking, Hotdoggit, I'm gonna leave the jacket right here, just hop out like I forgot it, and gon never see it again.

A big woman taking up most of the back seat called out to the driver, "Driver, now there ain't but so much room back here. You don't needs to be picking up nobody else till you gets rid of some of these peoples you already got." And the crowded cab of folk laughed as the car shot on down South Parkway. Man was sitting backwards facing the big caramel complected woman all dressed up in a blue brocade suit and coat with a fox collar. On her lap, she was balancing a stack of Christmas presents.

Man was hoping Solly had a bottle of whiskey. But lately Solly had been buying cheap sweet wine. Man liked bourbon, when he could get it. But it didn't make no never-mind today. He'd drink sweet wine if he had to, nasty as it was it would do the job. But Solly might have some whiskey. And Man knew that Solly enjoyed drinking with him as much as he liked drinking with Solly. Solly needed some comfort, somebody to talk to, his drinking buddy. Solomon Thigpen, best blues guitar picker north of the Mason and Dixon Line.

The jitney pulled over to the curb at Thirty-fifth. Man handed the driver the coins then hopped out and started running. He could hear the big lady calling him, but he acted like he didn't hear her, just kept going.

> Boogie, man, boogie,
> Boogie all night long,
> I say, boogie, man, boogie.
> Boogie all night long.
> You better make tracks and don't look back.
> Make you some long tracks, man, and don't look back.
> Boogie, man, boogie,
> Boogie all night long.
> I say boogie, man, boogie.
> Boogie all night long.

Solly's lady Holly came to the door, laughing, and said, "I hear you knocking but you can't come in. Merry Christmas, Fred." She was always joking with him like that, saying things like that, like he was not welcome or something. The apartment had a toasty smell. He looked at her. She was good to look at, regal, dark brown–skinned lady with a strong face, wide forehead, high cheekbones like an Indian's, a quick smile, a full heart-shaped mouth. She was a real dignified lady. Never smoked or drank. And never nagged Solly for his bad habits. Lucky dog, that Solly. Got a woman what puts up with all his shit. Man liked her fine with Solly but he couldn't imagine himself with her. Not his type. Too easygoing, too soft-spoken. He liked himself a woman with fire. One that had a mind to talk back. Hard to get along with but he'd hate having one like Holly, the quiet, smiling, gentle type, taking everything, good and bad.

Man laughed and said, "Holly it too early in the morning for yo mess."

"It's afternoon, Fred. Come on in. He's in there on the couch hugging his guitar." One of those pearl-inlaid Epiphone Deluxe babies. As he followed her in he thought that nigger probably sleeps with that fucking guitar.

And there was Solly, a little guy compared to Man. A bit lighter complected than Man himself, Solly must have weighed a hundred and fifty wet. Man was two hundred pounds most of the time, sometimes he dropped down to one-eighty but those were the times when he was running lean and working too hard to love Cleo right and to enjoy life. Solly was lying down on his back with the guitar resting on his stomach. When Man walked in he just turned his head sideways and looked at him and started grinning.

25

"Hope you brought a bottle," Solly said.

Man laughed. "Me? I was hoping *you* had one."

Man stood there, grinning, looking down at him.

Holly went by past the little puny Christmas tree they had over near the table and on into the bedroom. There was an opened box under the tree and a pink playsuit for a small child spread out on the floor on the wrapping paper from the box.

Man sat down in the armchair. One of the springs was pushing out the back, so it wasn't very comfortable leaning back. With his elbows on his knees, he leaned forward, looking at Solly. "What you gon do, Solly? Just lay there? Don't you want a taste?"

"Yeah, but I ain't got no money." Solly looked at him like he thought Man might surprise him and say, Come on nigger, I got some money, let's go get mellow. Man'd done that to him a few times. Then again, one time when he hit the numbers, he was right out front with his bread. Said, "Let's go get a setup!" And that was the time Man wrote *Policy Number Blues*, right on the bar napkin, beating out the rhythm on the bartop. But he never wrote down music notes because he didn't know how. It was just all in his head. He wrote down the words and he knew how the melody was supposed to go. He and Solly sang the song to the bartender. She thought they were crazy:

> Hey, bartender lady, pick up the bottle and pour.
> I say bartender lady please get yo bottle and pour.
> I put all my dough, this morning, on forty-four.
> Oh, Lord, this morning, my wife, she gave me hell.
> I say, this morning my wife, she gave me hell.
> Forty-four didn't come in, it never rang a bell.
> So, bartender lady, pour me another double shot.
> Ease my conk-buster, pour me another double shot.
> Tomorrow I may be sleeping in a vacant lot.

But Man said, "How bout—" then he stopped, still grinning, and pointed, jabbing his finger in the direction of the bedroom.

Solly shook his head. "She spent it all on Christmas."

Holly had a job as a nurse's aid at Cook County Hospital. He knew she'd been paid Friday two days ago. Holly wasn't like Cleo. She'd give Solly money for liquor if she had it. Sometimes Man and Solly were long time between slaves—not music jobs, music jobs they loved—and Holly would come through and get Solly through such times when he didn't have any money coming in. And she never nagged him and never tried to make him feel bad. Cleo wasn't like that. He loved Cleo but she wouldn't take any shit off him. She never thought he had any kind of right to just do his music and not work a slave for a living.

Man first saw Solly in Washington Park playing his guitar with an old beat-up straw hat on the ground in front of him. Had a dollar and some change in it just to encourage people to contribute. That was last year, 19 and 48, nearly a year and a half—last summer. Solly was just out of the service, though he never saw no action over there in Germany. He was in a colored company that went in after the war ended.

Solly's guitar made this beautiful sound, made you want to dance. Fact is folks were jitterbugging to his guitar right out there on the tough, worn-down, brown grass. Must have been some kind of holiday, maybe Fourth of July. But lots of folks—children and grown-ups—were there hopping around him and grinning and carrying on. Man had his harmonica in his pocket. You never know. And he was itching to get in on the fun too. But he didn't know the thing Solly was doing. It was one of them fast numbers, a little too fast for Man, but he paid attention to it for a few minutes, caught the rhythm, and picked it up on his harmonica. Many times he did that. Open your door, I ain't no stranger, honey. Got into the deep blue sea. Did some hoodoo spells.

That day they collected a whole bunch of money and went and got drunk as two skunks. Had a lot of fun. Hung out together from then on. They used to go out on the street corner, anywhere where there were lots of folks. Lots of times, Man took his sax and blew. Switched to the harmonica. But mostly he did the singing and Solly did the picking. Sometimes Solly would borrow a violin or he'd be switching back and forth from the guitar to the violin. One time he got hold of a base fiddle and went to town on it.

People were funny though. Sometimes Man and Solly could play on a corner for three, four hours and nobody dropped a penny in the hat. Then other times they'd almost fill up the hat with nickels and dimes. That way it'd take a long time to get enough to buy even a half pint. But his wife, Cleo, never did approve of him playing in the streets. Bullfrog in mud. Said it was lowlife, showed no self-respect. Holly never said anything like that.

◉

Anyway, sometimes he envied Solly for having such an understanding lady. But he didn't believe Holly spent all her money on Christmas. Not Holly. She was too practical to spend all her money on one thing, not even on the kid for Christmas. There was only one present under the tree. He was just starting again to feeling the pain from the buckshots. He figured the liquor would taken the edge off.

"Come on," Solly said, sitting up and putting his guitar down on the couch. "I know where I can get some money. Let's go."

Solly went in the bedroom and Man waited for him at the door, then Solly came back and they were ready to hit the wind, and Man said, "You know, it don't seem like Christmas Day to me. How bout you?"

"Just another day."

Man started singing, "Just another day . . ." Going down the hallway toward the front door he said, "By the way, I got shot last night." He looked at Solly, waiting for what he knew was coming.

"You what?"

Outside, walking along South Parkway, Man said, "The nigger Cleo with shot me."

Solly laughed. "Then how come you ain't dead, nigger?" He looked like he was waiting for Man to say he was just kidding.

"I'm serious, nigger. The nigger shot me—with buckshots. They didn't hurt much but he did try to kill me. That a fact. He coulda, too. Coulda put out my lights. Coulda hurt me had the nigger hit me the right way, cept the window was open just a little bit and the glass caught most of it."

"Manfred, you better start from the beginning."

"I went over there."

"You what—?"

"Yeah. I know I said I wouldn't."

"That ain't all you said, nigger. You said you never wanted to see Cleo again. Glad she was gone. You was the one spose to be happy to be free again."

"I know, I know. But last night, shit. I got to thinking bout last Christmas Eve and how happy me and Cleo was with the baby just six months old. Something got into me. I got drunk."

"That ain't nothing new."

"I got drunk, went over there, climbed up on the fire scape. Trying to open the window when he shot me. I heard Cleo scream."

"Police come?"

Man told Solly how he walked to the hospital and got himself treated and about his little trip with the police back to the reverend's place.

"And here you is walking around free. Man, you know the cops coulda throwed yo ass in jail and dropped the key in Lake Michigan. Now what you gon do?"

"I been thinking bout going out to Omaha to see my sister, maybe stay with her for a few months. I been talking with her on the phone. Getting to know her. I ain't seed her since I was about fifteen. If I hang around this town no telling when I might go off again and head over there."

"Omaha, huh?" Solly shook his head.

"She say they got a great blues place out there. She already told the owner bout me. Sound like I could go right out and start. Weekends, you know."

"Omaha? Omaha, Nebraska? Who do I know in Omaha? Knew a drummer once from Omaha. Boy by the name of Greg Wakely. Just came here on a visit, trying to get a band started. Mean drummer too. Talk about talking drums! The cat could beat the fuck out of some skin." Solly stopped and turned to him. They were standing at the curb waiting for a red light. "Listen, this old gal we going to see probably don't like liquor and drinking, so be cool. I'm just gon borrow a few bucks off her. I ain't never dicked her or nothing."

"You talking about Cindy?"

"Naw. Me and Cindy broke off. Her daughter hate me. I got tired of putting up with that bullshit. This woman I met when I was working as a temp out at the stockyards. She in Bacon. A wrapper for Swift. Estelle. She a older lady but she still real fine. Live up on Forty-third and Calumet. You wanna walk?"

"Naw, man. Let's take a jitney. I got enough for a jitney."

"Okay. Better stop here in this booth and call her first. Don't wanna go there and get turnt away."

"YALL COME ON IN," SHE SAID, HOLD-
ing her apartment door open. "Merry
Christmas." She was this big fat yellow
woman, looked kind of like Lady Day, big strong
chin and a straight nose, except Estelle had those dimples that gave off a
sweetness and you knew she was a kindhearted woman.

They said Merry Christmas to her.

Solly introduced them to each other.

Man took off his cap and unbuttoned his jacket. So did Solly. Estelle
took their jackets and hung them there on her coatrack. Man stuffed his
cap in one of the pockets of his jacket.

Estelle, her big fine self, stepped out in front of them and walked down
the hall leading them into her little dark living room. She didn't have a
Christmas tree or nothing. Man looked at her and wondered. He was
already writing himself a song about her—

> Oh, mama, mama,
> Won't you go tell Estelle I'm in jail,
> Oh, mama, sweet mama,
> Won't you tell Estelle I'm in jail,
> If she don't come for me by night,
> I'm gon be shot by candlelight.

"Have a seat, gentlemen. I don't have a tree this year. I said to myself a
tree just too much trouble. Just me by myself now. No man, no children.
Just me. No point in a tree just for one person. Can I get you something?
Coffee, tea, whiskey? I got some eggnog in the frigerator. I made it
myself."

They sat down on the couch and she stood in front of them just
grinning.

Man looked at Solly and smiled. How lucky could they be? He smiled
back. Man thought he was going to blow the whole thing and laugh.

But Solly said, "That mighty nice of you Estelle but I gon just take a
little whiskey in a separate glass. My partner here take the same."

She looked at Man with surprise. "You sure you don't want eggnog
with your whiskey, Mister Banks?"

"Naw—" Man waved his hand. "Soils the freshness, the crispiness.

You know. But I'll be pleased to have some of that eggnog in a separate glass. I bet it real good."

While her back was turned and she was at the icebox fixing their eggnog he and Solly gave each other a quiet five.

When Estelle came back she was carrying two water glasses full of this eggnog mess and handed them to them. "I'll bring the whiskey in a minute but first I just want to see what you think of my eggnog."

She sat down in the armchair facing the couch and looked at them like they were children about to drink fresh milk. Man needed the whiskey real bad. These were some hard times. And this was not funny. He gave Solly a look and saw that he was going to drink a little bit of it so Man did too. He took a swallow and it was really good. Right then for the first time in twenty-four hours Man knew how hungry he still was. The soup hadn't helped much. He was hungry as a mule that's been plowing from cain't-see to cain't-see. Still, hungry or not hungry, he didn't want to put out the fire before it started.

"My, my, Miss Estelle, this is mighty fine eggnog you done put together here. Your own formla?"

"Sure is. Handed down in my family from my great-grandmother to my grandmother to my mother and me. Alabama wisdom." She laughed, showing them her big pretty teeth like rows of white corn all even and smooth. She was a great-looking woman. Man gazed at her and thought: Yeah, this here is a mighty fine upstanding woman.

Then Solly said, "This would be a nice chaser with the whiskey."

She jumped up like somebody goosed her. "Oh, yes. I forgot. The whiskey. It's Old Crow. Is that okay?"

"Yes, ma'am. No bird like Dirty Bird," Man said, grinning at her, then giving Solly a sly wink. Beats Jim Crow. Crow Jane, Crow Jane. Man ribbed Solly but Solly kept a straight face. Now Solly, he knew how to control himself. He was really good when he wanted to be.

She brought the whiskey in short glasses, about an inch in each. Man took the first sip and felt the burning liquor go down like fire. He was happy as a hog wallowing in shit. Happy as a Mississippi frog sitting on a log. His eyes opened. He took a deep breath and took another swallow. Two more hits and his would be gone too. But he needed the kick. And if he took it slowly he wasn't about to get the sock.

Solly crossed his legs and Estelle sat back down facing them. She was watching them with that big pretty smile. "What kinda of work you do, Mister Banks?"

"I'm a musician."

"Oh, how nice. Like Mister Thigpen. I was so impressed when Mister Thigpen invited me to hear him play at that place down on Thirty-first and Cottage—"

"What place? When?" Man stretched his eyes.

Solly took a swallow of his whiskey and frowned. "You know. I tolt you about it. Place called Ease On In Tavern."

"Oh, I know that joint."

"Mister Thigpen played with such feeling I was really stirred up."

Man ribbed him. "What you play, Solly?"

Estelle spoke up first, "He played *All I Got Belongs to You* and *St. Louis Blues* and *Baby Please Don't Go* and that funny one. What was the title, Mister Thigpen?"

"*Got a Gal in Town with Her Mouth Chock Full of Gold.* I took requests too. It was one of them sentimental nights. Folks had me playing things like *What Can I Say After I Say I'm Sorry* and *Sleepy Time Gal.* Man, be glad you wont there."

All right. Man took him a sip of his whiskey.

"This is mighty good whiskey, Miss Estelle." Man took another swallow and finished it. "Sure is good. But quite naturally it's going to be good if it's Dirty Bird."

She smiled a little bit and he could tell she was getting nervous. "You haven't drunk your eggnog, Mister Banks."

"I was working at it." He was hoping she'd ask him if he wanted more whiskey. But she was watching Solly now, just looking and grinning. Then Solly finished his whiskey too. He smacked his lips.

"Would you gentlemen like some more whiskey?"

They looked at each other as if they were giving the thought serious consideration. Being gentlemen they didn't want to overdo anything. They knew how to be polite. They kept looking into each other's eyes, measuring the thought seriously. Then Man nodded to Solly and he turned to Miss Estelle and gave her a big smile. "What the hell, it Christmas. Folks is spose to have a good time. Right? Sure. Give us some mo. Nothing wrong with relaxing a little bit."

Man could tell it wasn't the answer she wanted to hear but she got up, took their glasses anyway, and reluctantly walked over again to her little kitchen area and took the bottle down from the cabinet again and poured again, this time less than an inch worth of booze into each glass. They were watching her. When they saw her being stingy with the stuff, Man figured Solly was thinking the same thing he was thinking. Solly would have to hit on her for some bread. Christmas, but that didn't make no never-mind: they could go to one of those bootleg joints and cop a bottle. Such places were all over the South Side.

She brought the whiskey over to them. "Yall still ain't drunk your eggnog much. You don't like it, do you?"

Man said, "I likes it, I likes it, Miss Estelle. It mighty fine eggnog. See—" He took another sip, held it on his tongue, hog-tied against swallowing. Then he had to swallow before he could talk. "See. I drink it down. It real good stuff." Then Man put the glass back on the sidetable and took a quick sip of the whiskey.

She was looking seriously at Solly. Just standing there with her hands on her hips. "Mister Thigpen, are you going to drink yours?"

"Sure am. Here go. Down the hatchet. See." And he put away about half of the eggnog, sighed, and put the glass down.

Man was about to crack up, knowing Solly had put a damper on his high just to please her. Poor innocent nice lady she was. And they were a couple of crab lice to be treating her like this. She deserved better.

She sat herself down again and said, "So, what you gentlemen up to this Christmas Day?"

"Oh," said Solly, "we just out strolling and thought we'd pay you a visit. Have to stop in on a few other friends too. You know how it is. Christmas and all." He drained his whiskey from the glass. "That remind me. I done left my wallet at home. Estelle, can you lay a nickel on me, just till next week?"

"What?" She looked puzzled.

"Borry me five dollars till next week?" Solly said.

Estelle caught her breath and held it and Man watched her bosom swelling. It was some big bosom poking out there, held without breathing.

Man caught himself holding his own breath. Waiting.

And Solly too. He could tell. Grinning but holding his breath.

Then she grinned and said, "Sure, Mister Thigpen. Let me get my purse." And she got up and went into the next room and came back with a five-dollar bill, and waving it like it was wet and she wanted to dry it, she then waved it in front of his nose and said, "Here you are, sir."

"Thank you, Estelle." He stood up.

Man drained his whiskey glass and got up too.

Solly stuffed the money in his pocket and followed her to the door where she took their coats off the coatrack. "Well," he said, "it sure was nice seeing you again, Estelle. I'll call you next week before I come."

They got into their coats and said Merry Christmas again and she said Merry Christmas again too and that was that.

◉

Man and Solly knew this bootleg joint where they always had a good supply on Sundays and holidays. Over on Thirty-first and State, State where the trucks travel night and day, rumbling along carrying all that stuff people use from city to city, passing through Chicago. This bootlegger, little dude with a big salt-and-pepper gray beard by the name of Professor DuBois Canon. He wasn't any real professor. Folks called him that because he had the chemistry of whiskey-making down to a T. And he talked with them big words. Had three women living with him. Miranda, brown. Sandy, yellow. Vada, black. Spose to be sleeping with all three.

Man and Solly walked down and over there. It wasn't that far.

Apartment in one of those old, old buildings on the west side of State, so dark and dingy you could fall down in the hallway and break your neck. Ground floor. They knocked. They knew the steps. Somebody inside would look through the peephole before opening the door. Man could tell by the "Who is it?" that it was Miranda.

"Manfred and Solly. Is the professor in?"

She opened the door. You could see right away down this long dark hallway that there was a lot going on in there. The professor always had a bunch of drunks hanging around, sometimes passed out on the floor. Man had been in some low-down places but the professor's took the cake.

Miranda was smoking a cigarette as she led them down the hall to the living room. Real dark in there, all through the place. The professor was sitting behind a desk in his usual way. Somebody on the radio singing *All I Want for Christmas Is My Two Front Teeth.* Six or seven drunk jokers were in one corner watching some kind of Christmas special on television. It was just starting and the announcer said they were going to have on a whole lot of stars—Bing Crosby, Sid Ceasar, Imogene Coca, the Billy Williams Quartet, and Liberace. Some old drunk joker said, "Perry Como sing *White Christmas* better than Bing Crosby." Somebody else said, "Fuck naw, nigger!"

Around the room were small groups here and there smoking and arguing about one thing and another. Room full a smoke. Smelled of white lightning.

Sandy, the yellow one, came over to meet Solly and Man. "What can we do for you gentlemen?" She was smoking her cigarette in one a those long holders you see Bette Davis with in the movies.

Man showed her his pretty teeth. "We here to do business with the professor. Want a fifth of lightning. Best you got. Want yo special discount price too." He laughed.

"I got your special discount price, motherfucker," Sandy said. "You pay three-fifty just like everybody else." She laughed like one of those hyenas.

The professor waved them over.

Man had to step over a drunk to get to the desk. Sometimes Man didn't have any sympathy for drunks. Himself included.

Solly—bless his respect for all of God's children—walked around the poor man on the floor.

Professor DuBois Canon took the cigar out of his mouth, reached

34

across the desk, and shook Solly's hand then Man's. "Nice to see you boys. Let's see how green your money is."

Solly took out the nickel and handed it to the professor. Solly said, "Do us right, now, professor."

The professor reached under the desk and came up with a fifth of white lightning and handed it to Solly.

Solly held it up to the light, what little light there was. Man looked too and it looked good to him, nice and clear.

"Here you go, Solly," said the professor, handing him a dollar-fifty change. Solly took it and stuffed the money in his pocket.

The minute Solly had the bottle in his hand here came three jokers from the crowd in front of the television.

Miranda called out from across the room, "You drunk niggers leave them boys alone."

Drunk nigger number one had a harelip.

Drunk nigger number two had one eye.

Drunk nigger number three had yellow teeth, two missing in the front.

Number one had slobber running down his chin. All three smelled bad. "Hey, man, hey," the slobbering one said, reaching for Solly's shoulder. "I'm your friend, ain't I? How's about a little taste for a friend?"

"No dice, my friend," said Solly.

"Well that's all right, motherfucker, if you wanna be like that, fuck you motherfucker. Fuck you and yo mama in the asshole. You got that?" the drunk nigger said.

Drunk nigger number two said, "Yeah. Who you think you is anyway? It's Christmas. Don't you love your fellow man?"

Drunk nigger number three said, "Yall leave the nigger lone. You heard him. He don't want to give you niggers none of his liquor."

The professor said, "None of that in here, Tucker," speaking to drunk nigger number one. "That goes for you too, Huff, and you, Jenkins. Leave the customer alone. Go watch Lassie."

"Fuck you too, professor," said drunk nigger number one.

"You want me to throw you out of here?"

All right. That got their attention. They wandered back toward the television group, muttering to themselves, "Motherfucking nigger . . ."

The professor said, "I do believe mankind is declining, boys. Still, I try to keep an optimistic view, though, of my fellow man. But this sort of riffraff—" he pointed at the drunk niggers, "makes it difficult."

One of the drunk niggers said, "You think you still the mayor of Chicago."

The professor took the misuse well. He ignored the drunk nigger. Looked at Man and Solly. Said: "Three years ago, when I was advisor to Mayor Kelly, one day I said to him, 'Ed, what are you going to do about this city—two to three hundred murders a year, two thousand assaults, three to four thousand robberies.' And the mayor shook his head. Said, 'Well, Professor DuBois, look at it this way: It could be a lot worse. We're not at war anymore. Troops still overseas, sure, but they're coming home. Chicago boys coming home. There was more killing over there than Chicago ever had.' The mayor went on to say he thought Mister Truman was doing a fine job in the White House. Eisenhower, he said, doesn't believe there will be a third world war. I said to the mayor, 'Ed, the colored folks fought in that war and the boys are coming back here and they still can't vote places in the South and there aren't any decent jobs. You could make a difference here in Chicago, Ed.' I told him just like that. You know what he said? He said, 'We're doing all we can to improve the economy. Why, I got a theory. A project like the Dearborn Street–Milwaukee Avenue subway—which they just finished—will create all kinds of new jobs for everybody. The airport too is big business now,' he said. 'The way I see it, Professor, we got a lot to be grateful for.' I just looked at him and said, 'Well, Ed, those things may be a sign of progress, and a few things to be thankful for, but as long as one man tries to establish his dignity by stepping on another's face, then we're getting nowhere. Lynch mobs are tolerated in the South just like they were back in the 1880s. Factory bosses refuse to provide safe and fair working conditions for workers up here. They tell them just being white is enough. They don't need any other advantage. It's a plot against them, Ed. People use many ways to humiliate, degrade, and destroy one another. And of course when you humiliate and degrade a person long enough he may soon start believing he deserves it. And he'll start doing it to himself.' Ed Kelly gave me this funny look and just walked away. But I never held back my thoughts when I was advising him—"

Vada came over. "Is the professor telling you boys lies about working for the mayor again?"

The professor said, "They are not lies, Vada. Not everyone in this world is a skeptic, like you."

Then Vada looked over at the drunk jokers. She grinned. She was real pretty. "You boys having trouble with them clowns there?"

"Naw. Nothing we can't handle," Man said. "We was just leaving."

"Well, Merry Christmas to you both."

◉

In the hallway, just before they stepped outside, Solly screwed the top off and took a hit then passed it to Man. It burned real nice going down. Man shuddered, shaking his shoulders. Said, "Yes indeed!" He was happy. "Professor something else, ain't he?" Man handed Solly the bottle.

Solly laughed. "Sure is." He took a slug. "You got your monica?"

"Always."

"We can go over to my place and celebrate Christmas. Get some music going. Holly like that. Play something she like."

"Sound good to me."

⦿

Walking back they kept stopping for a taste. Stopped in front of the Catholic school on Michigan for a taste. Man hit it and handed it to Solly. He said: "You ever feel you just ramming yo head gainst a iron wall trying to get somewhere with yo music in this town?"

"Hell yeah," said Solly. "Too many goddamned blues guitar players in Chicago."

"It like Mister Lee say, this the mecca of the blues. They told me *that* down in N'Orleans. Fact is, that why I come up here. Everybody kept saying Chicago where it happening, go to Chicago, go to Chicago, N'Orleans a thing of the past."

"And you been here, what, four years?"

"Got here summer 19 and 46 and still ain't got nowhere. And I know I'm good. It ain't that I ain't good."

"You good, nigger." Solly laughed. "I can tell you that. And I ain't no expert. But—"

"Yeah, but there is a whole lot of other blues singers in this here town just as good."

"And better."

"I don't know bout no better, now."

Solly laughed. "How long you hanged out in N'Orleans?"

"Oh, man, let me see. I left Atlanna right round the time the war ended, in the wintertime that year. Everybody was saying go to N'Orleans, that where you can get work as a singer, go to N'Orleans. So I went to N'Orleans and never got nothing but handouts. Peanuts!"

Solly said, "N'Orleans and Chicago big towns. It hard to get anybody to pay any tention to you in a big town."

Man said, "I know. That why I gon go where I can be a big fish in a small pond."

"What you mean?"

"I got a lot of reasons to get out Chicago."

"So, Omaha, huh?"

"Yeah, Omaha. You know, it hit me: I coulda lost my life last night. I'm gon get outta this town while I can."

Solly didn't say anything.

"Solly, you ought to come on out with me. Debbie say they like the blues in that town. In a place like Omaha we wouldn't have so much competition."

"I got a family, man. But it sound good though." Solly handed him back the bottle.

"Move your family with you." Man hit it and handed it back. "We could turn that town out with soulful sounds."

"Yeah, yeah." Solly took a swig, wiped his mouth. "Here."

"Think about it, Solly. We can get a fresh start." Chugalugged one more time. Man held it out to him.

Solly waved it away. Man put it in his jacket pocket.

"You need a fresh start. I don't need no fresh start. But, say, what about Cleo? You give up on her?"

"Naw. Love that woman, man—"

"I know you do, nigger—"

"But I know I ain't about to get her back by pulling some drunk-ass trick like I did last night. I got to walk straight fore I can fly."

Looking at Man, Solly laughed nervously.

"I ain't lying," Man said. No question about it, he knew what he had to do now.

Solly wiped his mouth and his hand trembled.

A few moments later Man said, "This stuff all right but sho wish it was some good Dirty Bird." Then he started singing—

> The jailer gave me whiskey,
> The jailer gave me tea.
> I say the jailer gave me whiskey,
> The jailer gave me tea.
> The jailer gave me everything but the key.

And Solly cackled at the ditty, saying, "You is a case, a real honest-to-goodness born case."

◉

They stopped again at the corner of Indiana for a taste. Man was happy. Good liquor and a good friend. It was like he hadn't even been shot and his life wasn't getting away from him.

When they got back Holly had company. Sherry, girl from upstairs who was about Holly's age. She was nice-looking, kind of gypsy-looking with a sexy mole that Man liked though he knew she painted it on her cheek right there by her mouth. And she had these great big blinking eyes like everything was new to her. She had a kid too, a boy, year older than Annabel. Sherry was on welfare.

Annabel was sitting on the floor playing with her Christmas present, a pink doll with blue eyes.

Sherry didn't want a drink. "No, thank you," she said with a smile.

Man knew Holly wouldn't touch the stuff.

Solly got his guitar, got two glasses and poured himself and Man some joy juice, then settled back in the armchair.

Sherry said, "Guess I better get back upstairs. Andy going to wake up soon."

"Naw," Man said. "Stick around. I'll sing you a song. Just for fun. It Christmas, lady. How they say?—Be of good spirit."

Holly laughed, then Sherry kind of laughed too. She sat back down.

Man pulled a kitchen chair over and sat next to Solly, took out his harmonica, put his glass on the floor between his legs. He warmed up a little bit on the harmonica.

Solly tested his strings. "What we gon do?" he said.

"Whatever comes natural." Man started patting his foot. Held the harmonica with both hands. Hit the middle register, moved on up higher and higher. Breathing smoothly for more action, keeping control of the flow of air. Letting it come nice and easy. Now and then he held his nose, to get the breathing stronger. Now he hit a low note, and a lower one. Real soft-like. No spit. He never spat in the harmonica. No, sir. Said to Solly: "Ready?"

"Follow you."

Solly said, "Les go!" And Man cut loose with—

> I'm so sorry to tell you,
> So sorry to have to tell you,
> Yo mama Miss Sadie is a bald-headed lady.
> Yeah, yo mama Miss Sadie is a bald-headed lady.
> I hates to talk about yo mama, Miss Sadie.
> I sho hates to talk about yo mama, Miss Sadie.
> But you leave me nothing else to choose,
> You leave me nothing else to choose.
> She got hair growing on her feets
> So long she can't wear no shoes.

Sherry and Holly were falling out, cracking up.

Man was thinking now this is the way to live. This was better than driving one of them big old pimp roadhog fish-scale diamond-dusted decorated Cadillacs with black-out tape on the windows, silver hubcaps, and tail fins long as canons, better than drinking good liquor and smoking Cuban cigars, maybe even better than most belly-grinding. Times like this he knew why he and Solly became friends. Why they stuck together. The music. Nothing but the music. They came alive in and lived in the music like pollen lived in a flower. And he remembered how they seemed to just understand this the first day they met. Understood it without talking about it. It was a recognition warm and big as a bowling alley. What they shared was always there. They could be together for days without talking and it was as though they were still telling each other all kinds of things, Man with his harmonica or voice and Solly with his guitar, a guitar with such a pretty sound you could've put a pleated skirt on it and some fool would have wanted to marry it.

Now Little Annabel got up and wobbled over to her mama and climbed up on her lap and sat there just looking at her daddy and Man. Didn't crack a smile. She was like that.

So Man wouldn't have to stop, Holly came over and filled his glass again. Bless her heart.

WHEN HE GOT HOME IN THE EARLY
evening, walking straight pretty much but
feeling good and tight, mellow-like, with the
high just starting to come down, he opened his

CHAPTER SIX

door and what did he see. Cleo. Cleo was sitting on the side
of his bed. Just sitting there like she had never left. Breast out. Baby in
her arms. Breast-feeding Karina, and looking pretty as a picture. He was
glad to see Karina but she sure did look too big to be still breast-feeding.

Yet he didn't know what to make of it or how he felt about Cleo being
here. He knew now he was mad as hell, wanted the devil to take her, God
to strike her dead, something, anything to happen. But Lord knows, at
the same time, he was happy to see her and all his feelings started moving
as if in his blood.

He remembered the first time he saw her. Thought, Oh, Lord, let me
down easy. I'm in love. Let me down easy. I'm about to die. This was the
most beautiful woman he'd ever seen in his whole life. Time, baby. Take
yo time. She was pushing a stroller in Jackson Park. Some men were
playing golf near where she was walking on the path. He was sitting on a
bench with his sax, blowing something sweet. He tipped his cap to her.
She smiled. It was one of those blue clear days, you know, when you feel
happy just to be living, with your eyes open. The baby was sucking on
a bottle one minute, the next he threw it on the path. Quicker than
Superman can change, Man got it and handed it to this pretty young
lady. Tipped his cap again. Told her his name. She said, "You a musician?" She said she'd just come up here from New Orleans to live with
her older sister. He told her he was in New Orleans a couple of winters
ago. Funny. The baby was her sister's. The baby's name was Maxwell,
Max for short. But he didn't look like no Max to Man. He laughed at
that name on a baby. Just didn't seem right. So he walked with her, carrying his sax strung around his neck, walked her along the path. Turned
out her name was Cleopatra Queneau. She was twenty-one that summer,
1947. They got married three months later, October eighth, in the
Greater Harvest Baptist Church at Fifty-seventh and Indiana Avenue. It
was her sister Shawn's church. The preacher, Reverend Stu Kesson, was
this bowlegged happy-faced man with a big gap between his front teeth.
Looked like a water buffalo all dressed up in one of those expensive pin-
striped suits.

Man and Cleo had them some happy times at first. Cleo loved the picture show. Till he came north he hadn't seen many movies, mostly cowboy shoot-'em-ups. Then suddenly with Cleo he started seeing all the new movies, some of the old ones too.

When they went to the Loop he felt a little out of place among so many white folks, but it was still nice being with her. They liked the Tivoli too. But most times they went to the Regal or the Met on Forty-seventh. First movie they saw together that summer was *The Best Years of Our Lives*. Double feature with *Song of the South*. Old Hattie McDaniel playing mammy to this white family. They saw *The Razor's Edge* too. They saw *Pinky* too. Story about this white-looking colored woman who wanted to go on and be white, and the other one was *Lost Boundaries*. Same subject, sort of. And when they weren't going to movies they walked in Jackson Park near her sister's house.

But sometimes Cleo wanted to just stay home and read these thrilling romance stories about heartbreaking love and that kind of carrying on. She read *Gone with the Wind* fifteen zillion times. He never did have any patience for reading. Picture shows other than shoot-'em-ups, now he liked them once he got to going to em. But his favorite type of entertainment was to have a drink in his hand in a bar with a lot a happy people and good music. That was heaven for him next to making the music himself. But Cleo didn't care for bars and the people in them.

Man would never forget the first time he met Cleo's sister, Shawn. He was sitting at Shawn's kitchen table. Cleo was at the sink opening a bottle of beer for him. Shawn walked in. Cleo turned around and introduced her sister to her boyfriend. First thing Shawn said was, "Where is Max?" Cleo told her Max was sleeping. Then Shawn, a tall, all-get-out good-looking woman with light brown skin and big, clear eyes, glared at Man and said, "Cleo said you're a musician." He said, That's right. And Shawn glared harder. Said: "Is that *all* you do?" And Man thought of saying, Naw, I can boogie, I can fuck all night, I can throw a pot of pig knuckles out the window, run outside and catch the pot before it falls without spilling a drop, I can howl better than a wolf, I can raise the dead from the swampland with my blues, I can scoobedoo you and yo mama, I knows how to haul ashes and I can put a spell on an audience. But he thought better of saying anything like that. Folks, old timers used to say, if they ain't bragging they complaining. So he just grinned at Shawn, hoping she might grow to like him. But it never happened. He couldn't think of a thing to change that frown. She had it every time she saw him.

Karina was born that next September. On the twelfth. Those were some happy days right along about then. He was working at the time out at Chicago Steel. Manpower had sent him out there but they kept him on longer than they usually kept temps because there was a strike going on.

He was also sent to Ford and other plants. Some chicken-scratch was coming in from music gigs too. Hard to get a regular gig in this town with so many blues singers all over the place. Club owners had it made cause if you didn't want to work for what they offered they could always get somebody else. He played clubs on Sixty-third mostly, three of them right along the strip. The Red Tiger. Sixty-Third Street Tavern. Blew harmonica one night for Jimmy Reed at Ducky Wucky's. But that was chump change. He just did it anyway because he enjoyed it. And Cleo, at first, used to come and listen too. He thought she loved his music. That was back when a pig foot and a bottle of beer seemed like they were always going to be on the table. Hard times hit them winter of 19 and 48, the baby's first winter, winter before this one. People everywhere—up and down Sixty-third, in the cafes, in the taverns, on the jobs—were bitching about the economy and because things were so bad President Truman just barely got enough votes to be reelected.

Now Cleo was gone.

◉

And here she was back again. She had the radio on. Brenda Lee was singing one of them light fluffy things that made her famous. A different kind of play from, say, Lil Johnson's playing with the blues, getting a man with a good hot dog, or getting her stove stoked. Lord, Lord.

Cleo!

But he wouldn't let himself dare think she was back for good. He wanted to believe it but he also wanted to believe a lot a things he hadn't seen come true—he wasn't going to be rich in the next ten minutes, Arthur Godfrey wasn't going to invite him on his show. But he held his breath anyway. Hell, she was here to get after him about last night. He said, "Hey, Cleopatra."

And he walked on into the room. Now Johnny Mathis was whining one of them ballads. Man walked over to the bedside table and turned off the radio.

Cleo looked back to see him. "Hello, Manfred."

Good God Almighty she sure was a fine-looking woman. Always that calm at the center of her face, even when she was full a fire. A calm-like inside her. She got this peace or something always going on, like nobody can touch her there. No matter how upset or mad she got, it seemed to be always there. That was one of the things about this woman that attracted him in the first place. That calm. Remembered the night he had to rush her to the hospital. She was ready to go. Baby was due. A hot September night. Had been over a hundred degrees that day and the heat was still in the air. He couldn't get a taxi to come out to the house. And Cleo was getting closer and closer. He was, you know, how they say, frantic. Yeah, frantic. Running around. He ran next door to this neighbor who had a car, old broken-down thing. But maybe he'd drive them down to Cook County. Old boy by the name of Jacob Bush. Janitor at Montgomery Ward's downtown. Regular family man. Well, they got Cleo out in the car all right, but the fucking car wouldn't start. They raised the hood and looked in there. Jacob looked so dumb there, looking under his own hood, Man wanted to punch him in the mouth. But shit, he was doing him a favor so he kicked the sonofabitching car, kicked the side. Hurt his foot too. This other neighbor from across the street, somebody Man didn't even know, saw them from a window and came over and asked if he could help. Man said, "Yeah. You got a car? My wife having a baby. Got to get to the hospital." They shot down there, going all the way down State just barely missing hitting one car after another. It was a wonder the police didn't stop them. The way they were ducking around those big transfer trucks like nobody's business. Just going. And all through this Cleo was just as calm as you please. Smiling even. Later, on the way back, he made the neighbor stop and fill his tank, and Man paid for it. Man figured there were some good people on this earth, and sometimes they showed up when you needed em.

⦿

Cleo was holding Karina so he saw only the top of his daughter's round head. For her age—she was just over a year old—she still didn't have much hair. She looked just like him, like he spat her out. People always said that. He wanted to see her face so he moved around to the side of the bed and looked over Cleo's shoulder.

Cleo said, "She took her first step by herself the other day."

He didn't say anything.

Karina was sucking away at Cleo's big thick long nipple with her eyes closed. How he loved them nipples before the baby was born. After Karina, Cleo didn't like for him to touch them anymore. Got so he didn't even try. Heap of times, he felt even shame of himself for wanting to.

Cleo said, "I've been away from here now two months. Two months, Fred. I thought you were the one who said you never wanted to see me again. And like an idiot I believed you, thought you were glad to see me go."

He felt like a fool. "Yeah. I know. I just got to thinking . . ."

"You just got to thinking about what?"

"Bout my wife and baby."

"Fred, you might have a wife and a baby but you don't have any way to take care of a wife and baby. You can't take care of yourself hardly. Look at you. Drunk now. Drunk every day."

"I'm not drunk. Just feeling good."

Cleo laughed one of her sad laughs, like she thought he was hopeless. "If you're not drunk I'm not a woman," she said. "Slurring your words. Can't stand up straight. Fred, I thought we had an agreement. You agreed. I left here on peaceful terms with you. You agreed that it was the best thing. We couldn't keep food in the cupboard, couldn't feed the baby, refrigerator empty. It was too hard on the baby, Fred. Eddie is good to her, she gets everything she needs—diapers, food, everything."

"I know. You right. I'm no good for you or anybody." He sat down on the side of the bed just behind her, almost believing it, but feeling a tight-bed of muscles in his stomach he thought of as his ambition to succeed.

"Don't pull your self-pity act on me. You know I don't fall for it. You can do better than you do, Fred. You can work and do your music on the side. You don't have to always be getting drunk and . . ."

"I tolt you I don't get drunk. I gets mellow. It inspiritualration for my music. I'm a person with feelings, Cleo. I got a powerful feeling to be more than just a working man, slaving way his life. I gots something fine in me, Cleo. For better or worse." He felt really strong about what he was saying. If only he could make her understand.

"I know you do, Fred."

He thought he saw tears in her eyes. "But does that mean you don't have to have consideration for anybody but yourself?"

"I tried, Cleo, I tried." And even as he heard and hated the whine in his own voice at this minute, he knew he would try again, even harder. But he felt he didn't have any good way just now to make her believe this new hope and desire in him. How could he show her he intended to ride the wings of his own energy all the way to the top of the sky?

"You didn't try hard enough, because I tried ten times harder than you and things still didn't work. You just put your music first every time—and your drinking. I wanted you to put me and the baby at least on a level with your music. If only you could lay off the bottle—"

We not talking bout the same thing, he thought. Said: "Cleo, listen, my pride won't let me beg, but I wants another chance. You hear me?"

"I wish I could believe you, Fred, but when the drinking and the music come first—"

"If you axing me to give up my music, Cleo, I ain't coming. You know I ain't coming. I just can't see why you got to put the music up against the marriage and say one or the other, it ain't fair, and it ain't the only way. They don't got to be gainst each other like that."

"I'm not asking you to give up your music, Fred."

"Well, good, cause, the way I figures it, one of these days, I knows I can make it bring in some bread—"

He saw she was looking at him with pity and he hated it, wanted her to know she had no need to pity him. Just one piece of good luck, and—

"You're talented, Fred. But—"

He cut her off: "Cleo, like I said fore you left, if you can't take the heat, go. And you did go. And like I say, it was wrong of me to come over there like that."

"If you do it again, Fred, Eddie's going to kill you. He already trying to make me take out a peace warrant against you. You know if he kills you he won't go to jail. You know that, don't you?"

"Listen here. You don't have to talk down to me, Cleo. I'm a grown man."

"Sometimes you don't act like it. You act like a little boy with no self-control. I wish you'd grow up. I love you, Fred."

"You know what I did the night you left?"

"What?"

"I sat up all night, right here on this bed and sang to myself, humming and singing, blew a little harmonica. And I was doing all right till last night. Just something about Christmas Eve. That a nice snowsuit."

"Eddie gave it to her for Christmas." Cleo reached down and kissed Karina's forehead.

Then Man leaned over and kissed the same spot.

Cleo gently touched the back of his hand and smiled, looking directly into his eyes. "I do believe in you, Fred, most of the time."

He grinned. "I'm gon show the world my stuff, what I got. I can make it cause I got faith in myself."

"How bout God?" she said.

Man laughed. "He got faith in me, too."

"Sure, you can make anything you want of yourself right here and now, Fred. If you try."

His face clouded. "All them great blues singers and blues songwriters got they songs stolen from them—W. C. Handy, Leadbelly, Big Bill, all of em. But that shit ain't gon happen to me." He was very agitated now.

"Well, listen, I've gotta go. I just want you to promise me you won't pull any shit like that again. Promise me."

"I promise."

"Because I don't want my baby's father dead. I love you, Fred. You hear me?"

"You mean it, Cleo? Because you do, I mean, knowing that, you see, give me a lot to hope for. You see, I'm going out to Omaha, get myself set up, get a fresh start—"

"You gonna stay with your sister?"

"Only a little while. Getting my own place. Get set up with the music, get a job on the side till the music catch on with the people. But if I knowed you'd come out there and be with me, baby, don't you see—"

"Fred, I can't promise—"

"Not axing for no promise, but something for you to think about. And if you can say maybe, just maybe, thas enough for me. Can you say maybe you come?"

She was just looking at him with her special smile. Then she finally said, "Okay, maybe, but only maybe."

"You do love me, don't you?"

"Sure, I still love you. I just said it a few minutes ago. I'm not going to lie about that. I told you that the day I left here. We just can't make it. Maybe some day in the future when you grow up, when things change."

"When I grow up? I'm twenty-five years old, Cleo."

"So?" She was putting her breast away and Karina was sleeping now. Cleo pulled the hood over the baby's head. "I've got to go," she said, making a restless upperbody gesture. Rhythm woman, rhythm woman, who named yo dance, why you leave me in a trance?

He frowned at her. "Do you gots to go now? Couldn't you stay a little longer, Cleo?" He put his hand on her shoulder and gave her his loving look. He meant it for real. He wanted her bad.

"None of that, Fred. No way am I going back to Eddie with your smell on me. Besides, if I do that it'll just make it harder for you to stop thinking about me. You got to pull yourself together because no matter what happens in the future, we can't be together right now." She got up and started moving toward the door.

He followed her. "Cleo?"

"What?"

"I serious about Omaha."

Cleo gave him a long look and didn't say anything. Then she said, "If that's what you want. It might be just what you need right now. A different city. A smaller town might be the right place."

Then he took her in his arms and pressed his lips against hers, the baby between them. She pulled away. Said: "You're crushing her. Stop!"

But he got her sideways and kept the kiss going till he felt her giving in to it then he felt her tongue shoot in his mouth and he knew she wanted him, needed him, even if only for a few minutes more. He knew Cleo's weakness. He reached inside her coat and under her blouse and felt the smoothness of her slip. Her belly was warm. He saw her eyes on him but he wouldn't look into hers then because he was scared she might be half putting him down and he didn't want to put up with it. Then he felt lower and slipped both hands around her, holding her by her bottom, the flesh of his hands against the flesh of her ass and he felt the heat rise from her and he knew he loved this woman like life itself. And he remembered the first time, always remembered the first time he got in her, that great-God-Almighty feeling of peace and pleasure, he'd never forget it long as he lived. Like having come home from somewhere without ever even knowing he had been gone. Long time, long time, baby, gone. That feeling was still stuck back there in that summer in his room. At the time he had a room in a rooming house on Fifty-ninth and Stoney Island. They stayed in his bed for hours and hours, loving real gentle-like, touching, kissing, hugging. Beautiful, beyond this earth it was so beautiful. He wanted that feeling to come back. It went away slowly. And never came back after the baby got here.

He could have cried. Fact was, tears were in his eyes. Had he blinked she would have seen. He didn't care and he did care. Because he was still kind of mad at her too.

Then she whispered. "Okay. Let me put the baby down before you wake her." She moved back to the bed and eased the baby down, then she turned back to him. "All right. Just this one last time, Fred. But not on the bed. We'll wake her. Sit in the chair."

He looked in those eyes, the eyes of that sweet little New Orleans woman, once he called his own. Oh, Lord. Sweet little mama. Coffee grind, mama. Biscuit roll, baby. Yo love hits me like Gene Benson hits a home run, knocks me out like Joe Louis knocks out some sucker. Talk nasty to me, sugar. He didn't say anything, but sat himself down in the chair. Sweet, sweet little woman. Closed his eyes. Sweet woman. Sweetheart. My my.

Then he felt her hands working at his fly. And she was doing what he thought she was about to do. He got hard. Lord, have mercy. Sweet woman. He felt the weight of her warm bottom, her naked skin, come down on his lap. She was straddling him, her wet warm tongue kissing his neck. And he felt himself sucked into her hot and slick. Lord! Have mercy! Then he knew she had him where he wanted to be. And all his loneliness and coldness was gone.

SATURDAY AFTERNOON. THE TRAIN— Chicago, Burlington & Quincy line—kept on stopping, seemed like, in every little town—Avoca, Minden, Neola, Underwood, Weston—then it stopped in Council Bluffs, Iowa,

CHAPTER SEVEN

and Man knew the next stop after that would be Omaha. He reached inside his breast pocket and took out a couple of folded sheets and reread the song he wrote in the night, thing he called *Not the Doctor, Not the Judge*. It turned him on. Kind of catchy.

He was wide awake now and sober as the train crossed the Missouri River. The wide stretch of brownish-green surface reminded him of bad pea soup or green shit. At the same time the sight of the river gave him the sudden and joyous feeling that he was crossing over out of his old life into a new one in a place where he could cut up without being cut down, could sing and shout without being hushed up.

He looked out the window at the farmland passing by. Little traces of snow along the edges of the winter fields. He remembered from shoot-'em-ups this was once all Indian land. Standing Bear. The Ponca. No more. The train was making a kind of music to the land. Whine, baby, whine. Rag, sugar, rag.

All through January he'd messed around, thinking about leaving Chicago, hanging out with Solly, getting drunk. Then February nineteenth, his birthday, he woke up in a cold wet dream about Cleo, and he made up his mind for real. He was twenty-six. Shit, I'm going to get the fuck outta this city. He scraped together every penny he could get his hands on working odd jobs.

Music gigs that week? Called Mister Lee over on North Lincoln. Lee came through this time. A saxophone player had just cancelled his engagement at the Jefferson. Man took fifty dollars in two nights. Had to give Mister Lee half. Came close to getting a gig at the Checkerboard Lounge on East Forty-third Street. But ended up running a dishwasher in Howard Johnson's for three nights. Paid off his rent. Packed. Left Chicago with just over a hundred dollars.

◉

During the brief time he'd slept he dreamed of a church, some storefront church, probably in Chicago or Atlanta. He was on a street corner watching the church. Word was somebody was using the church as a front for a bootleg or gambling racket. What he was hoping to see or why he was watching wasn't clear to him. He remembered being surprised by somebody using a church as a cover. Why hadn't he thought of that?

As the train rumbled itself on toward Omaha he wished to hell he'd bought him a whole fifth. He'd finished that little half pint of Old Crow he'd tucked in his bag in Chicago, finished it during the night. Couldn't get to sleep. Kept on thinking about the last time he saw Cleo, Christmas Day. Her coming over like that. Seeing his daughter. Doing it in the chair. That was over a month ago, going on six weeks. If you don't like my peaches, baby, please don't shake my tree. And he had kept his word. All the time he was getting together enough money to leave. If you don't like my cucumber don't hang round my vine. He never once called her or anything. Thought about it. Ain't gon lie. Thought about her, sure, kept on dreaming about her just about every night. Waking up thinking she was right there in bed beside him, hoping in his sleep, and waking up by himself, lonesome. But didn't force himself on her. Didn't want to do that.

> You may be gone now,
> But you won't be gone always.
> You may be gone for now, baby,
> But you sho won't be gone always.

He wanted to show her he could control himself. He kept thinking: One of these days, sweet mama, you gon want your daddy back again. Hoping it more than believing it.

◉

Now on the train all night long, half asleep, he had heard his own words in his mind, his *Plantation Blues*. He meant it to have that kind of rhythm, the train-on-the-tracks sound, going rag, mama, rag, whine, baby, whine, over and over. And he kept on repeating the words—

> Goin down to the railroad station.
> Take me to that railroad station.
> Goin down to the railroad station.
> Take me to the railroad station.
> Point me to the Omaha track.
> Goin to Omaha and ain't never comin back.

—as they entered the city, heading for the final short stretch to Union

Station, he saw dreary gray-and-brown railway yards, saw the long stretch of the power plants. Then finally, the train jerked to a stop inside the Marcy Street Station. Through the window he saw people everywhere, swarming. Well, mercy me!

The conductor was coming through calling, "Omaha! Omaha! This is Omaha!"

The minute Man stepped down off the train he saw his sister Deborah—Debbie they called her—looking at him and grinning and waving over the heads of the closer people. Even after ten years, he could still spot those big eyes and that soft brown complexion anywhere in any crowd. She waited right where she was. When he got to her, he was grinning and she was grinning, and she and he couldn't say anything. Cat had their tongues.

Then she threw those big fat arms around him and pulled him against her bosom, saying, "Lord, Lord, Freddy, you ain't changed a bit. Look at yourself. Looking just like you looked ten years ago. Just like Daddy. What was you then—fifteen, sixteen?"

"Something like that. You looking good, Deb." He turned her loose and held her back by the shoulders to see her face. "Yeah. Sure is good to see you, girl." She was big for a woman. They were all big, a big family.

"Come on," she said, "let's go."

On the way she carried his saxophone and he brought his suitcase. "Lord, Lord," she said, "you finally got yourself a wife and settled down. I remember Mama telling me about it two years ago. And they said, well maybe baby brother will finally get himself together and be happy. And then here you come calling me just before Christmas—wasn't it?—saying you and your wife separated. Any chance of getting back with, uh, Cleo?"

"I don't know."

"Would you like to?"

"Sho, but cain't we talk about this later?"

◉

In the Tenth Street parking lot across from the train station they got in Debbie's brand new 1950 lemon yellow Cadillac.

"Girl, you must be living high on the hog."

"We doing all right. I told you I got my own beauty parlor now didn't I?"

"You or Mama tolt me in a letter. Lyle still at the steel company?"

"Yeah, and he got promoted to crew boss." Bragging, she gave him a look to see how impressed he was.

Grinning, he tried not to look so dry-long-so.

"So, this is Nebraska. Wrote a song last night bout coming here."

"I didn't believe you'd really come, Freddy. It's so good to see you, boy! A song, huh? You still writing songs."

He sang—

> I'm gon pack my bag, baby,
> Gon be traveling bound.
> I'm gon pack my bag, baby,
> Gon be traveling bound.
> Don't expect me, baby, to be around
> Cause I'm moving outta this old town.

"Boy, you still got a good singing voice. I'm going to have to get you in my church choir. You used to sing in the church when you was a little boy in Lexington."

Man laughed at the memory, him singing with a bunch of other young'ens. He laughed because he knew she wasn't serious about getting him into church. He backslid so long ago he didn't even feel bad about it anymore. Never could understand why church didn't make him as happy as sin. God's dangers weren't as much fun. But he figured if there was a God he didn't have to go to any church to sing for him. Folks talked about the blues being sinful, but in his judgment, any God in his right mind was going to like the blues much as he liked the spirituals. Blues done saved as many lives as church songs.

Debbie started the engine and turned on the heat. Warm air shot into his face and it sure felt good. "Hey! If you're interested Lyle can get you on out at Lomax. You'd have to start out as a helper but that's how he started out and he worked his way up. They treat the colored boys well out there. Not like so many of these jobs where they try to keep the colored boys down at the bottom, mopping the toilets. They got good insurance and a union, cost-of-living raises. The company did well during the war and a lotta people working then stayed on and invested in Lomax Steel. In a few years Lyle going to become a part owner too."

But Man was thinking about getting some kind of music job in that Omaha lounge she told him about on the telephone. Thinking about calling Solly, too, trying to talk him into getting his ass out here to work with him. Could get a regular thing going. He was going to try hard as he knew how to get Cleo too to come on out here so they could start over again. He wasn't going to lie. He thought about that. Deep down, hoped for it. At the same time, he told himself he had to keep on keeping on right now, not live in the past.

Debbie said, "I got to make a quick stop, pick up some wigs I ordered. Won't take but a minute."

All right, he said, and he was thinking about how thirsty he was for a drink, something to take the travel-dust out of his throat. Double shot of Old Crow or even a pint of white lightning wouldn't be too bad.

She was pulling out the Tenth Street lot across from the train station now. Man saw yellow taxicabs lined up along the curb. Painted on their doors was: 20¢ PER MILE. Debbie said, "Got to be careful in this here town, Freddy. You can't do but twenty in the downtown area. Thirty-five tops anywhere in town. And they watch Negroes something terrible."

They were waiting just behind a red Ford with a white lady at the wheel. Another white lady next to her. The white lady stopped and stood a long time before driving out into the street. When the white lady left, Debbie eased her new-smelling Cadillac out on the street and headed north on Tenth.

"But it ain't a bad town to live in, to raise children in. When we first came up here everybody seemed real nice. The Negroes and the white folks were getting along pretty well. Presidents stop here—Roosevelt and Eleanor and Hoover the same year. And everybody just recently been proud of this colored boy, Charles Jackson French, who was a big war hero. And Truman stopped here last year and even got out of his car and walked in the streets with everybody. I ain't saying some bad things ain't happened. Back some years ago a mob broke into the courthouse and threatened to lynch the mayor if he didn't hand over this puny little old colored boy they thought had raped some white gal. Told the mayor they would burn down the courthouse if he didn't hand over the boy."

She drove north on Tenth, then west on Douglas. He noticed a music store right away. Looked like a good one. They passed a pet shop with dogs in the window on one side and cats on the other. But she finally stopped for a light and got distracted looking at two black women crossing the street headed for a department store, a grand white building that stretched the whole city block they were facing. He looked at the street signs. Sixteenth and Douglas. "Both of them my customers. Claim they can't pay me but got plenty of money to go in that expensive Brandeis. I'm telling you, colored folks is a blip!" Debbie said. "What was I talking about?"

When the light changed she drove on for another block and turned left and parked alongside the store she called Brandeis.

"Telling me about Omaha."

"When I come back, baby brother."

He watched her push her way through the revolving doors, bigger than anybody in sight.

He sat there watching the white folks. Well-dressed folks falling in and coming out of the big department store looking like they were day-dreaming or mad about something. White folks, they strutting or jumping to the same rhythm anybody else strutting or jumping to. They must got they blues when it comes to love, like us, dreaming in the moon, like us, high-toned marrying down to common, like us, they die in the arms of peoples who love them, like us, they dream they hearts gon mend and be thinking love gon overcome everything, like us, try to make it they North, they South, they Sunday and they Monday, they forever, like us, and they too got this way of seeing theyself in the face of the peoples they love instead of the face of they love one, like us. He sighed.

At that point in his thoughts he saw his sister coming toward the car carrying four big boxes. He reached back and opened the back door, and she carefully set the boxes on the back seat.

Huffing and puffing she climbed back into the driver's seat, shooting a glance at him, saying, "Baby brother, you should see inside that store. It's something else! All these high ceilings and fluted columns and giant plants and stuff. I just feel rich walking through there."

"See yo two friends?"

"No, and I'm glad. I don't like for my customers to know where I get my wigs from. Them wigs I order all the way from Egypt. Boy, I'm telling you, colored ladies love that long straight black hair. Specially the bald-headed ones." She giggled, shaking all over.

And in his mind:

> I may be yo best pal,
> But you listen here bald-headed gal,
> I say, I may be yo best pal, baby,
> But you listen here, bald-headed gal,
> I ain't gon give you no mo money, honey,
> To buy you all them wigs you keep wearing,
> Cause, baby, you got me drinking and swearing.
> I may be yo best pal,
> But you listen here, bald-headed gal,
> I may be yo best pal,
> But you listen here, bald-headed gal,
> I sho ain't giving you no mo money, honey,
> To buy you all them wigs you keep wearing,
> Cause, baby, you got me drinking and swearing.

"What were we talking about, baby brother?"
"Omaha."
She pulled away from the curb and entered traffic.
He said, "Just wondering what folks do round here."

"Oh, yeah. In the summer everybody around here go to the racetrack. Oh, I remember what I was saying. How they lynched that boy—William Brown—shot his body full of bullets then dragged it through the streets and burned it. Lynched him right over there on the corner of Eighteenth and Harney—about five or six blocks from here."

"So what this about the racetrack?"

They were leaving the downtown area. Debbie drove to Twenty-fourth and headed north. In a few minutes Man saw nothing but rows and rows of square dull-looking wooden houses, poor shotgun houses, the kind he'd seen in Atlanta's black section, worse-looking than the house he himself was born in.

"The racetrack. Yeah. That's out at Ak-Sar-Ben Field, out on Center and Sixtieth. I just take a limited amount of money out with me. That way I don't get carried away. They got a good track out there too. A mile long. Lots of people from North Omaha play the horses, guys from Swift and Cudahy and Armour go out there and throw away their money like crazy. I'm sure glad Lyle ain't like that. But it's lots of fun. Horses. You like to gamble?" said Debbie.

"Sho. I do some gambling. But I ain't never been to no horse race. Stock car race, but not no horses."

"I go out two, three times a week. I'll take you in the springtime when they start. It'll be fun."

They were still moving north on Twenty-fourth Street. Debbie said, "This is the colored folk's main drag. Everything happens here. My shop is just two blocks up."

"So, what else colored folks do around here?"

"Lots. Halloween we got a big parade on this street. It's something to see. Folks in costumes they made at home. Got two Negro newspapers, the *Messenger* and the *Monitor*. I take just the *Monitor*. But there lots of Negro-owned businesses out here. We're like our own little town—separate from the Italians. They got theirs. The Germans, the Jews, the Swedes, the Greeks, the Irish. Got their own sections, own businesses, churches. We do too."

Looking out the window, he said, "I never knowed there was so many Negroes out in Omaha. When I heard you moved out here I thought you musta been living with the Indians and cowboys or something." He laughed.

"No, honey. We about twelve thousand and white folks about thirty or so. Negroes been in Omaha before most of these here Italians and Poles and Welsh people. We came out on the trains, working as porters and in the sleeping cars back before the 1890s. Most of these folks came after World War One."

"Pretty cold right now. Get any colder than this?"

She laughed. "It can get down to thirty below. What you talking about? Chicago cold too."

He shuddered. "Maybe I came to the wrong place. Lynchings and freezing weather don't agree with me."

She kept laughing. "Now your summers can be nice. But it can get so hot and humid you can't breathe. Last summer it was over a hundred degrees for two weeks. And *humid*. I mean it was *bad*. But that don't happen too much. We suppose to get rain between April and September but it ain't been happening much here lately." She sighed. "Lots of things you're going to need to know, like the barbershop, where to cash a check, little stuff like that. Lyle goes to Walt Calloway's Barbershop, it's the best of the two colored ones out our way."

SHE STARTED PULLING OVER TO THE
curb to stop. The cross-street sign said
Grant. Man knew she lived on Grant but
this was a business section of town. He looked
about. In many ways it put him in the mind of
those rundown neighborhoods around Decatur Street, southeast of
Five Points, what they called the East Side in Atlanta. Blind Willie's
trucking point.

CHAPTER EIGHT

This place called Omaha had the same kind of easygoing feeling
Atlanta had. In shabby shop windows he saw these jacked-up prices
just like on Decatur Street. He saw a place called Miss Etta's Tavern
on the west corner of Twenty-fourth and Lake, and across from it on
the east corner, another place called Bob Jones' Entertainment Palace.
Must be the place Debbie wrote him about. Big sign out front said: LIVE
ENTERTAINMENT! Boys hanging out front a the local poolroom down
the street. Jivers sitting on the curb talking shit. Fat daddies cruising by in
their big new Cadillacs and Lincolns. Secondhand stores, greasy spoons.
If my folks ain't bragging they complaining. It's the way of the world.
You hear babble in the rabble. Vendor on the corner, head sticking out of
his booth, calling, *"World-Herald!"* Man thought, This just might be my
kinda place. A place where the blues could live and be appreciated, a
place where his own life might become a song.

> Gots to change my luck, baby.
> Sho gots to change my luck.

Then he saw the torso of a big black man moving along the sidewalk
in front of Miss Etta's at about three feet from the ground. Man stared
hard. Legless, the man's torso was fitted into a square wooden box with
low sides. But how was the box moving? Man's gaze didn't waver. From
where he sat, it looked like the amputee was scooting along on eight
skate wheels, two in each corner. The man was using his hands, pressing
his palms against the sidewalk, propelling himself forward at a fast
speed. His arms were long and thick and they reminded Man of chimpanzee arms. "Deb, who is that?"
"Who? Oh, that's Poppa Leon, a numbers' runner."
Man shook his head and laughed. There'd been another joker who

looked just like Poppa Leon in Atlanta, legless and fitted into a box. But that joker was a pimp, yes, a pimp, not a policy man, friend of Miss Gazella Bellamy of Butler Street. Everybody knew Thurgood the legless pimp of Decatur Street.

Seeing this Omaha Twenty-fourth Street, he remembered Atlanta now with affection. Decatur Street all over again for sho. On Friday and Saturday night Atlanta's Decatur Street got a spirit about it and started jumping. That's the way Decatur was. Decatur and Butler! Decatur and Piedmont! His first stopping place when he left home. He hung out there, picking up the sounds, shooting craps, playing the numbers with the older boys in the barbershop, the shoeshine parlor. Fellow in the shoeshine parlor could make his rag talk like a musical instrument. Yeah, this Twenty-fourth Street looked just like another Decatur. Place where everybody come out in their best, strutting and jiving when they got some money in their pockets. He saw strollers moving up and down Twenty-fourth, not warmed-up yet, but just wait till later, tonight, they were going to have a little more strut in their stride.

He and Debbie came to a stop in front of Debbie's beauty parlor—with the words TRUDY'S AND DEBBIE'S BEAUTY SALON FINE HAIR-DRESSING AND MANICURING painted on the showcase window—and in the window display: hair, nail, facial products, and wigs.

As they got out, three small boys with big curious eyes came toward the hot hood and stopped, just staring at them. Man looked at Debbie trying to figure out what was happening. Debbie smiled. "Hey, there, Willie Lee. What yall up to?"

"Nothing," one of the boys said. "Just wanna see your brother what play every instrument in the world."

Debbie said, "Boy! Wash your mouth out with soap. I never said no such lie!"

Willie Lee, looking up, said to Man: "Is you famous?"

Man laughed. "Naw."

Lord, Lord. Ain't well known, jes here on loan, sho ain't well-known, jes here on loan.

"Miss Debbie says you is famous."

"Willie Lee! Go on way from here boy with your lying self."

The boys just looked, mouths slightly opened.

Debbie said, "My sons started this whole mess, got all these boys worrying me half to death, Freddy."

A heavyset woman came out of the beauty parlor grinning. "You must be Manfred, Debbie's brother. Welcome to Omaha. Ain't like Chicago, is it? My name's Beverly—"

"How you do, Beverly?"

"Deborah, he is big, I mean *big*. And good-looking too. How come you didn't tell me you had such a handsome *good-looking* brother?"

"Because I know you don't know how to behave yourself."

And they busted out giggling like schoolgirls flirting on a playground with the new boy.

"Come on Freddy, come on inside. I want you to meet my business partner, Trudy Craig. Trudy's a lady. She knows how to behave herself around mens."

Beverly poked her bottom lip out and frowned at his sister but she was just playing. Didn't mean any harm. Said, "Wait till the next time you ax me to do your hair."

The boys followed them to the door then Debbie said, "You children run on and play now. You all over the man before he's in town good. Give him a chance. Get now! *Get!*" And she waved them away.

Inside the small shop there was the sharp chemical smell of shampoo, hair oils, creams, and the burning smell of hot combs and pressed hair. The woman he took to be Trudy was working on a customer's head with a straightening comb. The customer was straining trying to see out of the corners of her eyes. Trudy stopped pressing hair and gave Man a big big smile.

Trudy said, "Well, well, so you is Mister Manfred Banks. Man, if you only know how much your sister talk about you. Whew! She so proud of you. You must be something."

He tried to smile. Said, "Debbie, she good at making a big to-do over nothing."

"I just stopped by so yall could see Freddy. He got all his stuff out there in the car. I got to get him up to the house so he can unpack. I'm cooking two rabbits for dinner, so we got to get going. Come on, Freddy. See you, Bev, Trudy. I'll call later about my appointments for tomorrow. Did Miss Jones call back?"

"Miss Thing? No."

"Bye."

And they were back in the car. Debbie turned left on Lake and drove uphill till she came to Thirty-first Street, swung in and, mercy, mercy, came to Grant Street again. It wasn't a through street. But here Grant was again, up here, and it was a neighborhood street. Downtown it was business. "This is our house right here."

"Lyle got this place with his GI money, didn't he?"

"What you talking about? I helped buy this place. Lyle had the GI Bill and didn't even use it. He got some musting-out pay that helped a little bit with the down payment. I bet you glad you had flat feets, huh?"

"Naw, not really. I wouldn't a minded going to war."

A truck tire hung by a rope from a tree in the front yard. They got out and went in. The house was a simple little frame job with a front porch and swing. Screen door on the front door. Hole in it like somebody kicked it.

Debbie showed him his room upstairs, an attic type room, had to stoop to keep from bumping the ceiling over by the bed against the wall. Then she went back downstairs. There was a little radio on a table by the bed. He turned it on to see if it worked. Newsman said something about the Rosenberg trial, the North Koreans attacking the South. He thought: Looks like another war coming. American boys probably going to get sent to this one too. Then the man said Ezzard Charles said he could knock Jersey Joe out again, that his winning the title wasn't just a fluke. Man turned off the radio.

By the time he put his sax under the bed and hung up his few clothes in the closet, he heard stomping feet and voices downstairs coming in the front door. He knew it was the boys, Wade, twelve, and Marvin, fourteen. They were whispering down there. And he heard Debbie say, "Yall don't have to whisper. Uncle Freddy ain't sleep." And louder, to him: "You sleep, Freddy?"

Then he went down and there they were tall as him, at least the oldest one was. He hadn't seen them in ten years. Wade was going on two and Marvin going on four then. Debbie and Lyle were in town at the same time staying with his sister, Miss Henrietta, woman Man never knew well. Fact was, never knew any of Lyle's people well but he had a bunch of them there in Atlanta too.

Man had already left home. Had his own place in a rooming house—found it from an ad in the *Daily World*—a kind of gambling house on Butler Street. The lady, Miss Gazella Bellamy, who ran the place had some women rooming with her but they were working for her too, they did a little business upstairs on the QT. Man was like a son to them. Only one time did he have something to do with one of them and it was because she—Ada Douglas—took his thing out and made it hard in her mouth. She came in his room in the attic one Sunday afternoon and did that. Said it would make a man of him. And fact was he did start feeling his oats. But he wanted to be a man in other ways too so he made himself some money by running numbers for Miss Gazella. That's how he got enough money to get out of Atlanta. Took a train from there to New Orleans because people said that was where all the music was in those days. Everybody was talking about New Orleans. Played his harmonica and sang on the streets for handouts. Old Peg Leg Howell once told him he was good, but also told him to go up to Chicago.

Debbie's boys? He couldn't get over how big they were. He spoke to them. Said, "Yall member me?"

They come just to grinning. Marvin, lanky with shifty eyes, said, "I think I do. You used to ride me on your leg."

"That's right. I was your hoss. And you member that too. Boy you was just a little old thing. I took you down on Decatur one time too, to the barbershop. You raised hell and the barber, old George Willis, said we should nickname you Tenderhead."

"I remember that." He was grinning.

"And you Wade wont even walking good."

Debbie, standing in the doorway between the dining room and the living room, said, "And do you remember I made you go to Big Bethel one Sunday with them?"

He did. Said: "Sho." But he remembered feeling all kinds of mixed-up feelings about going into that church with his sister. Big Bethel A. M. and E. was just a few doors down the street from Miss Gazella's place—corner of Butler and Auburn. And he was fearing the girls from the house would see him going in. You see, he was supposed to be in the sporting life, running numbers and living there. He had a different kind of life from the church people's. Thought the girls might laugh at him, wonder if he was about to get religion, give up his music and leave the life. That church always scared him anyway, what he heard tell of it, saved folks and sinners marching down the aisle together and all those hundreds of women and men singing in there together like voices down from heaven passing judgment on everybody.

Then out of nowhere Debbie said, "Wade, why don't you pull your pants up. I don't like to see you wearing your pants down on your hips like that. Reminds me of some old lazy nigger down South."

Wade gave her a look. "Mama, there you go, picking on me again." He looked embarrassed.

"I'm not picking on you, Wade. You my baby." She laughed.

His lips were poked out. "Yes you is," he mumbled, taking off his jacket. He threw it on an armchair in the corner.

"Hang up your coat, Wade," Debbie said. "You know better than that."

The boy pouted but walked over and picked up the coat and stamped out of the room.

"Uncle Freddy, Mama say you can teach me how to play any instrument I wanna learn. Can you learn me the saxophone?"

"Depend on can you catch on to the saxophone."

"I wants to. I got a chance to get in the school band. I'm in music appreciation but they don't teach us how to play nothing but the piano."

"What's wrong with that? Piano is fine instrument, boy. Get yo mama to play you some Roosevelt Sykes, some Speckled Red, some Little Brother, Otis Spann, Champion Jack, and Jimmy Yancey."

"His mama's going to spank his butt if he don't stop nagging his uncle. Listen, Marvin, your uncle just got here. Don't be all over him talking about no piano lessons. Go on, boy, do your chores."

"What chores?"

"You know what your Saturday chores is, boy. Now get!"

He too left the room with his bottom lip hanging down low enough to touch the floor. Man laughed because it put him in mind of himself, always fighting with his daddy when he was coming up. Daddy wasn't so bad. Man just didn't want anybody always telling him what to do.

After a while Man walked out into the front yard and looked around at the neighborhood. It was still cold but warm for February. You may be gone now, but you won't be gone always. It hit him: All this time since leaving Chicago he hadn't stopped thinking about, brooding on, his wife. All the while he talked to his sister and nephews, Cleo was there just behind his words in his thoughts. You sho won't be gone always. He shook his head, trying to nail himself down to the here-and-now. Heartsick with love for that woman. Didn't seem like a Saturday to him but then he spent Friday night on a train. No people out except one man over across the way shoveling snow off his walkway. Man waved to him, the man waved back.

◉

Lyle was over at a buddy's house helping him fix his truck. He'd been gone all afternoon. Man and Debbie were sitting in the living room watching this dance show, all these white kids doing something like the jitterbug. They looked pretty cute. Put their own little twist to it. Ain't nothing wrong with that. Then she said, "Wouldn't it be nice if Mama had a telephone? We could call her and talk. We ought to put one in her house. But she wouldn't use it. She'd probably run from it when it ringed." And Debbie laughed. But he wondered how that would be, being able to talk on the telephone with Mama. He had never heard her voice on a telephone. He didn't even know if any colored folks in Lexington had telephones. Not even many white folks, he bet. But behind this train of thought on another track he wished with all his might he could call Cleo, just to hear her voice, just once more, to hear her say, "Maybe . . ."

◉

Man wasn't paying much attention to television when Lyle came in around six-thirty, dressed in a hunter's red-and-black striped jacket. Man wondered if Lyle had some liquor in the house. Never heard nothing about Lyle not being a drinking man. Man knew he should have brought himself an extra because he now had that I-don't-know feeling. Just came over him like a cloud ruining a nice day.

But here was Lyle. He didn't look all that different from the way Man remembered him. Lots of muscle. Tired-looking, sleepy-eyed. Weak smile. Little hair over the top lip. Real dark-skinned, almost dark as his own. Lyle came on in and Man stood up and smiled. They shook hands. "How you doing, Lyle?"

Lyle slapped him on the shoulder. "Good to see you, boy. It's been many years but I can still see little Freddy. Say! You look more and more like your daddy."

Lyle was taking off his jacket. He still had that crooked smile at the corner of his mouth. His overalls was dirty.

Debbie said, "Lyle, don't sit on the couch in them overalls."

He waved her away. Said: "All right, Deb. I hear you." So he just stood there.

Lyle looked at Man. "How long ago, Freddy, is it been? How old was you—?"

"I was sixteen last time I seen you and Debbie and the kids. Member, I left home when I was fifteen then I seen you all in Atlanna that one time. I was sixteen then."

"You hear from your mama?"

"Yeah. I always stay in touch with my mama, you know. Once I won fifty bucks in a crap game in New Orleans and I got me a train ticket, a new suit and took myself back to Georgia just to see Mama." But even as he said this he was remembering how he had longed for his Aunt Ida. He missed her something terrible.

"Where was you living when your daddy died?" Lyle said.

"I was still in New Orleans." He remembered being hungry most of the time in New Orleans, remembered soup lines in charity stations, sleeping on the streets or in flophouses, playing his harmonica in the French Quarter for handouts.

Lyle said, "We didn't see you at the funeral did we?"

"I didn't know about it till he was already in the ground."

"Nobody knew how to get in touch with you, Freddy. Daddy died June seventh, 1943."

"I was nineteen then. You was, what, twenty-three?"

"Yeah and the year after that Lyle and me and the kids moved up here."

"I liked Quincy," said Lyle. "He was always nice to me."

"That's cause you was taking a crumb-snatcher off his hands."

"Freddy!" Debbie shouted at him. "What a thing to say! Daddy liked Lyle because Lyle was a nice boy."

"Thas true. Didn't mean any harm, Lyle. You just never had to put up with his stuff."

Lyle said, "What's for dinner, honey?"

"I baked two rabbits. Turnip greens. Cornbread. Baked a sweet potato pie, your favorite. The boys out somewhere. But we can eat anytime you two hungry." Then directly to Man: "They both picky about food, specially rabbit. Lyle can tell you. We don't have to wait for them."

◉

At dinner Lyle said, "Debbie said you might be interested in hiring on out at Lomax."

Man nearly choked on the rabbit. "Uh. Yeah, Lyle. You think they'll take me? I did work for a little bit at Chicago Steel, you know."

"What you do there?"

"I was a helper. Nothing special."

"I see. Well, it'd have to be like that here too. But you could work your way up, if you want to. I just made crew boss."

"I know you did. Debbie told me. Gratulations."

"Thanks. They got a janitor job open, too. Pays more than just a bay helper's job," Lyle said.

"I was wondering too if I might be able to get a gig, you know, in one of the bars."

Lyle said, "Tending bar?"

Man laughed. "No—"

"Lyle, he means his music. You know Freddy's a musician."

"Oh, yeah. Sure. You could do that on the weekend. I bet, uh, what's her name—"

"Jorena?"

"Yeah, Jorena Jones. She's one of Debbie's customers."

"Miss Thing they call her. Lady lover."

"I see," Man said. "She owns that tavern?"

"Her daddy left it to her," said Debbie. "Bob Jones. Cancer got him few years back. But before the war they said that place jumped. Talk about Speckled Red and Roosevelt Sykes. He had them and Tampa Red over from Chicago."

Man could hear Tampa Red putting down his jive, singing, "If you want me to love you, you got to take all your money, throw it against the wall, you take what sticks, I take what fall."

And Debbie was still talking: "Peoples like old dirty mouth Lucille Bogan. Blind Blake. Even had a white guy there once, Mezz Messrow. Honey, when Jorena come to get her hair done she talks up a storm about her daddy and all the great folks he knew in his day. Half of what she say, I swear, has got to be a lie."

Man said, "I noticed the place when we was coming down Twenty-fourth. I like to see inside."

64

"Don't worry, you will."

At that point the boys came busting in through the front doorway.

Wade was crying, "Mama, Marvin, and Willie Lee got stopped by the police down on Twenty-fourth."

"What? What you crying for?" Debbie jumped up from the table and rushed over to the boys standing right there between the living room and the dining room.

"Marvin hit me."

"Because he such a blabbermouth."

"What the police stop you for?"

"I don't know," said Marvin. "All we was doing was walking down the street."

"What they say?"

"Told us to go home."

Debbie told the boys, "Yall go on upstairs, wash up, and get ready for dinner."

The telephone rang.

Debbie went in the living room and picked it up. "Hello? Oh, hi, Bev. Yeah. I'm listening. Uh-huh. Well, that's a nice idea, Bev, but I have to ask my brother. Hold on."

Debbie was looking dead at him. She put the phone down and came back to the table and stood right by him and whispered, "This gal is really gone on you. She wants me to ask you if you'd like to go to a social with her tonight, just to meet some people, get to know people. She belongs to one of the social clubs, you know."

Man shook his head no.

Debbie said, "Ah, go on, Freddy. It's a good way to meet people. It's not like Beverly would be your date or nothing like that. I'll tell her you'll go."

"Okay. What the hell." He thought it'd be a good way to get out of the house and get something to drink without being direct about it. Besides, get to see the town a little bit. Get my mind off Cleo for a minute or two. Thinking bout her sho ain't gon bring her out here on the next train. Need a lucky rabbit's foot. Need some hoodoo power. Get out and see the town, man.

Debbie went back to the phone. "Bev, he says yes, and thank you, girl. You so thoughtful. You coming by to pick him up?"

Debbie came back to the table.

He just looked at her. "Another fine mess you got me in," he said, trying to imitate Oliver Hardy talking to Stan Laurel. But he was joking, sort of joking. But this was easy. Didn't even affect the larger plan. He knew what he had to do now.

TURNED OUT MAN AND BEV DIDN'T
stay at the club more than an hour—under
an hour. This is what happened: Miss
Eudora Woods, lady hosting the party in her
home at Twenty-second and Maple, had set up for

**CHAPTER
NINE**

Blackjack. A fifth of Wild Turkey was on the card table. Four big greasy-looking jokers were sitting around the table, two with cigars in their mouths. Five or six women were about the living room chatting. The record player was spinning some kind of rock and roll. Bev—who looked real nice in her pink cotton-candy dress—took him around to everybody introducing him. Miss Eudora, at least ten years older than the rest of them, he guessed, showed him her purple gums. But her eyes weren't too friendly. The jokers playing cards didn't offer him any Wild Turkey and the ladies eyed him with suspicion. He got around to asking Miss Eudora for a glass of water, thinking she might get the hint, but she marched him in the kitchen and showed him the tap. That was it, far as he was concerned. He said to Bev, "Why don't we hit the road, go on down to this place called the Palace?" On the way they stopped at her house, which was one block over on Corby.

Bev said she had to check her stove, make sure she turned off the gas. "Come in." And he did. Front porch light on, light on in the living room window. Yellow house. Swing on the front porch. Nice house, friendly-like. Following her lead, he wiped his feet on the doormat then stepped inside behind her. Everything lacy and neat, rug down the middle of the hallway, rooms off to the sides, laid out just like Debbie and Lyle's place. Yeah, looked like lot these houses in North Omaha were pretty much shotgun style.

"You live here by yoself?"

"I sure do. And I like it like that." Bev made a pretend-serious face, making her mouth tight and throwing her head, snapping it a little, like putting a finish on what she said. "Come on back to the kitchen. You can have a quick beer while I check the stove."

Thinking about Cleo—

> The woman that I love,
> Lord, Lord, she gives me high blood.
> I say, the woman that I love,

She gives me high blood.
Yes, Lord, that woman that I love so deep,
She got me screamin and hollering in my sleep.

He followed her back there, looking at her big yellow legs and her huge rump. He was feeling a little turned-on to her. She wasn't exactly his type but he hadn't had any since that time with Cleo over a month ago. Beating his meat was getting old. But he was surprised by the sudden guilt he felt. What was this sense of loyalty to his wife, right now probably in the arms of that preacher man? He could hear Solly say, "Fred, is you a fool?"

"Look in the icebox," Bev said. "Opener in that drawer."

He opened the icebox and took out a bottle of Budweiser, got the opener from the drawer as she checked the stove knobs then went on back, he guessed, to the toilet. A door closed and a minute later the toilet flushed.

Still thinking about Cleo—

The woman that I love,
She won't make me no cornbread.
Yes, the woman that I love,
Won't make me no cornbread.
The woman that I love,
She'd rather see me stone.

He drank about half the bottle in one swallow, suppressed a belch, and wiped his mouth on his sleeve, then looked around the kitchen. On the wall were two photographs in old-time frames. One of an old man, the other of an old woman. Must have been Bev's mama and daddy. The woman was for sure colored but the man looked white. Bev had the old man's forehead and eyes but her mama's cheeks and mouth.

Bev came back into the kitchen pulling at her dress where it had stuck to her stockings and slip. That kind of pulling. She looked right nice doing that. Kind of got him hot because she showed some thigh, not on purpose, just from yanking and pulling. If you like my potatoes, mama, please dig up my vine. He finished the beer and put the bottle on the sink. "Thank you," he said.

"You welcome." Her smile was bright as a sunflower. "What'd you want me to call you?"

"Anything you feel like."

"You know, I like you." She walked right up to him and put her arms around his shoulders and pulled him against her. He had to take her around the waist to keep from falling off balance. Strong for a woman.

They kissed, soft at first, then hard, then tongued. Now Bev pulled back and said, "Yes indeed, I'm going to like you."

They went back out to the car and drove down to Twenty-fourth and Lake, and just as they drove up a red 1947 Cadillac was pulling out from the curb so they took the spot and parked right out front of Bob Jones' Entertainment Palace.

On the way in Bev said, "The owner of this place is a knockout—freakish. I mean, sometime I think she just what everybody say she is, a bulldyke. It's just her cool way, and she ain't never been with no man that anybody know about. And she hinkty too!"

Man grunted a reply, thinking, who cares. Not everybody needed to dance to a robinson or call hay bop-a-re-bop to a hairy chest. So what if some women, like men, liked the tickle of a Josephine Baker feather, the glow of a turquoise headdress, the touch of a flashing body covered with blue sequins and emeralds?

The place was all lit up with flashing and blinking lights. People, men and women, were hanging around the entrance and just out front on the sidewalk, lots of them, talking and jiving. The jukebox music inside was blasting out some good stuff, Speckled Red hitting hard at *The Dirty Dozens*. Hearing that, Man knew this was the right place for him.

He figured it was too early for live music, being only around eight-thirty. Suddenly, he felt happy—but it was a sad-happiness. In rhythm with the music, he snapped his fingers and whispered, "Yeah."

Bev glanced at him and frowned.

The minute they stepped inside Man sized up the place. It was oblong and country-swank with dark blue-and-purple drapes at the two windows that flanked the entrance. The same type of drapes hung alongside the small stage at the back. A small dance floor in front of the stage around which were gathered about fifty tables and chairs, all occupied by well-dressed people drinking and laughing and talking. The walls were mahogany paneling. Many people were also packed at the elegant bar which was to his right with a wall-size mirror behind it. Cigarette smoke hung lazily in the dark air. Speckled Red stopped. The jukebox was now playing Billie Holiday.

A woman stopped Bev and started chatting. Man looked around. People all over the floor, some of them dancing to the jukebox, so many of them packed at the bar, Bev and he couldn't get anywhere near. Planning to cut down soon, but right now he was hurting for a real drink. He could see over heads, behind the bar rows and rows of bottles—scotch, vodka, and those giant bottles of Old Crow, Jim Beam, Jack Daniels sour mash, Wild Turkey, Early Times, Ancient Age, and he thought, Lord, Lord, any one of them would do. Big black fella back there tending bar. A woman too.

Bev finished and bumped his arm. "Sorry. She's one of my customers. I can't go anywhere in this town unless I run into somebody I know. I swear, I know half the people in this place."

"I want to meet Jorena Jones," he told Bev.

She gave him a big-eyed look.

"Is that Jorena Jones behind the bar?"

"She's the one."

They pushed their way through the crowd and found two empty seats at the bar. They sat down together. Bev was on Man's left. Two jokers to his right were turned the other way, arguing up a storm over who the greatest hitter was in the Negro Leagues, Gene Benson of the Philadelphia Stars or Josh Gibson of the Pittsburgh Crawfords. The big black bartender leaned over in their faces and told both of them they didn't know shit, that Chet Brewer of the Kansas City Monarchs could hit circles around both Benson's and Gibson's heads. Johnny Ace now singing on the jukebox. Ace was one of the few popular singers Man had lots of respect for. Po boy could sang.

"Hi, Beverly."

"Jorena, this is Debbie Chaney's brother, Manfred Banks. He just got to town. He's a musician."

"Hello, I've heard about you." She had such a sad-sweet smile. The skin of her face and arms was a creamy smooth light brown. She had this way of twitching her little mouth. Younger too than he would have thought. Man grinned at her and said how do you do.

He wanted to ask her about a singing job but he didn't know how to bring up the subject gracefully. Take yo time.

She reached across the bar and held her hand out to him. The hand, he didn't expect that from a woman. Never knew any woman to reach out to shake hands like a man. But she did. And he shook with her, looking her smack in the eye. He told her she had a nice place here. She kept right on smiling and said thanks.

Then she said, "Debbie tells me you've done some singing in Chicago clubs."

"Yeah, lot of clubs." Thinking: And on the streets too.

There was a waitress working the floor, bringing empties back to the end of the bar from where she called out her floor orders. Bev spoke to her, calling her Drusilla. When she smiled Man saw a big gold tooth right in the front of her mouth.

Then he looked at Bev and she had turned away, leaning on the bar, talking to the big black bartender.

Jorena went on down the bar to help somebody down there needing a drink and Bev turned to Man and said, "I ordered myself a Budweiser. What'd you want, Fred?"

He told the bartender, "Double shot of Old Crow. No ice." And dropped a ten-dollar bill on the bar.

Bev pulled back, eyes stretching, mouth opened, and the bartender just gave him this half-ass grin, like he knew all about him from scratch. And Bev said, "You don't play, do you?"

He grinned at her. "I'm celebrating us meeting."

"Don't tell me you going to turn out to be one of them jive-talking jokers."

"Naw." The bartender brought the drinks and took the ten. Man held up his glass and touched it to her bottle of beer then took a sip and the bourbon burned sweet and nice going down. He said to Bev, "I'm for real—as real as stink, hard as the kitchen sink. Baptized by a preacher with a prize. I stay on the right track, never look back." He laughed.

She laughed. "So, you can talk jive but you ain't a jive joker. Right?"

"Thas right." He lifted the whiskey glass and took himself another good long shot. He was feeling pretty good. Looking around, he saw people looking happy. Rise Sally rise, wipe yo weeping eyes. Yes, he was about as happy as a sad stranger could be in a new town his second mind never told him to come to in the first place.

The music was nice and gritty. Now Sonny Boy Williamson on the jukebox tearing up that harmonica and singing the blues like nobody's business. Then the record stopped. The stage light came on.

A good-looking man in a light blue suit stepped up on the stage and spoke into the mike: "Good evening, ladies and gentlemen. I'm Greg Wakely. Just as soon as we get somebody to unplug that jukebox we going to start bringing you some real live music up here. All right?"

The crowd was ready. "Yeaaaah!"

Jorena Jones came back down the bar and stopped in front of Man. And there was that soft smile again.

He told her he sang and did some harmonica and played around with the sax a little bit too. He didn't want to sound desperate or something.

Bev said, "He's got so many talents."

Jorena looked at Bev and kind of winked at her. Then Jorena leaned a little closer to him as she wiped the bartop. Said: "I could use a good singer here in the Palace. In fact, this town could use a good singer."

He felt suddenly excited.

"You interested?"

"I been interested fore I left Chicago."

"Good. You met Greg yet?"

"No. I just got into town today." Man looked back over his shoulder at Greg Wakely on the stage. He was an average-size dark brown–skinned guy with a pear-shaped face. The bass man and the trumpet man joined him and were getting set up.

When Man turned back he saw Jorena waving Wakely over, eyes squinting like she was working spirits on him. And Greg came over.

She introduced them and Man told Greg what he could do. Greg wanted to know if he was union. When Man told him no Greg said, "Well, the guys and I in the union but you don't have to be."

There was something about Greg, Man thought, that wasn't quite right. But he couldn't put his finger on it.

Man told the bandleader where he worked before, telling him names of some clubs in Chicago. Well, Man could tell right away Greg was impressed by just the fact that Man was from the big city and had done some clubs there.

Bev and Jorena were listening to them, watching them talk.

Man asked Greg if he knew Solomon Thigpen.

"Sure do. That cat's a motherfucker on the guitar, ain't he? He'd be famous if there was any justice in this here world."

They slapped hands, giving each other five.

"Solly and me worked together all over Chicago."

Greg's face broke out in a big grin. "You want to sit in with us, have a little fun?"

Man scratched his head. "Not tonight, man." He looked at Bev and picked up his drink.

Bev said, "Go on, Fred. I'd like to hear you sing something."

Jorena said, "Yes, I would too."

Then he said, "All right." Don't need hair on my chest to pass the test. Got the stuff, don't need to bluff. Take a seat, have a treat.

Then Jorena clapped her hands together and laughed.

Man looked back over at the stage. The guys were warming up, Bobby Peck testing his alto and Little Brother Garcia, a huge dude in a dark blue silk suit, was picking slowly at his bass fiddle, with his head cocked to it, meaning not to miss anything it was putting out and down.

⊙

A hour later, after the band did four numbers—*Crawling Black Snake, Come Back Baby, I Wonder Why, Is You Is or Is You Ain't My Baby?*— Greg introduced Man. Big blues man from Chicago, all that lying shit.

The audience went wild as he walked over, taking his third glass of whiskey with him, and hopped up on the stage. He was feeling damned good, suddenly popping his fingers along the way, dancing a little bit too. Don't rush, don't blush. People were on the floor cutting up. Everybody having a good time, a rocking good time, as Dinah Washington would say. Now, this the way to live.

Man thanked Greg and the crowd and went right into singing *Going to Kansas City Blues,* kind of keeping big bad Jimmy Witherspoon's voice in his mind. But it all came out his thing, you know. Then he said, "This here is one I wrote myself. Called *Not the Doctor, Not the Judge.* Goes like this—"

> I may not be the doctor, baby,
> But I sho do gots the cure.
> I may not be yo doctor, baby,
> But I sho do gots the cure.
> Let me tell you, sweet mama, I don't play:
> When I love you, baby, it be bound to stay.
> I may not be yo judge, baby,
> But I damn well can be yo juror.
> I may not be your judge, baby,
> But I damn well can be yo juror.
> Let me tell you, sweet mama, I don't play:
> When I love you, baby, it be bound to stay.
> Baby, baby, you know black-eyed peas is brown,
> Yes, baby, baby, black-eyed peas is brown.
> Baby, baby, you know black-eyed peas is brown,
> Yes, baby, baby, black-eyed peas is brown.
> If you let me love you right and tight, baby,
> I swear I never leave yo town.
> Baby, chitlins is gray.
> Yes, baby, chitlins sho is gray.
> Baby, chitlins is gray.
> Yes, baby, chitlins sho is gray.
> Let me tell you, sweet mama, I don't play:
> When I start to loving you, mama, it be bound to stay.

And they went crazy, begging for more. Then he sang *Sixty-Third Street Blues.* And hopped down while they were still howling for more. Always good to leave them hungry. You know you can come back sometimes.

When he got back to the bar he saw Jorena grinning from ear to ear. And he knew right then and there he had it made with her. She said, "That was great!"

"Thank you. Then I got the job?"

"If you want it, it's yours."

And Bev had already bought him another shot of whiskey. Bless her heart. He looked at Bev trying to figure her out. She struck him as a strong-minded person who was pretty set in her ways. And he felt he could trust her as long as he didn't cross her. Like Cleo, she probably wouldn't take no shit. Yeah, he felt real good. He had a feeling right then the rest of the night was going to be all right. If he had trouble in mind, it was going to sleep for a while. He was riding high, feeling mellow, in spirit with good-time people. He was feeling so good he could have turned himself into a little red rooster or a big black kingsnake. He was feeling that good. High and mighty. Felt so good just to be breaking new ground. Like sudden freedom. Pretty as some of them crazy patched quilts old folks down South make. Like walking by the National Recovery Administration Center and not needing to go in. Hot dog! A good feeling like you get when you got good seed in the ground and your seed is just starting to pop up in straight rows under the sun. In other words, he felt about as good as liquor could make a poor miserable young man feel on a winter night in a new town.

AFTER THE FIRST NIGHT WITH BEV—
and he'd spent that first Saturday night
with her—he started sort of seeing her on
some kind of regular basis, mostly on the week-

**CHAPTER
TEN**

end, spending Friday and Saturday night with her.
They had an understanding. But she had some joker, Larry Taylor, yellow
nigger like herself. She showed Man his picture. As if he needed to see it.
"The women go crazy about him," she liked saying. Larry Taylor had
been out in Los Angeles, a couple of years now, but she was still madly in
love with him. Man could tell by something in her eyes when she talked
about him. But it didn't look like Larry was about to come back to this
little old hick town any time soon. Bev wrote to him a lot and once in a
while she got a postcard.

"My father, he comes to see me once a week," she said. "So I don't get
too lonesome. How about your wife?"

Man told her about Cleo and how he still felt about her. So Bev and he
were just keeping each other company. He liked her cabbage, and she
liked his neckbones, so to speak. She liked those naughty songs by
Memphis Minnie, the hoodoo lady, and when he was just sitting around
in her kitchen sipping some whiskey and she was cooking dinner and
drinking beer, she'd put on some of Minnie's old records and sing along
with her, songs about real life—what the ice man can give her and how
good the butcher man can cut her pork chops.

◉

Monday morning Lyle took Man down to Lomax Steel and the boss
hired him for the janitor job on the spot. He wasn't excited about mopping toilets but, hey, he needed work.

Now, with two jobs, all he needed to do was work on getting Cleo out
here. Still, he couldn't call her. But he had to figure out a way to reach her.

That next Saturday morning Man stopped in at Walter Calloway's
Barbershop on Twenty-fourth between Maple and Corby, left side of the
street, and got a haircut. The barbershop was on one side of a house that
had been partitioned down the middle. It was a friendly place full of
men, old and young, arguing politics and sports. Man felt right at home.

◉

By the middle of March Man wrote to Solly and put in his sister's telephone number. He said: "See if you can get in touch with Cleo for me, tell her to call me."

⦿

The second week in April, Man came in that Wednesday and Debbie told him Solomon Thigpen called from Chicago, said he would call again later that night. Man told Debbie not to pick up if it rang. He was dying to hear news of Cleo. He went up to his room and rested on his little bed, a bed too small for him, a bed in which he could never get comfortable no matter how many times he turned. And after six, the phone rang. Leaping up, he trotted out into the hall and picked it up.

"Fred? That you?" Who you think, nigger? "How you doing?" Solly was doing just fine, had caught T-Bone Walker the night before at the Checkerboard and the cat was a gas. Solly told Man that Big Bill Hill, this blues radio disc jockey, had had him on his show. Man felt jealous though he himself had never thought of trying to get on Big Bill's show, even though Man knew Big Bill, used to run into him on Sixty-third all the time. And Solly said, "So, what you doing? What this Bob Jones place all about?" And Man told him he ought to come on out—bring his wife and kid—work with him in the club. They could tear the joint up, keep em hollering for more, keep the place jumping night and day, the two of them together. Solly said, "I don't know, man." Then Man asked if Mister Lee got him any more gigs. And Solly said shit naw. "Racist motherfucker," said Solly. "Hey, man. Maybe I will come out there, try it. I been talking with my old lady about it and she keep on saying it up to me, if I wants to she willing." And Man thought: What else would Holly say?

Finally, Solly said, "Hey, Fred, I saw your ex–old lady Cleo yesterday, on Forty-seventh and Drexel coming out the check-cashing place. I been meaning to find her and give her the phone number you sent. Then there she was. She wanted your address. Hope you don't mind. I gave it to her."

Mind? This was the break he'd been waiting for!

And Man told him yeah, giving Cleo his address was all right with him, but he was figuring in his head fifty-leven different things all at once as he talked. Why did Cleo want his address? Was she still with that preacher nigger? Solly said she gave him her address and telephone number. "Here. Here it is." And he read an address on Drexel between Forty-fourth and Forty-third. "And here's the phone number too."

Man wrote down both of the numbers on the edge of the Omaha Telephone Directory right there on the table. Well, she was at a different address all right. And he sure wondered what that meant. Man almost let himself hope she was free. But he caught himself, fearing he might be setting himself up for another big hurting. Still he couldn't help himself. Did she know Solly was going to give him these numbers? And he said, "She didn't say nothing about not giving them to you. Go on, nigger, call her. You know you still crazy bout that woman. If a man answer just hang the fuck up. You ain't got nothing to lose."

And he was right.

He dialed the number right after he hung up talking with Solly.

A woman's voice said hello.

Man said is Cleo Banks there.

And she said just a minute and next thing he knew Cleo was saying, "Hello?"

And sure enough it was her pure-sounding voice. He said, "Cleo it's me, Fred. How you doing?"

She said she and Karina were doing fine, then she said, "I was hoping you'd call, Fred. I ran into Solly . . . I was going to call you if you didn't call me in a few days. How're you doing?"

He told her about the janitor job and gigging at the Palace on weekends.

She said, "Like my grandmother used to say, a little hole in the pocket is worse than a big one at the knee." She wanted to know if he was happy. He said he was pretty well. As happy as a lonely man could be.

He asked about the woman who answered the phone. "That was Shawn. Didn't you recognize her voice?" He hadn't. She said she and her sister, Shawn, moved in together and they were sharing the rent. She herself was working at a restaurant on Forty-seventh near Cottage Grove. Good restaurant and she got good tips because the place served home-cooked meals, and regular folks ate there all the time, working people, not any winos and straggerbums.

Then his heart acted just like a fist when she said, "But I miss you, Fred. I really do, honey." It was like some kind of Black Cat Oil had worked, like some rootman had removed a jinx from his life. Made him happy enough to hop up and dance and shout. See the gal with the red dress on? Baby, I'm on my knees, come back to yo sweet loving daddy, will you please.

But he just listened to her, eating it up. Thinking, I got a cure for yo snakebite, mama. Making it up. I say, baby, I got the cure for yo bruise. Got a cure for yo every need, Cleo, mama. You don't chew it. And it ain't weed. Make it up. I got a cure, baby, for yo heartache. It ain't liniment. And it don't taste like peppermint. I say, lissen here, mama, everybody, lissen to me. My Cleo coming back to me. I got the right thing for my baby's heartache. It ain't something you bake. But it sho will make you sing. You can call it Uncrossing Powder but I call it love. Long time, baby, long time.

Then she said, "Karina ask about you all the time. She knows your face because I show her your picture all the time. I want her to know her father, Fred."

Hearing this gave him more happiness than he had a right to feel. He said, "Well, les see if we can do something bout it." Rainy day, rainy day, no mo rainy days.

"You mean you want to try to make a go of it again, with me?" She sounded hesitant.

"I never stopped wanting you, Cleo."

"I guess I knew that. But I wasn't sure if you'd found somebody else by now."

"Naw." He thought of Bev. She wasn't going to fault him for this, going back to his wife. She would go back to Larry at the drop of a hat if she had a chance. Bev was a nice lady—she was no streetwalking woman, no whiskey-drinking woman like so many of them women down on Twenty-fourth and Lake.

Then Cleo said, "Well, how are we going to do this?"

"I'm gon buy you and Karina a train ticket. Thas how we gon to do it. When you gon come?"

"Soon as you send the tickets and soon as I pay off my bills."

"I'm gone send the ticket tomorrow."

"Fred?"

Something in her tone told him to brace himself. "Yeah?"

"We got to make it work this time. Okay?"

"Oh, yeah. Ain't nothing gon stop us."

"Are you still drinking?"

He hesitated. "Uh, yeah, but I'm cutting down. I gots two jobs, I gots to cut down—and I wants to cut down. You gon see, we gon be happy."

"Good. Then I'll be waiting for the tickets. I love you."

"I love you too," he said awkwardly but meaning it completely.

Then he heard her say good-bye and hang up. This news put the devil back in his hole and now he was going to stay there. Man felt strong enough to lasso a tornado, strong enough to wrestle an elephant to the ground. Hallelujah!

⊙

Hot dog! He was happy. Man found Debbie in the kitchen and he grabbed her and hugged her. He was riding high. The blues, like blood-hounds, lost his trail. You can tell yo mama, you can tell yo daddy.

Hotdoggit! He sat down, jackknifed his legs, stuck a cigar in his mouth, threw his head back, grinning, and said: "Debbie, me and Cleo's getting back together. She coming out here!"

"Well, I suspected as much," said Debbie, grinning. "Yall welcome to stay here till you find your own place."

Good-hearted Debbie! Her goodness was big as the countryside. He couldn't remember a time when she hadn't come through for him. Just one of them good-hearted peoples. And he couldn't remember a time when he had done anything for her except maybe share a candy bar with her. She never seemed to need any help or anything. Even when they were kids she used to lace his shoes and even hold the handkerchief for him to blow his nose. Saved him many times from a crabapple-switch whipping. When he was five he tried chewtobaccy, got sick, and she saved him from a beating by Charity or Quincy by not telling on him. At eight, she taught him to Camel Walk.

He told Debbie he was going to try to find his own place before Cleo got there, and she said suit yourself. She looked a little bit unhappy. He couldn't figure that. Said, "What's the matter, Debbie?"

"Nothing. I was just thinking about Bev. What you going to tell her?"

"She be all right. Me and her got a understanding. Beside, she got a boyfriend out in Los Angeles. Somebody she still in love with."

"Larry? Larry is a no-good jive so-and-so."

"Don't matter. She love him. Told me herself."

"I know she still got feelings but she's better off if he never come back to this town."

"I'm gon tell her bout Cleo. Don't worry. Whas for dinner?"

"Neckbones and rice."

◉

After dinner Man went back upstairs, took a long drink from the bottle he had hidden under his bed then stretched out on the bed. May not be the doctor, baby, say I may not be yo doctor, baby, but I sho got the cure. A long while since he'd felt light as a breeze, easy as one-and-one-equals-two. Make tracks and don't look back. Hot dog! Cleo was coming home. Home? Cleo was coming back. Let me one time hit yo town. Lord, Lord.

A few minutes later there came a light tap on his door. It was Debbie. "Look," she said. "Here's a two-bedroom apartment down on Twenty-fourth and Wirt. It must be upstairs over that little variety store up there near to the old folks' rest home." She had in her hand the folded Classifieds from the *World-Herald*.

He sat up and took the newspaper. "Thanks, Deb." Debbie went back downstairs and he walked out into the hall and picked up the telephone and dialed the number. A woman answered, said her name was Sofia Sweeney. He told her he was interested in the apartment for rent.

Later that night:

He is flying. It seems so easy and natural. Flying across a night sky with his arms stretched out in front of him, the tips of his fingers leading the way. Flying to a scoobydoo beat behind the stone mountain down there back against the blue-black sky. Dark clouds in front of him are doing the Sconch like a ballroom full of dark girls and boys. "Hell, this is easy," he whispers. "I can take it to the limits. But take it slow. Don't have to take it home. Take it slow. Talk that talk. Easy as the Texas Shuffle. Oo-bla-dee oo-poppa-da oo-bop-she-bam. Hot dog!" He's really flying! Sashaying along like nobody's business. Nobody can sell him down the river. Nobody can send him on a humbug. Slick as a mosquiter's peter! Nobody can play the dozens with his uncle's cousin. Nobody can touch him! He's flying higher than the sun, so high, in fact, he's going to be able to put the sun in his pocket and bring it back down with him. Rooftops and treetops below look so friendly from up here. A train cutting its way across the land looks like a toy. Railroad Bill might jump out from behind a bush and take it for all it's worth. Can hear a dog barking but can't see the dog, can't see people, people in their houses, pecking, loving, lying in bed sick, running games, being chinchy with the bread, smoking spliff, trying to outsmart the bear at the front door, can't see that sweet little straight-up-six-o'clock woman down there called Cleo either but he knows she's down there. Lean Sweet Mama String-bean! And he's coming down to her but right now it's so nice gliding along. It doesn't matter where he's going.

THE NEXT EVENING, EARLY, HE CALLED
Sofia Sweeney again, and she said in a tiny **CHAPTER**
but friendly voice to come on over and look at **ELEVEN**
the apartment. In his room he took himself a
long good shot from his secret half-pint bottle of Old
Crow, then stuck it in his back pocket so his jacket would hide it.

He walked down the hill and turned at Twenty-third and walked up
past Corby and at Maple he went on over to Twenty-fourth, stopped in
the shadow of a tree and took himself another long good shot. He knew
he had to talk with Bev real soon about Cleo coming.

◉

A white ambulance was parked in front of the old folks' home next door.
Sofia Sweeney's doorbell jiggled as he opened the door. The shop smelled
of wax, dust, and candy. The little old thin, very white woman behind
the counter smiled. She was alone.

Man took her to be Sofia Sweeney. She was a ghost with white hair
standing there behind the counter in a little old black wool dress hanging
on her like it might hang on a scarecrow. Her narrow, bony face, with its
big dark eyes, seemed at once full of pleading, fear, and kindness. She had
an old ratty sweater around her shoulders.

Man tipped his cap and smiled at her, watching her eyes real closely to
see if she was going to act scared on sight of him like so many white
women did. Watched for that wild crazy look they get, like a caged animal in mortal fear looking for somewhere to run. But she looked away
quickly so he couldn't see her eyes.

◉

He told her he was there to see the apartment. And without looking at
him she said, "You must be the gentleman who called." She reached in
her pocket for a ring of keys. "It's upstairs."

And she came from behind the counter with her arms folded across her
flat chest. He kept his distance on her so she wouldn't smell his breath
and he didn't want to scare her. Mack the Knife with blood dripping
from his teeth. God only knows what she saw. Then he followed her to
the door where she stopped and turned the CLOSED sign around.

They stepped outside and she locked the door, clinking her keys and cussing under her breath. "That key always sticks." Then he followed her into a hallway just next door and up a long narrow, dusty flight of steps. Two doors at the top. They turned to the one on the right. She said: "There's a woman living there, Daffodil Grover. Has a little boy. They're quiet. Do you have a family?"

She opened the door and pushed the light switch. Lights came on in the hall. They stepped inside.

Man told her he had a wife and a daughter who'd be two this coming September. She gave him this look, and he knew what it was about so he said, "She a good girl. She don't cry." And that got a laugh out of Sofia Sweeney.

She said all children cry. And he said he guessed so but Karina didn't cry much.

"When were you planning to move in?"

He told her the first of next month, May first.

Just inside the door was a long hallway curving all the way back to the kitchen. To the right just as they came in there was a little bedroom with a window facing the street. They paused at the doorway and looked in, then he followed her into the next room. She turned on the lights. This was a big bedroom with a living room joining it. Going up into the living room, he looked out the big windows down on the street at the sidewalk in front of the shop. "This pretty nice," he said.

"You'll have lots of room here. Just the three of you. Where do you work, Mister, uh—?"

"Manfred Banks. Lomax Steel."

She said, "Uh-huh." He could tell she was impressed by his employer so she didn't ask him any more about work.

They walked into the next bedroom down. It had two windows. One looked out on Wirt and from the other you could see the back porch.

Coming out of there, they walked kitty-corner right into the kitchen. She hit the light switch. A big square dirty spot on the linoleum where an icebox had sat. He went to the stove. It seemed to be in good shape, no chickenbone special.

Sofia Sweeney opened the back door, and he followed her out on the back porch. She turned on the back porch light. She said, "Nice thing about having the landlady downstairs is if you and your family want to vacation sometime I can look after your place for you, make sure nobody breaks in and steals your belongings."

He started to say we won't be going nowhere. Then it hit him that this thing white folks calls vacation—going on vacations—he didn't know anything about. He himself had never been on one. Or maybe he had been on one all his life. They went back inside. She said, "Well?"

"How much is the rent?"

"Eighty dollars a month."

"I take it. Can I give you forty down to hold it?" He nervously took out his wallet.

She took the four tens, they turned off the lights, and went back downstairs. He noticed two men in white uniforms carrying a body on a stretcher from the old folks' home next door toward the white ambulance.

Sofia Sweeney put the lease papers on the glass-top counter and he signed them. She said he'd have to give her a damage deposit of, say, eighty dollars. He could pay it forty dollars at a time long as he got it paid off before moving in on the first of May.

◉

He walked on from there, stopping to take heavy sips so he would be done with the whole bottle by the time he got to Bev's place. Easy to drink on dark streets. People were in their warm houses with their lights on. Nice walking on the sidewalk past their houses, keeping himself warm inside his coat, with his good liquor, feeling mighty mellow just strolling along. But carrying this tight knot in his belly was no fun because he wasn't sure how Bev was going to take the news. He guessed he wanted to get a little mellow before telling her. Buffer. But, like he told his sister, he didn't think Bev would mind too much, being as she had her heart in Los Angeles all the time.

Just before he got to her house he finished the half-pint of Old Crow and stuck the bottle down under a hedge by the sidewalk.

On Bev's front porch he could see her lights and hear the radio on. She wasn't expecting him, he know. A Thursday night. But he could hear voices inside.

Bev always told him she had her daddy over on Monday and Tuesday nights. He'd come over and spend the two nights with her. He'd take a bath in her clean tub. And she'd make him drink orange juice and rest. She'd comb his thin hair and pamper the devil out of him. That's how she said it. She babied him for two days. Man imagined her rubbing cream on the dry, wrinkled old age-spotted colorless skin of his back, as he lay on his stomach. She'd cook lots of good biscuits and gravy and eggs for him for breakfast, and for dinners she'd go all out with cornbread and baked chicken or make a beef or pork roast and slice it real thick and serve him this good meat with collard greens or peas and squash.

Many times she and Man would eat leftovers from what she cooked earlier in the week for her daddy. He was a very old man—name was Brett Prade—and he was white. Now, her name was Frye, because Prade was never married to her mother, Colette. In the old photograph on the wall Man could see the mother was in her day a real knockout colored woman.

But Prade was a pure-dee white man. Lived downtown, down by the railroad tracks, Seventh and Jones, in one of them dollar-a-night stumblebum hotels, called the Pioneer. She made him come out here like this so she could get a good meal into him at least once a week. Said he didn't ever get any good food downtown in them grease pits called cafes where he ate the rest of the week.

So, he didn't expect her father to be there. But somebody was. He knocked and Bev didn't come so he knocked again. Then she came. He could see her through the glass on the front door coming up the hall. She was in her jeans—she liked to wear her jeans around the house. Wouldn't be caught dead in them outside.

He could tell by the expression on her face when she opened the door and saw him that he'd come at the wrong time.

She stepped out on the porch. "I'm sorry, Fred. My father is here now. He's not feeling well. I'm taking care of him. He took ill. I made him come on out in a taxi."

"That all right, Bev."

"Was there something wrong?"

"Naw. Not much. I mean, nothing wrong. It just that I wanted to talk with you. I gots something to tell you. I gots to talk to you pretty soon. But I guess it can wait till Friday night."

"Tell me. What is it? You been drinking a lot, Fred. What is it?"

"Let it wait till Friday night."

"Tell me now, Fred. Just tell me. Are you leaving town?"

"Naw. It not that."

"Don't keep me guessing. I don't want to wait until Friday, trying to figure out what's on your mind."

He looked her in the eyes and said, "Cleo, my wife, and the baby—"

"I knew it. They coming to Omaha. Right?"

"Yeah. Thas what I wanted to talk with you bout."

Inside, he heard her father calling, "Beverly! Is that somebody at the door?"

She looked back over her shoulder and shouted, "Yes! It's nobody, Dad. I'll be there in a minute."

"I better go," he told her. "We talk Friday." Nobody?

"So, this is the end. Huh?"

"We talk Friday, Bev." Nobody?

"Well," she said. "I guess I expected this all along. That's why I didn't let myself get too serious. We'll still be friends, though. Huh?"

"Yeah. Ain't nothing to stop that. You better go back to your daddy." Nobody?

And she closed the door. Nobody?

◉

Walking back down Twenty-fourth he hit a rhythm. Doing what he did lots of time, composing in his head. Hearing the beat and the words to the beat, that offbeat. Sorry baby. Hate to do you thisa way. Sorry baby. Hate to do you thisa way. Getting something nice going. He felt real bad. Heart confused, heavy heart, feeling pained in the heart. But happy too. Happy Cleo was coming back. It was like he wanted to cry. Trouble in mind, happy sad tears. Yes, indeed. The half of it, he thought, ain't never been told. How do that song go? Until the real thing come along. Well, bless my soul, the real thing was coming back.

By the time he hit Twenty-fourth and Lake he felt nearly sober, so he ducked into the Palace for a drink. The place was kind of quiet. Jorena's bartender, Herbert Lawson, was sitting behind the bar looking like he was half asleep. Tampa Red and his Hokum Jug Band cutting up with *Come On Mama, Do That Dance* on the jukebox. Man said, "Hey, Herb. How ya doing, man?" And as usual Herb just kind of grunted. Man ordered a double shot of Dirty Bird. Herb fixed it and put it in front of him. He took out a fiver, just because he felt like it, but Herb wouldn't take the money.

◉

Almost right away, during lunch break, Lyle started showing Man how to weld. "Hold your rod like this. You don't want it touching, just moving smoothly along the line like this. See? Now try it again."

And Man took the iron, lowered his borrowed face-cover, and bent down to the beam where he was aiming at the line of a stud resting on the top surface. He tried with all his might to move the rod along the line without touching the surface but the bright orange light of the flux was blinding him. He couldn't see the line let alone see how to move the rod the right way. Like being struck in the face by one of them Bible angels Mama useta talk about.

Only four black men, counting Lyle and him and two others, Cecil Paley, big guy in coveralls, and Bernie Mungo, little thin guy, were working there and one black woman, Bernice Short. She'd been there since the start of the war when Lomax had more War Department contracts than any other steel fabricating company in the Midwest.

One day at lunch, Man, Lyle, Cecil, and Bernie were sitting together.

First thing Bernie said to Man was, "If you work your way up from janitor you'll be the first in history. You can believe that."

Cecil giggled. "Bernie, why you wants to discourage the man like that?"

Lyle said, "You guys lay off my brother-in-law."

◉

The boss, Eliot Selby, an ex–union man, kept on telling Man, "When you're ready let me know."

The old-time welders knew Man was trying to prove himself and they were teasing him all this time. There must have been seventy workers there total but the ones he knew best were the ones in the center bay where Lyle worked. Oliver Fergus, little bald-headed guy, five years on the job, standing at the urinal shaking his peter, saying, "So, Fred, when you get promoted to welder, you going to buy yourself a Cadillac? Hehehe." Or Amos Mozzella, saying, "Get any last night, Fred?" And he almost told him, Naw cause I didn't run into yo mama. And Mark Harvey, another welder, always saying, "Hi, hotshot. How's your peter hanging? You get your ashes hauled this weekend? How are them little colored gals out there on North Twenty-fourth Street?" And Louis Irving, another welder, saying, "Fred, you bring yourself some water-melon for lunch today? Hehehe." Or Vincent McElroy, welder too, had this way of playfully bumping against Man's big shoulder, then saying, "Excuse me, Fred, didn't see you. Hehehe." All of em—the crane opera-tors, Lenny Ludwig, Todd Stone, the guys on the sheers, especially Ralph Roberts—were like that except one old guy who called him Sir John. Don't ask why. And one young guy his own age who was studying to be a minister. He just ignored Man, which suited him fine.

At night in bed he thought about the trouble the jokers on the job were giving him. In his dreams he sometimes pulled a Bat Masterson on them, mowing them all down, sometimes whipping a Nat Turner on them. But big as he was he was strapped as though to a public torture rack, like a black man in a circus booth sitting on a stool over a bucket of water with a sign over his head: HIT THE BULL'S-EYE, KNOCK THE NIGGER IN THE WATER.

One day, while Man was cleaning the lunchroom, he overheard Amos talking with Cassidy DeMaris. Turned out they both had been at the same South Omaha high school, both from Catholic families. "I was an altar boy then a choirboy at Saint Philomena's. All of those festivals in the streets, cotton candy, popcorn." Man looked at Amos then. How could this little shit ever have been a choirboy?

But it didn't make no never-mind to Man what these suckers said. The larger plan was still being worked. He knew what he had to do. Words didn't hurt him. So he told himself. Far as he was concerned, they were just a bunch of ignorant redneck Okies and hillbillies. He did his job and stood his ground, making them walk around him, get out of his way much as possible, and he practiced the welding at lunchtime. If he had wanted to he could have knocked the stuffing out of any one of them at any time. They knew it too, big as he was. But they also knew they were white and he was black and because of this they had a lot of muscle, of another kind, backing them up.

He rode to work with Lyle in his car. And not one time did Lyle bad-mouth the white boys, some of them working under him too.

◉

One morning Man walked into the locker room at work and Eliot Selby was pissing in one of the urinals. He said, "Hey, Fred, this place looking kind of shitty. When was the last time you cleaned it up?"

Man was standing at his locker when he turned around to answer. Looking across the room at Eliot, he started to tell the truth and say: Cleaned it this morning but the guys shit it up in five minutes throwing paper towels on the floor and shit. But now he needed the job more than ever. He remembered his mother saying, "Always have you something to fall back on." And so far the music wasn't much but it was his happiness and not getting a lot of money wasn't going to stop him from living his music. Yet and still, he didn't want to be tied down to no shit-eating slave.

All day that day he did his work—mopping the toilets and cleaning out the face bowls, the urinals, the toilet bowls, emptying the trash cans, cleaning up the lunchroom and the locker room, did it all like he was walking on air, doing the *Cow Cow Boogie* at Jamboree time, his mind on Cleo. Let the good times roll. Unsung feelings now came to the surface and kept him grinning.

He was sweeping the men's locker room when Louis Irving came dragging his depressing ass in and stood at a urinal and started pissing. Looking back over his shoulder, Louis said: "Fred, how's your pecker hanging?"

"Ask yo mama," he said without looking up or stopping the broom.

"What you say?"

"You heard me."

He finished and came over to Man, looking up at him, red in the face. "I said repeat what you said?"

"Who you think you is?" Man said, looking him in the eye, squaring him off.

"Whoa. My, ain't we high and mighty this morning. What's got into you, boy?"

Man grabbed his crotch. "I got yo boy right here."

"Name calling, huh? Okay, nigger, if that's the way you want it."

"Get the fuck out of my face, Louis." Man spat the words in Louis's face. He'd knock that peckerwood to Ginny Gall where they eat the cow up skin and all. Knock him wise and otherwise.

And Louis backed off. Not too many little fuckers like Louis were going to mess with a guy Man's size. Unless they had a pack of other white suckers behind them. Man could make him eat dirt from moon to moon.

He'd messed up Man's good feeling for a little while but in a couple of hours Man got that spirit back up. Glad he hadn't exploded and gone up against the peckerwood. Remembered his mama's words: When you goes down the street, try to be nice and neat, watch yo step long the way, and be careful what you say. What she didn't add, he knew, was: You a black boy and the slightest wrong move can get you kilt.

He went about the rest of the day feeling really good. That morning he'd sent Cleo the tickets. He could almost hear the train whistle blowing! Now it was just a matter of waiting till the last week of the month. And meantime he didn't want no bullshit from these rednecks.

Cleaning the women's locker room that afternoon, he felt this turning and twisting inside, like all kinds of new life in him. Like a freshness— a birthing of something. Yeah. Come on back, baby. Yes, mama, person to person. Cleo and me again. Hot dog! Don't call me on the telephone, woman. Bring it on home, mama. Yeah. He was happy. Don't call, just come.

Yeah, he was happy. This was happiness.

Nobody there at Lomax knew but Lyle.

◉

It was two in the morning that next Saturday night when Man trucked out of the Palace carrying his saxophone in its case. Felt like he had made a lot of folks happy, sent them home feeling like their hearts wouldn't have to go to bed hungry. In a way Cleo was with him. Had been all evening.

He loved night air and it never felt better. At the corner of Twenty-fourth and Lake he paused at the curb out of habit though there was nothing coming. Then a joker wearing a newsboy's cap that hid most of his face approached him coming east on Lake. Man saw only his thick lips. Man's first thought: Somebody about to tell me how much he enjoyed the show. The joker said, "Hey, Jack, dig, can you lend me a—"

And before the joker could finish his sentence Man felt a blow from behind—like the Rocky Mountains landing on him. Something heavy and hard against his head, then something like the full force of a shoulder hit squarely against his lower back, knocking him forward into the street, and the saxophone case shot out into Lake Street.

There were three of them and they all scuffled for the saxophone, one of them grabbed it and they all ran just as he lifted himself up to one knee. He saw them as shadows hightailing it first across Twenty-fourth and on east out Lake.

By the time he got to his feet he couldn't even hear their footfalls. Couldn't have been a day over fifteen or sixteen. Just boys. His anger was snake blood in his mouth. He held a rage he couldn't release. Suddenly he cried out as loud as he could, "Goddamned sonsofbitches!" It came out as a roar. He was shaking all over with rage. Tonight he himself would go to bed with an empty soul and a hungry heart.

THE NEXT AFTERNOON AT WORK
Eliot Selby came in the men's locker room **CHAPTER**
while Man was making his rounds to empty **TWELVE**
the trash cans. He said, "All right, Manfred.
There just might be an opening for a welder third
class. Now is your chance. You've been practicing your welding. You
want to show me what you can do?"

"Yeah." Man set the trashbag down on the floor and followed Eliot
out into the main bay. Sparks from welding rods up and down the rows.
The crane moving on its lines overhead. Bernice Short, nice lady, waved
to him from the crane cab. She winked too. He waved back, then got the
hood he'd been using from the rack and his iron from the rack just there
next to the time card rack by the lunchroom door.

Side stepping a stack of rebars, he caught up with Eliot.

Cecil Paley and Bernie Mungo were working right close to each other,
on one end of a long beam for a bridge, welding studs to it. Eliot walked
over by them and stopped.

Nearby was a rail that was to be attached to the beam about five feet
from the end. It had to stand at a forty-five-degree angle. Man knew this
because he saw the finished ones over in the center bay all had rails
standing up like that.

Eliot gave Man this cold-ass look then picked up a rod and handed it
to him. "All right. Weld this rail onto the beam just the way it's standing
now, right where it's marked."

Cecil grinned. "Go, Fred, go!"

Sweet Lucy Brown!

Man put his hood on but kept the face-cover pushed up, looking
around for his brother-in-law. Took him a while to spot Lyle. Lyle was
way over on the other side of the main bay, pointing to something on one
of those big beams and two fellows were looking at what he was pointing
at. Lyle had taught Man what he knew, and Cecil and Bernie helped.
Man felt nervous but he knew he could do it. Yet and still, he kind of
wished Lyle was here. Then he was glad he wasn't because he might have
been even more nervous.

Bernie was grinning too. "Show your stuff, Fred."

Eliot said, "If you can do this right I might get Personnel to hire you
instead of advertising the position."

He adjusted the rod onto his iron. Then he lowered his face-cover. Took a few minutes to adjust to the view. It was hard to see through the plastic. Because it was all scratched up and everything. But he got it. Then he could see the rail standing there all right, the place where it was resting, the markings. Man got himself in position. Okay, don't bluff, do yo stuff. Time. Take yo time. He pressed the iron, getting it ready. Then he touched the rod to the crevice where the rail and the beam met, right at the corner marking. Hoping like hell that the damned rod wouldn't stick. He'd had such a hard time with that in the beginning, keeping the rod from sticking to the iron. Yo touch just gotta be just so. You had to be like a surgeon. Time. Had to take yo time. He knew this and broke out in a sweat when he saw and felt his hand shake.

Lord, have mercy. Man kept the rod up just the right way and at the right angle. He saw the bright orange flux laying out in a smooth line behind his rod and his hand stopped shaking. He kept it going like that, real smooth, and got one whole side done without the rod sticking one time.

Now, if he could just get another side done like that. He stood back, lifted his face-cover and wiped the sweat from his face with his sleeve. Time, baby. Take yo time.

Cecil laughed. "All right! Boogie woogie, Fred!"

Bernie said, "Don't gratulate him yet. He ain't done."

Eliot was watching but he didn't say anything, and he wasn't smiling either.

Mark Harvey, coming out of the locker room, stopped by Eliot's side to watch. Then Amos Mozzella, on his way to the lunchroom, stopped too.

Eliot said, "You guys get on back to work." And they moved on.

Then Man got into position on the other side of the beam, dropped his face-cover and eased the rod down to the point where he could see the marking. The first drop of bright liquid flashed. He was careful not to jerk the rod. Kept on telling himself, like in music, take yo time. Time, time, baby, time. Take yo time. This here welding had its own kind of rhythm. He kept the bright line thin and straight. Kept it moving right along the crevice, like holding a note high to the end. He held on. And it was done.

He heard Cecil say, "Look at that! Straight as a arrow."

Man lifted his face-cover. Sweet Lucy Brown! Let's go to town!

Eliot was nodding and looking at him. "Why you sweating so, Fred? You doing all right. Now do the other two sides."

Man moved in place and he lowered the face-cover again. This time he liked to have overdone it at the start—the rod stuck just a tiny bit but he didn't let it shake him. Instead, he eased it back and held it smooth and let the liquid pour on along the line behind his rod. Halfway along he almost fucked up again but not too badly. Didn't stick all the way. He was sure Eliot saw what was happening. And he was already wondering if Eliot was going to fault him and not give him the job.

But when he finished and lifted his face-cover the line looked straight as the other two, nearly as good anyway. One more to go. He thought, Lord, have mercy. Let me get this one perfect. Thinking he could hear the thump-thump-thump-thump inside his chest, he willed his hand to move with the firmness of Shine's swim-stroke from the sinking Titanic. Yeah! Make it sweet in the crevice, crisp without a miss, nice as a gentle kiss.

He got ready and started his line, this time he was going to end where he started and that was a danger spot because at that point it was really easy to get the line too thick. Nervous about that as he moved the line to the finish, he held his breath, then he stopped holding it, because it might break his rhythm and throw him off balance.

Then he heard Cecil and Bernie and—yeah!—Lyle cheering. Lyle had come over from across the way.

Man didn't even know he finished. So scared of fucking up the finish he nearly stopped before he reached the finish but he guessed he got it just right. Then he lifted his face-cover and stepped back from the beam.

Looking around, Man saw the three splibs laughing. Cecil was slapping his thighs. "Good God, look at that boy sweat!"

Lyle slapped Man on the back. "Real nice work, brother-in-law."

Eliot said, "Not bad, Fred. I'll see what I can do. I can't guarantee you nothing, you understand. It's only a possible job. I don't even know if they'll let me hire another man right now, even though we need one."

"But I thought you said—"

He started shaking his head. "No guarantee. It's just a maybe. We will have to see."

And Eliot walked away, back over to his stand out at the far end of the bay.

Lyle kept his hand on Man's shoulder, "Don't worry. He's always like that. You'll get the job."

Louis Irving walked by and gave Man a nasty look.

Cecil said, "Ain't no way they can say you don't qualify."

Bernie said, "If you don't get the job it won't be because you can't weld."

◉

One day soon after this event, his sister Debbie came in from the shop and said, "The tracks opening tomorrow out at Ak-Sar-Ben. You ready?"

Although he had forgotten about the track, he was ready. Besides, it was good to kill time in any way possible while waiting for Cleo. She would be out as soon as she got her bills paid, in about a week or so. The woman I love. I say, the woman I love.

So Man and Debbie headed for the horse races the next day around eleven but on the way, Debbie stopped in front of the shop. Said: "I always take they bets for them. I ain't never—but one time—brought back no money for anybody. And that was Beverly. She won about thirty dollars."

It was a beautiful day with a sky full of unsinkable clearness. He waited in the car listening to Frank Sinatra on the radio. Money burning a hole in his pocket.

On the way out, Man turned off the radio and, taking out his harmonica, blew it a while then sang *Ain't It a Crying Shame*. Debbie took Twenty-fourth south and by the time she reached Dodge, Man was on his third song. As they passed the university and Elmwood Park he was into *My Brownskin Sugar Plum*. And Debbie was laughing and singing along.

When they got out to Sixty-sixth and Leavenworth it was just like he expected—crowded, mostly white folks in lines buying tickets at little windows. Then the same folks standing along the railings or sitting in the grandstand, watching.

Down South they'd let blacks in only if there was room to spare, and they had to stay together in one corner of the grandstand. The first race was ready. He had three tickets on a horse named Godiva. Deb had two or three tickets on two or three horses, plus the tickets for the women back at the shop. He watched her lose her money. He lost his too. In the third race he put five dollars on a horse called Ramona's Luck. He lost his five dollars. Here come beans and rice.

> Lickety splurp, lickety splurp,
> Roll them dice, roll them dice,
> Tonight you eating beans and rice.

This was not like the gambling he'd done with jokers from the delta and slick suckers in zoot suits in Atlanta and New Orleans as a greenhorn. Crapshooting got you by the balls and made you dance to its magic. Rolling the dice, waiting for snake eyes, got the blood moving fast in the veins, put a zing in the head. African dominoes was a favorite, a game he'd learned in New Orleans. The only problem with dice gambling, as he now remembered, was the chance that somebody might have loaded dice and some sucker would get his African up and want to kill somebody. Or with cards somebody might have a stacked deck and get to see his own blood on a switchblade knife just before he died. But these horses were different. You didn't feel you had any control over them like you had over the dice and cards. You couldn't make them sweat in the palm of your hands, couldn't feel them, couldn't see that certain, secret sliver of light shining from their surfaces. This horse racing stuff was for ciddity folks.

◉

Later that night in his sleep:

The moment is as hazy and yellow as an old snapshot of people nobody any longer remembers. He's a jockey. Jorena is looking up at him. She's in a light blue floral dress with tulip print thin as a drunk's promise not to drink. He's not used to this pretty look, this stretched-out, sweeping look. But he's in his glory on horseback and his horse is a noble brown paso fino. They've just won the race and are at the finish line with people gathered around. But he sees only Jorena's big smile. And for a minute Jorena looks like Cleo. And paso is sweaty-tired as Man throws a leg over and climbs down and a black boy leads the horse away. Somehow not himself, Man stands facing Jorena and she presses her lips against his as the gathering of well-wishers begins to split. And again her face turns into Cleo's and it doesn't seem a bit odd but when the kiss is broken and Jorena says, "You're wonderful, I just love the way you sing," he feels a smile inside his face that won't come out. He says, "Wish Cleo understand me like you do." "You just have to give her time," Jorena says. And he says, "But I'm running out of time."

CLEO AND KARINA WEREN'T DUE IN till ten o'five that night, only five days before they were to move into their new apartment upstairs over Sofia Sweeney's variety store.

CHAPTER THIRTEEN

It was all he could do to keep Debbie from going with him to the station. She didn't want him to take her pretty yellow car because she swore up and down his license wasn't any good. Then she gave up and said go on, baby brother, but you better not wreck my car. All right, all right. I know how to drive, sister-woman. Nothing gon happen to yo mellow yellow hog. He wanted to be there by himself to pick up his wife. Make it romantic, just the two of them and the baby. Didn't anybody need Debbie there to help. But he knew she was dying to see Cleo.

In his room he had himself a half-pint of vodka. He didn't care much for vodka but he figured it was the best thing because you can't smell it on the breath. And since he was going to pick up Cleo he wanted her not to smell whiskey first thing. Trying to get off to a good start with a good impression. Some folks say if you try a little bit people will meet you halfway. He'd gotten a little mellow before dinner on some whiskey but after dinner he only took a couple of shots of vodka in his room before going down.

Debbie and Lyle were sitting at the dining room table playing cards. The boys were next door at Willie Lee's doing something he was sure they weren't supposed to be doing. "All right, Debbie. I'm going now. Where yo keys?" She gave him a disgusted look and nodded toward the living room. He saw the keys on the lamp table beside the couch.

It felt just like a warm summer night already as he got in his sister's big bad car. Yeah! I ain't the driver, ain't the driver's son, but I'll do the driving till the driver comes. He took care and drove out from the curb smoothly. He hadn't driven a car in a few years, it was true, but he still had the feeling for it. Time was back when he had a little old Ford he picked up off a boy in 1945 because Uncle Sam was shipping the boy off to Europe to help put the finishing touches on the war. That car didn't hold out but a couple of months. The boy had dogged it, so Man couldn't get much life out of it. He'd gotten his license back then. Kept it renewed too. It had been his best means for cashing checks from temporary jobs. Anyway, he had intended to get himself another car in time. But time just slipped on, and in Chicago you didn't need a car all that often. He walked pretty much most places. But on top of that, Man never could get himself enough money at one time and in one pocket to afford a car. But, shit, he could drive. Drive like a motherfucker! Drive east, drive west, some folk say I drive the best. He grinned to himself.

He got to Union Station—a long white building with rounded edges at the top—at Tenth and Marcy around a quarter to ten, parked in the Tenth Street lot, turned off the lights and sat there in the warm dark car looking vacantly ahead at the street, seeing only the shape of his thoughts in a chase chorus. Conjuring up an image of Cleo, he closed his eyes, remembering what she looked like the last time he saw her. That ofay-like hair, her soft light brown skin, the tenderness of her fingers when she touched him.

And he remembered photographs of her taken when she was a little girl. Pretty as an apple blossom! One was of her on a sunny day, in a cotton dress, squinting, standing by a fence. Somebody he would never know had snapped her picture. He often tried to imagine her as a child the way she might have been, with her older sister, Shawn, holding her hand while the two of them walked to school, carrying their little red tin lunch buckets, each containing a red apple and a peanut butter and jelly sandwich.

Cleo had given him impressions and images of herself when she talked lovingly about her childhood. She grew up in and about her parents' restaurant, a popular creole and soul food place called Cafe LeRoi. Her mother, Marie-France Le Fontaine, a beautiful Creole with light eyes and light hair, great-granddaughter of a slave-woman, Nina, and a Frenchman named Pierre something-or-other, did all the cooking.

Her father, LeRoi Michel Queneau, also Creole, but darker, manned the cash register. They had a young woman named Eliane working as waitress when Cleo and her sister were very small. Cleo grew up happy. From an early age, she and Shawn worked after school in the restaurant, setting tables, changing tablecloths, sweeping, dusting, seating customers when they were old enough, and running errands when their mother ran out of a particular spice or went to get fresh French bread from the Jean-Claude Bakery nearby or vegetables from the market.

◉

Man felt very excited. My turtledove coming! My angel coming! My creamy brown stick-around sugar coming! Just wished he had better news for Cleo. Wished he could tell her he'd just been promoted to welder three. Just you wait, sun gon shine in our back door some day.

While he sat there he got this idea for a song for Cleo. He got a pen out of Debbie's glove compartment and quickly wrote it all down. It was about how much he loved Cleo, about the birds and trees, flowers and bees, about being poor but serious about his love for her. Some folks say to write a song you gots to be smart but I say all I needs is a start. Called it *Rice Pudding*.

All right. All right then. Then he got to thinking about Eliot. Why was Eliot doing him the way he was, getting his hopes up then telling him he might not get the job. It was a crying shame. A dirty crying shame. A dirty dog shouldn't be treated that way. Man closed his eyes and rubbed them with his knuckles. He felt sober by then. Sober as a closet full of dead folks' bones. Wished he had brought the vodka bottle. Naw. Good thing he hadn't. Got to cut out that shit. Fly right.

Then he heard the train rumbling in. Train, train, running fast, cain't see nothing but the trees shooting past. He could imagine her on the train looking out seeing dark trees. He got out of the car, closed the door, walked across the street, into the big cool building, through the lobby, and out to the platform, and stood there with the people while the train was thundering in, window lights flashing by like big lightning bugs in some kind of strict formation. Man was trying to see the faces inside, to see Cleo, but they were all moving too fast. Time.

But he remembered her face well. He'd always thought she looked a bit like the young Josephine Baker. He first said this to her when they went to see Josephine Baker at the Regal. She entered from the rear of the theater, surprising everybody, walking down that candy- and soda pop–sticky aisle with her million-dollar white-and-pink evening gown trailing a mile behind her, entering in all her glory, creamy brown arms held up, waving to everybody, and with the biggest, toothiest smile he'd ever seen. And she was beautiful. But Cleo was even more beautiful than Josephine. Then a couple of weeks later they went to see Pearl Bailey, who knocked everybody out making a mock Josephine Baker–type entry, but, in her playfully caustic way, saying, "I don't care what yall say, honey, I ain't dragging my expensive gown on this filthy floor for nobody." And everybody cracked up. But, yes, Cleo was prettier than Josephine Baker. And the whole world knew Josephine Baker was beautiful.

Then that big mary stopped huffing and puffing down at the front end. Thought of Leadbelly singing *Going to the Station*. Could hear that beat, almost feel that hand hitting against the strings of that old guitar. Going to the staaay-shon. Then he could hear old Leadbelly singing, "Let the Mid-night spe-cial shine her light on me . . ."

Man started moving up the platform, not knowing which car she would be stepping down from, but he couldn't stand still, he just kept on moving, moving and looking back and forth, all around, trying to make sure he wasn't going to miss her the minute she stepped down. Folks were stepping down all the while, mostly white folks, hugging their relatives, people screeching with joy, laughing, and a few even crying.

Then way down there he saw Cleo's face, her light brown small face, sticking out the door of the car, looking over the heads of people, saw her, saw her seeing him at the same time. And he broke out running to meet her. Lord, Lord, he'd not felt so excited in a long, long while. A feeling he forgot he could get into. Almost laughing, remembering that old song about the black man outrunning the devil. Man couldn't run fast because he was so big but he hopped on up there, waving at her on the way, feeling his face locked in a giant grin he couldn't stop if he knew how.

And he got there just in time to help her down from the high step. And there was his baby girl in Cleo's arms. He reached for her and took her in his own arms and brought her to him. For just a minute he thought she was going to cry but she stuck her thumb in her mouth and held on to his arm. He held her and she looked back for mama. His whole body was singing.

It was like the meaning of his life suddenly revealed itself to him. Ain't gon sing the blues no mo. My baby girl never seen new shoes. No mo, long time. My wife buys her dresses at the Salvation Army store. No mo, long time.

He placed his free arm around Cleo's shoulders and pulled her close and they kissed. Sweet Lucy Brown!

Then Cleo laughed this nervous kind of laugh. And she said, "Fred, you look real good."

"You looks good, yoself. Where yo suitcases?"

"I guess they'll unload them down there by the engine."

They started walking toward the station where the engine had stopped. Never felt happier than when I held my baby in my arms. Hearing Karina say, "Daddy, Daddy."

He hugged Cleo again and this time kissed the top of her head. Sweet Cleo Leo!

Then he kissed Karina's cheek. Sweet Cleo trio! She was just looking at him with this frown. Wasn't about to take her eyes off him. And wasn't turning that thumb loose either.

◉

Man took his time and drove slowly.

Karina was on Cleo's lap, looking out at the street, the houses, the buildings, maybe the trees too. Cleo said, "Any good churches in Omaha?"

The question took him by surprise. "Churches?"

"Yeah." She laughed. "Don't you know what a church is?"

"Sho. Omaha full of churches."

"Good. I have to have a good church any place I live."

Sure. He knew this about his wife. Why had it taken him by surprise?

◉

The boys, Lyle, and Debbie were all in the living room when he brought his family in. Debbie was already at the door with her arms opened, ready to take Karina. She said, "Lord, have mercy, mercy me. Look at that beautiful child! Well, I never in all my life—"

But Karina, in Cleo's arms, grumbled and pulled back, holding tight to her mother.

Cleo said, "Don't be like that, honey. This is your Aunt Debbie. Why don't you let her say hi to you? She just wants to say hi."

Debbie kept holding out her arms to the child.

Lyle had come over and was standing there beside Man looking at Cleo. Lyle said, "So, you're Cleo. Good to meet you, at last, Cleo. Come on in."

And the boys, shy, back there behind them, were just looking.

Debbie, in her proper voice, said, "Cleo, honey, come on in and make yourself at home."

They all sat down in the living room, Debbie beside Cleo. She kept on holding her arms out to Karina, and Karina just looked at Debbie's hands and sucked her thumb. Debbie said, "She's talking now ain't she?"

"Sure," said Cleo. Then to Karina: "Can Mama's big girl say hello to Aunt Debbie? Go on, Karina. Say, Hello Aunt Debbie. Take your thumb out of your mouth and say hello to Aunt Debbie." Cleo gently held Karina's arm and by force moved the thumb out. "Go on, say, Hello Aunt Debbie."

Then Karina said, "Daddy, Daddy." And she pointed to Man.

And everybody laughed. Man too. He felt tears in his eyes but he didn't want anybody to see.

Cleo said, "You want to go to Daddy? Here, Daddy, take her."

Man was sitting in an armchair across from them. He leaned forward and held his hands out.

Cleo set Karina down on the floor and let her stand there. She held on to Cleo's skirt and just looked back at her.

Debbie said, "Just as pretty as she can be. Looks just like you, Freddy. Look at them eyes!"

The boys were watching everything like they smelled something bad.

Lyle said, "She's trying to make up her mind."

Cleo said, "Go to Daddy, honey. Go on—"

And she took a step in his direction, wobbled on her feet, stopped, then started again and stumbled on over to his hands. And he lifted her up on his knee and she rested against his chest and he held her like that.

But he felt kind of funny sitting there with his daughter on his lap. Then he just naturally started rocking her, like his mama used to do him when he was little.

Then Debbie said, "She's no little baby, Freddy. You don't have to rock her."

Then Karina suddenly looked up at him and grinned, and she started laughing. She said, "Daddy." Then again, "Daddy." And kept on laughing.

That was the beginning of their new life.

◉

That night Man sat out on the front porch with his harmonica. Cleo beside him. The baby upstairs sleeping. He felt devilishly happy, happy as a hoodoo doctor in a slip-in, joyful as an all-night kicker in a dance joint. He started blowing, then he stopped and closed his eyes.

He started singing—

> I gots me a long tall lady,
> She so long and tall she sleeps in the hall.
> I say I gots me a long tall lady,
> She so long and tall she sleeps out in the hall.
> But when we start to loving we sho have a ball.
>
> She won't let me mess around.
> She jes won't play my game.
> She won't let me mess around.
> She jes won't play my game.
> But Lord knows I love that woman jes the same.

He was having fun.

"I *know* that's not about me," Cleo said.

He cackled. "Naw, my beedle-um-bum." Leaning over, he kissed her cheek.

"What's a beedle-um-bum?"

"A beedle-um-bum is a beedle-um-bum and you is a beedle-um-bum."

And he started the song over again.

◉

Later that night, upstairs in his little bed, after Karina was asleep, they held each other and kissed, naked belly to naked belly. He was too young to be a poppa-stoppa but he felt energy popping in his muscles. His desire was big as the ocean, his joy wide as the western sky. Yeah, tell it like it is! Tell the truth! The warmth of Cleo's stomach against the surface of his spread hand sent rippling currents up his arm to his brains and throughout his body. He felt her hand busy at his crotch and he relaxed and let her lead him where he wanted to be.

◉

The day they were moving in, Man called a taxi, loaded it up, and rode to Twenty-fourth and Wirt sitting in the front seat with the driver. As the driver helped him carry the first trunk upstairs an ambulance pulled up and stopped in front of the old folks' home. While they were huffing and puffing with the second trunk two men in white uniforms were on their way into the rest home.

◉

It didn't take them long to get set up in the apartment. He had already bought, at the Salvation Army, an old refrigerator, a small bed for Karina, a double for Cleo and himself, a wooden kitchen table and four chairs painted enamel white, a couch for the living room, an old, dark, cheap rocker and a floor lamp. Got all that for two hundred dollars. And none of it looked too bad either.

Debbie let them borrow some sheets and pillows, a couple of plates, knives and forks, stuff like that, till they could get their own.

◉

One afternoon while Karina was taking a nap they silently undressed and stretched out on the bed. The bedroom door was closed. He softly blew his harmonica then sang to her—

> Wooh-wee, sugar,
> You sho knows how to pick me up and put me down.
> Wooh-wee, sugar,
> You sho knows how to pick me up and put me down.
> Wooh-wee, sugar-baby,
> You sho knows how to turn me round and round.

Then he slowly and hesitantly turned toward her and gripped her smooth hips with his big rough hands and pulled her to him. When they were belly to belly, they hugged each other. Man felt her warm soft breasts with their hard dark nipples pushing against his chest. He held her like this for a second as they kissed at least a dozen times, tongue to tongue, nibbling, stroking, sighing, breathing harder and faster.

Then he slid down slowly and kissed her belly, licked its tiny nearly invisible bed of hair. She was now dragging her fingers along the big muscle in his neck. Felt good. He thought: My Cleo, my high-classed woman, Cleo. Love this woman more than life itself. He felt playful, relaxed. Yeah. Light-skinned woman don't use no comb. Blue-gummed nigger like me ain't got no home. Light-skinned woman wear fine shoes. All a nigger like me got is the blues. His erection was big as a house between them and he felt her tiny soft hand trying to do something with it. Love you, sweet mama. Do it bottom or top, sweet mama. Tell you no lie. Love to eat yo cabbage. Drink yo pot liquor. Hey, pretty mama.

Cleo whispered, "I've missed you so much, oh so much." And she reached down and lifted his chin and kissed his big mouth with her wet, slightly parted lips, and he felt her tongue again slide smoothly in between his teeth. Go on, call the cops and turn out the lights. This was heaven. Go on, make me want to cry. When my baby gets to loving me, all I can do is scream. She was moving her head, causing her lips to shift and turn against his. Good-looking woman make a dead man come. Don't you know, a good-looking woman make a dead man come. Lord, Lord. Good-looking woman make a preacher throw away his Bible. She kept grinding her mouth against his. And his erection was so intense it was painful.

Then he lay back and felt her hands all over him and her tongue on his left nipple then the tongue moved slowly down his stomach.

> Sepia baby with pretty thighs,
> I a crawling blacksnake with two eyes.
> Sepia baby with pretty eyes,
> I a crawling blacksnake with two good eyes.
> High-class sugar, you my high tone.
> Ain't no way I gon to leave you lone.
> High-class sugar, you my high tone.
> I'm gon love you right down to the bone.

And though he knew this woman was Cleo there was a newness to what was happening. Like being with somebody for the first time. You thought about your timing, you kept your eyes half closed, and you kept your movements slower, easy, cautious because you didn't want to feel foolish. Even if this woman was your wife she was not the same woman who left you. She changed and you changed. Now you were trying to find your way back or a way to go on in a new way.

Her tongue was exploring the left side of his body along his ribcage. She had one hand on his midnight steeple. And though this woman had seen his body many times, she had not seen it recently. They hadn't felt comfortable making love at his sister's house. Naked, he wasn't sure about his big body, yet the uncertainty was slipping away slowly, slowly, especially now as Cleo seemed so sure of herself. She squeezed him and somehow the pressure eased the pain he was feeling. She was now stroking the patch of nappy hair around it. He spread his legs farther apart, beginning to feel proud of his big body—a thing he'd so often felt ashamed of. Through half-closed lids he could see her head, the side of her face. She no doubt felt his eyes on her and looked up at him and smiled. Said: "I love your blackness. You're so beautiful, so smooth." And he closed his eyes and wondered what she saw when she looked at his blackness. Blue-blackness? Did she see a light in that blackness? Something so powerful and so strong that it was really a burning light of beauty. Did she see his arms and his ashy, thick hands as beautiful? His chest muscles, the scars from the buckshots, his stomach, his long, black, uncircumcised dick, were all of these parts of him also beautiful to her? She was now nibbling at the huge muscle of his inner thigh. Was that too beautiful? She worked her way on down to his calves and to his ashy foot with its broken toenail. Then she shifted to the other foot and started back up.

She stopped at his crotch and lingered there a while, then she slid back up beside him. He lifted himself on one elbow and looked down at the delicate yellowish brown tone of her skin in the afternoon light. He saw it as a beautiful kind of music that touched something in him. Hesitating for a moment, because he remembered how she could be about her nipples, he slowly sucked her nearest hard dark nipple, then the other one, pulling at them gently with his teeth, such long beautiful stems, and all the while, touching her gently with his free hand, stroking her stomach and down to her center and between her thighs. I may not be the doctor, I may not be yo doctor, baby. But I sho got the cure. Sho got yo cure. And while he sucked he felt her stroking his thick, woolly, knotted hair with her long slender woman-fingers. Then she reached down and pinched his right nipple with her left hand and he felt a whole network of shivers race out from that point moving throughout his body.

Without losing rhythm, he licked her stomach where he'd licked before. Oh, Lord. If I ever had the blacksnake blues. If I ever had the blacksnake blues. Them blues is now old, old news. Then he spread her thighs farther apart and looked again seriously for the first time in what seemed like years at that part of her he had once known so well. He felt heat spread behind his eyes and that old electric energy he once knew shoot out from his center down and up to the top of his head. Lord, Lord. Make a blind man throw away his cane. Lips curling flames, folded back but rising from a raised mound firm and smooth. Smooth as sunrise. Alive as a whole raining forest full of steamy moonlight.

And he lowered himself to her and tasted the sweet salt of her, ran his tongue along the flames, tasting and feeling the coolness of the fire. And memory. He remembered her this way, this part of her, yet this was new and this was happening for the first time. And she started to talk back to him with little cries, moaning, and giving him whisperings freighted with strings of words that were getting along very well without any meanings at all.

And when she sent up a cry from her guts, shook all over, closed her thighs, shivering and shaking and bit into the cover to choke her own screams, he pulled back.

And he pushed the tip just inside the flames and stopped, watching her reaction. He was feeling the way something in him connected him to the rest of the world, to all of life, to flesh and air and water and everything else beyond these poor walls and his body. Her head was turned to one side and she was biting her fist. When he moved deeper she gripped him with her arms and thighs and held him with what seemed like all her might. And they began moving with a kind of music slowly together, like two people who once knew a song, who once sang a song together, but who were now learning how years later to sing it again after having forgotten all of the words.

Later they both slept.

Then he woke and watched her sleeping. It was like they had never been apart. Felt that familiar. He knew this. It was like time had always been now, leaving him the full sense of themselves complete as one. Her eyes closed, her head against his bosom, he believed he would never know a greater peace than the peace of this moment.

SURE WAS GOOD BEING WITH CLEO again, as husband and wife. Long time. Long, dry long time. He loved him some Cleo. Yes, Lord. But already this new sense of responsibility he was feeling toward Cleo and Karina shook him. It felt like chains.

CHAPTER FOURTEEN

◉

One morning, early, before getting up, they were wide awake, and he suddenly said, "What happened? Or is this the wrong time to ax?"

"No. I can talk about it. Eddie got so he was trying to control my every move. I couldn't breathe without him all over me checking out how many times I took a breath in one minute. He was a jealous fool. It got so bad he wouldn't let me out of the house. When I saw him following me one day I knew I had to get away. I got scared of him. I thought I might end up killing him if he didn't kill me first. He started knocking me around."

"How you get away?"

"I just packed my stuff and Shawn came over and got me. We moved it all into this apartment down on Forty-fifth and Drexel. Shawn and I got together. That was early in March."

"Did he try to find you?"

"I'm sure he did. I was scared to even go out of the house half the time. He'd told me many times if I ever left him he'd kill me."

"If I'd knowed about it, his ass woulda been mine."

"I think you mean that, don't you?"

"Damn right I mean it." And he did.

"Fred, it was awful. I lost my sense of humor. You know me. I've always been able to laugh at things. I couldn't laugh at anything anymore. I could barely take care of Karina. But somehow I got myself together because I knew her life and mine too depended on my getting out of there."

"Glad Shawn was there, glad she helped you. I know she ain't never liked me but—"

"Shawn is Shawn. She don't dislike you. It's anybody I'm with. Even when I dated in high school. That's how she is, Fred. It's not you. You shouldn't take it personally."

"I just member how she useta bitch at you bout me fore we got married. Talking bout you picking up some common nigger in the park. That hurt my feeling."

"Well, you can't live in the past. And Shawn knows my life is mine and hers is her own. She's my sister and I love her but she can't live my life."

"Is she with anybody yet?"

"She had some young man hanging around for a while but now all she does is go to church when she's not at work."

"What kinda work—?"

"She's working as a waitress in a catfish and black-eyed peas restaurant on Forty-seventh—same one I was at. I told you, remember? I worked there too right up till I left to come out here. But the boss got these hands that were too busy for me. I don't like people touching me without my permission."

He kissed her. "I love you, woman."

"I love you too." She kissed him back. Then she lay back on the pillow. "So, what has your life been like since you left Chicago? You involved with a woman out here?"

He was hoping she wouldn't get around to asking that question. But here it was. He said: "I wouldn't call it involve. I been sort of just seeing somebody off and on, you know. But she got somebody else and I knowed from the beginning. It wont like we was fooling each other. She knowed how I felt about you cause I told her, and that was long fore I ever knowed for sho you gon come back. You believe me?"

"I believe you, Fred. I'm glad you had some female companionship. If you'd had that in Chicago maybe you wouldn't have risked your life like you did that—"

"I was too messed up in the head then to be bothered with anybody. I didn't want nobody."

"Let's try to make it work this time," Cleo said. "We both have to try harder than we did before. Karina deserves it. She's got a right to her mama and her daddy."

He kissed Cleo again on the mouth. His hand slid down her belly and between her thighs to her mound of hair. She opened her legs and he reached in with two fingers and started playing with her. She always liked that.

⦿

He took Cleo with him to the Palace one Saturday night soon after she got to town. He introduced her to everybody—Jorena, Herb, Greg, the guys in the band, folks he didn't know all that well—and introduced her proudly as his wife. And she did him proud too. He was showing her out. That was true.

Jorena leaned on the bar in front of Cleo and said, "You know Fred is looking a hundred percent better since you got in town."

He laughed and they laughed too.

Jorena said, "I don't know what you doing for him but it sure must be the right thing."

Cleo laughed and held onto his arm. "Is that right?"

He said, "She got it right."

A tall dark Watusi-looking joker walked in. Jorena called out, "Hey, Percy!" Then to them: "That's Percy Norman, night boss down at Sears. He and his boys come in here a lot. Oh, by the way, Percy told me long time ago to tell you he really digs your singing."

Man looked back at the tall man going by. With him were two shorter men.

Then guess who walked in. It had to happen sooner or later. Bev. The minute she was inside the door her eyes, like daggers, hit him, then Cleo.

She headed for the other end of the bar but he reached out and touched her arm. "Hey, Bev. Got somebody I want you to meet."

She stopped, looking surprised and angry, with her nostrils flared, then looking Cleo over, looking him up and down like she never saw him before. Then she said, "Oh?"

"This Cleo. Cleo, this Beverly. Miss Beverly Frye."

They just looked at each other. But Cleo was giving her this smile. Cleo held out her hand to Bev. "Hi, Beverly."

Bev looked at Cleo's hand, grunted like some old hog in slop, threw her nose up, and walked on to the back. Man watched her go.

That act—and acting like he was nobody—opened up his eyes. He never would have thought Bev would be like that. She went on back to a back table where there were a bunch of jokers clowning and acting the fool. These were low-life jokers she, any day in the week, wouldn't give the time of day. And she sat her big fat yellow ass down with them and started a lot of fake laughing, like something was really funny to her. Peoples is a bitch.

Cleo shrugged. And that was the end of that.

Jorena fixed him a double shot of Old Crow and brought Cleo what she wanted, one of those lady-fied drinks in a tall skinny glass, pink with green plants stuck down in it. He took himself a good long swallow of bourbon and set his shot glass down. It was just about nine-thirty.

Greg mosied over and said, "Hey, Fred. How about opening the show tonight? We could do something everybody knows, say, something like *Sleepy Time Gal* or *I'm Nobody's Baby*. You do that kinda number?"

"Naw, man. I don't know the words but maybe I can fake it." He was grinning. Teach me but don't bleach me.

Greg started humming the melody to *Sleepy Time Gal*. Then he said, "What you like to open with?"

◉

Man answered Greg's question a half hour later when he took the microphone and put it right up close to his mouth. Said: "Good evening folks." People kind of settled down, stopped so much chattering. "I feel good tonight. Real good! Happy as a man can be tonight cause my baby here. But you know my baby don't stand no cheating. No midnight creeping." They laughed. "She's got what it takes. I don't have to wait till the real thing come along. Don't have to go to Kansas City or Chicago to get what I need. The very thought of her sends me. I'm hers body and soul. You know that song, *I Let a Song Go out of My Heart*. Well, I let a song fly into my heart. This here song I'm about to sing—called *Rice Pudding*—is dedicated to my wife, Cleo. Right over there at the bar." He pointed. "The love of my life."

Everybody—except one—clapped.

He got real close to the microphone now and got his voice down low, making that bedroom sound, and sang:

> Baby, baby, you sho knows how to do it right,
> You sho knows how to wake me in the morning.
> Baby, baby, you sho knows how to do it right.
> You sho knows how to wake me in the morning.
> And you sho knows how to put me to sleep at night,
> Baby, baby, you sho knows how to make it tight.

Here he put some fast-talking harmonica in, then sang it over again, making slight variations. Baby, you sho can boogie, boogie without a light, boogie on outta sight.

Now he put a little happy harmonica in right along here, letting it say what he say, repeating what he said. Then he went on, still adding, extending, playing with it, insisting rather than repeating.

The crowd screamed, going crazy. They loved it. He put everything he had in the singing this night. And he kept his eyes right on Cleo while he was up there.

Then, while the crowd was carrying on, Bev got up and walked through the bar, with her nose up in the air, and out the front door.

◉

That night when he and Cleo got home, a little after midnight, the taxi let them out on the Wirt side of the building.

Right there where they got out, Man saw a light on in the back of the variety store, where Sofia Sweeney lived. He figured she must be still up doing something.

Walking by her side window, he saw her in there, leaning on her dining room table. A fifth of White Horse scotch, more than half shot, near the edge of the table. She looked like she was sick, throwing up or about to throw up. Head hanging, spittle dripping from her mouth—an ill ostrich.

Cleo pulled at his arm. "It's not polite to look in people's windows. Come on. You wouldn't want anybody looking in on you. Would you?"

Just as Cleo pulled him away, he could see Sofia's mouth moving. She was talking but he couldn't hear what she was saying.

Upstairs, while Cleo was across the hall at Daffodil's picking up Karina, he walked in—catching a whiff of the staleness of his own dwelling place—and turned on the light in the hall, sauntered down to the kitchen, and opened the cabinet over the stove, yanked down a fifth bottle of Old Crow, took himself a long pull straight from the bottle and, smacking his lips, recapped it. For real, got to cut down on this shit.

Then while standing there he heard this voice, Sofia's voice downstairs, through the floor. But he couldn't hear it well so he walked up the hallway a little and stopped where the voice came through more clearly. Sofia was saying, "So sick of these goddamned niggers. Sick! Sick! Sick! Sick to death of sonsofbitching niggers! Niggers! Niggers! Niggers! Everywhere I turn, niggers! Goddamned niggers! Stupid asshole niggers! Rotten no-good asshole niggers! Niggers! Niggers! Niggers! Niggers over me, niggers all around me!"

And Man smiled. So, it like that, huh.

◉

He's in a house somewhere—it's hard to know where. It feels like New Orleans then again maybe it's Atlanta. The room is dark gray-yellow. He's in bed with Cleo but when he turns over and kisses her Cleo turns into Jorena. But somehow it's not surprising. He looks at her in the moonlight coming in through the window. Actually the top part of the face is Jorena's and the cheeks and mouth Cleo's. He moves down and kisses her bosom, pecking little kisses all over it, lingering only briefly at each nipple. This is Jorena. But the breasts belong to Cleo. See the tiny mole on the left? Ah, it doesn't matter. This woman is both and he loves her. She's the perfect woman. And he works at her with his fingers, trying to get her hot, and she quickly gets hot. She turns fully to him and opens her warm thighs and he moves into her warmth. They hug and kiss and start their hips moving to a Dupree Cabbage Greens–beat. Love my greens! Boogie! Going back to New Orleans! Boogie! And they're going at it strong, grinding down the shady lane, down between the low cabins, through Angola, under the low-down dog, past the black cow standing in the high weeds, when suddenly the door is kicked open and a bright white light pours into the room, a cold light, and through it comes none other than Sofia Sweeney, saying, "You people make too much noise," and Sofia reaches down with both hands and grabs the bed and yanks it from beneath them as though it were a sheet of paper. And they plop to the floor.

THAT MONDAY WHEN HE AND LYLE got to work Eliot was sitting in the lunchroom with a cup of steaming hot coffee in front of him. Other guys were coming in through the lunchroom door, going on into the

CHAPTER FIFTEEN

locker room to change for work. Eliot turned as they came in and grinned. "Well, Fred, looks like you're getting promoted, boy."

Hallelujah!

Man felt a rush of excitement. It was like another piece of the plan had fallen into place. But, wait a minute. Boy? Why always this "boy" crap? His stomach felt like a cake of lard was resting on it.

"I got the okay to hire one third-class welder. Looks like you're it. Have to be on a trial basis. You understand?"

"I do. Sho." Hey! As he stood there looking at Eliot he felt scared to let himself get too excited because it might all blow up in his face. He just kept his fingers crossed and told himself, keep on keeping on.

"Okay," Eliot said. "You start this morning. They got a new janitor coming in this afternoon. Boy named Kermit. You'll have to take time and train him in-between time."

"Thata be fine, Eliot. And thanks. I preshate it." He kind of resented thanking Eliot. If only Eliot hadn't made it seem like a favor. He knew it didn't really apply this time but old folks used to say: When somebody wants to do too much for you, be careful. He also remembered them saying: Watch out when folks give you everything you wants: a fat hog ain't long for this here world.

But Man knew Eliot could have hired some white boy off the street. And it was only a miracle he hadn't.

◉

Lunchtime. Guys packed in the lunchroom. The women ate in their own lunchroom. For the first time Man sat down with the guys on an equal footing. He was one of them. Opening his bag, he took out his roast beef sandwich Cleo made for him. Everybody was eating and talking at the same time. He sat there next to Lyle eating in silence. Amos Mozzella asked Louis Irving what his old lady fixed him for lunch. Louis said none of your fucking business. Oliver Fergus said what kind of Italian name was Amos. Amos told him to go fuck himself. Louis then said that Amos must have been one of them little choirboys who pee in their pants every time they see a priest. Amos told him again to go fuck himself, that Italians were better than his type any day in the week. Cassidy DeMaris seconded the motion. Oh, yeah? Sing *Santa Lucia* for us, Amos. Yeah, said Oliver Fergus, Let us see you make some spaghetti, Amos. I'm hungry, Amos. Make me some spaghetti. Get off my back, you guys, Amos said. Yeah, said Eliot, You guys cut it out. Yeah, said Mark Harvey, cause Amos might start crying. A lot of them laughed. Lenny Ludwig laughed the hardest, choking on his sandwich. Vincent McElroy started singing *Santa Lucia* like a castrated angel.

◉

Eliot brought Kermit over to Man where he was welding and introduced him. So Man stopped what he was doing. "Show him what he suppose to do, Fred."

"Okay." Man put down his welding iron.

Man led Kermit to the janitor supply closet where the brooms and cleaning stuff were, then he led him around through the locker rooms, the lunchrooms, showing him where the trash cans were, showing him what to clean, telling him how many times in the week he had to clean what.

Kermit was a ditty-bop type joker with a mean strut—stepping like somebody trying to avoid jimson weed—and with a cocky tilt to his head. He had long curly hair and kept running his fingers through it. Probably his proudest possession. Kermit had a look that said: I ain't the janitor, ain't the janitor's son, but I'll keep it clean till the janitor comes. Man had never seen him out north anywhere. Was he new in town? Turned out he was fresh up from Saint Louis. Man got the joker started and was glad to turn his back on him.

Then Man strolled back to his welding.

◉

That next Saturday—with a good Dutch Masters cigar stuck in his mouth at a cocky angle—he again went to the track with Debbie. Cleo wasn't interested and Daffodil wasn't around to babysit Karina anyway. At the track he lit the cigar and ordered a beer before placing any bets.

He felt good!

> I got me a good hand now, baby,
> And I gon play it right.
> I got me a good hand now, baby,
> And I sho gon play it right.
> Watch you and me, we gon get real tight.

Humming to himself, humming: Got me a good hand, baby, gon play it right, got me a good hand now baby, sho gon play it right, watch you and me, we gon get real tight.

This time he had the feeling he was in touch with something magical, that he'd be able to pick the right horses. Maybe he could make these horses dance for him the way the dice used to dance in his hand, and dance even after he threw them on the ground and snapped his fingers, crying Hah! Tell me my name. Hah! Talk to me. Hah! Get way down with me and tell me my name. Talk to me, tell me them horses' names while you at it. But Queen of Comedy let him down in the first race, Cynthia came in fourth not first in the second, and Running Foe was out-flanked by Blue Regina in the third. He refused to bet on second- and third-place positions. No sense knocking on a door not even there. Knock, knock. Anybody home? He needed a drink.

By the end of the fourth race Man was ready to go, and Deb was just getting warmed up. She said, "You know, to catch a ride back, all you got to do is go to the parking lot. Anybody will give you a ride back to town."

So he pulled his cap down over his eyes and walked back to the parking lot and waited at the exit gate with his thumb out. Two white guys were there too, both with thumbs out. They were laughing about having lost all their money.

A white man stopped and asked them which part of town they were headed for. They said south and got in.

He was alone, waiting now.

Then a dark blue Chevy was coming. He held up his thumb.

But when he saw the driver, a pretty young white woman, he dropped his arm, but she stopped anyway.

With a big smile, she leaned down so she could see his face. "You want a lift?"

He hesitated, then said, "Yeah, I do."

He opened the door and got in.

She didn't ask him his name and he didn't ask her hers. She talked though, about her bad luck at the track, laughed it off as the price she paid for her day away from the kids. She lived out in northwest Omaha, near the Country Club. She had a deal with her husband. If he could waste money at the Country Club, she could throw away a few dollars at Ak-Sar-Ben. Her husband said she could have her fun like this if she promised to bet only twenty dollars and come home no matter what. The kids, two boys, were with the sitter, a nice colored lady named Fernie Mae.

She drove him to where he wanted to go, Twenty-fourth and Lake. He thanked her, took a five-dollar bill from his wallet and offered it to her.

She smiled. Dimples. A light of kindness in her eyes. "No, that's okay." She waved it away.

So he got out and closed the door. Nice lady, he thought, as he headed for a drink. Just one to get the track dust outta my throat. Yeah, a nice lady. Now that just goes to show you all white folks ain't evil. Ain't no mo evil than niggers or anybody else. Old folks useta sing bout evil niggers: niggers walking on the cross. Yo soul loss. Yo foot slip and you bust yo lip. Everybody, he thought, was subject to devilment. Just had to fight it all the time. Me? I gots it all in me, he thought, as he pulled himself up on a bar stool. Just gots to fight it, fight it. And gots to cut down on this alcohol.

⦿

That next Monday morning when he and Lyle got to work, first thing, Eliot, looking mad as a wounded bear, walked over to him at the time clock and said, "Fred, Bernice is out sick today. I want you to operate her crane."

He looked up at the rails and the empty yellow crane-cab, at the darkness inside. He laughed to himself. Well, ain't this a bitch. Just starting as welder and here comes Eliot asking him to run a fucking crane too. Ain't the operator, ain't the operator's son, but I can operate till the operator comes.

Lyle said to Eliot, "Nobody else around?"

"Not that I can spare. I need all my men on the welding and sheers today. Lyle don't you got an operator you can spare a little while to show him how to run the thing?"

"Hell, I'll show him myself." Lyle looked at Man. "You should be able to do it, Fred. Ain't much to it. Come on. I'll go up there with you."

Yeah, he thought. But he couldn't help wondering if he somehow fucked up last week. He hadn't thought so. No bubbles in his lines. He was real careful.

Eliot said, "Yeah. Lyle'll show you what to do. Just take it easy up there."

Lyle went up first and Man climbed up after him. They sat side by side in the old cab. The view from up here was pretty nice. The welders down below making their orange sparks. The cutters operating the sheers along the side. Old Ralph Roberts down there at his sheers talking to himself and slamming steel. Man liked it up here, looking down on them all.

Lyle took the lever and said, "There ain't but two ways you can go with this baby: left and right. Left this way, right this way. Okay? For the lift you have to be careful. It goes like this, up and down and out like this and back. But you gotta take it easy or you might hurt somebody. You could even kill somebody down there if you let the load start swinging. Okay? Larry down there will be your crane follower. Hey! Larry—"

Larry looked up at them. "Yeah?"

"I'm sending the chain down. Hook up something. Trying to show Fred here how to operate the crane."

Lyle lowered the chain.

Larry was this old bald-headed guy with teeth missing in the front. He took hold of the chain, bent over and hooked the chain around a small beam. He waved his hand in a narrow circle with his forefinger stuck up above his head. "Take it away!"

"All right," Lyle said to Man. "You take charge here. Go on. Take it easy now."

Man pushed the *up* lever and when the chain got tight the beam started lifting off the ground. Time. Take yo time.

Lyle said, "Take her easy. You got to make sure the load don't start swinging everywhichawhere. Just bring it up slowly. Bring it on up. Little higher. You want to be sure to clear everybody's head. Bring it higher. Yeah. Right there. Now just ease up on the *up* lever. Stop it slowly. You got it. Okay. You're going down there where Eliot is standing. See them iron horses? Down to them horses. You going to set it down on them two horses. Ready? The trick is to start the crane moving slowly so the load won't start rocking. Got it? Go ahead. Start. That's it. Gentle, now. Keep the load straight. It's swinging too much. Slow down, Fred. That's it."

Time. Take yo time.

And when he got even with the two iron horses down by Eliot's little station he came to a slow stop.

"That's it. That was good. Keep everything nice and smooth. You're all lined up now. All you got to do is move the load out to the place where you want it, then let it down nice and easy right on the horses. Larry will direct it on. You don't have to worry about that. When you get good like Bernice you can move loads around without a follower. Okay. Go head. Put it down."

And he started it down. By then Larry was standing there by the horses where the load was going down and Larry grabbed it when it came down close enough, and at the same time held up his wiggling forefinger telling Man to inch it down.

Man was letting it down slowly, taking care.

Then Larry turned red in the face, and looking up at Man he started shouting, "Let the goddamn sonofabitching load down. Down! Do you know what *down* means?" And he swore under his breath, mumbling to his old crazy self.

Lyle whispered, "Don't pay Larry no mind. He's just a old mean fart.

That's all. Ignore him. Don't let him shake you. While you up here, keep your cool. That's the main thing."

Larry unhooked the load when it was resting on the horses.

◉

After that Lyle got out and went down, leaving Man up there by himself. He made up his mind he was going to do this the best he could. And the rest of the day went pretty good. Larry bitched at him, cussing and shaking his fist at him off and on, but he was getting the hang of it all right. By the end of the day Man felt he could operate a crane.

On the way home Lyle grinned and said, "You keep learning things out there, pretty soon you going to know how to do it all. Then they have to make you boss."

◉

Man was feeling good as apple pie about his promotion to welder and learning the crane. Before dinner he had himself a few drinks and smoked a Dutch Masters cigar on the back porch. Cleo was in the kitchen cooking. Mama in the kitchen cooking, daddy on the porch looking. She kept dropping things in there.

At dinner he was telling Cleo about the crane work today while she was trying to get Karina—sitting in her high chair—to eat her mashed potatoes.

"Fred, you think we can get a telephone? I got used to having a telephone when—"

"When you was with—?"

"Shawn. I meant Shawn. Now, don't get mad. There isn't anything wrong with getting a phone. We can't even call the police if there was trouble."

"The *police!* When we do gets a phone I sho ain't gon be calling no fucking police on it."

"Fred, let's not talk anymore if you got to cuss."

"Excuse me for swearing." He put a spoonful of mashed potatoes in his mouth but he was so angry he couldn't swallow.

Cleo said, "I'm happy you got this new job, Fred."

"Yeah. Me too." He swallowed. "I need a beer with dinner. Any beer in the icebox?" He had been feeling great a minute ago. Now he felt like shit. And he couldn't figure it out. Just that quickly. He couldn't even remember what she'd said that ticked him off.

She got up, went to the refrigerator, and brought him a bottle of beer.

He opened it and took a long swallow.

Cleo said, "I want things to go right this time, Fred. I want us to have some fun. We never used to have any fun. All I'm asking for is for us to do things together sometimes, go places."

"Do what? Go where?"

"I mean, is this the way life is going to be here in Omaha? Me at home like a good little wife, sending off the payment for gas and light to Omaha Public Power, doing the grocery shopping, just me and the baby at home and you coming home from work wanting to get drunk before dinner?"

He looked at her, pissed. She was making him feel small. "Cleo—"

She looked down at the table. "I'm sorry but—"

"You ain't been here a good month and already you starting to nag."

"I'm not nagging, Fred. I just said can't we have some fun sometimes. And do you have to drink *so much* all the time?"

"Cleo, don't start on me. I gots me a good job. I gots this place here for us. The baby gots thangs. What you wants from a man, Cleo?"

"Listen, Fred. I don't want to argue with you. Maybe what I need to do is find myself some kind of job, get out of here. You think Jorena would give me a job tending bar?"

"What? You crazy? You gotta have a license. And who gon take care of Karina?"

"Daffodil said she would if I want to go to work."

"You got it all figured out, huh?"

"Don't sound like that, Fred. What's wrong with me working?"

"Listen here, Cleo. You see that baby-child there? A baby needs her mother."

"Yes, but Fred, what good is a crazy mother to a baby?"

"What you mean, woman?"

"I mean I'll go nuts in this place. I want to go to work."

"All right, if you want to work, Cleo, fuck it, go on, work. See if I give a shit." He bit into a corn pone and chewed it angrily.

A few minutes later, he jumped up from the table and grabbed the bottle of Old Crow from the cabinet and poured a water glass half full and walked out on the dark back porch and sat down. He took himself a hard long drink and looked up at the blinking stars. Couldn't help it. Here he was feeling happy about his accomplishments at work, feeling mellow, with his family, and here comes Cleo with her shit again. Yet he wasn't all that sure what she had said to set him off. Feeling like nothing had changed, he wondered if she was going to be on him all the time no matter what. The thought made him want to hit something.

He took out his harmonica and blew some nameless melody, something that seemed to speak on its own, and he listened to it, wondering. Poot or shoot. Just let me down easy, greasy.

A little while later, Cleo came out with Karina in her arms and sat down beside him. For a long time she didn't say anything.

Karina said, "Daddy, Daddy."

"Yes, baby," he said. He held the harmonica out to her. She touched its hard surface with her chubby little fingers, then grinned.

Then Cleo said, "Give me a sip of that."

Surprised, and curious, he handed the glass to her. Sweet Lucy Brown! come to town with her britches hanging—

She took a little sip and shook her head, frowned, no, tried to turn her face inside out, and, holding her throat, made this sound like she was choking to death.

He smiled to himself and said, "You know you don't like it. Why you drink it?"

"I just wanted to see what it taste like."

"Cleo—" He put the harmonica back in his pocket.

"Yes?"

"Cleo, all I wants is to be happy with you. Can't you see that? I likes me a drink. I ain't gon lie about that. I don't see no harm in it. You useta bitch about me not working. Now I'm working. I gots my music going again. I'm not doing any rambling or nothing like lots of mens do." He took a drink and went on gazing at the stars.

"I know all of that, Fred. I appreciate it too. But we're not getting any younger. I want us to be happy. If I go to work that would be helping us to a better life. I left Eddie because I still loved you but I also left him because he was making me suffer. I didn't come out here to just be depressed all the time. Love or no love."

"You depressed?"

"Yeah. Most of the time. It's no fun just sitting around here with nobody but Karina to talk to."

"Daffodil next door."

Cleo laughed. "Daffy is all right but she and I don't have anything in common. I mean, if I could get out, there would be more variety. You see—"

"I ain't stopping you from going to work. But I still say what about Karina. And variety, now: I don't know what you mean. Life is life. You try to make things happen but when they don't you still got to just go along, dry-long-so. I have to do a lot of shit I don't want to do." But even as he said this, he was wondering why he himself hadn't figured out a way.

"You don't understand. You're a man. You just go about your business, do whatever you want to do."

He was angry. Mend sails or chew nails. "You ain't heard a word I said, have you? I tolt you many atimes, I ain't likes other mens. If I was I

117

be dead by now. Like old folks used to say, heap of good cotton stalks get chopped down from just being mongst the weeds. I stay way from weeds."

"Then what'd you call Solly?" She laughed suddenly.

He had to laugh too. Couldn't help it.

Just then Man saw somebody, a shadow, down on the sidewalk by the backyard looking up. He said, "Who there?"

"Uncle Fred, it's me, Marvin."

"Come on up, Marvin. That gate ain't locked."

The boy came up the back steps.

Karina said, "Boy."

Cleo said, "Yes, honey, Marvin's a boy."

Again Karina said, "Boy."

"Whas going on, Marvin?" he said.

Marvin said, "You got a long distance phone call from somebody in Chicago. He wants you to call him right away. This the number." The boy handed him the piece of paper.

Man looked at Marvin. "Who was the call from, Marvin?"

"Mama talk to him. I didn't. I don't remember the name."

He laughed. "Boy, you come all the way down here without the name of somebody who called me from Chicago?"

Marvin giggled. "I forgot. It started with a *P* or a *T,* I think."

"Thigpen? Solomon Thigpen?"

The boy giggled again. "Yeah, I think so. Think Mama said something like that."

Cleo said, "That's a hard name for a child to remember, Fred."

"Yeah, but Cleo, this boy—" Man couldn't finish. He laughed.

Cleo said, "Wonder what Solly wants that's so urgent. Probably wants you to wire him some money."

He stood up. "You don't know that, Cleo. I'm gon call him."

Marvin said, "Bye yall." And he ran down the steps.

Man called out, "Bye, Marvin. Thank you."

Cleo shouted, "Say hi to everybody, Marvin."

But he was gone.

Karina said, "Boy, boy, boy."

◉

Not having enough change to use the phone in front of the rest home, Man walked down to the drugstore on the corner of Twenty-fourth and Emmit and asked the sleepy-eyed woman behind the counter for two dollars' worth of change. He handed her the two bills. She gave him the change. At the back of the store he got in one of the booths and closed the door. Got a dial tone, got the operator, and put the money in. A man said, "Hello?" and he asked for Solly Thigpen. The man said, "He must be the new guy back in the back. Wait a minute." Then he waited and a couple of minutes later he heard Solly say, "Hello?"

"How you doing, motherfucker?"

"Oh, man," Solly said. "Glad you called. Listen, I been thinking bout coming out there. I mean serious. I mean right away. You know? Soon as I round up the bread for a ticket."

"All right, Solly, but what about Holly and Annabel?"

"Oh, man. We kinda broke up. Holly staying with her mama right now out on Seventy-eighth and Phillips. I mean, we ain't mad at each other or nothing but it was the best. You see?"

"Yeah. Well, listen. Come on out. Like I told you, I'm cutting up on weekends at a place here. Your boy Greg Wakely there too. You could get in there too with yo guitar and raise hell."

"I just want to get the hell out of this city right now. Ain't nothing here for me no more."

"Yeah. So come on out."

"Hey, man. Can you borry me fifty bucks till I gets out there and gets myself together?"

"Solly, I ain't got no fifty bucks, man. I would if I could. We just paying the rent and buying food. Getting by, you know."

"I see," Solly said with a little hurt in his voice. "Well, I'm gon raise the money anyhow and get on out there."

"Let me know when you gon come. I be looking for you."

"I got yo address from yo sister. I'm gon call you at her place when I'm ready. Think it might be sometime next week. That what I'm counting on."

BACK AT HOME HE TOLD CLEO SOLLY
was planning maybe to come out next
week, that he and Holly separated. She was
washing the dinner dishes. Karina was sitting on

CHAPTER SIXTEEN

the kitchen floor banging a pan on the linoleum. When he walked in she said, "Daddy, Daddy," and stopped banging the pot.

Cleo turned halfway around and said, "She's better off."

He sat down at the table. "What you mean, better off?"

"Forget it. Why is he coming out here?"

"What you mean, why is he coming out here?"

"Just what I said, why is he coming out here."

He didn't know what to say to this as he looked at the side of her pretty face. Cleo, Cleo. What a woman! This was one of the reasons he loved her, loved her toughness and independence, though he wouldn't have put it in those words. Loved her spirit. The woman's got spirit. Standing there with her skinny arms just about up to her elbows in suds. She ain't the teacher, ain't the teacher's daughter, but she'll teach the class like the teacher taught her. This was his Cleo. "Solly coming out here, Cleo, cause Holly and he separated, cause this here a free country."

"What kind of an answer is that?"

"You smart, you figure it out."

"Is he just going to hang around, standing on the street, dragging you with him, drinking, or is he going to try to get a job and be a regular kind of person?"

Man got mad. Shit! What right did she have to ask him questions like that about Solly? She got the wrong attitude. That was the way he saw it. Then he had a second thought: Cleo had her way of seeing things. He knew he needed to try hard to remember that, to give her some credit for having good sense. She was nobody's fool. Maybe the way she saw Solly wasn't so off. Admitting this, or half admitting it, meant that he too was not all he should be or could be. But he knew that. Nobody's perfect. Shit, what did she expect. A man had to do what he had to do. Why somebody got to be there passing judgment? He said: "Cleo, what is it? Is it that you just don't like my friends?"

"What friends, Fred? You don't have any friends that I can see, except Solly. And all he's ever done is bring out the worst in you. Remember, everybody who grins in your face isn't necessarily your friend."

120

Now he was really mad. He remembered old folks saying that. Really mad because it hit him like a metal pole in the forehead that she was probably right. But he couldn't imagine himself without Solly's friendship. Not that they had ever had much to say to each other. It was just the feeling of being together, enjoying each other's company, tasting a little bit. "My mama didn't raise no fool," he said.

"You know you and Solly get together and nothing else matters. He throws away all his money the minute he gets it. And you don't do that unless you're with him."

"Thas a bald-headed lie! You trying to call me a fool?"

She said, "No. I just hope when he gets here you don't start up again the way you two were in Chicago. I can't stand that anymore, Fred."

"Start up—what?"

"Don't act like you don't know what I'm talking about, Fred." She kept her back to him, still washing the dishes as she spoke.

Karina, in an anxious voice, said, "Mama, Daddy, Mama, Daddy."

"Cleo, you don't make any sense to me, girl. All I'm axing you is to make sense to me."

"I said what I got to say. I'm warning you now. If you start that stuff with Solly again, all that drinking and staying out all hours and stuff, falling in drunk—" She wagged a finger at him.

"Go on, finish what you bout to say."

Karina said, "Mama, Mama."

"I said what I wanted to say. I'm just warning you."

"Watch yoself, Cleo, you threatening me. Thas what you doing."

"Call it what you want, Fred. But I'm not taking it. I came out here because you agreed to act right."

Karina said, "Daddy." She was pointing at him with a chubby finger.

Looking down at his daughter, he had a sinking feeling. He was a heavy man going down into the depths of the ocean effortlessly, unable to swim but not resisting the plunge. Just looking at her this moment, seeing suddenly her confusion and fear, he felt without anchor. But there was also the sensation that he had not hit bottom. He looked at Cleo. "I'm not axing you to take it. And anyhow, how come you can't act like a wife? I'm the man in this here house." And even as he heard himself say these words he heard his father's voice saying the same words. How many times had he felt sick with anger hearing his father bark those words at his mama?

"You might be the man but I got rights too. I don't deserve to be treated like you treated me in Chicago."

She was right, he knew that. And even as he continued this line of defense, he disliked the pettiness of his own position. He wanted to be a bigger and better man than this. But he felt so small, so very small in the world, small, broke, but not completely broken. He knew he still had some fight in him and something in him knew he wasn't using it the right way. All he could say: "You not the onliest one with rights, Cleo."

"I'm not going to take it, Fred. You start that again, next thing you know you won't be able to hold your job."

He thought: It must be even harder for Cleo, depending on somebody like me. Would I depend on somebody like me? The thought shook him. "I ain't give up my job. Did I say I was gon give up my job?"

"No, but nobody can drink like you do with Solly and get up and go to work."

Getting up, he kissed Karina on the top of her head, and walked out of the kitchen. Cleo was right. That was what was hard to face. He went and stood on the back porch, seeing nothing. Need me a stroke of good luck. Could make it big if I got the chance, just the right connections, cut a record, get going big. Something got to happen. That's for sho.

●

Two or three days later at work, he was welding a triangular rod to a beam over by Bernie and Cecil. Those two were working and shooting the shit at the same time. Man was just doing his work when Eliot stopped by him and said, "Hey, Fred, that's not the way you suppose to do a corner. You know how to do a corner. Why you fuck it up like that?"

Man looked at the corner where the triangular rod came to a point. "You mean this corner?"

"I don't mean the corner of the fucking building."

"What wrong with it?"

"You can't see what's wrong with it?"

He looked again at the corner.

Eliot put his finger on the thread of flux. "It's too thick. This is not first-class work. We take pride in our work here. We can't send out crap like this. We'd start losing contracts from the big construction companies. This gotta be done over. I want to see it corrected, and I don't give a shit how you do it. Just get it done." And the motherfucker walked away. Lord, Lord, what I ever do to be so black and blue?

Man watched him go. Cecil was laughing in his hand. Dumb nigger. Bernie came over. "What's the matter, Fred?"

"Eliot pissed about this corner. Say I got to fix it. And I don't know what the fuck to do to fix it."

"Here, let me show you." He took Man's rod, dropped his face-cover and went to work on the corner.

Man looked out across the bay, saw Eliot looking at them. Soon Eliot started coming back this way, shaking his head.

Before Eliot got there, Man said to Bernie, "Here come Eliot. You better let me do it."

Bernie looked up and handed him the rod.

Eliot stopped by Man and said, "All right, Fred. Come on with me."

"What?"

Eliot started walking up the bay.

"Where we going?"

"I got a job I want you to do. Come on."

Man followed Eliot up to the first of the big shears at the end of the main bay. Old man Ralph Roberts was at the shears slamming a huge sheet of steel against the straightedge as usual. Ralph was talking to himself as he worked. He was just going to town when they walked up. The machine noise was loud. It was impossible to hear what Roberts was saying. But when he saw Eliot he took his foot off the peddle and let the damned thing rest. Man was already wondering what kind of shit Eliot was trying to pull on him now. Shit! Talk about love will make you drink and gamble. Fuck! Job like this make you see red and kill a motherfucker.

"Ralph," he said, "I want Fred here to work with you today. Show him what you want him to do." Then he winked at the sonofabitch. Man knew what that meant.

Eliot walked off in a hurry.

Ralph grinned and looked at Man. "Okay," Ralph said. "I could use some help." His head was shaking from this nerve disease that caused him to shake all the time. And his lips were moving too, like he was still talking to himself.

Man just looked at the old fool. He already had a sheet of steel on the table about ten by seven, ready to be cut.

"All right," Ralph shouted at him, "don't just stand there. Grab that end. We got a lot to do here." Man was over by the straightedge.

He took hold of one end of this sheet. Ralph had the other. And before he could get a good grip on it, the sucker started ramming the damned thing into the mouth of the shears so fast Man couldn't keep up with him. Ralph kept hitting the peddle, chopping the sheet into strips of about two foot, the long, thin things falling in a pile behind the shears. Man didn't even have time to put on his gloves. He cut his hand and got blood on the steel as he was trying to hold onto his end. Fuck! Ralph's face was a neon sign of contempt for Man's good sense.

Ralph shouted over at him, "Push, push, goddamnit, push!"

Grunting, Man pushed the sheet across the table into the shears. But he shouted back at Ralph, "Hey, Ralph! I gots to get my gloves."

"What?" the old man shouted back.

"My gloves!"

"What the fuck for? Who need gloves?" He looked at his own gloved hands.

Man said, "I gots to get my gloves. And you ain't got to talk to me like that, Jack."

"My name's Ralph. Okay, okay. When we finish this sheet." And he kept on ramming the sonofabitching thing into the shears and hitting the foot-peddle. His hands bleeding, Man turned it loose just for a minute. His left hand was bleeding so badly it caused him to fuck up the cut. Then that old bastard started cussing up a storm: "Goddamnit, what the fuck do ya think this is? You just ruined two or three cuts when you let go. You can't let go like that." He stopped, took his foot off the peddle. "Okay. Go get your goddamned gloves. I ain't got all day." He looked at his watch.

Man walked down the bay by welders bent over their work and fabricators at this and that kind of small machine, along the sides, to where he had been welding. His gloves were on the beam where he left them. He picked them up and strolled on into the locker room to the face bowl.

While he was washing the blood off his hands, Ralph came up behind him. "I thought you was going to get your gloves. You didn't say nothing about going to the toilet."

"I'm washing my hands."

"Goddamn, man. You got to wash your hands to put your gloves on? You think you a fucking surgeon?"

"Hey, man, you don't have to shout. I can hear you."

Man started to hit the motherfucker but changed his mind. Then he walked over to the urinals and started pissing. He just finished and wiped his hands on a paper towel, wrapped some paper towels around both his hands and slipped them into the gloves.

Man then headed back up to the shears before Ralph finished and was standing there waiting for him when he got back. Motherfucker!

Ralph said, "You know you just caused me to waste the company about three or four hundred dollars in just them few minutes?"

Man didn't say anything. Ralph turned the goddamned machine on again and grabbed his end of what was left of the big sheet and started pushing.

When they finished, Ralph looked at him. "Well, what the fuck you waiting for?"

"Hey, man, you ain't got to cuss and shout. I can hear you."

"Then get the fuck back there and get that stuff stacked."

Man didn't know he had to stack the shit too. But he guessed that was what the helper did, stacked the shit, did all the shit work.

So, Man drifted on back behind the shears and the sucker had about ten of those big sheets cut down back there. Man started stacking the strips on the four-wheeler standing there. He thought: Shit, I'm a grown man. That motherfucker don't have to talk to me like I'm a dog. He was mad. For a minute he thought he was going to go around the shears and beat Ralph over the head with something till he couldn't move anymore. But he kept on stacking the strips.

Suddenly that sapsucker Ralph started running the shears while he was back there. Man didn't know much about shears but he knew you weren't supposed to run shears while somebody was behind them. Danger signs all over the plant about that. And that old bastard knew he wasn't supposed to be hitting that peddle.

Man shot around the shears, hot as hell, ready to knock the shit out of Ralph but he stopped and stood there, wide-legged, fists tight, ready.

He saw fear in Ralph. Ralph grinned, showing bad teeth, said: "Sorry. I just had them few little pieces to do on this other job."

Louis Irving was walking by and started laughing. Man gave him the finger and Louis gave him the finger back.

Man sauntered on back and finished stacking all the strips. When he was done he walked slowly back to the front. There was old Ralph standing there shaking and talking to himself while he fumbled with the job order paperwork on his clipboard hanging up on the face of the shears. He looked over at Man. "Ready? You gotta move faster than that. Took you too long back there."

Man didn't say anything, just helped him lift another two-hundred-pound sheet from the stack and slide it onto the table toward the mouth.

And this shit went on like that all day.

By quitting time, Man was pissed as hell, tired as a slave or somebody on the goddamned chain gang. All his muscles and bones were aching. His mouth was so dry he couldn't talk. The world was still mostly green but everything inside him was now gray, the color of held-back rage.

On the way home Lyle said, "Saw you on the shears today. What was that all about?"

"Don't ax me. I think Eliot got it in for me—moving me around like this. Don't know what he trying to do. He come over this morning and get on me bout my welding. And it wont that bad. I mean, I seen worser stuff pass right under his eyes and get shipped out. No problem. But he get pissed cause Bernie was trying to help me fix it. Then Eliot come back and put me working with that crazy sonofabitch, Ralph."

"Ralph insane. Redneck from way back."

"I figured. The bastard give me hell all day. Look at my hands. If he wont an old man I woulda kicked his ass and kissed the job good-bye." Man spat out the window.

Lyle laughed. "That's what happens when you work the shears. You better wear gloves."

"I don't tend to work the shears no more."

Lyle looked at him. "What if you have to? What if Eliot tell you to?" Lyle pulled up to a stoplight at Sherwood Avenue and stopped.

"I'm spose to be welding. Ain't that what he said he wanted me to do? You was right there when he told me. Member?"

The light changed to green and they started again. Lyle drove over to Lake and kept on going.

"Yeah, but you see, Fred, when you a welder third-class, you can get moved around like that. Eliot within his right to move you where he want you. I do that to my mens. I have to take mens off jobs they trained to do and put them to doing other things. That's the way it works. You just gotta play along."

"I ain't gots to be treated like no fucking dog while I'm playing long. I ain't gon take it. Shit naw."

"Ralph you talking about? Don't pay no tention to Ralph. Just do your work and let him grumble and mumble. Just hold your ground and he'll leave you alone."

Man saw that Lyle didn't understand so he just shut up.

Lyle let him off in front of Sofia Sweeney's variety store. Said: "See you in the morning."

"Yeah." He got out and slammed the door.

An ambulance was parked in front of the rest home and two young men in white were bringing out a body on a stretcher. Man stopped and watched them slide the body into the ambulance and close the doors.

Then he trudged upstairs.

◉

Nobody was home. He walked straight back to the kitchen and took down the Old Crow and poured himself a water glass about half full. Went to the toilet and pissed, watching his pretty yellow stream while taking the first taste.

Finished, he flushed the toilet.

Then he washed his wounded hands. After pouring isopropyl alcohol straight onto each hand, he put the bottle back in the medicine cabinet and dried his hands, thinking about Eliot and that crazy Ralph. That's all right: What goes around comes around. May be crazy but I ain't stupid.

He slammed out on the back porch, wondering where Cleo could have gone. Probably grocery store. Or maybe next door. He sat down and propped his feet up on the banister. A car went by on Wirt toward Twenty-fourth. He took himself another sip. Couple of school kids, girls about ten, walked by, probably headed to Kountz Park over there on Florence.

Man took out his harmonica, dried his lips by pressing them inward,

126

then ran the instrument across his mouth, warming up, trying to feel his way into something right. He'd been playing with some lyrics to something he called *Undertaker's Blues*. He ran a few chords to see if he could hit the right melody for the lyrics in the back of his mind. He hit a melody that was like walking up a tree. A good Havana cigar would've been really good right now.

He rested the harmonica on his thigh and thought, Shit, why I gots to put up with this kinda shit on the job. He might be poor but he sure didn't have to be nobody's dog or slave. They can take that job and stick it up they ass fore I'm gon let em treat me like a dog. Then he heard something inside, turned and tried to see through the screen door. "Cleo? That you?"

He heard her coming down the hall. Karina was stumbling long beside her. "It's me. Hi, Fred." She came to the screen door. "How you doing?"

"I could be doing better."

She came out on the porch, holding Karina's hand. Cleo looked prettier than usual in her black pinstripe double-breasted dress with six goldtone buttons down the front in two rows—another Salvation Army special.

Karina said, "Daddy."

"Hi, baby," he said. "Give Daddy a hug." He took his feet down from the banister and sat his glass up there.

Karina stumbled over to his leg. He picked her up and sat her on his lap.

"She's wet. Be careful," said Cleo.

"Why she wet?"

"Because we were out. I haven't had a chance to change her."

Karina said, "Mama." And she pointed at Cleo.

Cleo said, "What's your name?"

"Krena. My name Krena. Mama, Krena." She pointed at Cleo.

"Aren't you going to give Daddy a kiss?"

Karina leaned over and kissed his cheek. He rubbed her hair.

"So, where you go, Cleo?"

"I went to the beauty shop. See?" She held her arms out and turned around. She looked real pretty like always.

He looked at her hair. Said, "Look nice. You went to Debbie?"

"Yeah. Debbie did it. Didn't she do a nice job?"

He took another swallow of liquor. "I said it pretty. Look real nice."

"You don't sound like you mean it." She leaned against the banister and looked in his eyes. "You're not drunk already, are you? How long have you been home?"

"Cleo, shit! I just got home. And, naw! Fuck naw! I ain't drunk. Why you gots to start every time?"

Karina started crying and Cleo lifted her off his lap. "I got to go change her." She picked up the child. Said: "By the way, I found me a good church today."

"Huh? A church?" He smelled something, and he felt he didn't have to be a chemist to know it was shit.

"Yes, Fred, a church. Your wife is now an official member of the North Star Baptist Church."

"That that little old storefront up the street?"

"Yes, Twenty-fourth and Pratt. The people, they are real nice. I really like the minister's wife, Sister Spalding. She runs the nursery school behind the church."

Man realized it was the baby he smelled.

He wondered why in hell Cleo always had to get herself mixed up in some goddamned church, but he didn't say anything.

She turned and opened the screen door and sprinted in.

◉

Then she came back out a few minutes later and said, "I didn't cook any dinner today. I thought we could go out somewhere and eat. Maybe down to Carter's?"

He didn't say anything.

She said, "Is that all right, Fred?"

"You go on. I don't feel like it. I'm not going to eat nothing." He thought: She ain't even noticed my hands. But then the palms wont that easy to see.

"What's the matter with you?"

She sounded more angry than anxious or concerned.

He didn't answer. Said, "Where Karina?"

"She's right in here on the floor, playing. I asked you, Fred, what's wrong? You're like *that* again."

He took another long swallow of bourbon. Said: "Like *what?*" Already he was beginning to see double. Glancing over at her, he saw two versions looking at him with alarm.

"You know what I'm talking about. You're upset about something. You mad because I went and got my hair done? Because dinner isn't done?"

"Cleo, get off my back. Okay?" he snapped.

"Why can't you just tell me what's bothering you?"

"Okay, okay. I had a hard time at work. All right? Look at my hands!" He held out his scarred palms.

"What happened?" She ran her fingertips along the surface of each of his palms, giving him a worried look.

"Eliot put me on the shears." His eyes narrowed.

"What was wrong with that? Sounds like you're learning to do a lot of different things. I don't see anything wrong with that. Didn't you wear your gloves?"

"Yeah, but the motherfucker I had to work with give me a hard time. He kept fucking with me." Too hard to explain about the gloves. Couldn't find the words.

"Fred, maybe it's *you*. Maybe you're the one who's being too touchy. You're not trying to find some excuse to quit, are you?"

That pissed him for real. Too mad to say something back, he just looked at her, hearing a drumbeat in his ears maybe like womb-kicking. He felt angry enough to smash something. He gazed at Cleo. He'd never hit her and was determined to keep it that way. He would not become his father. If he did nothing else in life, he meant to rise above that shit his father was. None of that low-life, dull, stupid shit. He would never stoop that low, hitting a woman.

"You looking at me like you could kill me. But you know yourself you made up reasons many times in Chicago to quit jobs just because you didn't like what somebody said to you."

Even while he was determined to control his anger, he heard himself saying, "I'm warning you, Cleo. Get off my back." And he pointed at her. Feeling one way and trying to think another. Lord, save me. Drifting like a ship on the sea. Drifter's blues. Get out of my face blues. It hurt my jaw to talk about it blues. Hurt like hell. He knew the best thing to do now was to try not to talk anymore.

"Okay. Be like that. Refuse to talk to me. That's what you do all the time. You just clam up and refuse to talk."

When he finished his whiskey he got up and walked by her and went inside, walked by Karina on the floor and put the glass down in the sink, walked on up the hall, opened the front door, stepped outside, closed the door behind him, and went down the steps.

He was thinking: This ain't living. Fuck naw, this ain't living. Do a man got to just take the life he been dealt? Couldn't he change things. Lift himself up. Do something different. If you stand still long enough people throw dirt on you. Outside, his head cleared a bit.

On the way down to Twenty-fourth and Lake, he struck on to the right melody for *Undertaker's Blues*. It had to be like walking across the sky—that soft, that clear, like a canyon of grief-driven clouds. And he heard the melody over and over, refusing to let anything else in, as he strolled along the sidewalk looking—he hoped—like a young man going some place important, like a young man with a mission.

THE PALACE WAS QUIET AND JUST about empty. He sat at the bar and Herb put a double shot of Old Crow in front of him. He said, "How you doing Herb?" Herb grunted and gave him a sour look, pushing his lips out. Then he sat on his stool and rubbed his chin. This joker reminded Man of some kind of junkie always in a nod or the voiceless straight man in a black blackface comedy routine. But Man didn't give a shit, he just wanted to get halfway drunk. Not have to think too much. Not wanting to be too far out of control, he wanted to just get mellow. Let liquor bend his heart like a cloud does a midnight moon.

CHAPTER SEVENTEEN

Restless, Man got off the stool and wandered over to the door and looked out. Across the street Poppa Leon, in his little box, was wheeling himself along, to a riffing rhythm, like he was in a hard-driving boogie, with his long chimpanzee arms, a big grin on his wide black face, white cigarette stuck between his purple lips. Seeing that man smiling caused Man to feel shame. Some suckers don't know when they lucky. Talk about being a diving duck ain't never coming up. You didn't go down with the Titanic, nigger, and yo name ain't Shine. You can still boogie, cain't you? Look at Poppa Leon: he cain't boogie but he ain't nobody's monkey man either, he be his own man, and got a good attitude about it too.

Returning to his stool, Man thought he'd try telling Herb a joke. Said: "You hear the one bout the nigger and God, Herb? Nigger out on a cliff looking at the valley and the cliff start crumbling under his feets. Nigger start falling down the valley. On the way down nigger praying to God, God if you up there, please God, help me, answer me, God. I ain't got much time God, I'm falling, answer me please—quick! God finally say, Yes, nigger I hear you but you ain't lived a good clean life so how you spect me to help you. I'm sorry, God say, there ain't nothing I can do. Nigger thought about this then called out in a loud voice: Hello? Is anybody else up there?" He commenced to laugh watching Herb but Herb never cracked a smile. Stubborn joker.

Man finished his drink and walked out. Restless. Shit. He wasn't about to go back home just yet. Scuffle his ass off and no preciation. Always there: thought of just saying fuck it, hit the road, catch a train, going anywhere: train, train, running fast, cain't see nothing but the land go past. Good feeling, real good feeling. Fast moving feeling, sweet as sweet potato pie.

He walked across Twenty-fourth and into Miss Etta's Tavern. The place was stark and smelled of piss and old beer. Or was it the smell of death and dead dreams, rot? He breathed in the fetid air. Lyle had told him a bunch of drunks and cheap whores hung out here. A place of weekend stabbings, it was also known for great blues on the jukebox. Right across the street from the Palace, this was a whole different world, the bottom, the gutbucket.

But this kinda place, he thought, is a place of unprettified truth, and the bare truth is healing. Here, every tub sits on its own bottom.

A pistol-packing-mama woman, sepia-colored, about three hundred pounds, was behind the bar, sitting her giant bottom on a poor little old stool, smoking a cigarette. She was leaning across the bar talking to a woman who looked like a full-blooded Indian. In the back an old man was mopping near the silent jukebox. On his head was a porkpie hat that looked as permanent as the tomb of a pharaoh.

Three other women sat at the bar talking together. They were dressed in what Man thought of as whore outfits—thigh-tight skirts, off-the-shoulder blouses, high heels. Everybody looked up at him when he came in. Just inside the door, near where he was now standing, a drunk young man called out to the three women at the bar, "Hey! When one of you no-britches-wearing bitches gon gimme some of dat pussy?"

Two of them igged him but the third one shouted back: "Clean up yo-self! Yo mama didn't raise you in no doghouse!"

But it was doubtful he heard her because the young drunk had stumbled on halfway outside, mumbling to himself like a hoodoo ghost. Man gazed at the pathetic creature and wondered how a man could let his life go down that low. True, a black man's life ain't shit in the eyes of most peoples but you a piss-po excuse for a human being if you got to join them in thinking of yoself like that. Man shook his head in disgust.

Man sat at the bar three seats over from the Indian woman.

Big woman behind the bar said, "Yes, sir? Can I help you?"

He took out his wallet and threw a ten on the bar. "Double shot of Old Crow, no ice, if you please." His second mind told him: Don't throw yo money round like you a rich man. Mama's voice whispering in his ear: Fool and his money soon part. Fool always throw the wrong card.

Man then took out a Dutch Masters cigar and stuck it in his mouth, picked up a book of matches from the bar, struck one and touched it to the tip of his cigar, waiting for his drink. He felt important when he was lighting a cigar. Just holding it or sticking it in his mouth gave him a sense of greatness, made the very space his big body occupied important.

He liked himself better with a cigar. The three women farther down were still watching him.

It took the three-hundred-pound woman a long time to get off the stool as she was grunting and breathing heavily, but she made it, wobbled over to the liquor bottles, got the Old Crow, made his drink and brought it to him and he paid her, then took himself a good long swallow and sat the glass down. He could smell the huge woman. Her odor was not the ranky pissy scent of somebody who never takes a bath but rather the fume of fresh sweat covered with cheap perfume and powder—somehow a sexless odor. He wondered what it must be like to be her.

The big woman took the ten, and put nine back on the bar, but she kept on standing there in front of him. Then said, "Ain't you Manfred Banks?" Frowning like she was looking at a tough crossword puzzle.

"Yeah—?"

"Thought so. You the new singer over at the Palace."

"I never seed you in the audience."

She laughed, showing her big mouth full of yellow and gold teeth, and all her huge rolls of fat shook. He took her to be about forty though she looked older. "My name is Miss Etta Oliver, I owe this place. There ain't nothing going on down here on Twenty-fourth and Lake I don't know about. Shoot. When you singing we can hear you all the way over here. That band too. We just turn off the jukebox sometime. Don't make no sense to keep it on." She took a rag and wiped the counter.

The Indian woman looked at him with a blank gaze for the first time. "You wanna buy me a drink, Big Timer?"

Now he looked directly at her. She was pretty drunk already, but what the hell. "Sho." And he told the bartender, "Give the lady a drink. Whas your name?"

She said, "Matilda," and kept her eyes on her wine glass.

Etta took a bottle of sherry and poured the woman's glass nearly full. "Fifty cents," Etta said and waddled over and grabbed a single off the bar from his change, stuffed it in her pocket, and dropped two quarters down by his other singles. A kind of energy seemed to take charge of her whole body for a second.

Miss Etta called out, "Hey, Niggerdemos, come on up here. Get some quarters. Put em in the jukebox. Play something good, something lowdown and lawless." She wiggled her big shoulders and stuck her purple tongue out. It was as though she might suddenly go spinning off across a dance floor or some unexpected thing like that.

The old man leaned his mop against the jukebox and commenced his slow drag to the front, all bent over. And for a sliver of time Man saw himself, in the future, bent like that, slow like that, if he was lucky enough to live that long.

This was something he hadn't thought much about: this getting-old stuff. But look at it this way, like the great old blues singers always say, everybody got to come to this party and do the jitterbug. And he remembered what old folks used to say: You gots to walk that lonesome valley by yoself.

While Niggerdemos was coming Matilda said, "One of them girls down there called you."

He'd heard the woman call him big-timer but he'd missed the rest of it. And one of them had whistled. Lord, Lord. A whistling woman and a crowing hen ain't never gon come to no good end. Mama's words.

His heart felt crisscrossed as he looked down at the women. Couldn't hear himself saying to one of them: I ain't no doctor, no doctor's son, but I can doctor you till the doctor comes. Besides, he was already spoken for. Wasn't he? Yet and still, sometimes I think I will, sometimes I think I won't.

But what the hell. And his gaze didn't break as he saw the one on the far end fingering him to come there. She looked like she must have been about thirty-five, not ugly, not pretty, gold tooth in the front, a thin, brown-skinned rough-looking woman with a scar on the left side of her neck where somebody once tried to sever her head from her shoulders.

He knew the game. Didn't spend time in an Atlantic whorehouse for nothing. And why not go down there? He took his money and drink with him and stood behind her. She turned around on the swivel stool and faced him, legs crossed, cigarette in the corner of her mouth, one fist on one hip, the other hand resting on her bare knee. In a husky voice, said, "Wanna get your big dick sucked?" And she reached over and grabbed his crotch and squeezed. "Want me to whip some of this tight pussy on you?"

If he was stuck in Georgia mud, he suddenly came unstuck. Despite himself she got a rise out of him, a rise he didn't know was in him because he felt so full of anger, desperately full of the need to be wild and free of himself—drunk. A diving duck, not giving a fuck. Swing low, sweet mojo. What the hell, ring my bell. Lay it on me strong. I ain't done nothing wrong. Ding my dong.

Niggerdemos shuffled by, going to the jukebox.

The other women weren't looking back, just keeping their backs to him but he knew they were all ears. And he could see them watching him in the bar mirror. Slick, ready for any trick.

Again despite himself, he grinned and something shifted in his feelings as he said, "Yeah. I might." But even as he spoke he felt a creeping sense of guilt because Cleo was visible—but transparent—before his eyes as though reflected on window glass. His throat felt tight.

"I'm Lolita. I know who you are. This here is Roxanne, and she's Aileen. They're my friends."

He looked at Roxanne—young, plucked eyebrows, smooth damp

skin. She was in a sleeveless glittery red dress, fitted in front where a row of buttons ran down at an angle from her left breast to her right thigh. He saw a long embossed razor scar on her left arm.

"How yall do?" He didn't want to grin but couldn't stop. The guilt was growing like that newsreel shot of the atom bomb explosion—an expanding cloud.

The other two looked at him sideways and then sort of sullenly grinned too.

The one called Roxanne said, "You sure is a big guy. You box or lift weights or something?"

"Naw." He felt himself beginning to blush, something he hadn't done in years, possibly since he was a child, he couldn't remember the last time somebody gave him reason to blush.

Niggerdemos dropped some quarters in the jukebox. The first song to come up was somebody singing Bessie Smith's *Careless Love Blues*. Ah, shit, he thought. One of his favorites.

Lolita patted the seat beside her. Said: "Come on, honey, let's talk business." And he took himself a deep breath and put his stuff on the bar and sat down, refusing to evaluate what he was doing. A man didn't need to always understand his actions. Now the jukebox was giving out another Bessie Smith number by the same singer singing *Ain't Goin' to Play Second Fiddle*.

Lolita leaned over close to his ear, trying to work her mojo real slow. Said, "I got the best tongue in the whole Midwest. I use my teeth too, but I won't hurt you, sugar." And she stuck her long purple-pink tongue out, lifting her lips back, and when he laughed, she slapped his shoulder. "You know you can't resist that. Or this—" And she slowly pulled her dress hem up higher and at the same time opened her thighs.

Man looked down, deep down in the jungle, and saw savannahs. Wouldn't be surprised to see a flock of geese fly up outa that tangle. Saw the best years of somebody's life gone, and Lolita was saying, "Go on, touch it. It ain't gonna bite you."

Instead, he laughed and took a long drink of whiskey, feeling the sudden force of his deep love for Cleo, wife, mother of his beloved child, roughly grab his throat and begin to choke him with two mighty hands. He shook himself, trying to dislodge the image. But she hung on. If Cleo found out he messed with a whore she'd leave him sure as a hard head makes a soft behind.

Lolita laughed, probably at herself, her acting. The other two women laughed too. The one called Roxanne, under her breath said, "Lolita you gointa kill the po man, drain him dry."

Aileen, who looked like she was about thirty, grinned with one of her front teeth missing. Fat cheeks. Short hair put through the straightening comb so many times rigor mortis had set in at the roots. One of those firm-looking colored women who looked like she'd been through a lot of shit and still had a lot to say and do before she was ready to check out. Definitely not somebody's Aunt Jemima.

Roxanne, now, on the other hand, was a lot younger—maybe ten years younger than the other two. He liked her fine brown frame. And he could tell you'd have to get up at early-bright to pull something on her. She couldn't look at him. Her light yellow-gray eyes glanced at him like a cat's. But he could tell she was a poor girl, maybe eighteen, maybe twenty.

Looking at her scar, he said to Roxanne, "How old is you, girl?"

"Old enough to know fat meat is greasy," she said and turned away from him.

"She's my cousin." said Aileen. "She old enough to know better. She ain't never going to be no member of the Elizabeth Club. I can tell ya that. Nobody can put nothing over on this girl."

Man didn't believe the cousin story, he knew from his days in Atlanta and New Orleans that good-time women were all the time saying they were related. If one copped a nod, the other stood guard. If one did the Cootie the other did the Crawl. If one pushed, the other pulled. If one shot smack, the other held the needle. Maybe because they formed family feelings toward each other. They were often tighter with each other than with their pimps.

Lolita said, "I'm ready when you ready, daddy. I got a room round the corner."

"Okay, I'm ready, let's go," he said. Blacksnake got a mind of his own. Blacksnake know the way to the henhouse. Man took himself a long hard swallow. Stuck the cigar in his mouth but the fire had gone out. Still, it gave him courage and seemed to help him resist the image of Cleo in his mind.

Aileen smirked and said, "Now, Lolita, don't you kill the man, now." She covered her mouth.

A little voice in his head whispered: Fool, is you blind in one eye and cain't see out the other? Long as you got money everybody wants to be yo friend. Lord, Lord.

And Roxanne cracked up, leaning on the bar and wiggling her shoulders. She was the one who'd whistled. Whistling woman, whistling woman.

"Don't worry. I'm gon take good care of him. Ain't I, sugar?" And she got down from the stool and pulled at her short skirt, standing with her legs apart so that the skirt stretched across the fronts of her heavy dark thighs. She too smelled of cheap perfume and sweat but her smell had sex in it.

Miss Etta was up there still talking with Matilda as Man and Lolita

135

headed for the door. They hadn't even looked down this way. Nigger-demos had gone to the back with his mop.

As they walked out, the same young drunk came in off the street and sort of stood just inside the door like he was trying to figure out why he came in. Talking to himself, he was looking at the floor. Now he put his right hand out and started counting on his fingers. Said: "Fuck all yall." Then he turned around and staggered back out.

◉

Her room was a chinch-pad, no bigger than some people's closets with an old lumpy bed taking up most of the room. No toilet, the chamber of commerce was down the hall. She closed the door and turned to him, and held her hand out. No chorus of do-wah singers upon their arrival. Man suddenly had fever-dry lips. This nitty-gritty sister excited him in a twisted way. She turned on the light—a bare lightbulb suspended from the ceiling.

He dropped a ten into her palm, worried about the clap, but not worried enough to turn around and hightail it.

She stuffed it in her bra. "Take off yo pants, honey, and get on the bed."

In this light she looked older. Skinny, bony, and twitchy, she was a worrisome-looking woman. He'd put any money on her having many things bothering her mind. You see that look in women with lots of babies and children hanging on them crying and carrying on. It was a process of one life falling away and another emerging. Or maybe she had lost her man in the war. There was a picture of a soldier boy with thick lips pinned to the wall by the bed. "Who that?" he asked before he thought about the wisdom of asking such a question.

She got shifty-eyed, swallowed, then looked at him straight. "His name is Pete. We have a child. He's going to be getting outta the navy in six months." Oh, yeah? Mama in the kitchen cooking lima beans, Daddy out on the ocean fighting submarines.

But suddenly he felt strange—unable to breathe. Unable to look at her face, he felt an overwhelming strong need to beat it, to be anywhere but here, to run, even. And he remembered he hadn't wanted sex, he'd wanted to get splibby. And there, suddenly stronger than before, was the image of Cleo's face smiling at him, smiling in that special kidding way of hers, about to wag her head and say something like, "When are you going to straighten up and fly right, Fred?"

Then he glanced at Lolita as she came closer, reaching for his crotch, but he caught her hand. "It's okay. I ain't into it. You keep the ten."

She gave him big eyes. "You strange. You pussy-whipped or something?" Pushed her lips out.

"Yeah." He turned and walked back out into the hall, thinking, Naw,

I'm the son of drums, your star-crossed, jump-back-in-the-alley harmonica man, the man with the charleswheatstone blowsuck nobody can touch. Naw, you don't know me, baby. I'm gone. I never was here. I'm somebody else.

Lolita came out too and closed the door. "Here, here's five back. I'll keep five for the trouble you put me through."

Hey, she was all right, he thought. Woman got a heart.

◉

Man got a pint from the liquor store. Gotta cut out this shit. And he started walking home, taking sips on the way. Gandering slowly, thinking, just thinking. Pussy-whipped, hell. Son of gutbucket pussy-whipped? Got me a woman with a light round her shimmering but just cain't seem to get along with her. Maybe if I groom slick, wear zoot suits, act like one of them black juice-stealing preachers everything would be all right. Naw. That ain't the way. I know I got something. A new front door ain't the answer. It was like he was holding something precious in his hands and standing barefoot on a bed of fire and holding this precious thing—the most valuable thing he'd ever touched or known—and trying desperately not to drop it, not to burn, trying to keep from dropping this precious thing that meant everything to him. This thing, this thing, this thing would save his life. All he needed was a tiny piece of good luck to pull it off, make it stick, lickety-stick. Something like a bolt of lightning seemed to hit him. He suddenly saw what was wrong: He himself was his own worst problem. Got a good wife. A good kid. A great future. Just got to change my mind. I am changing my mind.

◉

Sofia Sweeney was sweeping the sidewalk in front of her shop, using the light from her showcase windows, windows where she had lots of little things—chess sets, crossword puzzles, playing cards, comb-and-brush sets, matches, lipstick, fingernail polish, cheap jewelry, pens, stationery, teddy bears, Bibles, greeting cards. She also sold newspapers, magazines, and paperback novels. He and Cleo sometimes bought the *World-Herald* down there. For a change, no ambulance was pulling away from in front of the old folks' home.

"Hi, Sofia." Just the sight of her rose sympathy in him, sympathy, not pity, sympathy. Hearing her drunken rage through the floor gave him a strong bond with her. Come to jick-heads: take one to know one. It was strange but stronger than this black-and-white race shit. He knew her suffering. He knew sure as death they were down there in the same ocean of clouds together unable to stop the storm. He didn't know about her, but he knew he could learn better how to read the weather forecast.

She glanced up at him and gave him one of her crooked smiles. Under her breath, said, "Hi, there." Then she stopped sweeping and rested on the broom. "Banks, I've been meaning to have a talk with you."

"Yeah?" He knew some shit was coming. She was stinking of scotch. But he knew his own breath didn't smell like wind over a mint field.

"Can you and your wife try to keep the child from running so hard across the floor? Down there in my place you have no idea how loud it sounds. Makes my ceiling shake, my lights, everything. I know she's just a small child but she runs hard."

"Oh, yeah. All right." We been trying.

"Can't you put her out in the backyard?"

He thought: You crazy, you coo-yon? Said: "We stop her. Don't worry." Fuck that backyard shit. My child ain't no dog. Keep yo cool, keep yo cool, don't be a fool. You been to school, you know the rule.

"Just try to keep her from running so hard."

"Don't worry." Cool now.

Upstairs, he heard Karina running to meet him as usual, stumbling along in that awkward way of hers. When she ran like that he always thought she was going to fall on her face. Sometimes she did. And there she was, crying out, "Daddy, Daddy."

She'd lost one shoe. He reached down and picked her up and held her against his chest, kissing her cheek. Then he caught her big toe between his thumb and index finger and sang—

> Twinkle twinkle little toe,
> How I wonder what you know.

And she giggled and snuggled close to him. And Man tucked her closer and walked on into the bedroom. He felt her little heart beat and it gave him a good sense of life. He loved her for herself. His love for her was like a big tree, giving him all the shade he wanted. And he was glad he'd fox-trotted on away from Lolita's chinch-pad, her fishhooks, and her kindness. Po Lolita.

Cleo was just lying there with all her clothes on staring up at the ceiling. It was about eight, maybe eighty-thirty, first dark outside. Looking at his queen, he felt lower than a splat of chewtobaccy on the sidewalk.

He sat down on the side of the bed and stood Karina on it. She stood there holding his arm. "Daddy," she said, then pointed to Cleo and said, "Mama, Mama. Mama bed. Daddy."

But he was watching Cleo. He said, "You sick or something?"

Her eyes moved slowly to him. She spoke: "I found a job."

He blinked. "A job? Where?"

"Your sister's beauty shop. I'm starting tomorrow."

A job? What about Karina? What about . . . many things? "What about Bev?" he finally said.

"Didn't you know? She and Debbie had a falling out. Beverly accused your sister of flirting with her boyfriend, some guy from Los Angeles. Debbie says she never even looked at the man. Anyway, Bev walked out in a huff. Somebody in the shop said she left town. Maybe she went to Los Angeles with her man."

"Naw. Not long as her father living."

"Her father died a month ago."

"Yeah?" Man rubbed his chin, looking at Cleo. Said: "You cain't do no hair. What about Karina?"

"I'm doing nails and washing hair. Daffodil will take care of her two days—Wednesdays and Thursdays. Mondays, Tuesdays, and Fridays she's going to be at the nursery school down at North Star."

"You?—washing other women's nappy stinking hair?"

"It's work, Fred. We need the money."

"Ain't no way it's gon be much."

"Any little bit helps. Where did you go?"

"Down to the Palace."

"Yeah?" She gave him her unbelieving look. Sometimes he wanted to take that look of hers and put it in a blues song or make love to it, but he had no words and no body for it.

Then he told her about Sofia's asking them to stop Karina from running across the floor.

Cleo sat up suddenly. "That drunk bitch got a nerve to complain, the way she carries on down there every night, throwing and breaking things and cussing."

He said, "Yeah, but it's her building."

"I don't give a damn. She's still supposed to have some kind of respect for her tenants."

He hadn't seen Cleo so mad—at anybody except him—in a long time. When Cleo got mad she could pitch a bitch. Her anger could make a buck-tooth shark come out of the water, hop in an Eldorado, drive downtown, buy himself a pair of wings, and fly around the world and land in Bermuda to blow off steam. When Cleo got started all the angels in heaven finger-popped their way down to earth just to back her with do-wahs. He believed she had strange connections. Angels swung their chariots low for her.

THERE WASN'T ANYBODY TO PICK UP **CHAPTER**
Solly at the train station. He got in while
Man was at work, first Tuesday in June, **EIGHTEEN**
right smack in the middle of the morning. And
Debbie had too many customers to get away that
morning. But Man had already told Solly to come on out to the house.

Yes, guitar man, too, was part of the plan.

So, Solly was sitting in the living room playing his guitar for Cleo when Man got home that evening around six. Cleo was sitting across from him. Karina sitting on the floor tearing up a newspaper and singing her own song.

"Hey, man!"

"Hey!"

Solly jumped up and came to him and they slapped each other on the back, playfully punching each other in the stomach.

Man was happy. Couldn't stop grinning.

"See you made it."

"Yeah." He looked a little thinner but not much different.

Cleo said, "Fred, I cooked a pot of ham hocks and greens."

Man looked at his wife. She sounded proud. True, she didn't like cooking but when she put some effort into it she wanted to crow about it. And she had been known to put on a pot, to truly burn. She was dynamite when she wanted to go all out, say, with some hog maws or tripe and crackling cornbread. He just looked at her. It pleased him to no end that she would cook for Solly. She was giving Man a fixed smile. Lord, Lord.

"How about a drink, Solly?" said Man, still grinning.

"Thought you'd never ast."

Man went back and got some glasses and a fifth of Old Crow, then took out his harmonica.

After a good long shot of whiskey, Man cut into—

> This evening, this evening
> Gon find me a lucky rabbit foot,
> This evening, this evening
> Gon find me one lucky rabbit foot.
> This evening gon change my luck
> Cause I'm a man knows how to truck.

And Solly, with his belly-fiddle against his stomach, backed Man up with some crying strings, long whining, low-down, bluesy whimpering strings. Cleo sat with Karina on her lap listening and clapping their hands. Lord, have mercy.

⊙

By dinnertime they were both pretty mellow, nearly drunk. And Cleo didn't seem to mind or at least she was pretending not to notice. Man thinking: This is the life. If I be on the wrong track put me back. If I sneeze I cain't touch my knees. Gon give you a bushel and a peck if I ain't hung by the neck. Some folks say. Yeah, some folks say. But I say. What I say?

After dinner, his eyes half-closed with pleasure, Man took out a couple of Dutch Masters cigars, gave one to Solly. Struck a match to his own and held the same match for Solly.

"Say, Fred."

"Huh?"

"What was you saying bout starting a blues band?"

"Yeah, we might wants to do that out here. But right now I ain't thinking bout nothing that hard. Good cigar, huh?" He grinned.

"Yeah," said Solly, holding the cigar out and looking at it.

Cleo was clearing the dishes from the table. She stopped and opened the window by the stove for extra air. He was looking at her: Most beautiful woman on earth. Make a blind man see. Preacher throw down his Bible. Ain't she already done it? Love like a red rose. Mahogany brown eyes, creamy smooth thighs. And free-hearted.

Man said, "Come on into the living room. I'm gon run down next door and call Greg. I'll be right back."

He took the bottle of Old Crow back to the living room with him, humming to himself: Don't wanna hear a peep, even if I drink so much I stagger in my sleep.

Man ran out and down the steps, the night cool air feeling good on his oily face. He stepped into the booth in front of the rest home and dialed the phone. No need to go up to the drugstore this time cause he had change. Hey, go get Greg, tell em bring a keg, les sit back in a chair, see if we cain't get somewhere. Waiting. Humming. Give me a bottle of beer. Humming. Sweet mama, my honey dear. A bottle of beer. Serve me red beans and rice. Sweet mama. Serve me twice. Humming. Waiting. Lots of rice. And come on treat me nice. Don't throw no dice. At the same time he saw an ambulance pulling up in front of the rest home. Two young men in white got out and walked up the walkway toward the entrance. When Greg picked up, Man said, "Hey, Greg! Guess who here. Yeah.

141

Come on over. Have a drink. We just sitting round. Come on over." And he hung up. Then ran back upstairs.

From the bedroom, Cleo said, "Fred, open the living room window if you going to be smoking those cigars up there."

"Okay, okay." Yeah, she was right. It was hard for him to remember cigar smoke wasn't sweet to everybody. But with a good cigar, a full belly, he could be all right the rest of the night.

Man took up the half-finished fifth of Old Crow and held it up to the light. It wasn't so much the sparkle of light through the amber liquid that mattered. It wasn't the fact that a good portion of the stuff was still in the bottle that counted. No, it was the good time it surrounded and the smile the liquor put in the belly. Tell the truth snagger-tooth!

Man was still grinning and looking across at Solly on the couch with his guitar when Cleo came in. "I'm putting Karina to bed now, Fred. I hope you all ain't planning to play none."

Karina was back there somewhere crying to the top of her lungs. She didn't want to go to bed.

Solly was pouring liquor.

Man said, "Ah, hell, Cleo, it only nine. Let her stay up a little while longer."

"No! Don't start. Why can't yall go over to Greg's?"

Solly handed Man a glass of whiskey.

Man said, "Cause this is my house too. I scuffle and work and you mean to tell me I can't even relax in my own house lessen you try to run me out. Cleo, come on." Love that woman but she sho can be tough. Puts her foot down. Gotta respect her though. Thas my little lady.

He could tell she was going to stand her ground. Those hands on her hips said so. Even if she blue and blind, she still be mine. Blues half my life, other half my wife. She said: "Fred, I know Solly just got here and everything, and I don't mean to be rude or nothing, but don't forget you got to get up at six-thirty in the morning. You know what happens when you drink after dinner."

Solly laughed, looking at Man. It was the unnatural laugh of a man who wished he was not in the room.

"Why don't you tell me?" Man snapped. He felt like she was talking down to him and it hurt his pride, yet he knew she was right. But knowing she was right didn't make it any easier to take.

"You can't get up. That's what."

Anger landed in Man's temples with the lightness of a jay settling on the tiniest limb of a wafer ash. He was mad at both his wife and his best friend. But he turned his back on her and sat down in the armchair, holding his whiskey glass. Just hold tight, don't get in a fight. Keep on the light, potato-head, jitterbug. You can cool it. You got a mind, rule it.

The doorbell sounded and he looked back at Cleo who was still there in the bedroom but was now looking up the hall. Wonder woman of my heart, give me a head start. Love is here to stay, you can count on it every day.

Without saying anything, Man got up and went by her, up the hall, and opened the door. "Greg Wakely, drummer supreme of Bob Jones' Entertainment Palace."

Greg was all smiles. "Hey, man!" Something in his voice saying: Cut out the shit, it's just me.

"Come on in." Man held the door, at the same time holding a static grin that felt unnatural. And something like the truth hit Man: He didn't like Greg. Didn't from the beginning. But didn't know it till now. For the first time, standing there, facing him, Man tried to figure it out. Greg seemed to hold back. But Man felt pretty sure Greg also didn't like him. They were just pretending. And why? They had to work together. Uh, had to? Well, Man wanted to hang on at the Palace. Getting better there and better known all the time. And he got along well with Jorena. He knew Jorena liked him.

Greg, dressed in a white shirt and a necktie and a pair of slacks—always the dapper dude—stepped inside, rubbing his neck. Greg, the self-proclaimed poppa-stoppa, had arrived.

"I see you got the joy juice going. I need me a drink." Putting his proper Negro voice aside, Greg was into his splib voice now. But there was sneering in it, even contempt. It was like he said to himself: Okay, I got to slum with you low-down niggers, let me just get myself in the groove here. Man thought: Sho don't like this nigger. Why I call em? Had to call em to see Solly. Greg said: "Hi, Cleo."

Cleo was behind Man. She returned his greeting with a cool, not-too-friendly hello.

Man looked at Greg. His expression said, What the fuck did I do? Excuse me for living. Then he said, "Hey, did I come at a bad time?"

Man said, "Naw, man. Come on in the living room."

Behind Man, Greg said, "I can't stay long, man. My bed might get cold."

He think thas funny. Man just looked at him. He started to say to Greg: Dog that bring you a bone will turn around and carry it somewhere else.

Stepping around them and going into Karina's room, Cleo sneered with a grunt at Greg's remark. And Man knew Cleo could spit out a long list of things she didn't like: A womanizing man was at the top.

Man decided to tease the nigger. "Greg, ain't no kinda way yo bed gon get cold, man. I know you got you a different woman every night." Throw the dog a bone, have some fun, watch him run.

"That's what I mean. I want her to still be there when I get back." His laughter was forced, unnatural, like hot mashed potatoes in your front pocket.

Solly was standing when they came into the living room. Standing and grinning, hand outstretched.

Greg, now grinning too, said, "Hey, cat. Been a big bit. How you been?" Walking toward Solly.

Solly still grinned. "You know, man, just getting by, keeping with the music. You looking good."

And the minute they were in touching distance, Greg and Solly got to going through this greeting bit, slapping the palms of their hands together once, then playfully punching each other on the arms. Man watched with a fixed grin on his face. Didn't even know it was there. Do they like each other? Cain't tell.

"Good to see you, man," said Solly. "Still fucking with them drums?"

"Yeah. Got to keep my tum-tums sending out that heartbeat, you know. Stay in touch with the stuff." He stopped and looked at Man, then back at Solly. "Hey, Solly! You gon bring your guitar down to the Palace ain't you?"

"If you cats want me to."

Man said, "What kinda question is that?"

Cleo came into the room with a water glass and handed it to Greg. She smiled. Over her anger?

Man looked at her like she was some kind of wonderful miracle come down from the clouds, a saint stepping down to bless three sheepherding boys on a hillside. Straight out of the Bible or a story old folks told.

Greg thanked her and Solly got the bottle and poured some liquor into Greg's glass. Greg stopped him. "That's enough, man. I want to be able to walk outta here. I can't drink this old heavy shit like you niggers do."

Solly burst out laughing—a forced laugh.

Cleo left the room, mock fanning her face with her hand.

Suddenly there was loud knocking—THUNK THUNK THUNK—on the floor beneath them.

Greg sat down. "What was that?" He'd never been here before. He was looking around. "You got a big apartment here."

Man looked at the floor. The knocking had stopped.

Solly said, "Sounds like somebody downstairs hitting on the ceiling with a broom."

"Fuck her," said Man, knowing he was sounding badder than he felt, catching a tiny glimpse back there in the swampland of his mind of Sofia with two giant pink-faced, beer-bellied policemen in the doorway and Sofia handing him an eviction notice. Memory of Chicago and being often one step from eviction for one reason or another.

Greg laughed. "Who's down there?"

Man said, "Fucking bitch, the landlady." Angry more at the fact of her power making him feel helpless.

Greg sat down and took a sip of his whiskey. "Man, you going to get evicted, motherfucker." And he laughed, bending forward, holding his stomach.

"Why don't we go down to this joint called the Palace?" said Solly.

"You want to go to the Palace?" said Greg. He sounded like he couldn't quite understand the request.

"There ain't much happening in the week," said Man. Through the week, he remembered men of his father's generation saying, white folks got me gwine, but on Saturday night and Sunday too, thinking of that little gal of mine.

"I don't give a shit," Solly said. "We can hang out. Leastways we won't get you kicked outta your apartment."

"Yeah," said Man. "Come on, les go."

Through the floor, faintly, Man heard Sofia Sweeney in her rage: "Goddamned niggers, goddamned sonofabitching no-good niggers, fucking no-good goddamned niggers."

Po woman, what she must be suffering.

Solly said, "What she saying?"

Po woman, what she must be going through. Yet and still, she pisses me off.

"Sounds like she's cussing us out," said Greg, laughing. "She calling you motherfuckers niggers. Let's get outta here before she gets her pistol."

"Or fore Cleo gets hers," said Solly, giggling.

Man was first to stand.

◉

The Palace was so dead Man stopped them at the door. "Les go across the street."

Solly took a quick look. Said: "I like the joint. Good stage."

They could hear the cry of the blues from across the street—old Charley Patton's voice singing about some low-down whiskey-drinking woman of his.

Greg looked at Man. "Man, you go in that place?"

"They got some good blues on the box."

"That place is the pits, man. Niggers kill each other in there every weekend."

"I don't give a shit long as the music is good," Man said. He felt good and free right at this moment, a way he liked feeling, but as innocent as what he was doing now seemed, something back there was pulling at him: Cleo's disapproving face transparent on a window glass in his mind. "Besides, it ain't the weekend."

Solly said, "Let's check it out."

They turned around and walked back out onto the sidewalk. A couple of cars pointing north stood waiting at the intersection for the light to change to green. By the time they were halfway across, Charley Patton was singing *A Spoonful Blues*—the dressed-up version, not the sporting house original.

Together they pushed into Miss Etta's.

The place was slow-rocking with old Charley's gravelly voice and was packed with rambling and stumbling shadows, and shadows just standing packed at the bar. The place smelled stale just like it did the first time Man came here.

Miss Etta, big as a prizewinning hog in a pink dress, was behind the bar on her stool. A thinner black-skinned woman in a blue sack dress and a shiny-eyed old man in suspenders were waiting bar. Miss Etta just sat there by the cash register Buddha-like watching everything, especially the money.

Greg said to Solly, "Your first day and Manfred brings you to the worst place in town." He shook his head.

Man laughed. Some folks say you gots to get down dirty if you wants to play but I say you can play any old way.

Solly giggled. "That's my man!"

The three of them wormed their way through the thicket of shoulders and got to the bar. Man was already hating tomorrow like shit. Remembering that old blues song about being too lazy to work and too lazy to steal. Lord, Lord, have mercy. And hating those motherfuckers, especially Eliot, that two-faced motherfucker.

When they had drinks in their hands, they moved back from the bar to make room for people trying to push in to order. There was Niggerdemos over behind the bar down at the end. He seemed to be washing glasses.

Then Man saw Matilda, the Indian woman. In that kind of don't-walk-by-me-without-speaking pose. She was stone drunk all right with that hard, unseeing look, but Man saw she saw him. She was standing right in front of him, a big wide woman with that long slick black hair pulled back in a single long braid, overalls over some kind of little silly flower-print dress. Bottle of beer in one hand and the other in one of those big loose pockets. Seemed to be looking at him but, no, maybe through him. He couldn't be sure. Man chuckled, said: "Hey, lady. How you doing?"

She grunted. Said: "I'm fine. I remember you. You and your friends want to join us back there?"

"Back where?" Man said.

Matilda slowly turned and lifted her glass and with it pointed back over heads somewhere.

Greg made a face. He had his nose high like he smelled something bad. He looked at his watch.

"What the hell," said Solly. He slapped Greg on the back.

So they started following Matilda back. Man was right behind her. Matilda stopped in front of him. Somebody was getting up from a chair and was stepping back into the clearing. But the man stepped back only two or three feet. Then he was falling. Man felt Matilda fall back against him. Or she was knocked back. The falling man hit her. His arm flew out. Two or three women screamed. A shot rang out—POP! then again, POP!

Now people were ducking and running, screaming and pushing. Man saw the joker with the gun. Little biddy fellow at the table where the man had been sitting. The falling man was clutching his shirtfront and blood was pouring from beneath his hands. Stumbling back, the man fell on another man sitting with his back to the action, and both of them went over on the floor.

The sucker with the gun got up and started waving the thing. He was shouting something. Man, Matilda, Solly, and Greg dropped their drinks and ducked to the side, behind the fellow, and flopped down on the floor with a bunch of other people, keeping an eye on the gunman. The floor was greasy and dirty and smelled like a sewer.

Greg whispered to Man, "See. This kinda shit don't happen at the Palace." His teeth were glowing in the dark bright as his eyes stretched. Man clucked at him. Ease up, scrapper. Don't put me through no changes I don't need.

Turning from Greg, Man saw Lolita crouching on the floor just up ahead of him. She was packed down with a bunch of other people, watching the drunk man with the pistol as he staggered toward the front door. People were getting the hell out his way fast, falling over each other, clearing passage.

Then he was gone and slowly everybody started coming back to standing positions, brushing off their clothes, complaining, talking—"Ain't that something?" "Just like that—BAM! BAM!"

But Man said to Solly and Greg, "Les get outta here fore the cops come."

On the way out they saw a bunch of people crowded around the shot man on the floor and Miss Etta was trying to push her way through them to get to the man. So was Niggerdemos.

Outside they ducked around the corner, away from streetlights and when they stopped Man saw that Matilda had come with them. He laughed. "You know them people? The man what pulled the gun, the sucker wasted?"

She took a long pull from her beer bottle. "No. But I heard the one with the gun say, Stay away from my wife. Next thing I knew he was shooting." She drained the bottle and threw it in the gutter. It made a sequence of sounds—ping clang click, glass against stone—but didn't break. "You boys want to come over to my place?"

Too quickly Solly said, "Yeah, but let's get a bottle first."

Matilda said, "Liquor store back there corner of Lake and Twenty-fourth."

Man looked at Greg. Greg said, "I got to go home. See you cats later."

Just what Man expected Greg to say. Greg: Quick to quit, quick to split. Bye, bye, drummer, home-bound minute the scene break down.

And Greg headed across the street and vanished in the shadows. Man watched the darkness that swallowed Greg and for half a flicker of a second saw it as a lighted passage, one of wisdom, caution, and he envied Greg's ability to just pull away like that, to change his mind.

Man said, "Okay. Les get a taste."

"Shit," said Matilda. "I can't drink whiskey. Stomach." She rubbed her huge belly. "Get me some beer. I'll wait here. I'm not going back down there."

They trotted down and came back with a brown bag. "Here's a opener," Man said and handed Matilda a beer with it.

He screwed off the top of the pint of Old Crow and let Solly hit first, then he took a swig while they walked.

He and Solly walked with Matilda in the middle till they came to the corner of Twenty-second. The houses along Twenty-second, as they gandered north, were dark with yellow-lighted windows. They seemed so peaceful, but back there on Twenty-fourth and Lake, they could hear the sirens approaching and then coming to a stop.

Man wondered if Solly really wanted some of what this woman was putting down. He must be pretty hard up. As they walked Man smelled her, she smelled pissy. Pretty soon she gave out a large fart-sounding belch. Aside from that belch she kept a troublesome silence as she stumbled along bear-like.

Matilda led them up steps and into a house in the middle of the block on Miami between Twenty-second and Twenty-third, and down the hallway. She unlocked a door and led them into a smelly, dark room. Turned on a light. A table, a bed, three straight-backed chairs. A picture of a serene Jesus Christ torn from a magazine and tacked to the wall over the table. On the table itself, five or six empty wine and beer bottles. The floor, covered with old linoleum patterned with orange-brown kestrels and the leaf of a cobra lily, squeaked when they walked across it into the room. "You-all sit down."

Solly put the bag of beer on the table. He had a wild look. Maybe still shook up from the shooting. Chain me or train me.

Man sat down and took another drink of Old Crow. "Good stuff!" He passed the bottle to Solly. Solly turned it bottom-side-up to his mouth and handed it back.

Matilda was standing at the table, opening another bottle of beer. When it was opened she sat down and put her elbows on the table with the beer in front of her. She was leaning forward, her head down, chin on chest, eyes closed.

Man said, "You going to sleep?"

She shook her head from side to side.

He said, "You from around here?"

"I'm Omaha-Winnebago. Left the reservation ten years back. Ain't got nothing there for me. White man came in and let certain people own sections of the land until there was no reservation left for all the people. I'm forty years old. Do I look it?"

"Naw," Man lied.

"The Sioux and the Poncas, even the Pawnee doing better than us out there. What we need today is somebody like Standing Bear, like the Ponca had. I lived in North Platte for a few years. But they throw you in jail there, if you Indian or colored. So I moved to Omaha in '43, the year the Missouri flooded this whole town. Thought I was cussed by some kind of evil spirit to have walked into that much water. But not many Indians here. I like it that way."

Solly said, "You don't like your own peoples?"

She didn't answer.

"I said, Do you like your peoples?"

It was like she had closed them out, gone to sleep with her eyes opened.

Solly sat down next to her, at the edge of the table. He touched her arm. He had in his eyes that sex-look. A look that said: Ain't no dentist, ain't no dentist's son, but I can do yo drilling till the dentist come. Or: Ain't no miller, ain't no miller's son, but I can do yo grinding till the miller come. She slowly moved her arm away, then her other hand came up onto the table. In it was a silver dagger with a black leather handle. The whole thing probably sixteen inches long. Man could see she'd pulled it out of her overalls. Without even looking at them, she placed the thing beside her bottle of beer. Then just as slowly picked up the beer and lifted it to her mouth.

She belched again.

Solly looked at Man. Solly looked confused. Man handed him the

Old Crow, and he drank again, then looked again at Matilda. Solly said, "Hey, tell me. Why you want us to come here with you?"

She didn't answer, just drank her beer.

He said, "You hear me?"

"Her name is Matilda."

"You hear me, Matilda?"

"I hear you. Drink your whiskey." She put the bottle down.

"Drink my whiskey? That all you got to say? How bout some action?"

Her right hand moved toward the handle of the dagger.

Solly cleared his throat. "What you got the knife for?"

Her eyes were still closed. She picked up her beer and drank again, then put it back beside the dagger.

"I said why you carry that big-ass knife round, Matilda?"

She still didn't say anything.

Man stood up. "Come on, Solly. Les get outta here. Leave the woman alone, man."

"I'm not bothering her. Just asting her a question."

"Come on, Solly."

Solly stood up. "Okay. But there ain't no harm in asting a question. What wrong with her? Why she got to pull a knife on us? What we do to her?"

"Come on, Solly." Man took Solly by the arm. Solly was drunk. When Solly was drunk Man felt protective, felt like he had to take care of him, keep him out of trouble. Solly could get wild.

When they reached the door, Matilda turned and looked at them. Said: "Thanks for the beer." Po sad Matilda.

Solly looked at Man. "She say thanks for the beer. Just like that. Thanks for the beer." Solly didn't understand. Po Solly.

Po sad Matilda.

"Les go," Man said, pulling his friend out.

THAT NEXT FRIDAY NIGHT AROUND eight, Solly and Man set out walking down to the Palace. Man was mellow, stepping in a kind of rhythm like he heard marimba music in the background. Or bluesy bop or bebop. Bass walking. Or straight-up horn talking. Funky blues.

CHAPTER NINETEEN

Solly said, "Say, Fred, didn't you tell me you once played a mandolin?"

"Yeah, man, from Japan, made of redwood too, beautiful thing. Beautiful! I worked at a place that sold all these weird instruments from crazy places like India and China and Japan and Africa. That was back before me and Cleo got married. Manpower sent me out to this importer's factory. They kept me on out there—over on the north side—for a few weeks. They had all kinds of these barrel drums from the Gold Coast, congas, egg shakers, samba whistles, funny-looking flutes, African tambourines, cane fifes, a funny-ass-looking pretty harp-guitar from Germany, all kinds of whistles, bells, hoops, shit I never heard of. I used to try out everything that came through that place. One time I played this little old thumb piano. I even bought one of they quill flutes, you see, real cheap from them but times got hard and I ended up hocking the damned thing. I never knowed there was so many different types of instruments in the world. Seeing all them instruments opened my eyes to a lot of shit."

"What you mean?"

"I mean I started thinking, you know, bout stuff. Like you and me here doing our thing making music that make peoples smile, and there be somebody ten thousand miles away doing something just like we be doing, you know, making music and making peoples smile at the music, feeling the same thing we be feeling. It was the first time I ever thought about peoples being pretty much alike everywhere even though they be talking they talk that we can't understand and we be talking our talk they can't understand, yet and still, the same things make us happy and the same things make us mad."

As they passed in front of Walt Calloway's Barbershop, Man glanced in and caught Walt's eye and waved to him. The other two barbers, Halbert and Otis, waved too. The barbershop was busy—all three chairs occupied and four or five waiting. And Man saw one slim black guy standing, with his back to the row of seated men, facing Walt and violently waving his arms—sign that a heated political or sports argument was in full swing.

"If that true," Solly said, "then how come nobody cain't get along? I mean, look at white folks and us."

"Yeah, well, I don't know. I member down south one time, guess I was no mo'n' ten, and this white lady stopped her car and come up to the house from the road axing directions, and I was in the front yard playing my washtub bass. And she looked like she was beat out, tired from a long drive, and she kinda snapped at me. And I hadn't even done nothing to her. Hurt my feelings."

"You told me bout that damned washtub bass—"

"Yeah, but I ain't tolt you bout this time. She was standing there looking real mad like I wont talking fast enough for her. I think she wanted to know how to get to Winder. I scratched my head so she know I be studying on the question real hard when I seed she was looking at my washtub bass. She touched the cord, sorta flipped it with her finger to see it dance. And you shoulda seed that woman's face light up with a smile. She was like a changed person. Then she looked real close at the tub to see how it was tied to the broom. Then she axed me to play it for her. So, I started playing the tub, getting this real good deep bass, you know, and she started justa smiling, and said, 'How clever.' I still member the word cause it was the first time I ever heard that word: *clever.*"

"So what's the point of the story?" Solly said impatiently.

"The washtub music changed that woman just like that." And Man snapped his fingers together. "She come up there pissing mad at the world and left there smiling, even gave me a quarter. Quarter was a lot of money then."

"But did she ever find out how to get to Winder?"

"Yeah. My mama came out and told her which road to take."

◉

At nine, Solly was on the stage of the Palace with his guitar. Man next to him, in front of the microphone, his harmonica ready. Their first time together on a stage since Chicago.

Man said to the crowd, "Folks. This here is Solomon Thigpen, great guitar man from the big Windy City. Just got in town a few days ago. Mister Thigpen gon be joining us here on the weekends. Me and Greg and the boys lucky to have this cat. Hope you like him much as we do. So, come on give Mister Thigpen a big, big welcome."

And they did, with clapping, shouting, and foot stomping.

Behind them Greg was sitting at his drums. The other guys in place.

Greg said, "One, two, three, go!"

And they cut into *Done Somebody Wrong,* warming up the crowd, then they did *Careless Love Blues.*

At the end of that one somebody called out to Man, "Sing *I Got a Woman.*"

Solly hit a few strings, introducing the number, then Man closed his eyes, feeling the song start up from his stomach.

When he finished it, they clapped and cheered.

After that, Man whispered to Solly to back him with the melody of *My Baby Don't Stand No Cheating,* and again, the crowd clapped and cheered and whistled jamboree-style. Then:

> Hey, listen here everybody,
> At the track I can place a bet.
> I say listen everybody,
> At that old track I can place me a bet.
> But all my company want is my dirty sweat.
> Hey, listen here everybody,
> All that old union want is my dues,
> Listen everybody,
> All that old union want is my dues.
> So I got the sign-on-the-dotted-line blues.
> Hey, listen everybody,
> I say at the track I can place a bet.
> Listen everybody,
> Out at that track I can place me a bet,
> But all my old company want is my sweat.
> Hey, listen here everybody,
> I gots to punch that old time clock,
> Yeah, listen everybody,
> I say I gots to punch that old time clock.
> If I don't I'm gon sho gets a pay dock . . .

Solly hit the strings, crowding them in intensely on each other.

Man was studying the crowd as he sang. He'd gotten to know its moods. Tonight, it was a hard-drinking Friday night crowd and they were loud, tired, and blue, but somehow they seemed to hear and appreciate what was happening on the stage. When he finished, again there was loud clapping and shouting and whistling and foot stomping. By now folks were doing the Hully Gully, talking all at the same time, drinking fast, spilling liquor, giggling, strutting, sassing and jiving, woohwee-ing, waving dime notes, tapping their daisy-beaters and spoons, their fingers, the flat palms of their hands on tabletops.

Mercy me!

⦿

Saturday morning bright sunlight came through the yellow-tan window shade, and Man woke in a good mood. Not the slightest trace of hangover. He eased out of bed, trying not to wake Cleo, crept into the bathroom and brushed his teeth and came back and kissed her on the side of her face. She moved, turned and peeked at him, smiled, threw an arm around him and pulled him down on her breasts.

⦿

Early Saturday afternoon Man and Solly walked up to the nearby liquor store and bought a half-pint of Old Crow. Man stuck it in his back pocket and they stepped back out onto the sunny sidewalk and started walking slowly east on Spencer underneath the branches and in the shade of a line of huge box elders as they headed for the park on Florence. Man felt relaxed, almost peaceful but Solly seemed on edge about something.

They walked on without speaking till they crossed Twenty-third then Man said, "Say, you ever wonder what you gon be doing ten years from now?"

"Me? I be lucky if I can figure out what I'm gon do tomorrow," said Solly, with a snort of a laugh. "I know one thing: I gon be having some bad luck. Don't take no prophet to predict yo basic bad luck, cause it alway coming. But what kinda question is that, anyway?"

Saturday afternoon over this way was quiet except for the groans of a big delivery truck at the entrance of the supermarket on the east side of the park, the occasional hammering of a Saturday-afternoon woodworking hobbiest, and the shouts of small boys playing baseball.

"I gets to thinking bout life, the future, sometimes, you know," said Man, "and I be wondering what all this carrying on spose to mean. You know, you can go through life and miss everything in it if you ain't paying attention to what's going on. See, cause this stuff that be happening now sort of can tell you what you might be facing tomorrow, if you don't change." He looked at Solly. "You mean to tell me you never thinks about the future?"

Solly frowned. "Ah, sho, I thinks about the future: think about how I'm gon get some money. And some pussy, too." Solly laughed. "That's what I be thinking bout."

"Come on, Solly, you can't tell me you ain't never wondered what you gon be doing ten or fifteen years up the road, wondered if you gon be living or dead, by yoself or with Holly, rich or on-yo-ass po, or what."

"In my nightmares, maybe. Shit, man, I don't let that kinda stuff

154

worry my mind." He waved Man's remark away with a quick flash of his hand.

"Sometimes I wonder why I hang out with you." Man chuckled and shook his head. Guitar man, guitar man, whacha gon do without a plan? Eeny, meeny, miny mo, what make you so slo?

"You hang out with me cause you can be yoself with me, that's why— you can fart, get drunk, piss on yoself, do anything, and you know I'm gon still be yo friend. You know I don't give a good goddamn what you do and still I care bout yo black ass. You know I'd do anything I can to help you when you dead drunk or pissing blood like that time in Chicago. Member? I can be there like that, nigger, and still not try to put no strictions on you. I love you like a brother, nigger. Better than a brother."

Man had never thought about their friendship in those terms. He wondered how much truth was in what Solly was saying. Solly had never said anything like this before. "Yeah, maybe you right. Then, what you see in me?"

Solly laughed. "You want the truth? All right. I knows you gon be serious bout everything. Oh, I know you have a good time and gon ball and get mellow and stuff, but Manfred, man, you one serious dude, you know that. You gets heavy, man. You be laughing and stuff, but you be heavy." He touched his forehead with one finger. "You likes to talk gospel. You the wise man when you gets mellow, man. So I just sit and listen cause I know if you talk long enough you gon luck up and say something that make some kinda sense. I might have to wait a long time but, WHAM! when it comes there it is, the gospel according to Manfred, just like wisdom out of the Bible."

"Naw, Solly, come on, stop jiving me, I serious. What you see in me as a friend?" Solly was talking bull.

Solly raised his voice: "I'm telling you!"

"Solly, you know I ain't no smarter than you. Fact is, you be the one always talking shit, giving me advice."

"You want the truth—?" Solly's eyes stretched and his hands flashed out in front of him in a dramatic motion.

"Not if it just like the truth you just laid on me." Man gave his pal a thick grin, remembering his mama always saying: Tell the truth and shame the devil.

They were now crossing Twenty-second Street. One squirrel was chasing another along the curb then up a bur oak tree, rattling mossycup leaves. Boogie, little squirrel, boogie! Fly through the jungle.

"The truth is when I give you advice," Solly said, glancing down the street at two teenage girls coming this way, "it advice you done give me in the first place, I be just giving it back to you."

"Give me a sample, man," Man insisted in a tense voice, expecting Solly to repeat something he—Man—used to say a lot back in Chicago when they first met: I aim to jump high for what I want. It was an old saying: Jump high for what you want. The old folks down South said it to the children.

The girls turned at Spencer and headed west.

"I cain't think of no sample right now."

"Solly, you don't even know why you hang out with me, man. You just making up shit, man. Whatever comes outta yo mouth. You ain't even thinking bout what you saying."

"Don't have to think about it." He playfully punched Man on his big arm. "And anyway, why you asting me questions I cain't answer?"

"Cause everybody should think about the future, man."

"But you asting about death and all that shit. I don't know nothing bout death."

"Then what you wants me to ax you about—pussy?"

Solly laughed. "Yeah, matter of fact, I knows me a few things about pussy. Now, that a subject I can talks to you about. I'm somewhat of an expert."

"But ain't you never thought about death when you fucking? I mean, wondered about whas it like?"

Solly looked suddenly serious, maybe worried as he glanced at Man. "Why would I wants to think about some depressing shit like death while I'm getting my nuts off? I be having fun." His laughter was nervous. "You mean to tell me you think about dying while you fucking?"

"Not all the time, man, but the thought have crossed my mind. You know, you finish and you be laying there and you think about life and stuff, what it is, and one thought lead to another, and you wonder bout death, you know."

Man could see the park from here. A group of small boys were playing baseball in one corner.

Solly was silent.

Man started up again. "Anyway, I wont axing you about death. I axed you about the future. Member?"

"Yeah, the future." He snorted. "I think of the future as a good road and I know damn well it ain't every good road that gon lead to the best place. Anyway, if I don't die, I'm gon be finding out bout the future soon enough. You too!" And Solly burst out with uncontrollable laughter.

When they reached the park they cut across the grass to the farthest corner from the boys, and sat on a winter-dirty picnic table, and rested their feet on the bench below. Man took out the half-pint and ceremoniously broke the seal and passed the bottle to his friend.

"Member when we first met?" Man said, cocking his head to the side, gazing out across the park like somebody trying to see air.

Solly took a drink. "Yeah, in Washington Park. I was cutting up. Folks jitterbugging on the grass. And here you come with your harmonica." Solly cackled, handing the bottle back.

"You sho was playing up a storm," Man said, grinning. "Hearing you, I knowed right then you spoke my kinda talk. I jes got happy. Couldn't help myself."

"That's the trouble with mens like us," said Solly. "We gets lost in our music and the womenfolks just don't understand."

Man held his palm out. "Put it there, friend."

And Solly slapped Man's hand real fast like it was hot.

HE'S EASING THE LOAD UP, *holding the lever firmly and easing it back slowly, watching the load rise. A giant load, he's careful not to let it start tossing and turning. When he has it up above head level he reaches for the drive-handle without even looking at it, knowing it so well, and pushes at it so that the crane starts inching along the tracks. And he keeps his eyes on the load, making sure it stays straight. Then suddenly there is a loud scream—*EEEEEEEEEEE! *The cry of some male thing getting its balls cut off. And he looks around, back and forth, up and down the bay, trying to see what is going on. And in his panic he releases the lever and looks straight down below the cab. On the ground, lying spread-eagle is Eliot. Half of his head torn off where the edge of the stack of beams has torn into it. A gut-deep fear grips Man's bowels and he thinks he might be pissing in his pants. He's killed a man, a* white *man. Image of himself swinging at the end of a rope with the smell of kerosene all over his body and flames leaping up at his legs. Flames. Lord, Lord. And his eyes are turned up to the tops of the pines and he sees clouds drifting by above him and he knows, God, he knows sure as shit, he's going to die in a minute or two. And the rope touches his right cheek.*

CHAPTER TWENTY

He woke with a great sense of relief and dread. May not be alive but sho ain't dead. Went to the river, all I caught was a shiver. Cain't get across, cain't get back loss, cause of that goddamned boss.

⦿

Man knew from the minute he punched his time card that Friday morning, last Friday in June, payday, that getting through this day was going to be like swimming upstream in a river full of alligator shit.

How many mo years I gots to be dogged around?
How many mo years you gon dog me round?

Eliot was at the time clock looking like a wounded grizzly. Probably there waiting for him. Seemed that way. The minute Man punched his time card, Eliot roared: "Come with me!" Then turned tail and started booting it.

"Huh?"

Eliot stopped and looked back. "Manfred, I want you to work the drill today."

Man walked over to Eliot. "The *drill?*" He stood there trying to give Eliot a friendly smile. As if he deserved it.

"Yeah. I'll show you. Come on."

Man followed Eliot up through the main bay, past the welders, past Bernie and Cecil. Both winked at him. Ah, shit, Man thought. Something is up. Eliot pulling some shit again. Trying to shoot me through the grease. Man didn't know how much more of this crap he could take—being switched around from job to job when he was supposed to be a welder third class, not a shears helper, not a crane operator, and, fuck, not a drill operator. He'd heard the drill suckers complain about their wrists hurting all the time. They wore those braces on their wrists and they had lots of back trouble.

How many mo years—?

He followed Eliot to the west bay and to a big drill, thirty inches long, lying on a beam. A drill operator, quiet guy with dark curly hair, Cassidy DeMaris, who walked sort of one-sided with a limp, was busy drilling a bolt hole in one end of a beam just like the one Eliot now had his foot on next to the idle drill. Never knowed nobody to get a thrill outta operating a drill. They say whiskey will kill but so will a drill.

Man watched Cassidy balance the drill as it worked its way through the steel. Eliot was saying that his other west bay drill man, Richard Phillip, was off because he had to rush his wife to the hospital. She was having a baby. And Man was wondering how he was supposed to operate a drill without training. And he knew that union rules said he wasn't supposed be doing any of this shit. According to the rules he was supposed to be welding. He'd thought about bringing this up to Eliot before but had let it pass. Now it just came out. He said: "Hey, Eliot. I thought the union was against this kind of thing?"

Eliot looked him dead in the eyes, frowning. "What kind of thing?"

"You know, moving around, doing jobs you're not trained to do."

Eliot turned red. "*Fuck* the union. If you want to work here, Manfred, you're going to do as I say. You got that?"

Man shook his head yes. Said: "Okay." But he said it like it was a warning. Ashes to ashes, dust to dust, if you want yo job don't make a fuss.

"Here's the drill." Eliot picked it up. "You hold it like this. Here's the on-off switch. This is the safety switch. This button here on the handle releases the liquid. Don't let this liquid stop pouring, otherwise you burn up the drill. And if that happens you pay for it out of your paycheck. One of these babies costs a fortune. I can guarantee you that. Here."

Man took the drill. He switched it on then off. "These the markings?" Somebody had already chiseled in the dents.

"Right dead in the center of each of them. If you fuck up a bolt hole you ruin the whole beam. Each time you fuck up something like that you cost the company money."

Man knew lots of holes drilled in the wrong place were filled all the time and nobody said much about them. Bad luck don't hang out no sign. This was bad luck.

"You got it?" Eliot said.

"Yeah." He didn't look at the foreman.

Eliot bristled and walked away.

Standing there, holding the drill by its crossbar-handles, Man looked over at Cassidy, trying to figure out how to handle the damned thing. "Hey, Cassidy?"

Cassidy was about ten feet away.

"Yeah?"

"Nothing," Man said, hearing Cassidy's tone. Then straddling the beam, positioning himself, with the tip of the drill resting on the cross marking, dead in the dent, Man threw the switch and gripped the handles. The drill skipped out of the dent and started to jump and dance about on the surface of the beam. He held on like a longhorn buster gripping a set of horns.

How many mo years—?
Lord, how many mo years this got to go on?

Out of the sides of his eyes he could see Cassidy giggling. Two or three other guys nearby, a crane follower and a couple of west bay welders, stopped what they were doing and were watching him, snickering and cackling. You can laugh till you cry.

Man quickly turned off the drill and got another grip on it. Looking at the wet surface, he saw that he'd scratched a zigzag scar across the marking but hadn't started a hole. Mad, he felt something move through his body, shaking him. It pissed him off to have somebody laugh at him. For one blind half-second he thought he would throw that big expensive two-hundred-pound drill at Cassidy and knock that stupid grin off his face. But all he did was shout, "What the fuck you laughing at, motherfucker?"

Cassidy dried up real quick. "You talking to me?" He turned off his drill. He was touching his chest.

"Who the fuck you think I'm talking to—yo mama?"

Cassidy looked away then turned his drill back on and started concentrating on his work, ignoring Man. Man just watched him for a few minutes.

He took a pack of Spearmint Gum out of his pocket, slowly opened it and unwrapped one stick, stuck it in his mouth, started chewing, then walked over to a scrap metal bin a few feet from the beam and threw the gum paper in.

He took his time walking back to the beam.

Then Man got another grip on the drill and threw the switch, pressing down this time, down hard, forcing the tip to stay in the dent. Sweat broke out under his arms. He felt it running down his back. The muscles in his upper arms throbbed. Sweat ran down from his hairline past his eye, along the base of his nose to his mouth, and he tasted its saltiness but he didn't let up. Holding the drill like that, dead in the dent, he began to see steel shavings turning back from the point of action.

How many—?

It was a hard position to keep because he had to lean over the drill with his whole upper body aimed down on the point of action. And he had to keep it straight and keep up the pressure. John Henry, he ain't no hero of mine.

When the drill had cut into the steel about a half inch Man felt the drill begin to do some of the work. It was cutting its way now pretty well but he had to keep it straight and keep laying some weight on it, but not as much. John Henry, he died young.

Twenty minutes later he had finished the first hole. He knew what a bolt hole should look like. John Henry, he died too young. His was not very smooth but hell it was his first one. Who could expect perfection on the first try? Trying to make it smoother might enlarge the hole and that would be worse. Died with his hammer in his hand.

By the ten o'clock coffee break Man had finished five holes. A drill operator, in that amount of time, could do maybe seven or eight. He knew that. In the lunchroom he threw his gum in the trash and got himself a Baby Ruth from the machine. He was still pissed and didn't want to talk to anybody. On his way outside, he spoke to his brother-in-law, who was sitting at a table with Eliot and Mark Harvey.

Outside he started eating the candy bar, then he saw blond Darlene

Farrell, secretary to the personnel manager, Paul Sawyer, crossing the parking lot from the main office building to the personnel office. She was in a tight red dress and black high heels. On an average day she walked over there and back about a dozen times. Watching her make the trips was one of the pastimes of all the workers but especially the truckers who hung out in the lunchroom more often than anybody since they used it to do their paperwork. Man wondered—not for the first time—what it would be like to do it with her, what it would be like to do it with a white woman, period. It couldn't be all that different, as different as some niggers had made it out to be. His body felt a pull at the thought but part of his mind reacted with anger. Then biting his lips he felt shame and deliberately shifted his eyes away from her toward the line of trucks parked down to the right of the yard by the front gate.

He bit off another chunk of Baby Ruth and chewed it.

"Hey, nigger, what you doing looking at that good white pussy?"

He turned around. It was Cecil, grinning Cecil, Uncle Tom sonofabitch, picking his teeth with a toothpick, breath smelling of tuna.

"Hey, Cecil."

"What's the matter?"

"Ah, man, it's that motherfucking you-know-who still fucking with me. Put me on a drill in the west bay. And I don't know first thing about no drill. That's against union rules."

"Yeah, man," said Cecil, "Eliot can do some crazy things. He don't pay them union rules no mind. I mean, not until people call him on some of this shit is he gonna stop pulling it. But you see, he got you by the balls. If you refuse, he can tell you to punch out and walk. Say, did your friend from Chicago find a job yet?"

"Yeah. He's working the night shift at Sears."

"With Percy Norman and them guys?"

"Yeah. He likes it cause ain't nobody breathing down his back. Percy give him two floors a night, and he know he got to take care of them, get em swept and mopped and waxed fore the store open at eight. Want some candy?"

Cecil shook his head. "No thanks. Shit rots your teeth. Cousin of mine, Pee Wee, worked down there with the night crew. He didn't last long. Said them niggers go in there and sleep half the night up there in them beds in the furniture department. Problem with Pee Wee was he forgot to wake up one morning. Clerk came to work and saw this big black nigger in overalls lying up there in one of the beds and she liked to have had a baby on the spot." Cecil's big stomach rocked as he laughed. "You meet Percy yet?"

"Yeah. He stopped at the house once or twice. Solly rides with him. Pays for gas."

"Old long tall strange nigger, ain't he?"

"He seem all right to me."

"He's a good *straw* boss. That white man on the day shift stand by him through thick and thin. You know his old lady put a knife through his back two or three years ago. Said she did it just to *mark* him, make him hers. And that nigger, all the way to the hospital, kept saying to her, Honey, you got to take care of me now, nobody else gon want me. Francine a crazy bitch, man. Hard, gin-drinking bitch, man. If I was Percy, man, I'd have blown that bitch away. She'd be in her grave resting in peace. Your friend—what's his name?—get his own place yet?"

Man thought: nosy sonofabitch. Said: "Naw, not yet." He folded the wrapper back around the candy and stuck the unfinished bar in his shirt pocket.

"You trust another man at home with your wife, man, while you at work all day?"

Man looked at the bastard. He felt a rush of cold-blooded anger cloud his eyes as he looked at Cecil. Mule don't kick by no rule. No point in telling Cecil his wife was down at his sister's beauty shop washing hair and polishing fingernails Monday, Tuesday, Wednesday, Thursday, Friday, and Saturday afternoons from one to six while Solly was sleeping. Speaking slowly and softly, Man said: "Why don't you mind your own business, Cecil?"

"Don't go getting mad at me, Jack."

Man turned around, opened the lunchroom door, and walked inside, walked on into the locker room, a room he used to mop, and stood at a urinal, unzipped, and took it out, pissed, rezipped, and headed back to that goddamned drill.

Eliot was standing there looking at the holes when Man got back. "Not too smooth. Look at these holes you've made here. You've fucked up *all* of them. You're a big guy, you should be able to control the drill. What's the problem, Manfred?"

"The problem, Eliot, is you puts me over on this here drill specting me to do a first-class job and I ain't never even touched no drill before in my life. Now, that ain't—"

"Hold on, wait a minute. I'm not asking you to work miracles, just drill a straight hole. What kind of training do you *need* to drill a straight hole? What'd you want, huh, you want me to send you to *college* to learn you how to drill a simple hole in the end of a beam?"

"I want you to get *off* my back. That's what I want."

That did it. He could see Eliot's eyes narrow and his whole face turn red, his ears were like slices of beet. "What you want around here don't count worth one goddamned bit. It's what *I* want you got to pay attention to, boy. You got that?"

"What's this *boy* shit?"

"You heard me. You'll do as I say or you walk. You want to work or not?"

Man thought of Cleo and the baby. He picked up the drill and lifted it up so that it was standing on its tip. Went to the river, couldn't get across. Catch a nigger by the toe, don't let him go, if he hollers make em pay fifty bucks a day.

Eliot was fuming, agitated, moving about in front of him, and suddenly, leaning forward, he shouted in Man's face: "You can consider yourself on probation from now on. Okay?"

Man didn't answer.

"Do I make myself clear?"

Man threw the switch and started the drill.

Eliot reached over and switched it off. "I said, do I make myself clear?"

"I heard you, Eliot."

"Okay. After lunch I want you to report to me in the main bay. I have another job for you. I can't let you fuck up any more of these holes like this. In the meantime, I want you to pick up scrap metal."

"What?" Man shouted. It was a job men from Manpower did, a shit job done only by laborers hired on a temporary basis.

"You heard me. Scrap metal. Here—" Eliot kicked at a few scraps on the floor. "And over in the main bay."

Man put down the drill and just stood there like somebody who'd just been whacked over the head with a two-by-four. Between a rock and a stone-hard place, brain-lynched, Georgia boy, Georgia boy, he almost laughed he was so pissed.

Then suddenly he felt released from anger, if only for a moment, because he knew what was coming—if not today, soon. Not much difference between a hornet and a yellow jacket. And he knew, from what old folks used to say, a tin plate don't mind dropping on the floor.

As he watched Eliot walk back toward the main bay he noticed out of the sides of his eyes that Cassidy was snickering. Man decided to ignore him. Let the idiot laugh. He reached down and picked up a scrap, thought of throwing it at Cassidy's head but didn't. Instead, he threw it in the big bin about fifteen feet away in the other direction from the beam he'd drilled holes in.

AT LUNCHTIME HE WASN'T HUNGRY but he got his lunch bucket out of his locker. His plan had seemed out of focus all morning but he could still see it. Main thing was: he knew what he had to do.

CHAPTER TWENTY-ONE

But right now his stomach felt tight, and he couldn't sit in the lunchroom because he didn't want to have to talk to anybody.

So he went for a walk, down across the lot, and on out past the gate to the dusty road where the big trucks were shooting by. He had his lunch bucket. Walking up Commercial Avenue across the railroad tracks, he tried to figure out what Eliot had against him. It seemed personal, not racial. Just personal. But then why had Eliot given him a job welding in the first place? Eliot could have left him sweeping the floor.

Man stopped and sat down on a bench at the bus stop. Reaching in his shirt pocket, he found what was left of the candy bar. He sat there and ate the rest of it, chewing slowly, tasting the strong sweet sticky stuff and letting it slide down his throat. If he quit, walked out, he would be free of Eliot but he wouldn't have a paycheck.

Maybe he could run numbers. Get tight with Poppa Leon. Find out who was in charge, who were the kingpins. Naw. That wouldn't work. Hadn't worked down South. And Cleo wouldn't stand for it.

He felt star-crossed. Butting heads with the boss wasn't any fun. But looked like they always found something to jump on him about. Was it really that old hammer that killed John Henry? Po John Henry. Swing that pick. From cain't-see to cain't-see. Daddy wouldn't do it. Them boys gon kill they fool selfs working like that.

> Drive that pick,
> Push that shovel,
> Work till ya sick,
> Work like the devil.

True Cleo had that part-time job polishing fingernails and washing hair down at Debbie's but she wasn't making enough to pay rent and light and gas and to buy food. She'd mostly been using her check to buy Karina things. Love my wife, love my baby, love grits and gravy. Swing that hammer till the whistle blow, swing that hammer and don't be slow.

He hated to have to think about these kinds of problems. He opened his lunch bucket and looked at the two sandwiches wrapped in wax paper. Tired man don't feel like no food, mad man in a bad mood. How long fore the whistle blow?

Closing the bucket, he got up and started walking back in the direction from which he'd come. Let the sun go down. Don't care if it don't come up again. Let the sun go down. He had a good mind not to go back at all, just keep on going by the gate, on up Sherwood Avenue. Find the first liquor store, buy a half-pint and get nice and mellow. Forget about all this shit and worry. Blow that whistle, ring that bell. Give me my time card. Been here too long. It ain't early and it sho ain't late. Sho is a shame when a man got to choose between booze and shoes.

As he entered the gate, passing the personnel office, he was thinking he should just walk right in and ask Darlene for his check. He knew they'd be right there on her desk in a neat stack. Eliot didn't go over to pick them up till around five-thirty. Get his check, cash it, and take off, maybe hitch to California. Fuck, he said softly to himself. But that wouldn't solve nothing. Couldn't live without Cleo and Karina. Hate this trapped feeling.

How long—?

Eliot led him to the east bay, out in the middle, between one of the shears and a large scrap container, where three huge beams were lying side by side on wooden beams. Both were welded together with rails. Nearby, a trip-hammer lay on the ground hooked up to a portable generator.

"Okay. I want you to take these apart." Eliot pointed to one of the rails.

"What?" He looked at Eliot and frowned. When beams were incorrectly welded together he knew they were always burned apart. Old folks used to say a fisherman don't believe fish stink. What was Eliot trying to pull? Man knew one thing: A howling dog knows what it sees. And Man knew one other thing: Nobody can ride you lest yo back is bent. "Take em apart?"

"That's right." Eliot bent over and lifted the trip-hammer, straining from the weight of the thing, and balanced it on the floor, then switched it on. The thing started jumping about on the concrete floor. Big bad booger bear. He switched it off.

Man said, "Why you wants to take them apart with a trip-hammer? Ain't you spose to burn em?"

"Trip-hammer is faster. You get them started and I'll have a burner come over and finish the job."

"Who fucked em up in the first place?"

"Amos had the wrong paperwork this morning when he welded them together like that."

"Shit," said Man. "You can't do this with a trip-hammer."

"Are you working here or not?" said Eliot.

Man took in a deep breath and let it out in a big rush. He looked at the trip-hammer. True, he'd used one for a couple of hours at Chicago Steel once. But he had busted up a block of concrete at Chicago Steel. It'd messed up his wrist too. And he wasn't even suppose to be using equipment. Since he'd been sent out as a laborer, a cleanup man. This was a union job. A nasty, ugly, hard, mean job too. He kept looking at the trip-hammer and the way Eliot was holding the handles.

Man knew the crane operator, guy named Todd Stone, was watching from the cab of his crane above.

Man felt Eliot's eyes on him. "Well?"

Man looked Eliot in the face. Said: "Eliot, why you doing me like this? Cain't you talk to me like a man, man to man, face to face, tell me what I did to piss you off?"

Eliot grinned. "You haven't done anything to me personally. But I'll tell you, you're halfway out of the door, boy, already. If you want to work at Lomax you gonna do as I tell you. Now, here's the hammer. Get to work."

Man reached for it, took it by the handles, and Eliot stepped back. For a moment his eyes flashed. Then he turned and walked away.

Man watched him go, lumbering like a bear. Eliot didn't look back. Man shook his head, rain falling in his brain: It ain't pretty women killing me, no sir, it ain't pretty women killing me, it sho ain't dancing and gambling killing me. What I'm talking bout is the big steel, sho ain't no thrill, sho nuff ain't no thrill.

The rubber of the trip-hammer handles was damp, probably from Eliot's hands. Wet hands meant nervousness. It made Man feel good to think Eliot was nervous. Fuckface sonofabitch. Yo mama wear dirty drawers. Yo daddy ain't got no dick. Eat shit, motherfucker.

Feeling evil, Man lifted the trip-hammer up onto one of the beams, then rested the blunt blade on a mound of solder holding the two together. Nearby he heard snickering and looked toward the shears. It was Amos and the shears operator with their heads together, laughing, and looking in his direction.

> You can laugh till ya cry,
> Yes, you can laugh till ya cry,
> But I'm gon be gone
> And you be stuck here till you die.

He threw the switch and the hammer started jumping around on the narrow wings of the joined beams, hitting everywhere but the mound of solder. Who ever heard of using a trip-hammer on steel? He turned off the hammer.

Now he heard loud guffaws. Mark Harvey and Louis Irving had joined Amos and the shears operator and they were all laughing at him. Mark was bent double, red in the face cackling so hard he suddenly started coughing and gasping then choking. In a second or two he was purple, leaning back on the table of the shears trying to catch his breath.

Todd Stone started moving east now with an empty chain swinging gently just above head-level. Swing slow, sweet chariot. What you imagine Todd Stone saw? Here come a nigger, here come a bear, tell me which one ain't got no hair. Who cares? Pass the sugar, pass the tea, pass me anything you can see.

Then off at the right, Man saw Eliot coming up the east bay. The guys saw him too and broke up, scattering, heading back to their work. The shears man turned around and started operating the shears.

Throwing the switch again, Man tried to force the trip-hammer to dig into the solder, but again it jumped off.

Eliot came over to him and stopped. Said: "You haven't even gotten started?"

Man switched off the hammer. "Listen, Eliot, I don't know what you're trying—"

"Yeah? Go on, say what you're about to say," Eliot said, propping his fists on his hips, spreading his legs, as though ready to fight.

"I don't think a trip-hammer is the way to do this."

"Oh yeah? How would you know, Mister Smart-ass?"

"Hey, man, I don't have to be all them names you keep calling me." Man let the trip-hammer rest against the beam. He was pretty sure now Eliot was trying to make him quit. If he quit he wouldn't qualify for unemployment insurance checks. Suddenly his goal was to make Eliot fire him. He said: "I think you owe me uh pology."

Eliot turned red. His mouth and eyes twitched. He touched his chest with all eight of his fingers and two thumbs. "Me, apologize to ah nig— to somebody like you?" He spat—halfway toward the ground and halfway toward Man—and the glob of thick, coffee-colored mucus landed on Man's pants leg and dripped down to his steel-toed boot.

He just looked down at the mess on his clothes for what seemed like a long time, thinking this cracker don't believe fat meat is greasy. Nothing or nobody, not even Eliot, was going to foil his plan. This all happened in less than a wink.

Man wasn't even aware of his arm in motion till he felt his fist crack against the bone and cartilage of Eliot's nose and left cheek. His fist hit the nose and ended up squarely on the left eye, landing a Joe Louis punch. All right. This is it. You've done it now. It's all over: Mister Whistle man, blow yo whistle, punch my time card. I'm gone—like the crow cross a corn field, gone.

May done dug my own grave but ain't gon be no slave.

Eliot staggered back, stunned, holding his face. And the minute Man struck the boss the flash of a sharp, ugly memory flung itself against his mind: His daddy Quincy staggering into the yard from the mill where he worked, stumbling in with a bloody face and Manfred, maybe six or seven at the time, standing on the lopsided porch watching his daddy come. Oh, Lord! Banty rooster nightmare, high sheriff blues, hollering down the years with that choked-back memory. Tears, tears, but no weeping, only real tears falling through blue light like locust pods on a dusty dirt road. And it took days, maybe weeks, before he (the "little man" in short pants) began to understand that the mill boss had knocked his daddy upside the head with a two-by-four, knocked him coo-coo for sassing. And the bossman's men, all white as dirty sheets, flocked on Quincy and pounded him, making him cry and beg for his life. Then they sent him off fired without his final pay. And that was only one of the times Quincy had had a run-in with a white man.

A HALF HOUR LATER THEY WERE BOTH in the personnel office, Eliot with his eye patched up by the company nurse. On his cheek, a purple bruise.

CHAPTER TWENTY- TWO

Man and Eliot were seated, facing Paul Sawyer across his desk. Man knew what to expect as he watched the personnel manager's shifty eyes. A man with a huge gut and balding with gray temples, wearing blue suspenders and a red bow tie, Paul Sawyer was looking at whatever was in Man's employee folder. Suddenly he closed the folder and said, "You know Mister Selby here could press charges against you and you'd go to jail."

Nodding, Man didn't want to repeat himself. But the fact was he was pushed into hitting Eliot. Eliot had spat on him. He didn't want to have to say this again. So he didn't respond, hearing ancient voices of old folks whisper: Fore I be a slave, I be in my grave. Fore I be dogged—

Paul said, "Instead of pressing charges, however, we're going to do you a favor, Banks. I'm firing you. You can consider yourself fired. Do you have anything to say for yourself?"

Man looked up from his hands and focused on Paul Sawyer's eyes. "Naw. I ain't got nothing to say." How could he forget what old folks used to say: When you got yo mouth open make sho yo eyes open too. And all he could see with his own eyes now was two white men set against him. No question about it, this was not the time to say anything.

"Okay. Pick up your check from Darlene on the way out."

He got up then and without looking at Paul Sawyer or Eliot, walked out of the office and stopped at Darlene's desk in the outer office. With a faint smile, she sat there with her elbows on her desk, and in her right hand she was already holding his check between her thumb and index finger, holding it out toward him.

He took the check, returned her faint smile, and walked out of the office, closing the door gently behind him.

◉

When he found Lyle in the main bay he could tell Lyle had already heard or had guessed what was happening. Lyle said, "You shouldn't have hit him, Fred. Anything but that."

"He spit on me, Lyle. I had to hit him."

Lyle shook his head. "Yeah. But there got to be another way, buddy. You don't go round punching the boss in the face."

"He pushed me to it, Lyle. I'm sorry if I done messed up things for you here."

"No. Not for me. For yourself. Now what you going to do?"

"I'll find something. This ain't the onliest job."

●

In the locker room, he changed back into his street clothes, rolled up his work shirt and pants, and while he was stuffing them into a paper bag, Bernie Mungo came in. Said: "You leaving?"

"You see me, don't you?"

Bernie looked around to make sure nobody else was in earshot, then stepped closer to Man. Said: "You got fired?"

"Yeah." Man was impatient to leave but he took a long hard look at Bernie. Buzzard come to anybody's funeral. Cept this wont no funeral. Maybe a blessing.

"Since yesterday afternoon when I first heard this mess, I knew this was coming. I was gonna tell you but you was already gone when I heard them talking," little Bernie said, his eyes flashing like he'd stolen something and was afraid of being caught.

"Heard who talking?"

"The white guys talking about Eliot seeing you with a white woman."

Man was puzzled. "What white woman?"

"Don't you know? Eliot saw you in a car with some white woman."

"Not me. I don't even know no white womens." Color me blue.

"From what I heard they been talking bout it for some time now. He musta came in the next morning telling everybody he saw you with your white woman. That was just after he promoted you to welder. They said it was that week. The guys say he was really pissed off. All these crackers round here been talking bout it. Amos said she had to be a tramp. No other kinda white woman would look at a nigger."

This was all new. Man couldn't make any sense of what Bernie was saying. A white woman? Could Eliot have thought Cleo was white? Naw. Nobody would ever take a brown-skinned woman like Cleo for white. And he hadn't been with anybody else. Not in no car. Hey, wait a minute. He looked at Bernie. Said: "The only white woman I been anywhere near was some woman gave me a lift home from the track that time my sister wont ready to leave."

Bernie laughed. "Then she must be the one."

"I can't believe this shit," said Man. Color me green.

"It's true. That's why he been riding your behind. I heard him say many times if the good Lord intended white people to mix with the coloreds he'd a made them all the same color."

> You can color me blue,
> You can color me green,
> But don't you ever color me mean.

The door from the bay opened and Bernie jumped. Po boy. It was old man Ralph Roberts. He walked on by them over to the urinals and spread his legs, unzipped, and stood there, with his head thrown to one side like he was trying to listen to something behind him. They were behind him. Then Ralph said: "What you all dressed up for, Manfred? They promoted you to boss already?" And he laughed.

Man didn't answer. He said to Bernie: "I got to go."

"See you, man." And Bernie too walked over to the urinals.

Man walked on by both of them and out through the lunchroom, out the lunchroom door into the parking lot and daylight looked better than ever. He knew what he had to do. He knew damned well what he had to do.

He was crossing the railway tracks when he thought how much nicer it would be if he could just make himself some dough-re-me playing and singing and not have to put up with any old monkey-time job or broke-dick white mens—or tricky niggers, for that matter. Just make some bread doing what he loved. Is that too much to ax? Then maybe Cleo would ease up, get off his case. Life! What a tough fucking titty to have to suck!

As he climbed the hill toward Sixteenth Street, anger drained from his head, face, and shoulders, down into his stomach and formed there like a tight fist. Then, talking to himself, aloud he said, "Fuck it, ain't gon let Eliot or nobody slow me down."

WHEN MAN TOLD CLEO HE GOT FIRED all she said was, "I'm not surprised." She'd just walked in from work at the shop and it was six-thirty. She looked tired. "How long you been home?"

CHAPTER TWENTY-THREE

He said, "Bout two hours. Ain't you interested in why I was fired?" He was sitting in the living room with a glass of Old Crow. He'd been blowing his harmonica and humming some blues for two hours, trying out rhymes, trying to make up things: Looka yonder here comes the train, on the right track but in the wrong lane. Lulu Gal, Lulu Gal, will ya be my pal? Long tall yellow gal in a mary jane, if I ain't careful she gon drive me insane. Jump back in the alley, Sally, do yo stuff but don't treat me rough. Fed me coffee, fed me cake, but that girl, she wouldn't open her gate, said it was too late.

Cleo sat on the arm of the armchair and folded her hands in her lap, looking down at him. "Tell me why you were fired."

"Cause Eliot saw me with a white woman."

"What?"

"The boss saw me with a white woman."

Cleo's mouth opened and stayed that way. She smoothed her hair back on one side. Said: "Start over, please. You were fired because you were with a *white* woman? Who was this *white* woman and when were you with her?"

"I wasn't with a white woman," he said.

"You just said you were with a white woman."

"I was with a white woman but I won't really with her. She just give me a ride, member, that day I went out to the track with Debbie? Well, I caught a ride back with this white woman coming this way cause Debbie won't ready to leave—"

"Whoa! Back up! You expect me to believe this—?"

He was surprised. "Yeah. Why not. I was fired—"

"No, Fred, I mean about this white woman. I remember that day well. You never said anything to me about getting a ride home with anybody."

"Yes I did, you just forgot. But what difference do it make? Somebody I don't even know give me a ride home and I lose my job. I'm pissed off about that. How come you ain't?"

"If that's the reason you lost your job then that's a stupid reason but don't expect me to believe it's not true, I mean about the woman."

He couldn't believe what he was hearing, and he felt outraged, wounded, slapped hard. "You say you love me and you cain't even believe my word? If you cain't believe me what kinda love can we have?"

She looked away, maybe feeling guilty, maybe not.

"I ain't never not believed something you told me, Cleo." He felt truly confused. If you gon call me a lie, why should I try.

She still didn't say anything, just looked off toward the front windows. What she thinking?

He tried to x-ray her thoughts. You love me? Have to ball-the-jack to get you back?

> I'm Jack the Bear,
> I say I'm Jack the Bear,
> Put yo rope round my neck,
> Lead me anywhere.

He said, "I love you, don't you know that?"

She looked at him. "I believe you do, Fred, but—" She stopped and sighed.

> Let me be yo teddy bear,
> Sweet mama.

"But what?" Sweet, sweet mama.

"Men," she said.

"Mens what?"

"Men will play around on their wives even if they love their wives." She gave him her sincere, no, innocent look. "My daddy played around on my mama but she stuck by him. She used to say to him: Dogs don't bite at the front gate. In other words, if you're not creeping you got nothing to worry about. But I told you all this before." She sighed again. "It's not that I don't *want* to believe you."

"You should because it the truth. I ain't got no use for no other woman, specially no white woman. What I want wids nother woman, huh? And beside, I'm one man, don't be putting me with all mens. Don't know nothing bout what other mens might or might not do."

She stood up and walked over and sat beside him and touched his arm. "I really want to believe you, Fred."

"Seem to me I should be the one not trusting."

Suddenly she stood up, angry. "Why you say that?"

"You know why."

"No I don't. You tell me."

"If you don't know, forget it."

"No, I'm not going to forget it," she snapped. "If you're talking about my leaving you, you know goddamned good and well that I was justified in leaving your ass when I did. You know what you were doing—drinking up all the money and letting your own baby go hungry, not paying the rent. I couldn't even get out and work because I'd just come out of the hospital. So don't throw that up in my face. You're never going to make me feel bad about leaving you even if you talk about it from now until doomsday."

"All right, all right." He waved what she was saying away. "Les just drop it, okay."

"You brought it up."

"I brought it up and now I wants to drop it. Okay?"

He got up and walked out of the living room and headed back to the kitchen.

The door to the spare room back by the kitchen was closed. But Solly wasn't in there. Man had checked earlier.

Cleo followed him. Her arms were crossed.

He poured more whiskey into his glass and returned to the living room. If all the liquor was in one lake and I was a water snake. If all the liquor was in the clouds and I was a . . . was a what? He glanced back at her.

She followed him, arms still crossed defensively.

"Why didn't you pick up Karina?" she said suddenly.

The thought hadn't even crossed his mind. He suddenly felt ashamed of not having thought to pick up his own daughter next door. Actually, now he understood why. He'd been happy to have the little time alone with some whiskey and his harmonica. Not that he had been brooding or feeling sorry for himself but that he'd needed to think about things.

Cleo said, "Fred, you've been home two hours. You could've picked up your daughter."

"I get her." He put his glass down and got up, wobbled a bit, feeling relaxed, mellow.

"Don't bother. I'll do it." And she clumped out, and he heard the front door slam.

So he sat back down and picked up his harmonica and the glass of whiskey. Took a sip of whiskey, blew a few notes, took another sip of whiskey, ran a chord, got a bluesy whine going, then laid into it.

> Sitting here drinking Old Crow,
> Just sitting here drinking that Old Crow,
> If I drink this stuff all night
> By morning I'll be real tight.

The harmonica whined a long, long time.

> Old Crow, Old Crow,
> You so-and-so.
> Old Crow, Old Crow,
> You so-and-so.

And that harmonica whine again, like a baby crying.

> Yeah, I'm gon be outta luck,
> I'm gon be outta luck
> But I'm okay long as I can truck.

And he made the harmonica say yes yes yes mama, *yes* mama.

> Other peoples eat high on the hog,
> Other peoples eat real high on the hog,
> But I'm down here drunk and it's a shame
> I gots to always play this game.

But when he heard Cleo coming back with Karina he stopped, beat the harmonica on his thigh, put it in his pocket, finished his drink, and stood up. He was going to stop drinking. He knew what he had to do. But right now he wanted to get good and drunk, and he knew he couldn't do it here, not with Cleo looking in his face. It had gotten harder and harder to drink around her and Karina.

They met in the bedroom. She had Karina in her arms. The girl-child said, "Hi, Daddy."

And he said, "Hi, honey."

And she grinned and blushed and hid her face in her mother's hair.

Cleo said, "You going somewhere?"

"Yeah."

"Where?"

"Out."

She shook her head. "Fred, you're getting back into your old habits, you know. Why don't you leave your money at home."

He stepped around her. "Don't worry."

She turned and followed him into the hallway. "How can I not worry, Fred? If you go out and blow your check like you used to do in Chicago I swear I'm—"

"You what?"

She didn't answer but kept looking into his eyes.

On the way downstairs he saw Solly coming in. Hey, man. How you doing? Not too good. Solly said: "What's happening?" Man told him he got fired.

Solly said Percy Norman was waiting for him, he had to go. Said: "I got to run upstairs get my lunch. Go on out there and talk to Percy. He give you a job."

Job slinging a mop? The idea didn't seem all that pretty to Man at the moment. He wanted to get drunk, not go somewhere and push a broom. Yet—what the hell? He walked outside and across the sidewalk and bent down at the blue 1948 Ford sedan parked at the curb. Percy was at the wheel.

He turned his long black face toward Man. Said: "How you doing, Big Man?" Percy was a regular at the Palace.

"If I had me a job I be fine." He tried to stand far enough back so Percy couldn't smell his breath.

Percy frowned, looking up at him. "Ain't you still out there at Lomax Steel with your brother-in-law?"

Man coughed up some phlegm and turned and spat it down between the car and the curb. Said: "Got fired. Redneck boss saw me with some white woman gave me a lift from the track and thought me and her had something going. Never axed me nothing. Just started dogging me. And today I hit the motherfucker in the mouth. So, they fired me."

"You mean the peckerwood fired you cause he saw you in a car with a white woman?"

"It come down to that, pretty much."

"Sonofabitch!" said Percy. He squinted, looking sharply into Man's eyes. "When you ain't got no job you swimming with your boots on. I can put your big black ass to work, nigger." He laughed. "*If* you gon work—"

"I can work, man."

"If you work like you sing then you ought to be all right."

"I ain't got trouble with work."

"You want to start tonight? We start nine-thirty. Quit seven-thirty in the morning."

"I can start *tomorrow* night, Percy."

"How come you can't start *now?*"

Man looked up at the sky, took a deep breath and blew it out of his mouth. The sun was going down and the sky was yellowish orange along the rooflines. He looked back down at Percy. Said: "I wouldn't be any good tonight, Percy."

Percy studied him for a minute. "Okay. I understand. Go on, nigger, get yourself drunk. But be on time tomorrow. You riding with your ace and me?"

"Might as well."

Solly came up beside Man and slapped him on the back. "Percy, can you give this sorry-ass nigger a job?"

"I just did." He started up the engine. He looked at his wristwatch. "Come on, Solly. If you wants to run around a little bit fore we have to get down there."

Solly bopped around and got in and slammed the door.

Percy winked at Man. "Tomorrow, Mister Blues."

Man waved them off and just when he was about to head for Twenty-fourth and Lake, he heard somebody behind him making that come-here-but-on-the-QT sound: PSSSSSS. He looked back at the doorway, expecting to see Cleo. Nobody. Then again: PSSSSSS.

He looked up. It was Daffodil Grover looking out her window. She was calling him with her index finger. And she had this I-know-some-thing-you-don't-know grin on her kisser.

Dumbly, Man touched his chest with his index finger.

She slowly shook her head yes, narrowing her eyes and licking her lips. What's going on?

He went quietly up the steps, tipping, knowing if he walked normally, Cleo might hear him. And what you got to hide Mister Clyde? But he could already hear the radio blasting away in his own apartment so he knew Cleo wouldn't hear. But why the secrecy? You cain't be on both sides of the fence at the same time. He knew that. Knew too what old folks used to say: Never trust the moon to keep yo secret. Better leave a secret out in the open so sunlight can shine on it.

At the top of the steps, Daffodil had her door opened. It framed her tall big-boned body, standing there in a loose yellow-and-green cotton dress, one she wore around the house a lot. She was resting against the door frame, leaning on her left shoulder and her right fist was on her hip.

"What you want?" He didn't think it was going to be something about his daughter.

She was grinning and blinking her eyes like he'd never seen her do be-fore. "I like your friend Solly," she whispered. "Just wanted to ax you to put in a good word for me."

Man smiled, thinking, Why so many womens go for the jive-ass or the mean nigger? Some good womens gets mashed up like hamburger, go down, falling like rain. Raindrops cain't tell silk from burlap. Man looked at Daffodil. Daffodil, Daffodil, on one po wheel. She was blush-ing and waiting and he said, "Sho, Daffy. I'll tell em."

On the way down Twenty-fourth he hit a rhythm in his stride, thinking about Cleo, wondering why she wasn't as understanding about the music as was Jorena. And it hit him for the first time: Cleo got her own music. It's there in the church. And he remembered the first time he saw her get happy, in Chicago in the church where they were married. About a week after they were hooked, he let himself be dragged to Sunday afternoon service. And he sat there, feeling strange and full of sin, sure the whole church could smell his liquor breath. The choir was jamming up a breeze, shouting one of them happy-sad sorrow songs, he couldn't remember which, and there was Cleo right with them, grinning like a Halloween cat, clapping her hands, tapping her feet, and singing like nobody's business. The woman was in her heaven. Going to town clapping. Roll Jordan roll clapping. Calling Jesus clapping. This little light of mine tapping. Come on children, we all climbing up Zion's hill. These bones gon rise and talk, yes Lord! Great getting up morning! He'd never seen Cleo that happy before. And it happened every time he let himself be talked into going to church with her. He'd sit there beside her watching her and listening to her joy. And he'd wonder why *he* couldn't make her that happy? What did God have that he didn't have?

LATER, SITTING AT THE BAR IN THE Palace with a double shot of Old Crow on the rocks in front of him, Man was listening to Billie Holiday singing *Good Morning Heart-ache* when his brother-in-law walked in. This was not a place you'd expect to see Lyle but there he was. "Hey," said Lyle.

CHAPTER TWENTY-FOUR

"Sit down, have a drink. Kick up sand, join the band."

Lyle smiled faintly and took the stool on Man's left. "Didn't get a chance to really talk with you fore you left."

"Fore I was fired, you mean."

Lyle shook his head. "Eliot went too far this time. I think you ought to get the union on his ass."

"Fuck the racist bastard," said Man. And even as he spoke his second mind had a long arm and on that arm was a hand and the hand pulled his coattail—so to speak: Yo anger ain't eating nobody's insides but yo own.

"What's with this white woman stuff Bernie told me about?"

"Just some woman gave me a ride from the track."

"Bernie say all the guys been talking bout it for over a week. You and your white bitch."

"Lyle, I don't even want to talk about it. The cracker is sick. Thas all I can say."

Herb came up and stood in front of Lyle. They exchanged greetings. Lyle said, "I'll have a Budweiser." And to Man: "I told your sister and she's already trying to dream up another job for you."

"I got another one already."

Herb put the bottle and a glass in front of Lyle and walked back down to two women. Lyle picked it up and poured. Took a sip then said: "Already? Doing what?"

"Night cleanup crew downtown, Sears."

Lyle nearly choked on his beer. He put the glass down. "Naw, Fred. You can do better than that."

"It's just something till I see something else." He took a long slow swallow of whiskey. Nothing wrong with honest work. Ain't that what old folks always said? Even with captain-man on yo ass, forty-four-forty. Humbug, humbug. Whistle blowing sweat-time. Gwine when you didn't wants to go, but still honest. Member my mama on her knees on the white folks' floor pushing a wet rag. Hello, captain, hello. No-thrill steam-drill will kill. Hammer thud knock you in the mud. Don't wish captain no harm but wouldn't lose no sleep if he lost his arm. If captain goes blind won't come to work till half-past nine. Yeah, honest work honest work. But not much use for the kind they be talking bout. Heart not in it.

Then the door opened and in came Jorena in a purple outfit looking as flashy as all get out. Man softly whistled under his breath and as she passed by she slapped him on his back and spoke to Lyle.

Once she was behind the bar she talked quietly with Herb for a few minutes before coming up to where Man and Lyle sat.

"You on tonight, Fred? Greg suppose to be coming in around nine. When you gonna get yourself a telephone? I wanted to call you earlier to see what you and Greg had planned for tonight."

Sometimes when Greg was on Man didn't go on and vice versa. Other times both of them were on jamming.

Man said, "Yeah. That's a problem I got to take care of. I do needs me a phone. Matter fact I'm gon see bout getting one tomorrow." Tomorrow, tomorrow.

And Lyle said, "Then we wouldn't have to send the kids all the way down there just to give you a message."

"Yeah. Thas true." He took a shot. Then, looking at Jorena, he said, "Yeah. I'm on tonight. But, listen here, I just got hired working nights down at Sears. I'm gon try to keep Friday and Saturday night free but I can't promise less you gon pay me enough to live on." He winked at her, laughed, and drained his glass.

She smiled, saying, "Wish I could. What happened to your job at Lomax?"

And he told her the whole story, the abuse and all and how he had hit the boss. She laughed. "Good for you, Fred. Man after my own heart. Don't take any crap. You want another drink?" She was already lifting the bottle of Old Crow down.

One of the women down at the end went over and put money in the jukebox and a second later they got Nat King Cole singing *That Ain't Right*. It was new and Man liked it, liked the bass and the congos. Nat had great timing. Man was tapping his feet, listening closely.

The door opened and Man's sister, Debbie, came in, walked right over to Lyle. "Hi, Jorena. Hi, Freddy. Lyle told me what happened." And to Lyle: "I picked up some barbecued ribs for tonight."

Lyle smiled, and probably so did his stomach. Man knew Debbie wasn't used to the idea of Lyle sitting at the bar in the Palace on a Friday evening. Good family man. No riffraff. To his sister Man said: "Sit down, Debbie. Have a drink."

"No. I got a woman under the dryer. Got to get back. But I just wanted to tell you this woman I know named Ernestine Franklin, owns a house up on Twenty-fourth and Evans, say she knows somebody who just got hired on at this roofing company on North Thirteenth. Here, she wrote down the address and phone number. Don't know for sure if they're still hiring. And Trudy say her cousin just got hired at a asphalt company out Thirteen thousand and A Street. They do paving and make parking lots and stuff. Patch-up work for the city. Stuff like that. The pay is good too. One of my customers said they might be looking for packers down at Field Paper Company on Davenport. But you might even be able to get on out at the stockyards with one of the packing companies. Now, that's where the money is."

He cut her off: "Debbie, I already got a job." But he was thinking: Day job better cause it'd let me be mo free at night. But—

"You do? Where?"

"Sears. Mopping the floor at night."

Man saw his sister give Jorena a look. Honest work, honest work, drive that mop, drive that mop. They both had this look he knew but couldn't name. Soldier boy in Atlanta just back from the war: Born in Georgia, worked like the devil in Tennessee, nearbout died in Germ-a-nee. Then Debbie said, "Freddy, what I'm talking about is a *real* job, not some—"

"Give me the address," he said. And he took it and stuffed it in his shirt pocket, just to make her happy, then picked up his glass and drank the liquor down with his eyes closed. Worked like the devil most time, gon stop working don't care if the sun don't shine. Free as a bumblebee, don't bother work it won't bother me. Smacked his lips when he set the glass down. Roll that cotton, tote that bale. He thanked her.

Lyle grinned, looking at Man. "You drink that stuff like it's water. Your stomach must be made of cement."

Man thought: Jailer gave me whiskey, jailer gave me tea. Got the hesitation blues, gon put on my walking shoes. Little whiskey won't hurt the soul, throw it upside the wall, pick it up, put it in a bowl. Blues ain't nothing but a glass of liquor.

"Just like his daddy's," said Debbie, still standing. "I got to get back to the shop. Lyle, pick up some toilet paper, baby, on your way home, please. See yall." She waved good-bye.

Sho nuff. Man frowned as he watched her leave. Like my daddy? Ain't nothing like him. White folks called him coon but he be off on the moon. Got his type of blues but I sho don't fit his shoes. Thought Debbie knowed me better. Jailer gave me everything but the key. Gon make my own key. Open anything I wants.

Then Lyle left.

Herb left and Drusilla came on duty. And Man started humming and singing: It ain't whiskey killing me, no sir, it ain't whiskey killing me, it ain't gambling, it ain't dancing and gambling killing me . . .

◉

An hour later, Man was still sitting at the bar in the Palace with a half-finished double shot of Old Crow at his elbow. Jorena had left. A smooching couple at a table over by the jukebox. Drusilla was tending the bar. And in walked Kermit with a young white woman in pink flowered pants holding his arm. She had dimples and a pretty smile. You could see right away she was too young to be in a bar.

Kermit started grinning and profiling as he introduced the girl—Amy—to Man.

"Amy my sweet baby. Ain't you, baby?" Kermit said and kissed her behind the ear and hugged her.

She giggled and turned red in the face.

Man noticed that Drusilla was standing there with her mouth open in shock watching the white girl.

They sat at the bar and Kermit threw a twenty on the bar, stuck his chin out, and threw his chest out. "Sugar," he said, "You want to hear some music?" He motioned his head toward the jukebox. He gave her some change and she got off her stool and strutted over to the jukebox.

Drusilla whispered to Man: "I don't know who that boy is but he better be careful, he can get himself lynched around here."

Man nodded, slyly watching Kermit. Lord, have mercy. This po nigger think he really into something. Better not let Eliot know.

◉

That night his eyes were closed hard and he was in a yellow-gray fog—

> He and Solly are sitting side by side about halfway back on what seems to be a bus about to return to Chicago where Mister Lee has promised them a great job making a lot of money singing and playing the blues. In a blur he sees his sister waving good-bye from the platform, stout and firm, standing there holding her purse by its ridiculously long strap. He's sure the woman is Debbie though she looks a bit like Mama. Apparently she is seeing them off, probably has driven them to the bus station. Moments before, in the car, she slipped a roll of twenties into his jacket pocket. The gesture is like that of a mother stuffing a handkerchief into a son's suit coat as she is about to send him off to Sunday school on Sunday morning. And out of self-pity he'd steeled himself against letting tears flow by refusing to blink and by gritting

his teeth and telling himself not to cry. But now he and Solly
at the bus window are waving good-bye to her as the bus
pulls out. One of these mornings gon rise, one morning gon
rise. Up in the sky gon take a walk. The bus is almost full.
Man watches their journey east out of a city that surely
must be Omaha, and the bus moves along Jackson, and he's
watching through the big window the downtown strollers,
shoppers, workers, moving along the sidewalk. The bus
moves slowly past the St. Nicholas Boarding House. Still
moving, no stoplights, till they come to Tenth Street where
the big bus makes a slow left turn, heading north on Tenth,
going the four blocks slowly. He feels a powerful sense of
happiness at the prospect of the coming success. This will
mean a better life for Cleo, Karina, and himself. And Solly
too. Now Man is thinking about Chicago, about living there
again. It feels good to be returning with money in his pocket
and a bright future. Now the bus is making another slow
turn, this time right and onto Douglas, and still creeping
along till it comes to the Douglas Street Bridge, where, in the
distance, up the coast of the Missouri River, he sees the long
stretch of the old American Smelting & Refining Company
plant, with vertical rivers of black smoke lifting from it. A
place were countless men, like himself and unlike himself,
spent sweaty years earning a living. One generation passes
away and another replaces it. He feels lucky being on his
way to a way of life now that will touch people in a good
way. And before he can blink his eyes twice the bus is
crossing the Missouri River—something he'd forgotten was
there—crossing it into Iowa. But the river water this time
gives off a shimmering golden glow and he can see that
beneath that sunlit surface there is an even deeper brightness.

He turned over—

And right away he's in some small hot church with Cleo,
and there she is, happy as a morning glory drinking sunlight,
clapping her hands, tapping her feet and singing to God
while the church choir jams down hard on I Got Shoes. All
God's children got shoes! I got a derby, you got a derby!
All God's children got a derby! I got a robe, you got a
robe! All God's children got a robe! I got a crown, you got
a crown! Lord, Lord, have mercy! This was some happy
woman. He knows he's dreaming. He's had this dream before.

But he can't get over it. What is it about this place, a church, and shouting to God, that gets her so up? He sees himself sitting there beside her, wondering, trying to figure it out. Nothing else gets her going like this. Between songs he whispers to her, "Don't you love me any mo?" And she touches his cheek and says, "Sure I do, honey, you know I love you, but you just got to understand how much I love Jesus too! Praising his name makes me so happy! I just feel good all over. Just the thought of Jesus makes my skin feel warm. I feel Him all through my body." And as he listens to her he wants to say, "But why cain't you feel me all through yo body like that too?" but he doesn't—doesn't because somehow he knows it's the wrong question, a question that would push him farther away from her, a question that may even cut him off forever.

LIKE BLACK GHOSTS, THREE ABREAST,
they approached the side door of Sears
downtown on Dodge. It was nine-twenty-
five. Percy in the middle. Street quiet and dark.
Percy took a quarter from his pocket and tapped on
the plate glass door.

CHAPTER TWENTY-FIVE

Man had a hangover and a headache. If I blink I'll sink, if I sink I'll stink. Went to the river, went down to the river. Lord knows, it ain't pretty women killing me. Couldn't get across.

Now they were on their way to work.

They stood there waiting. Percy sucked his teeth. Said: "Old man Rosemond running late. Getting old, cain't make them rounds fast as he used to." He laughed, slapped his thigh, looking at Solly.

Solly said, "You gone be old one day, yoself—if you lucky." He laughed.

Man grinned, looking through the plate glass. "He already old. What you mean?" Then he saw the stout, elderly white man in a blue uniform, wearing a newsboy's cap, wobbling along toward the door. His back was bent, and in his right hand was a ring of keys. Man watched the night-watchman unlock the door.

The old man pulled the door open and held it for them. Said to Man: "You must be the new boy Percy told me about."

Percy, in his big bass voice, said, "Oscar, this is Manfred. Manfred here is not no boy. You know that, Oscar. Look at him."

The old white man frowned, trying to focus on Man's face. He had to lift his head and look up and it was clearly a strain. He sort of mumbled, "Yes, I see. I see."

Man just grinned, watching Oscar Rosemond, who looked confused. Then he fell into step beside Percy, and the three of them walked down a ramp till they reached a stairway.

Behind them Oscar called out, "Some of them already down there— Orson, Lorenzo, and, and—"

When they reached the next level down, Man could see that they had come in off the street at the mezzanine level and were now on the first floor. Ahead of them, sitting on benches, were four young men.

Percy led the way over. He introduced the fellows to Man. Orson, slouched down so low he seemed to be sitting on his spine, was a shifty-eyed big dude with closely cut hair. Maybe twenty-two or twenty-three. Lorenzo, legs crossed, pretty boy, skinny, long arms and legs, big blinking eyes like a girl's, a baby-fuzz mustache, same kind of stuff on his chin. Twenty-one or so. Bernard, older guy, short, light-brown, sleepy-eyed, always had this I-don't-give-a-shit look, maybe thirty or even thirty-five. Lunch bag on his lap. Hands in pockets. Unlighted cigarette stuck between his lips.

Bernard said, "I caught your show at the Palace last weekend. Me and my girl."

Man grinned. "You did? You like it?"

"Yeah, man. People all over town talking about you. You some kinda celebrity, man. But how come you got to be working a job like this you got talent like that?"

Man kept his grin. "It's how I gets my material."

Percy laughed. "Cause he gots to feed his black ass just like you. Now let's get to work. Come on. All you. Let's go get started. Orson, Lorenzo, Bernard. Solly don't do the floor backward again tonight so you have to walk across the floor after you buffed it. Come on, Big Man."

Guffaws.

Man saw Solly give Percy the finger behind his back.

They all walked over to the set of elevators and got on one. Orson mumbled something to Lorenzo and ribbed him, and both started snickering. Man saw Percy's long index finger push the BASEMENT button. The elevator shook, then Man felt the sensation of descending. It was a brief descent. And the door slid back, revealing a dark corridor. He almost laughed. Black sheep hide easy in the dark. Old folks talking. Go into the black, you may never get back.

He watched Percy disappear into the darkness and a moment later the corridor was flooded with dim light. Man followed the others out and along the corridor till they came to a steel door marked JANITORIAL SUPPLIES. Aside from the noises of humming electric sounds of machinery and those they were making, the basement was dead silent.

Inside the janitorial supply room, with the fluorescent lights on, Man saw in one corner about a dozen mop buckets on wheels with ringers constructed on top of them. To the left of the buckets was a row of three large concrete sinks. Farther left, on racks suspended from the ceiling, were about twenty cotton mops with wooden handles. Beyond them, on the same set of extended racks, were about a dozen dust brooms with long wooden handles. He shuddered at the sight of them. He remembered mopping the toilets and locker rooms at Lomax and shuddered again.

In the opposite direction, where the guys had gone immediately, were three rows of five lockers. To the right of the lockers were five silver buffing machines, heavy-looking weapons with long handles, like lawn mowers. Man eyed the lockers. All except three had locks on them. Man followed Percy over to them. The others were beginning to unlock their lockers and change into their gray work shirts and pants.

Percy said, "Here, Fred. This one here you can have." He touched a locker without a lock. "You have to get your own lock. See that big wooden closet over there. Clean uniforms there. Should be able to find one your own size."

Man looked at Solly, pulling on his pants, buckling his belt. He almost laughed at how silly Solly looked in his gray uniform.

Man found a pair of pants and a shirt—the largest size—that looked like they might fit, and he took them back to the bench in front of the locker Percy assigned him. The guys were jiving and joking and laughing about one thing and other. He stripped down to his underwear and put on the uniform. A bit tight under the arms and at the crotch but otherwise okay.

Man watched Percy go pick up a plastic bucket and stand by the door. He said, "Okay. Let's make it snappy, you punks."

One by one, he saw them take down a dust broom from the racks, take down a mop, and stack both on top of the ringer and push the bucket out of the supply room.

On the way out, Percy poured into each bucket about a cup full of industrial cleaning soap from the large plastic container.

When they were all gone, Man followed Percy over to the supplies and did as he did. Percy got himself a dust broom, a mop, and a bucket. He said: "They got water on each floor in the storerooms."

The door was open and Man could hear the guys down by the elevators talking loud and laughing.

When he and Percy got to the elevators the jokers were all gone. The dials above the two doors indicated where the elevators were. Number one elevator was on the left, number two on the right. Number one was already on the fifth floor. Alongside it, the lighted panel said GIFTS LUGGAGE ETC & KITCHEN APPLIANCES.

Percy pushed the button, lighted a cigarette, and spat a speck of tobacco from his tongue, all the while watching the lighted dial. "Solly up there," he mumbled as though talking to himself. The elevator light didn't change.

Man pushed the button for the other elevator. It was resting on the third floor. Housewares floor—pillows, bed sheets, drapes, pots and pans. He pushed it again. Then the light went off, then came on at the second floor where it stopped.

The fifth-floor light still hadn't changed. Percy said, "That must be old Oscar up there too, starting his rounds again. When he making his rounds on a floor he always props the elevator door open until he finish. Really screws us up when he do that."

Man looked at the sixth level. THE EAGLE'S NEST RESTAURANT. He said to Percy: "We got to do that too?"

"They got they own sanitation engineers." He chuckled. Said: "That's not Sears. But lots of Sears clerks eat lunch up there." He dragged on his cigarette, blew the smoke to the side, squinting his eyes. When he turned, Man could see a large embossed scar on his neck, like a deep knife cut, as though somebody had tried to cut his head off from the rest of his body but had lost balance and gone sideways. Man remembered the rumor about Percy's woman Francine Lincoln stabbing him in the back. Suddenly, Percy stood close to the elevator and shouted up at the ceiling: *"Send the motherfucking elevator down you dumb assholes!"*

Still the fifth floor didn't move. No way his voice could have reached the second floor let alone the fifth. He sucked on his cigarette once again, then threw it on the tiled floor and mashed it out with his pointed-toe black shoe. "If I have to walk up there, I'm gone kick some ass," he said. "Them niggers knows they ain't spose to hold on to the elevator like that."

Man laughed, still watching the second-floor light.

Percy shouted again: *"Hey! Up there! Send the fucking elevator down!"* Then he gritted his teeth.

Percy took out his pack and knocked a fag out and stuck it in his mouth, then lighted it and blew the fresh smoke at the door, his eyelids half-closed. Made Man wish he had a good cigar.

Man kept watching the light. Shine on, shine on. One two three four five six seven eight nine, work these floors till they shine. That's the line.

"I'm getting mad now," said Percy, spitting tobacco again from his tongue. He looked at Man. "If we ever get the elevator, I'm gon show you what I want you to do on the first floor. I've been doing the whole thing myself for a week cause this old boy we had doing it wont no good. But I'm not spose to be sweeping and mopping and carrying on. I'm the supervisor. These niggers can't seem to get that through they heads. I'm spose to be supervising them, making sure they do they job. So, when you gets broke in, you gon do the first floor and I'll take care of the mezzanine. If we had any kind of decent help here at night I'd be just like Jack Smith on days, a foreman. Smith don't push no broom nowhere. He answers the phone and send a man with a mop to whichingever department done had some kind of accident, whether it's perfume spilled on the floor or some baby done throwed up or something. But, naw, you see, here at night, I gots to be supervisor and mop-man and all this other shit. And, see, I can't even get them niggers to send me the fucking elevator."

Then suddenly the light on five went out and the elevator was coming down—four, three, two, one, and basement. The door opened and there stood Oscar Rosemond, big-eyed, looking like somebody had just slapped him from sleep. "Oh!" he said, looking at Percy. "You going up?"

Percy gave him a nasty grin. "That's right, Oscar. Been trying to go up."

Oscar walked off past them and headed down the corridor toward Bargain Basement. He called back: "Don't bother with the lights. I'll turn em off when I leave."

◉

On the first floor, Percy and Man parked their buckets by the elevator door. Then Percy took the ring of keys off his belt and stuck one into a slot between the elevator doors. All the ceiling lights across the entire floor came on.

He told Man to get his broom. Said: "Let's go. I'll show you where I wants you to start."

Man followed him through rows of suits on metal racks, then rows of sports shirts and slacks. Off to the left along the mirrored wall were more racks filled with jackets.

Percy reached the far wall and stopped and turned around with his back to the front door. Man looked through the plate glass of the revolving door, through the big plate glass windows. The street was dark and cool with just a sprinkling of light here and there. Percy was standing with his arms stretched out in front of him. "This your floor," he said. "Sweep from here all the way back to the Women's Wear. This going to be your territory. Got me?"

Man nodded. He knew what he had to do. Mopping floors was just one step along the way.

Percy said, "Look at this floor. It don't look dirty but don't let that fool you."

Man watched him, listening carefully.

Percy was now down on one knee and rubbing the palm of his hand across the tiled floor. He stood up. "See this?" He held his hand out in front of Man's face. "This why you got to sweep all of the floor, see. That spot didn't look dirty but it was. See?"

"I see it."

"When you finish sweeping everything back toward the storage room, take it up back there. Come on. I show you where to put it, where to get your water."

Percy started his slow, humped-back, long-legged stride down the center aisle, hands in back pockets, looking down.

Man left his broom leaning against a cashier's counter, and caught up with him. They walked down past the elevators and through Women's Wear and beyond into the storage room.

Percy led him to a big concrete sink against the storage room wall. "This where you get your water and dump it. Don't be dumping it in the men's room. One old boy fucked up the toilet that way. And these here—" he pointed at four tall trash cans. "You pick up your trash back in here. There your dustpan there—" Percy pointed to a dustpan hanging on a nail to the left of the concrete sink. "You got all that, Big Man?"

Man tried to grin. "Yeah." He was feeling woozy and a little bit sad. "Yeah, I got it," he said. Oh, Mama, won't you go tell Estelle I'm in jail. Gotta boogie fore you can woogie.

Percy said, "Okay. You on your own. When you ready to wax, come get me and I'll show you what to do. By the way, we knock off for lunch at midnight. If you didn't bring nothing there some machines up there outside Smith's office. We meet up there on the fifth floor, Snack Bar area. If you gon be on schedule you spose to have all your sweeping done by then and maybe half your mopping. Okay?"

"Okay," said Man, thinking: Top of the hill harder to find than the bottom. But he could see it, he had a plan.

Then Percy turned and walked slowly toward the elevators. He was whistling something Man didn't catch. Then he stopped.

Man walked slowly back down the aisle through the store, listening to Percy's footfalls going toward the elevator. When Percy was gone, Man stopped dead in his tracks and stood still in the middle of the aisle, listening to the silence, slowly shifting his eyes over the rows and rows of suits. In a far mirror he suddenly saw himself, a big lone dark figure among the glitter, the patterns of color. The sight scared him. He shifted away, then looked at himself again right away. He thought: I ain't no janitor. Fuck this shit! I'm spose to be the man with the good hand. That sho ain't me there in the mirror. He snorted. Ain't no janitor. That clown in the mirror don't know no better, I do. Lotta peoples I'm gon amaze cause I got a trail to blaze. And he started pushing the broom, but sweeping the floor good, glancing up at the mirror once in a while to see the clown at work.

As he worked, something like pieces of songs, lines, snatches danced across his mind to the rhythm of his back-and-forth arms. I may be wrong. Jell-O, Jello-O Mama. Spin your parasol. Sent for you yesterday! Yeah. Do anything for my baby. Eat Wonder Bread, eat baloney every day. Sleep in a hollow log. Do the Beer Barrel Polka. My mama done tole me! You gives me a thrill and you ain't Jayne Mansfield. You on the right track and you don't even drive a Cadillac.

He kept his rhythm, pushing the broom. If he could make Cleo happy he'd have the answer to the sixty-four-thousand-dollar question. He remembered a bed-conversation in the wee hours the other night. Feeling

Cleo's wakefulness he woke too. Voice low in his throat, he asked her: "Whas wrong?" And she said: "Just thinking, all I really want out of life is a good life for our daughter." And he said: "Is that *all* you want?" "That and a good church," she said. "Is that all?" And he could hear her breathing in the silence before she spoke, saying, "What else *should* I want?" and, hurt, he said, "Nothing, I guess." Yeah, he felt hurt but didn't really know why and didn't feel he had a right to what she was making him feel. One part of him felt he too should want exactly what she wanted but the bigger part of him didn't feel what she felt and didn't want what she wanted.

AT MIDNIGHT HE WALKED INTO the snack bar area, saw a row of candy, coffee, and cigarette machines and a few tables and chairs outside a closed soda fountain. The other suckers were lounging on a set of plastic couches against the far wall in the snack bar area.

CHAPTER TWENTY-SIX

Solly was slumped in one corner of the couch looking half asleep. Strange thing about Solly: He was different, like a different person, when they—he and Man—were in a group of guys like now. Strange thing about himself. Their friendship at such times seemed on the lay-away plan, suspended, on hold, in hock, for some reason. Man didn't understand it as he thought about it now for the first time. He remembered times in Chicago when he and Solly happened to be among a group of other musicians, street musicians, park musicians, musicians in nightclubs or coffeehouses, when they were just hanging out with drinkers in bars or in flophouses, anywhere. Most of the time folks knew they were tight but they didn't have much to say to each other at such times. Maybe, thought Man, it be our way of being equal with everybody in the group.

Percy was eating a sandwich. On a chair in front of him was a steaming cup of coffee. Solly was sitting next to him eating a candy bar. Orson had his feet up on a chair. He was eating an apple. Lorenzo was lying down flat on his back on the plastic, no shirt. Bernard was standing over him, saying, "Sit up, nigger. You think you gone hog the *whole* couch?" Bernard, lunch bag in hand, started lightly punching Lorenzo's naked shoulder.

Lorenzo jumped up, frowning, and leaned back against the plastic back. "Damn! Can't nobody even sleep round here?"

Percy said, "You spose to sleep at home, youngblood. This your *job,* not your bed. If you take your narrow ass home in the morning and get some rest instead of bopping around all day after pussy you be able to come to work and do your job. You wouldn't need to sleep on the job."

"I'm not *on* the job," said Lorenzo. "This is my lunch break. I can do damn well what I want with it."

Percy didn't say anything to that, just kept eating his sandwich.

Man paused, looking long at Lorenzo, thinking, now, there's a boy who don't believe fat meat is greasy. Act just like a engine ain't got no driving wheel.

Then Man walked over to the coffee machine, put a dime in for a cup of coffee with cream and sugar. His thoughts had shifted to Cleo. He wanted things to be right between them. Watch me and my baby get tight, gon play this good hand right. But looked like every time he turned around she was pissed at him or he was pissed at her or they were getting at each other. She just won't play my game. Just won't play my game. And I don't know how to play hers. But Lord knows, I try. If I'm not try-ing, I'm flying. But even as he thought this he doubted that he'd tried hard enough. When the coffee finished draining into the cup, he took it and stepped over to the candy machine and dropped in a dime for a Baby Ruth. Then sat down on a nearby chair, facing them.

Lorenzo looked at Bernard, now sitting next to him. Said: "You just mad because your old lady in bed with her sweet daddyman right now taking more dick than you got. While you down here doing the sissy with a mop she home sucking a dick big as a baseball bat, sticking her tongue up the dude's asshole, sucking his dirty toes. That's *your* problem."

Bernard coolly said, "Whatever gave birth to you, man, musta been in pretty bad shape, but, you know, she coulda done better. All your mama needed, Lorenzo, was a good hard dick. If she'd had something like this—" and he grabbed his crotch and shook it at Lorenzo, "she woulda give birth to something higher on the animal scale than you."

"There you *go*, there you *punks* go," said Percy. "I thought we agreed to cut out talking this shit every night. Talk *constructive* talk."

Lorenzo rolled his eyes at Percy. "This is my lunch break, mother-fucker. You can't tell me what to talk about. This is a free country, moth-erfucker."

Bernard grunted. "Not free to the likes of you."

"Bernard," Lorenzo said, "don't talk that shit to me, man. I know your problem. Your old lady's crying sweet tears of joy right now, with her big soft thighs wrapped around her daddyman. And that nigger be pumping dick into her like nobody's business, just pumping more dick than you ever had. But one thing I can say, he gets it real nice and juicy for you when you get there in the morning."

The guys were snickering and laughing.

Man sipped his coffee, watching Lorenzo.

Bernard looked at Percy. "Percy, if you don't want a dead worker on your hands, you better tell this young nigger to lay off."

"All right, Lorenzo, that's enough," said Percy. "Don't let your mouth write a check your ass cain't cash."

Lorenzo gave Percy a quick finger.

Man saw Lorenzo looking at Solly. He knew what was coming.

Finally, Lorenzo said, "Hey, Solly."

"What you want, nigger?"

"You get any pussy lately?"

Giggling, Orson pumped his fist up and down in front of his fly. And rolled his eyes.

Solly got his deadly look on. "Yeah. Matter of fact, I did. I did it to your mama couple of days ago—in the mouth, the ass, the pussyhole, everywhere. She loved every minute. And she got a good one, too. But not as good as your sister's. She's my honeydripper. You should see her stand on her head and suck my dick. Yeah. She my honeydripper."

"Your what?"

"You heard me," said Solly. "Your sister sucked my dick dry. That's what."

Percy said, "Okay, you cats cut it out fore somebody get mad and we have a fight on our hands. One nigger few years back almost killed another nigger right here on this couch."

"I ain't scared of dying," said Lorenzo, standing up, nervously walking over to the candy machine. He bent down and looked at the bars on display.

"How far you got, Fred?" said Percy.

Man said, "I finished the sweeping. Got that all done."

Orson said, "You running behind if that's all you done."

Percy looked at Orson. "Who's the boss here, Orson? Me or you?"

"You *spose* to be."

Lorenzo put money in the machine and a candy bar fell. He came back over. "Yeah, but I bet you don't make nowhere near the dough Smith makes. Yet and still you all suppose to be both of you foremen."

"Lorenzo," said Percy, "boy, can't you just shut your mouth for once at lunchtime? Didn't you just hear me tell you not to let your mouth buy what your ass cain't pay for? Every night, yackety-yak, yackety-yak. Cain't nobody get a word in edgewise."

"I'm going to take me a nap," said Lorenzo, and walked across the snack bar and fell down on his knees and stretched out on the floor beside the counter.

Percy said to Man, "Yeah. You gon have to move fast to be done with the waxing and buffing all by quitting time."

"I'll get it done," he said.

"It's his first night, Percy," said Bernard. "He doing fine for his first night. I didn't do that good my first night."

Percy said, "That's cause you walk slow, motherfucker."

Bernard laughed. "Listen who's calling somebody a slow walker. You one of them old-time jitterbugs. Your strut old as the hills."

"Yeah, but I gets where I be going."

Man laughed. Everybody laughed.

◉

When the clock on the wall over the snack bar said one o'clock, Man stood up, threw the candy wrapper and the coffee cup in the trash can by the coffee machine and headed back toward the elevators. If you not trucking you shucking. Percy was already ahead of him, Bernard too. Solly fell into step beside Man and said, "How you doing?"

"I'm doing okay. Wish I felt better. Motherfucking headache. Could sho use a drink."

Solly gave him a look that said something was up. Then he whispered, "In my locker." And Solly slipped him the key. In a good-natured tone, he said: "Don't finish it, motherfucker."

Man eased on down to the basement, took a long sloppy swig out of Solly's bottle, put it back, and went to work, with the strong strange smell of the wax burning his nostrils. He hit a working rhythm, a get-it-little-sister-rhythm, ignoring his headache, feeling the surge from the whiskey. As he worked he hummed, pushing a memory smooth as a cloud, hearing Blind Willie McTell's twelve-string guitar, remembering old Blind Willie on Decatur Street in Atlanta, and it kept him going. Blind Willie made each note and each word he sang clear and individual as a carved piece of stone. Man'd always tried to sing and play like that. Work, work with me, little sister. Push it. Keep on rocking. Country boogie. Before long he felt almost normal, sweating out the liquor, and he worked hard to do a good job on the floor, make it so slick he'd be able to see his own face shining back at him. Hearing his mama: Freddy, if you gots to do something, boy, give it everything you got, do it better than it ever been done before. If you ain't willing to do that, don't even start, stay outta the way and let somebody else do it.

PERCY PULLED OVER TO THE CURB AT
Twenty-fourth and Lake. Man, next to him,
opened the door. Said, "You sho you don't
wanna stop for a taste? Make you sleep better."
Sometimes Percy stopped with Solly for a taste. But

CHAPTER TWENTY-SEVEN

this time he said no, he wanted to go home and hit the sack right away. Man got out, and Solly got out of the back and slammed the door.

Percy drove away, his engine knocking and sputtering.

Coming along the street in his box was Poppa Leon with a cigarette in his mouth, grinning. He was wheeling so fast they stopped in their tracks, unsure where to jump to let him by, but Poppa Leon stopped right in front of them. "Morning, gentlemen! Beautiful morning isn't it?"

"Yeah," they said. Man wondering: Where he get his feel-good spirit?

Poppa Leon held up a finger of warning. "Remember boys, every shut-eye ain't sleep and every good-bye ain't gone." His smile was wide as the Missouri. "Also, just remember, boys, seven eleven, see ya in heaven." And he winked and wheeled himself past the newspaper vendor and on to the curb, bumped down, and rolled on across the street.

Man and Solly looked at each other. Man thinking how Poppa Leon's keep-on-keeping-on must be due to some strong hoodoo so deep it be in the bone marrow. And cheerful too. Just scooting along and joyful like a morning finch. Put all the rest of us to shame. Got nothing to complain about, boy, after that.

The vendor man was laughing at their bewilderment. They walked over to the vendor, still watching Poppa Leon scooting along. "What he mean by 'seven eleven, see ya in heaven'?" Man asked, wondering if the legless man heard himself some death bells all the time, death bells ringing, sail on, sail on. That made him appreciate life more than somebody who ain't never been tested. Been tested, arrested, and invested. Buddy Brown, Buddy Brown, go lay back down.

The vendor, an old man with every other tooth missing in his top front row, and murky yellow eyes, finally stopped laughing long enough to say, "Ah, shucks! Poppa Leon always say that—seven eleven, see ya in heaven. Say it to everybody he meet, day or night."

"How he lose his legs?" said Solly.

"Came back from the First World War like that," said the vendor just as a customer walked up.

It was eight-fifteen and Miss Etta's was already opened. The Palace, across the street getting the east sunlight, was locked and silent. The stumblebums and winos were drifting into Miss Etta's slowly from every direction. Solly and Man fell in line. Man thinking: Here come Spodee-O-Dee ready for a little of that spodee-o-dee, get my drift, spodee-o-dee, give me a little lift, spodee-o-dee.

This morning the dark interior was like a musty, damp cave, too cold. They spoke to Miss Etta and sat at the bar up front with the black window to their back. She was holding a beer mug under the tap spout when she called back, "How ya'll boys doing this morning? Just got off work? I'll be with you in a minute." Sucking her gums. For some reason didn't put her teeth in this morning.

Taking out his harmonica, Man ran it across his mouth. Cooking beans, eating em like collard greens. Said: "Listen to this." He warmed up. Nothing like a little music to sprinkle light in a dark place. People looked around. A new melody he done worked out, a song to make the springs screech on yo bed. Man put the harmonica away and said, "You know, I'm mo happy than I been for a long time, you know."

"What you mean?"

"I mean since me and Cleo got back together."

"Nigger, you just love you some Cleo."

"Sho nuff, I love me some Cleo."

"Love you some Cleo like you love yo Dirty Bird."

"Got to cut out the Dirty Bird," Man said, frowning. "Her going way like that teached me something bout myself. Worried me down to my last nerve but it learned me a lot. I love her mo than before because, you see, I done forgive myself."

"Forgive yoself for *what?*"

"For not liking myself. You know it kinda funny. I was always mistreating Cleo cause I was mistreating myself. Leastways I know now what I been doing wrong. I might not be able to change overnight but I'm sho gon try."

He saw Solly looking confused.

"It like this, Solly. When I mistreat Cleo I ain't doing nothing but hurting myself. Like yesterday. That didn't have to happen."

"Is you Manfred Banks or is you somebody different?" Solly pulled back in mock disbelief.

Man chuckled. "Yeah, I just made up my mind to try to do whas right. I mean, I know whas right. Guess I always did. But the difference now is I wants to do something bout it. I wants to keep my marriage. How bout you and Holly?"

"She coming back to me. I know that."

"I mean, you gon try to make it work this time?"

Solly frowned. "What you mean?"

"I mean what I said."

"If you mean am I gon give up stray pussy you gots to be crazy. A man is gon be a man."

"I'm a man and I'm gon try not to be tracted to stray pussy. Drinking is bad enough. Gon try to cut down. Be mo considerate of Cleo from now on."

"Fred, I swear, you sounding mo and mo like a fucking preacher every day. I always knowed you was meant to be some kinda preacher."

"Naw, Solly, you don't get it. I ain't got religion but I know whas right. My mama taught me what was right. I just forgot it for a long time. Maybe I had to run wild for a few years fore getting back to my mama's teaching."

"Well," said Solly, "here come the drinks. I'll drink to yo mama." He laughed.

When they had their Old Crow, Man said, "Hey, I forgot to tell you about Daffodil. Her nose is open for you, man." Man took a quick sip of the whiskey and it burned going down and he felt it settle and burn in his empty stomach. As he said this, he was struck by how cheap he felt delivering this message. "Daffodil's nose open a mile wide."

Solly laughed and lifted the glass to his mouth. "Yeah. I know. Here's to ya mama." And he laughed again. "Every time I walks out the door, Daffy door open and there she is grinning in my face."

"You gon tune her up?"

Solly laughed again. "Naw, man. I been cooling it here lately. You preach me on being good then ast a question like that? Well, tell you the truth, I been missing Holly. I talked with her a few days ago, and like I said, she coming on out, just a matter of time. Trying to get her to come on out here."

"Is she talking about it like she coming?"

"She might, she might, real soon. I been talking to her nearbout twice a week. Lost her job at Cook County Hospital. She on welfare. The folks in her business, all in the Kool-Aid, looking in her icebox to see if she bought any bacon, shit like that. She sick of it. Said her mother sent her a money order for forty dollars. She bought a pair shoes for Annabel. You know what that damned caseworker said? Said she musta got the money turning a trick and told her if it happened again they was gon cut her off. She bout ready to come out here."

"She be better off. You miss her, huh?"

Solly gave Man a sad smile. "I do. I'm trying to put aside a little bit of money to send for her. Soon as I get enough I'm gon get us a place.

I talked with Miss Ernestine Franklin about getting a partment in her building."

Man was happy to hear what he was hearing. Somehow if Solly could just turn a new corner, he felt, it might be easier for Man himself to change. Take my hand, lead me on. "What she say?"

"Said when I gets ready, if she gots what I want, she'll let me have it." Solly wagged his head.

Man laughed. "Well, well. Solomon Thigpen, sound like you turning a new leaf. I never knowed you turn down no woman interested in you. I must be looking at a changing man."

Solly chuckled. "Yeah. Maybe you is but don't put all yo money on it." He looked at Man and he suddenly seemed very serious, unlike Solly. Said: "Yet and still, I feel like I'm older, you know." Frowning, he drank his whiskey. Said: "Got a letter from my sister Billy Jean in Jackson. She just moved back in with Mama and Daddy cause that no-good nigger husband of her'n tried to kill her. It just made me sick on the heart. I don't want to be like that, Fred."

The stream of morning winos had stopped for the moment as they sat there drinking, then the door opened again and Man glanced back and saw Niggerdemos shuffling in, even more bent than usual. He waved to Miss Etta as he shuffled on down the length of the bar and past the juke-box and walked into the back room. Lord, Lord. Must be something terrible getting old. Don't care where you bury my body, it gon rise like the sun. Don't care where you bury my body, gon be getting up in the morning. Old folks' song. But Man wasn't even sure he believed in life after death. Sho believe in old age. You can see it. Yonder it goes, all bent over. But waking up in the sky after you die. Thas something else. Wants my lucky rabbit foot now, not in heaven. '

◉

Leaving Solly down on Twenty-fourth and Lake to shoot a game of pool with one of the regulars in the poolhall, Man started booting it north. When he reached Walt Calloway's barbershop, through the window he noticed Walt with an empty chair. Deciding to get a quick haircut—and he needed it!—he ducked in.

Halbert, the first barber, a heavyset, elderly man whose pants were always held up with red suspenders, and who always wore white nylon socks, was working on the head of another old man the guys in here called Gus.

Otis worked the middle chair. Now, Otis, he was the youngest of the three barbers. Twenty-nine or so, with five kids at home. Otis, a butter-scotch-complected, slender Negro, always wore himself a neat dress shirt and a little black bow tie. He was cutting Zachary's hair.

Man knew Zachary only from the barbershop. An average-size man, he was dark with pink splotches on his cheeks and the backs of his hands, maybe forty years old. Zachary worked out at the stockyards.

There were usually at least one or two, often more, guys in here just hanging around, not waiting for a haircut, just here to yack, lecture, preach, teach, and sometimes to listen. Two such fellows were sitting in the waiting chairs. Man remembered their names as Marion and Kenny. Marion was a waiter on one of the train lines. Kenny, like Zachary, worked out at the stockyards.

The minute Man stepped inside, he knew he had entered a verbal storm. A loud, knock-down-drag-out argument was in progress. Man grinned at the prospect. Said: "*Now,* what you niggers fighting about?"

Walt, sweeping around his chair, looked up and returned Man's grin, saying, "Zachary over there trying to say white folks more evil than niggers. Now, do you believe that, Fred?"

"I just walked in," Man said, looking at the waiting men, Marion and Kenny, and asking them: "Who next?"

"You!" shouted Walt, now, no doubt at least for the second time, shaking and snapping his white cloth free of the previous man's hair.

And Man bopped directly over to the chair and plopped down, letting Walt spread the cloth over his shoulders and down across his lap and secure it at the base of his neck.

Then Walt started combing and clicking away, while the argument raged on. Man closed his eyes and listened to the circus of voices, picking up on the lines of conflict.

Now Walt was saying, "What you think of that, Fred?"

"Think of *what?*"

Zachary said, "I *know* what I'm talking about. When niggers evil they be plotting behind your back. White folks right out in the open with they shit."

Otis shouted, "But I don't see no difference—"

Kenny said, "You all missing the point. Wickedness, moral depravity, sin, corruption, evil-mindedness, all these things you talking about, have nothing to do with the basic situation, which is—"

Walt: "Listen to Mister Intellectual—"

Man said, "Call it anything you wants to call it. I was born in the worst state white folks ever made, a state full of dumb rednecks who got no other way to feel like they is important than by shitting all over the Negroes, and—"

"White and black the same," insisted Otis, "when it come to devilment. All you got to do is look at—"

Kenny said, "I'm telling you, it's an animal thing. The human animal is like any other primate—"

"*Primate?* What's that?" shouted Walt.

Kenny said, "The human animal wants to survive. The way it survives is by brutally protecting its own interest."

Zachary said, "Don't see a whole lot of niggers able to protect they own interest. Just look—"

"Amen," said Marion. "It's like I told ya'll a minute ago: it ain't a black and white thing, it's a male and female thing. I say, the question is who the most evil, men or women, and women win every—"

Walt: ". . . and if you don't believe how evil, how venal, the white man is, just look at the record: using us as guinea pigs in experiments, selling us contaminated food. Every time you turn around some white cop done shot some black boy for nothing. I tell you the white man is a cannibal—"

Man said, "You cats can carry this argument anywhere you want it to go: You can say the South is more evil than the North, night is more evil than day, and—"

But Kenny was still talking above both Walt's and Marion's voices, saying: "So every thing this primate does is done out of greed, self-interest. The human animal can rationalize any vicious or baneful thing it does. But that's cultural. And to prove it—"

"Listen to him," said Walt, mocking: "'That's cultural.'"

Marion: ". . . and you can spend all yo paycheck to put some hair on a woman's head and she'll go behind yo back with some other—"

And Halbert was saying, "Ya'll better listen to Zachary. He knows what he's talking about. Ain't that right, Zachary?"

"Damned right!" Zachary shouted.

"And the black woman is more evil than—" Marion was saying.

"Blacker the berry, sweeter the juice," said Man.

Walt: ". . . and the proof that the white man is more evil than the nigger is in history. Ain't you niggers ever heard how the white man was created? The white man was created in a test tube by a mad scientist back at the beginning of creation. And he was put here to torment everybody else—"

They all laughed. Kenny bent double with his laughter, stamping his feet for emphasis.

Halbert said, "Walt, you ought to be shame of yourself talking that—"

Otis said, "It is true though, that the black man was the first man, God's man."

And Man said to Walt: "Don't take it all off, Walt."

"What difference it make, nigger? You going to be ugly with or with-*out* hair."

And everybody laughed again.

MAN WALKED INTO HIS BEDROOM.  Cleo was standing facing Karina, who was sitting on the bed with her legs dangling off the side. Cleo was lowering a cotton dress over the child's head. She stopped and looked at Man,

CHAPTER TWENTY-EIGHT

asked where was Solly. Solly stayed down on Twenty-fourth and Lake to shoot a game of pool. She gave him a weak smile. "How'd it go? I expected you earlier."

He stared at her a minute as though he hadn't heard her question, then said: "What?"

"Thought you'd get home before now."

He yawned, stretching his arms above his head. "Stopped for a haircut."

"Looks nice," she said, giving him a weak smile.

Karina said, "Daddy. Hi."

"The job. You *did* go to work last night, didn't you?"

"Yeah, yeah, I did." He looked around the room as though he had misplaced something. "I'm tired." He turned and bumped into the chair by the door. "Fuck," he said.

Karina said, "Fuck." And grinned.

Man looked at Cleo, expecting her to say something. She said: "See? You got to watch what you say."

Karina said pointing her finger at Man. "See," she said. Then again: "See. See. Fuck."

"Honey, don't say that word." Cleo finished pulling the dress on.

Man was headed for the kitchen to get a drink. He'd felt good just before coming home. Now shame made him angry—angry at Cleo, his witness.

Karina looked up at her. "Fuck," she said.

Cleo gave Man a look. "Will you keep her this morning? I've got somewhere to go."

He turned around. "Where you going?"

She hesitated. Didn't look at him. Held Karina's arm as she slid down from the bed to the floor. Cleo said: "Church." She kept her eyes focused on the top of Karina's head.

"Church?" said Man as though it was something nasty on his tongue. "Today ain't *Sunday*. What you going to church for?"

"I promised to help Sister Spalding bake some cookies for the nursery school this morning before I go to work."

"You *what?*" He raised his voice.

"What's wrong with that?" She looked at him with a steady gaze. She didn't look one bit afraid of him.

He told himself: She's lying. Sure as shit, she's lying. "Cleo, is you some kind of fool? What you look like up there helping them bake cookies? Huh?" Yeah, she lying or I'm flying. He kept watching her eyes.

"Just because you don't believe in helping anybody isn't any cause for me to be selfish."

Before he knew it he raised his hand to hit her, but suddenly he saw his father's face and his father's fist raised against his mother's terrified face.

Now, seeing his wife ducking, getting out of his way, Man shuddered and pulled back, trembling. He slowly sank to his knees then lay down on the floor and stretched his legs and arms out and started crying.

His second mind was talking to him: If you wants to see how much she gon miss you, stick yo finger in a glass of water then look at the hole it leave.

Yes, his second mind was talking loud in his ear: Let the past go. Stay in the shade of the tree of love. You gon drive her way. Gon be sorry. And sorry cheap as talk.

He could see her standing there looking down at him. He couldn't read her expression.

He whispered, "I sorry, I sorry, baby. I would never hit you. I don't know what got into me. I sorry."

She said, "Please, Fred! *Please* get up!"

Still deeply ashamed of himself, he sat up then stood up, acutely aware of his drunkenness and that he was hurting his wife even though he hadn't hit her, that his daughter was lying on the floor, screaming at the top of her lungs and kicking the floor. It was as though he *had* hit Cleo. He was suddenly scared of himself. He thought, Bless my soul. Let the Midnight Special shine its light on me. Ugly thing inside done cut loose. The worst part was: He'd *wanted* to hit her.

Man reached out for her and pulled her into his arms but Cleo quickly pulled away. She went and squatted down beside Karina. "It's all right, honey. Come on. Let Mama hold you." And she picked up the child and held her against her bosom.

Cleo sat on the side of the bed holding Karina against her. The girl rested her face on her mother's shoulder and gradually stopped crying. Finally she stuck her finger in her mouth and started sucking it.

Man reached over and touched Karina and she jumped away from his hand and hit at it.

Cleo shifted the child's position now and held Karina against her other shoulder.

He turned and walked into the kitchen and got the bottle of Old Crow down from the kitchen cabinet, found a water glass and poured about two inches worth in and took a long swallow, then walked back to the bedroom.

She was still sitting where he left her, just looking at him. Karina was resting her face against Cleo's shoulder, with a thumb in her mouth.

He said, "I sorry, Cleo."

She started crying, then suddenly stopped herself. Said: "I can't stay here Fred and take this. I've tried hard to give you a chance."

"I just ast you to forgive me. Said I sorry. It's not like I hit you. I *didn't* hit you."

"Fred, you don't understand. Next time you will."

"I said I'm axing you to forgive me. Just answer my question. Do you forgive me?"

She looked at the floor. "I forgive you, Fred, but it doesn't change anything. I don't want us to lose everything we have. I want you to give me a chance to be a good wife. Remember you talked about trust the day you lost your job at Lomax? I thought about what you said. It's true. I have to trust you. I shouldn't have accused you of the white woman. That was unfair. I had no proof. I had no good reason not to believe you."

"I *know* what you saying, Cleo."

"Do you?"

◉

He was surprised to see Jorena behind the bar when he walked in. Had expected the dark silent one. "Hey, lady whatchu doing here so early?"

No one else was in the bar, no finger-poppers, no red-eyed serious drinkers, just Jorena looking serious as cancer.

She was wearing one of those slick jet-black beaded dresses with a sweetheart neckline and fitted bodice. That was all of it he could see.

She looked up from writing something on a pad. "Oh, Herbert's coming in later. He had to go downtown this morning on business. How're *you* doing?"

Feeling like somebody who'd been planted and dug up, he climbed onto a stool and dropped his elbows on the bartop and, turning the corners of his mouth up, looked at her. Said: "I could be doing better."

With a steady hand, she was now pouring Old Crow into a glass. He watched her, thinking of all the things pretty as bean blossoms, all the things dangerous as beehives.

Jorena looked concerned. "What's the matter?"

He hadn't realized it, but he must have been looking like the guy who caught the dude who was playing with his stuff out the window. She sat the glass near his big, rough, folded hands.

"Life, I guess." He looked up, glanced at her, and shifted away toward the reflection of himself in the mirror.

"You feeling shot through the grease so early in the morning, Fred?"

"Yeah, I keep doing things to fuck up my own self. You know?"

"Like what?"

He took a deep breath, chest swelling, and let it out. He felt he could talk to Jorena, felt she was a friend. She was somebody who wanted nothing from him. And though he'd never thought to talk with her about anything on his mind, he'd long felt he could and that she would be interested enough to listen. Man said: "Ah, I had a fight with my wife this morning. Almost hit her." He looked quickly into Jorena's eyes. "I *didn't* though!"

"But you *wanted* to, didn't you?"

"I sho did." He shook his head. "I don't know . . ."

Jorena leaned closer to him and placed her small hands on top of both of his. "Listen to me, Fred. You're a *good* man. You're not like most men. You have a *gift,* and you have soul."

He'd never heard her talk like this or in this tone of voice before. He took a quick sip. He blinked, looking at her. She brings me down slow. He took another quick sip. Yeah, Jorena was all right. He laughed a little bit. She was still watching him. Maybe it was the daylight on her, but she looked older this morning. Good-looking woman make a mule kick down his stable, he thought, smiling to himself. Good-looking woman make a blind man see. Jorena was sho nuff first class.

He lifted his glass to her, smiling. "You give me inspiritualration."

She smiled faintly. "Inspiration, huh? Well, that's the way you make me feel when you sing, Fred."

He waved away her compliment. "My liquor be singing sometime."

"No, Fred. I listen to you. It's never liquor. You sing straight up from your guts. It comes out of everything that you are."

He was feeling better already. "Tell me some mo." He grinned.

"I'm *serious,*" she said, looking at him with mock skepticism. "Not that there's anything wrong with whiskey. I'm in the whiskey business. I'm the liquor lady, inherited the right from my daddy. Carrying on the tradition. But I'm honest about it. Some people can handle it, others can't. You're one of the ones who can't, Fred. Sometimes it takes a long time to know that."

He suddenly felt naked, completely exposed before her, and she kept looking him dead in the eye. He shifted on his seat and picked up the glass but hesitated before taking a sip. He said, "Yeah, yeah, yeah, I know what you're saying: If it make you feel good, watch out, it cain't be good for you. Old folks always say God didn't make yo body for liquor, tobacco, and dope. Well, I'm *not* religious."

"One of the reasons I left Creighton University," she said simply and flatly. "But I know a few things about people." She suddenly stopped. "But, hey, who am I to tell you not to drink?"

He looked into the layers of gold light in the glass, as he turned it slightly, watching the colors change.

Jorena said, "With your voice you could be famous."

He almost blushed.

"I don't care bout being famous. I jes wants to feel free, get along with my wife, care for my kid, stuff like that. Don't wants my body having to do one thing while my mind be doing something else."

"That's what I mean," said Jorena. "You ever seriously try to make a living singing?"

He shook his head no, not sure if he had or not, not sure how serious his seriousness had been, remembering cold days in Chicago when he felt like the whole world had rap-jacked him half to death whenever he went searching for a break in the blues business.

Jorena was saying, "If you could make a living singing, then your body and mind *both* would be in harmony. When I see you back there on that stage, I know you're complete, the happiest man on earth, while you're singing."

This talk was beginning to make him feel nervous. He didn't want to think about why. Jorena was sounding a little bit too much like Cleo used to sound back in Chicago.

She was saying: ". . . and I know there're other things in life beside ambition. If I believed ambition was everything I'd've stayed at Creighton."

Somebody had mentioned that she'd gone to college but didn't finish. Her education, he thought, was obvious. He was curious. "Was yo daddy still living when you dropped out?"

"Yes. It really broke his heart too. He wanted me to become a lawyer. After my mother died Daddy seemed to focus all his feelings on me."

North Omaha legend had it that Jorena's family was among the earliest. Jorena's father's father had come out here as a porter working on the trains back before the turn of the century. Jorena's mother, a frail, mysterious mulatto, had died in childbirth. People didn't know much about her mother's folks. Bob Jones, her father, had gotten his financial start with his father's help. Bob Jones, the grandson of a slave, had been *the* Negro, or at least one of the few Negroes, who went downtown and met with white men, good ones and peckerwoods alike, descendants of both patterollers and abolitionists, in fancy rooms at the Fontenelle, to speak for the colored folks out north. The white men thought of him as a leader. Many colored folks did too. But he had himself some enemies. Man had heard from Debbie that Bob Jones had been one of the leaders of the Urban League and on the board of the National Association for the Advancement of Colored People, helped finance both North Omaha Negro newspapers. A deacon in the leading Methodist church, he had the whole church rebuilt so that it was the best-looking one in the area. The only black person on the Omaha Grain Exchange, he invested early in real estate. When the colored boys started coming back from the First World War, Bob Jones sponsored a colorful North Omaha parade down Twenty-fourth Street to celebrate their victorious return. On his death-bed, winter 1940, he left instructions for another such parade when this one ended. And Jorena, with help from a few other black businesspeople, carried out her father's wishes four years ago when the boys started coming back. And Jorena was raised by her father and her aunt, Jorena's father's sister, who'd lived with them through those years. By the time he died of a heart attack he was the richest black man out this way. Bob Jones, folks said, died disappointed, if not heartbroken. He'd never gotten over the death of his wife. And Jorena's dropping out of college had not helped matters.

Man was curious. Said: "Jorena, you here reading me. What about yoself? Whatchu wants outta life?"

She propped her chin on the heels of her hands, elbows on bartop, rolled her eyes toward the ceiling then refocused on him and said, "Why don't you ask what's *really* on your mind? You want to know if I'm a lesbian, don't you?"

He blushed. He hadn't been thinking that. Scratching his head, he smiled. "I, uh—"

She cut him off: "I know what people say about me, Fred. I've got ears. North Omaha is a small town unto itself. Everything that happens here happens to everybody. I'm *the* lesbian in the community. The bull dyke. At first I had a lot of trouble accepting that role. In fact the role was assigned me long before I ever knew who I was sexually, before I had a sexual identity, back when I was just a girl in elementary school. It followed me everywhere. Even the white kids at Creighton whispered about me. I'm not sure if I was born attracted to women or the whispering caused me to feel the way I feel."

He was looking straight at her. Said: "I understand that."

"You do?"

"Yeah. You see, something like that happened to me. From the beginning everybody said I wont gon mount to nothing. Specially my daddy. That nigger laid into my ass all the time. Got so everybody down on me, teachers, the other kids. I musta said, Shit, if this what they think of me, then fuck it, I'm gon be what they say I am. I cut up a lot, beat up other kids, threw erasers at the teacher when his back was turnt. Stuff like that. Guess I bought they picture of me. And that's why I got into music, you know. I been trying to get myself out of being like that, the way they made me be. You know what I mean?"

"I sure do."

"Listen here," he said. "You ever been in love with a man?"

She smiled sadly. "That's the kind of question a man would ask. As if it proved something. Why didn't you ask me if I ever been in love?"

"Have you?"

"Been in love, you mean?"

"Yeah." But now he felt like he was prying and didn't feel right about it. He picked up the whiskey and took a big drink. He'd gone too far, he thought. But he kept looking at her.

She lowered her head and said, "I was in love once."

He wouldn't press her to talk about it. She looked like she didn't want to say any more. And that was all right with him.

Somebody came in and Man turned and looked toward the front. Herb walked in, glancing at them. Said: "Good morning." Mean-looking, grim as ever. He walked on past Man back to the end of the bar and went on in the back.

Jorena's face changed. She stood up straight and gave Man a faint smile. And her body was saying the conversation was over.

In a few minutes Herb came out, hands behind his back, tying his gray half-apron around his waist. He looked like a man ready to do the Saturday night fish fry.

◉

Still feeling restless as a hungry tiger, he walked over to his sister's shop and opened the door. Deb, Trudy, and the new hairdresser, Abigail Jackson, were standing behind their swivel chairs. Each had a customer.

"Oowee! Lord, have mercy, look who's here. Speak of the devil," said Trudy, grinning from ear to ear, glancing up at him, as she continued working at an elderly woman's short gray hair.

All six women in the shop laughed as Man closed the door and sort of stood there slouched to one side, grinning at Trudy. She gave her chair a little push, sending it into a half spin, so she could work and see him at the same time.

Playing like she was offended, Debbie said, "That's my baby brother there you talking about."

All six women laughed.

Man walked over and sat down in the manicure customer's chair but he turned the chair so he could look at his sister.

Abigail Jackson said, "You want a manicure, Fred? Cause if you do you outta luck."

Everybody laughed again, but he just grinned.

Debbie said, "Honey, my brother think that's sissy stuff."

Abigail made a face. "Manicure? Manicure ain't no sissy stuff. *Shoot!* I do my husband's nails every week. And I *know* he all man."

Trudy said, "Lots of men come in here and get their nails done. It ain't nothing—"

Abigail cut her off, saying, "But ya'll got to admit mens is different. You can take a big old rough man and paint his nails and ain't nobody going to blink an eye, but if you put some polish on some little old dainty fellow everybody start calling him a freak."

"Ain't it the truth," said Debbie. "Freddy?"

"Yeah?"

"You here for any special reason, baby?"

"Naw. Just stopped by . . ."

"Well ain't that something," said Trudy. "Just stopped by to see us work."

They all laughed again.

"How's Cleo and that sweet baby girl of yours?" Debbie said.

"They okay."

Debbie frowned. "You all right?" She looked suddenly concerned. "You're not sick or anything are you?"

"Naw, I ain't sick."

Abigail said, "Big strong healthy man like Fred? You can *look* at him and tell he ain't sick, girl."

The customer in Debbie's chair looked at him and said, "Lord knows it's the truth."

Laughter.

Debbie said, "Freddy, uh, did you want to speak to me, I mean, in private?"

He grinned. "Naw, Deb. I told you I just stopped by to see how ya'll doing."

"You never come in here when your wife is working," said Abigail. "You come to watch *us* work but you don't come to watch *her* work."

He just looked at Abigail and said nothing.

Trudy said, "Ain't nothing wrong with that. Lots of times I don't even wants to hear my husband's name, let alone see him."

Again they laughed.

"*Trudy!*" shouted Debbie.

Man didn't feel offended. He was just sitting there watching his sister and the other women and feeling pretty amazed by how they passed the time talking and laughing without seriously hurting anybody's feelings.

"All right, all right," Trudy said to Debbie, "I was just trying to say—"

"You said enough, thank you," said Debbie.

More laughter.

Abigail said, "Fred, don't pay Trudy no mind, honey."

"I'm not." And Man stood up. Said: "I'm gon catch ya'll later."

"Okay, baby brother," said Debbie. "Bring that cute girl to see me. Don't stay away too long."

They all said bye as he reached for the doorknob.

◉

Man strolled home and went to bed.

Hinky dinky parley voo. See if I can stop you. He is kissing Jorena fully on the mouth and his eyes are closed and she is moaning. Breathless, when he opens his eyes, he sees his wife's face smiling at him, and it's not odd. Yet he knows, rather thinks, he's still dreaming because she's already gone to work. Been here and gone.

TWO AND HALF WEEKS LATER, THIRD
week in July, Man and Solly were standing
on the train platform at ten-thirty in the
morning, a beautiful blue morning full of white
light, waiting for Holly and Annabel to arrive on the
ten-forty. Man had borrowed Lyle's car.

**CHAPTER
TWENTY-
NINE**

They heard the train whistle before they saw the train. Then there was the train coming along the curving track.

Now the train was charging in and Man looked at Solly. He could see Solly was excited, just like a kid about to open a present on Christmas morning. Made Man happy too, just the sight of Solly's dancing eyes. Solly's sleeves were rolled up like he was ready for anything.

> I'm going to the station, going to meet my baby girl,
> I'm going down to the station.
> At the station gon meet my baby girl.
> If she ain't at that old station gon sit right down,
> And stay right there till she comes into town.

When Man saw Holly two cars down the platform he started grinning and nudged Solly and pointed. And Solly broke out through the crowd, running to meet his wife. Boogie, Solly, boogie! Cleo had come in like this too. Wonder if they gon make it? Boogie, Solly, boogie.

Holly was carrying Annabel in her arms and a porter wearing a red cap was walking beside her pushing her four suitcases on a two-wheeler.

Man watched. Nearly knocking her over, Solly kissed his wife on the mouth then kissed his daughter's cheek. Man watched as Solly hugged them both. This was the Solly he liked best, a Solly who seemed suddenly more alive with warmth and tenderness. But then maybe that's what attracted so many women to Solly: Beneath the jive, this tenderness. He didn't always show it but he always had it.

Holly was laughing nervously.

Annabel looked serious as she studied her father from her perch in her mother's arms.

Man continued to watch from a distance. Holly was all dressed up, sharp as a tack, on the right track, in a light blue fitted suit with a single button, lace at the neck, stockings and heels. Man remembered the suit. Holly had gotten it at a Salvation Army store for five dollars.

The train whistle blew again.

◉

Man parked Lyle's car behind a pickup on the side of Miss Ernestine Franklin's building on Evans just off Twenty-fourth, one block south of Cleo's church, North Star Baptist, on the other side. Miss Ernestine's place was really just a big old two-story country house converted into tiny apartment units. Man had seen the one Solly rented on the top floor. Fact was, he'd been with Solly the week before when Solly put money down on it and left a damage deposit in Miss Ernestine's shaky brown hand.

As they now got out of the car, Man noticed Miss Ernestine in her first-floor apartment peeking out from behind her lace curtain, checking them out. He smiled, thinking, Yeah, yeah, it's us and we ain't high-tone. Ain't no dog looking for a bone. Look all you want, Miss Siddity from the hick city.

They walked up the sidewalk, carrying Holly's four suitcases, and around to the front and up on the porch. Miss Ernestine met them at the door, frowning. Always frowning, even when she seemed to feel all right. That frown had left a permanent crease between her eyebrows. Glaring through her thick glasses, she looked down at the small person, Annabel, and wrinkled her nose as though she smelled her.

A big light brown woman with big veined hands, Miss Ernestine was now refocusing on Holly and Solly. She continued to hold the door open with one of those big hands.

People said she had grown children who never spoke to her, children she hadn't seen in more than twelve or fifteen years. People also said she was a distant relative of Black Elk. And come to think of it, she did look like some sort of Indian. Supposed to have also been an unacknowl-edged relative of the Fontenelles. Sure had a high opinion of herself. She moved her lips, probably adjusting her false teeth, then said, "Mister Thigpen your apartment is ready. I just checked it. This must be your wife, and—"

"Yeah. Miss Ernestine, my wife, Holly. This here is Annabel," said Solly in an unnatural voice.

Man looked at Solly. His ever-loving guitar was in its old raggedy case strung across his back. Guitar man, guitar man, whatcha gon do without a plan?

Miss Ernestine glared again at the child, then drew her lips back from her big, very white teeth like a dog giving warning not to come a step closer. Man almost laughed, instead he bit his bottom lip and grunted, shifting the weight of the suitcases. She no doubt thought she was smiling. He was carrying two, Solly two, and Holly herself was carrying a large handbag.

Then Miss Ernestine turned around and marched herself back down the hall. They stepped inside the hallway and stood there at the base of the steep stairway, unsure of what to do next. Then Miss Ernestine came back carrying two keys on a ring. "I had an extra key made. Here." She looked at Holly and said, "Well, I sure hope you *vote.*"

Holly said, "Pardon me?" Her eyes stretched and they looked like the clear white of two boiled eggs.

"I said so many of these no-account Negroes in this town don't bother to vote. I sure hope you're the voting kind. We need more voters in Omaha."

Holly didn't know whether she should laugh or what. She looked at Man. "Vote for ... vote for what?" said Holly.

"Never mind," said Miss Ernestine, and she turned and walked quickly back down the hall and into her apartment, slamming the door behind her.

Strange woman. Man laughed and shook his head. He'd heard about Miss Ernestine's passion for politics, her dislike of young people, everyday good-time people. When she was young she'd stood up in Reverend Earl Little's church and told him his Garvey ideas were misleading the Negroes of Omaha. And when the Klan killed Reverend Little she went to the funeral and said what a great man he was. Old-timers still remembered that. She'd been among a group of North Omaha citizens who'd tried for years to get Bob Jones' Entertainment Palace and Miss Etta's closed down.

Man and Solly struggled up the squeaky steps with the heavy luggage, set it down at the lopsided door.

Solly unlocked the door, watching Holly's face. With a half-grin, Man watched them both and they walked across the linoleum-covered floor into the lopsided living room.

Holly walked over to the doorway of the kitchen and looked in.
Solly followed her.

Annabel whimpered and started wiggling in Holly's arms. Holly said, "*Say* what you want, girl? You can talk."

Holly then set the child down onto her feet and unsteadily Annabel gained her balance, holding onto her mother's leg for a second then letting go.

Solly said, "It a gas stove."

Holly said, "Uh huh." And she walked on into the kitchen. "This is not bad. Sure is better than what we had in Chicago, more room and cost less."

"Glad you like it, sugar," said Solly, standing behind her.

Man turned and went to one of the two living room windows. Between the two windows was a boarded-up door leading out to a fire escape. Looking to his left, from there he could see the bedroom area. It was separated from the living room by only a wide archway. Just inside the room, against the left wall, was a regular-size bed with a tarnished iron headboard and foot railing. An old shabby dresser with a cracked mirror sat in the dark space against the far wall.

He turned and looked down at Lyle's car on the street, then at the row of frame houses across the street. He looked at the fire escape, its black painted iron, and felt an itching inside his shirt where the buckshot wounds had all healed and left black embossed scars. Sonofabitch.

He turned back to the room.

"Got yo harmonica?" Solly said.

"Always." Man took it out and held it up.

Solly took his guitar out of the case and hit a few warm-up chords.

Holly said, "Not now, Solly. We got to get moved in."

"All right, all right," said Solly.

"Tell you what, while yall unpack I'm gon serenade you," said Man and settled down in the nearby ratty chair and leaned forward with his elbows on his knees and started blowing a little Decatur Street barrelhouse, flirting with McTill's Pinetop's Boogie-Woogie. Man felt lifted up, like he was flying.

When he looked up he saw Solly and Holly kissing in the kitchen doorway. He stopped playing. "Okay, you lovebirds. I'm gon get going, let yall make up for some lost time." He walked over to the doorway and put his hand on the doorknob. "Eight-thirty tonight, Solly?"

Annabel was standing near her mother, staring at Man.

"Huh? Yeah, Fred. I'll be ready."

◉

A few days later:

It was just a little after midnight, and the janitors were in the snack bar on the fifth floor.

Percy was sitting on a hard chair facing the guys—Orson and Bernard were on one of the couches. Lorenzo was sitting beside Percy, also on a hard chair. Man felt depressed, sick, tired, and dejected as he sat on one of the couches beside Solly.

Lorenzo, probably trying to imitate Percy, waved a hand at them. "Okay, you motherfuckers, hurry up and eat and get your asses back to work."

Man looked at Orson and Bernard when they laughed, and he wondered what they wanted out of life, if they ever had a thought about the future or anything. He looked around slowly at everybody, Solly too, and wondered and wondered why none of this was all right or even funny. Got to do better. Send a letter. If you can't spurt, squirt. If you outta place find some grace, waiting for daybreak for ya soul to take, cut a curve if ya got the nerve, get there quicker with a little likker, shoot loose with a little juice, stand tall if ya look like ya gon fall. Learn so ya won't burn. He felt sick. He had to find his way out of this nightmare.

Percy gave Lorenzo a sideways look and just shook his head.

Man was sitting on the couch eating a Baby Ruth. He'd been feeling sick to the stomach for hours and wasn't all that hungry but thought he'd better eat something. Before leaving home, he'd drunk about a half pint of Old Crow and had two cans of beer with some cold beans from a pot Cleo made the day before. They had not sat down to eat together since he'd almost hit her. Once when he woke up and found her sitting at the kitchen table eating lunch, he sat down across from her and she got up right away and took her plate out on the back porch. He hadn't had much interest in food lately. And just as often as he remembered, he forgot to bring a sandwich for midnight lunch.

Suddenly he stopped eating the candy, felt like he was going to throw up. Sick as a pup. Hit with grit—or was it shit. Gotta haul ass or fall. He tossed the rest of the candy into the trash can over by the coffee machine.

Orson said, "You shoulda been a basketball player, motherfucker."

Man felt cold sweat on his back and his stomach seemed to be turning inside out. "Hey, Percy," he said, "I'm sick, man. Feel like I'm gon throw up. Think I better go home."

Percy frowned.

Lorenzo giggled and tried to make his voice heavier, saying: "Hey, Mister Bossman, I gots a bellyache, please suh, let me go home," mocking Man.

Man said, "Watch your mouth, you little sucker. I can mop all these floors with yo ass in one hand and yo head in the other. And when I finish I can run yo ass through the ringer and then hang you up to dry."

Everybody laughed.

Lorenzo puffed out his chest. "I was just teasing you, Jack, you can't take a joke. Hey, yall, see how Fred is. He can't take a joke. He ain't regular peoples. Funny dude."

Man said to Percy, "I'm gon go home."

Percy frowned, looking at him. "Leave that panther piss lone, you'd be all right. Come in here and cain't work cause you got too much of that hooch in your guts."

Man looked at Solly. Solly was keeping quiet, as usual when they were in a group. They'd finished a half-pint before Percy picked them up at

Solly's. Sipping and slipping boohoo brew. Man figured Percy must have smelled it when they got in the car. The old sniff whiff.

Then Solly, surprisingly, said, "Listen who talking. Now, Percy you know damned well, man, you drink as much as anybody."

"Yeah, but I don't do it when I knows I got to come to work and be up all night. Ain't no kinda way you can do that heavy drinking and come here and take care business likes you spose to do. That's why I don't do it. If I'm gon drink, I do it in the morning when I gets off, then I sleep. You hear me, I *sleep* me a good eight hours. Then I'm fresh. You niggers just ain't learnt how to handle this kinda job. I *been* telling you."

Man stood up and started walking toward the corridor where the elevators were. Choo choo choo, bugaloo, best go home, rest. Never pass this test. Harder you try the lower you fly.

Percy said, "You can't get out by yourself. I gots to call Oscar to let you out." Percy got up, looking at his watch. "Last bus north leaves in twenty minutes. You might make it, otherwise you booting it, lessen you can get one of them white cabdrivers over by the train station or the bus station to pick up your black ass." He gave Man a glazed, curious look. "Come on. Let me see which floor he on."

Lorenzo called after them, "Don't let him shit you, Percy. Nigger just going home to check up on his old lady."

Man could hear Orson and Bernard laughing. Solly said, "Why don't yall just shut the fuck up. You ain't got no business talking about something you don't know the first thing about. So, just shut the fuck up."

And that was the last Man heard as he and Percy entered the corridor and walked down to the elevator. They looked up at the elevator dials.

> How long, how long—?
> How long, oh how long—?

Oscar had stopped number one on the mezzanine. It was a station for him. He often sat there in a straight-back chair and gazed out on the night street or dozed.

They got into number two, the one they'd come up in, and rode down to the basement.

When they got off, Percy was lighting a joint. He stopped and inhaled deeply then passed it to Man.

Man looked at Percy and hesitated. He didn't care much for reefer but he was feeling so bad, what the hell. It might make him feel better. It'd been maybe a year since somebody had offered him marijuana. He took it and sucked the smoke up into his head and held it there long as he could. Percy was grinning and watching him. "That cure anything you gots," said Percy.

Man passed the joint back to Percy.

In the dressing room, while Man changed, they finished the joint and got back on the elevator and rode up two floors.

They walked over to the exit where Oscar was sitting, watching them approach. He looked like an aging St. Bernard. Man could see from his dazed look that the nightwatchman had been sleeping and was probably awakened by the sound of the elevator or the sound of his and Percy's walking. In the silent store, leather against tile echoed throughout the entire floor.

Percy started talking before they got over to the old man. Said: "Hey, Oscar. Got a sick man wants to go home."

Oscar stood up, looking at Man carefully. "What's the matter?"

"Stomach," said Man, pressing his hand against his belly. Oscar was looking at him suspiciously. Thinks I might have something, gold watch, diamond ring, a refrigerator, maybe a mattress or something like that stashed under my shirt. Man heard that a few janitors before his time had been arrested for trying to leave the store with shoplifted things hidden in their clothes. What? A coffeepot? An eggbeater? A pair of living room drapes? An ironing board? A washing machine? Arrest me, test me. Send me to jail but bring the bail. I may be a thief but I ain't on relief.

"Sorry," said Oscar. "I got to search you."

Man said, "Go right ahead." He held his arms out. Search me, search me, just make it fast, don't make it last, cause I might throw up on yo pink ass faster than you can blink.

Oscar patted him down both sides and inside his pants legs then stood back. Said: "All right. Hope you feel better."

Man didn't say anything.

Oscar turned and unlocked the heavy plate glass door and pulled it open. Man walked through into the cool night air and headed toward the bus stop half a block up. If it was on time it should be coming in five minutes.

> Feel like dice throwed in gambling,
> Just like dice throwed in gambling.
> Lord, Lord . . .

HE UNLOCKED THE DOOR AND LET
himself in, closed it, locked it, and stood
still in the dark, quiet hall. To his right was
his daughter's room. Thought he could hear her
breathing but wasn't sure. He felt sick but didn't

**CHAPTER
THIRTY**

want to wake his daughter, if he could help it, by walking too heavily to
the bathroom. Felt like he was about to throw up.

> Feel like the dice throwed in gambling.
> Sho got to stop my rambling ways.
> Feel just like dice throwed in gambling . . .

So he tipped down the hall and turned into the bathroom. In the doorway, stopped and listened for Cleo's breathing across the hall in their
bedroom. Heard nothing. Then he remembered Lorenzo's signifying.
Stupid bastard. Yet . . . Man turned and eased across the hall and stood
in the bedroom doorway, trying to focus on the dark room. He could see
the windows, the shades with the streetlight illuminating them a black-
yellow. Below the windows was the bed but he couldn't see it except in
outline. He held his breath to listen for Cleo's breathing. Didn't want to
wake her. But just to be sure. He heard nothing. Then, softly: "Cleo?"
and again: "Cleo?"

He reached out and threw the light switch and the ceiling bulb—covered with a hazy glass dome—threw its yellowish light down on the
room. The bed was empty, completely made. She cross the hall. Had to
be. She wouldn't go away and leave Karina.

Turning his back on the bedroom, he lumbered down the hall into the
kitchen then walked in that direction and stopped in front of the room
that had been Solly's. The door was open. He reached in and switched on
the light. Empty. But it still smelled of Solly, of his sweat.

Man turned off the light and hotfooted it up the hall past the bathroom
and into Karina's room and directly to her bed. He leaned over the bed,
trying to see her in the dark. "Baby?" He couldn't hear her breathing now.
He reached out and touched the bed and found it flat. She wasn't there.
He then shot across the room and threw the light switch. The bed was
completely made. In its stillness, the room seemed completely empty.

Racing back down the hall and into his own bedroom he stood there looking around dumbly, sensing the same emptiness. Done been here and gone. Panic wrapped a big fist around his heart, and it beat faster and faster under the tight grip. His throat was suddenly dry and constricted. He felt hot all over.

Convulsions hit his stomach from the back of his spine. He bent double and ran across the hall to the bathroom. But he missed the toilet bowl. The vomit—rancid whiskey, candy, beans, beer slime—shot all over the toilet seat and the floor around it.

> Done been here and gone back,
> Done been here and now gone back.
> Been here and gone back on the fast track.

He fell down on his knees before the toilet and held on to the seat, and more stinking slime and mucus-slick chunks of god-knows-what poured up across his helpless tongue and into the bowl. Eyes closed, tears drained down his cheeks. She gone. He began to sob. His whole chest seemed to contract then swell with sobbing. A man's heart and soul bigger than the world but he ain't nothing but a pimple on the ass of time. And he threw up again and again.

> She gone,
> She gone.
> Have mercy, she gone.

He sat there gagging a long time with his face over the bowl after nothing else would come up. A pimple on the ass of time.

Then he pulled himself up, holding onto the seat, and finally stood on his own shaky legs, turned and wobbled out into the hall and down to the kitchen to the cabinet, took down the Old Crow. Old Crow, Old Crow, you so-and-so, you so-and-so. About a third left. A little old pimple on the ass of time, thas all. He poured about half of it into a water glass, and, leaning against the counter, drank long, feeling the liquor cutting its way down through his raw insides. If I was a fish. If the river was rye, I drink till I die. Ain't nothing but a pimple. He had to get a hold on himself. Think. Daffy next door. Yeah.

> Done been here and gone.
> She gone.

Carrying the glass with him, he walked unsteadily up the hall, opened his door, stepped across the hall, and made a fist and knocked two times. High as a kite, get up ramble all night. All night. Nothing. He knocked again, this time louder—three times. If it ain't you, fuck, it's somebody else. I swear. He knocked again. Come on, bitch. Even as the word *bitch* moved across his silent tongue, he disliked its taste, disliked himself for using it. Is yo mama a bitch? Is yo sister a bitch?

He heard Daffy say, "Who's there?"

"Me, Manfred."

The door opened and Daffodil, in a pink bathrobe, stood holding the knob, eyes stretched with animal fear. She was holding her robe together at the throat, not, it seemed, out of modesty, but out of fear. She no doubt saw something in his face that scared her.

He said, "What the matter with you? Looks like you seed a ghost."

"*You,*" she said and covered her mouth. "You look like you seen a ghost yourself. Talking bout me."

"Where my wife?"

She frowned suddenly. Her eyes shifted away from his face, blinking. "How should I know? I don't keep track of Cleo. Ain't she home?"

"She not home and you lying."

Daffodil's mouth opened and stayed that way. Eyes stretched. Neck snapped. Then: "You calling me a *lie?* Listen, Fred, I don't have to stand here taking insults from you. Find your *own* wife."

And she tried to close the door but Man's big foot suddenly came to rest just inside the threshold, blocking her effort. Daffodil turned red, lips poking out. "Nigger, if you don't *move* your foot, I'm gonna call the police."

"My wife in there. Tell the truth."

"Your wife is not in my house. Move your foot."

But he pushed the door all the way open and walked in past her. Just inside was a chair against the wall. He sat his glass down on it. Then he looked at her. She scared. He knew the look. His stomach erupted again but nothing came up but bile. He turned his head from her and lifted the bottle to his lips and drank, working the bile down with another slug of whiskey. Like swallowing your anger.

"Nasty pig," said Daffodil, rolling her eyes at him.

Man looked down the hall and called: "Cleo?"

The apartment answered back with a damp, warm, poorly lighted silence.

Then he heard Daffodil's boy, Ajax, say, "Mama?"

Man stumbled down the hall, turning on lights, looking first in the little bedroom by the front door. Empty. Though drunk, in his second mind he suddenly disliked what he was doing. How awful he must seem to Daffodil. But he kept on, driven by some madness he couldn't stop. He checked the bathroom. Nothing. Must be outta my mind. Then he checked Daffodil's bedroom, seeing her unmade bed. Must done gone crazy. Then, past a chair with a current *True Confessions,* July 1950, on it, on into the kitchen. The layout was like his own next door. Sink full of dirty dishes. In the back bedroom, he saw Ajax sitting up in his little bed looking at him. Room smelled of dust and too much stale heat. Boy scared. Said: "Mama?"

Behind him, Daffodil: "It's okay, Ajax."

Man turned to her. Said: "You see Cleo tonight?"

"Naw. I ain't seen Cleo." Her eyes shifted away again.

She was ahead of him as he walked halfway back up the hall. She lying, she lying sho as shit.

"Is my daughter here?"

"Naw! Ain't you got eyes? You don't *see* her do you?"

"Then where they at?"

Daffodil flashed an angry look at him. In the back room, Ajax started crying. "Fred, you drunk. Why don't you go on?"

"She made you promise not to tell. Didn't she?" He started toward her, hating himself, ready to grab her by the shoulders, but she backed away and screamed, *"Sofia! Sofia! Help! Sofia!"*

"Shut up! I ain't doing nothing to you," he said, making another move toward her.

Daffodil backed farther away up the hall and stumbled into the chair sitting against the wall, knocking his glass to the floor. She groaned and grabbed the chair by the back and beat its legs against the floor, screaming, *"Help! Sofia!"* Then she lifted the chair and held it out toward Man, shaking it, in the manner of a lion tamer in the circus.

Got to be crazy, outta my mind.

"Sofia, call the police!" she shouted.

He stopped, laughed a laugh strange to his own ears, laughed at her trembling fear, feeling disgust with himself, sick, diminished, stupid. Then he turned away, wanting to strike something, to hurt, and headed for the door, stopped, picked up his glass off the floor. He tried to drain the last drop out the glass while looking down the hall at Daffodil standing there holding the chair, glaring at him.

She was saying, "I'm telling you now, you get on out of my house."

And he laughed again—though his heart had started to beat faster with fear—as he walked through the still-open door back across the hall to his own apartment. He heard her slam her door and throw both locks.

◉

Walking through the kitchen, he poured more liquor into his glass, opened the back door, and stepped out onto the porch. How low can you sink? Got to cut this shit out. Know that for sho. The sky was clear, black-blue, packed full of stars, a big bright one twinkling like nobody's business. Do you got to drag everybody down with you? How low? Nothing but a pimple on the butt of time. Yet and still, don't understand, baby, don't understand, why you needs another man. Been here and gone. I say the woman I love.

> The woman I love
> Give me high blood.
> I say, the woman I love
> She give me high blood.

He stood there sipping rapidly from his glass, trying to think what to do next. Debbie, he thought. Damn it, yeah, Debbie!

Man stumbled back into the apartment, left his glass on the kitchen table, forgetting about the telephone they had recently had installed, not used to it, too drunk to remember, walked out the front door, down the steps, making a loud racket, feeling for change in his pocket, feeling a couple of quarters, nickels, dimes. Love the way you pout, you sho knows me in and out. Pick me up, put me down, turn me round and round.

> I say the woman I love
> Make me holler top of my lungs.
> I say the woman that I love
> Make me holler top of my lungs,
> Singing her my songs . . .

In the phone booth in front of the old folks' home, he dialed and waited. Two rings, three, four. As he waited he slowly focused on an ambulance parked at the curb. The back doors standing open. Then a sleepy woman's voice said, "Hello?"

"It's me, Deb. Cleo up there?"

"Cleo? You must have the wrong number. Ain't no Cleo here."

The woman—definitely not Debbie—hung up. By now he was having second thoughts about calling his sister this time of night. All drunk and everything. If Cleo wasn't there—and why should she be?—Debbie and Lyle would be pissed. Calling there would just give them another reason to think he was hopeless. If he'd gotten Debbie on the phone, and if Cleo wasn't there, he imagined Debbie saying "Freddy, didn't you know this was coming? Couldn't you see it . . . you treat that gal like a dog and you expect her to stick around and take it? I'd be gone too. You're my brother and everything but you ain't learned nothing about how to treat a woman. You talk about Daddy. Boy, you act like him. Check yourself out. She's not here, Freddy. Why should she be? She probably halfway to

Chicago by now." He could almost hear Debbie and he didn't want to hear that smack.

Yeah, he thought. He'd been thinking that all along. She was on her way back to Chicago. That goddamned sister of hers knows. Wrong house but the right street. Bring it on home. Mean woman make a dog eat a snake. Bring it on home. Mean woman make a good man throw his bottle down, leave town. Bring it on home. Lose yo sense of humor, believe the rumor. Bring it on home.

Two men in white uniforms suddenly came out of the rest home carrying a body on a stretcher. Don't worry bout my soul. Wake up and find my own self dead. Worry bout yo own soul. Nothing but a pimple. Little old bitty pimple.

> How long—?
> Oh, how long—?

He reached in his back pocket and brought out his wallet and address book. They were held together with a rubber band. Removed the band, returned the wallet to his pocket, opened the address book, shifting it slightly so that the streetlight hit it squarely. Turned the pages. Had trouble seeing the page, things on the page. Everything double. But found Shawn's name under Q, the only one on the page. Had trouble finding the coin slot but felt around till he found it, then dropped a nickel in, dialed 0, and waited. When the operator said, "Yes, may I help you?" Man told her his name, said he wanted to make a collect call to Shawn Queneau, gave her the number, and waited.

He was still seeing double. Everything was hazy, but he thought he was watching the two men in white as they pushed the body into the ambulance then closed the doors. Throw it upside the wall, run back in catch it fo it fall. She don't play my game but I love her just the same. Make him pay fifty dollars every day. He was babbling to himself.

> She won't cook me no hog-maws,
> She won't cook me no hog-maws,
> Won't kiss me on my jaws.

He heard Shawn answer and the operator say, "Collect call for Shawn Queneau from Manfred Banks." Shawn said, "This is Shawn." The operator: "Will you accept the charges?" Shawn: "No, operator, I won't." And Shawn hung up. And the operator said, "She can't accept the charges, sir. Is there any other call you wish to make?" He told her then that he wanted to pay for the call, asked how much should he deposit. While she was talking, he fished in his pocket for all the change he had and placed it on the counter beneath the phone, counting it out. Seventy-five cents total. But the line suddenly went dead. He dialed 0 again and got a different operator, told her what he wanted to do and she said, "Deposit thirty cents for the first three minutes, please." He did and waited. Shawn's phone rang, then it rang again. It rang a third time, then a fourth time. It must have rung twenty times before he hung up.

> The woman I love, she blessed from up above,
> I say the woman I love, she blessed,
> The woman I love, she blessed from up above,
> I say the woman I love, she blessed,
> Lord knows, she stands out from all the rest . . .

Back upstairs, he drank more Old Crow from the glass, standing in the kitchen, trying to figure his next move. Sweating and weak, he was beginning to feel better, but almost weightless in a strange way, as though his veins were filled with air instead of blood. His head was pleasantly without pain. But everything he saw—the glass in his hand, the icebox, the table, everything—he still saw double. It had happened a lot in Chicago. Then for a while when he first came to Omaha it stopped happening. But never saw any bearded men nursing babies or legs walking without a torso. Chained dogs did not spit fire at him. No corpses danced around his bed. No worms crawled out of his nose and ears. No one had tried to cut him down with an ax, thinking he was a tree. He knew it was the whiskey. But he wasn't hearing things or seeing things. No strange animals or being attacked by armies of bugs. He never woke up in the night screaming or any of that crazy shit people say you do when you got the d.t.'s. Seeing double he could handle. In a way it was kind of nice seeing two of everything. This way, you couldn't miss anything. If you didn't see one version real good you were bound to catch its twin.

> Won't make me no cornbread,
> Rather see me dead.
> Won't make me no kinda cornbread,
> Rather see me good and dead . . .

He finished the liquor in the water glass and automatically stumbled over to the cabinet, took down the bottle, and poured what was left—about two inches' worth—into his glass. See me dead. Good and dead. One hand on her hip, giving me a lotta lip. His head felt light enough to float or fall off his shoulders.

Glass in hand, he paced—rather, stumbled—up the hall, into the dark living room, back through the dim bedroom, into Karina's dark room, back down the hall, sipping the whiskey, into Solly's room, back to the brightly lighted kitchen and back through the whole process again.

Then he thought, She's down at that fucking church. He started grinning. It made sense.

He found an empty half-pint Old Crow bottle on the floor by the icebox among a bunch of Coke and Pepsi bottles, rinsed it out holding it under the tap, then sat it on the table and poured the whiskey into it slowly, spilling a little on the tablecloth. No top to go on it, he stuck the bottle in his back pocket and stumbled up the hall, out the door, closing it behind him, and stamped down the steps holding onto the railing because he knew how easy it would be for him to fall. Got to do better. And if he fell there was a lot of him to land. Lord knows. Nobody there to let him down easy.

AS HE STUMBLED ALONG IN THE dark street, feeling the warm night air on his damp face, going north he told himself: Just wanna talk to her. Thas all. Just wanna talk to her. Don't want it all, jes a little bit, jes a spoonful. No harm in that. Jes wanna talk to her. All I want to do. Try to reason with her. Jes a little bit. He stopped, took out the bottle, swigged, and returned it to his back pocket. Jes wanna—

CHAPTER THIRTY-ONE

A lone car went by also going north. He saw it double.

Stopping now, again, Man tried to remember where he was going. He couldn't. Cry mercy and shout cause I can't figure it out. Why was he walking north on Twenty-fourth? Get tight but don't fight. He took another drink, figuring he'd made a mistake, had meant to walk down to the scene—Twenty-fourth and Lake. Yeah, that's what he'd meant to do. For God's sake, get down to Twenty-fourth and Lake. He almost laughed.

Turning around, he walked back in the same direction, walked for what seemed a long, long time before he saw the storefront and remembered his apartment upstairs, remembered Cleo there, then Cleo gone. Been here and gone. She gone. He stood unsteadily in front of the store. A lone car went by, going south.

Taking out the bottle, he took another drink, swilled it, and put it back in his pocket. Yeah. She was down there with that goddamned preacher. What was his name? He couldn't remember. Slowly he turned and looked north. The church was that way. North. North Star Baptist.

In the distance a dog started barking and kept on. He could imagine the dog. The bark was insistent, snappy, small, fussy, nervous. Had to be one of those little fuckers.

Again, he set out in that direction, grinning secretly at his own confusion, delighting in the elusive games of his own mind. Talking to himself, "Jes wanna talk to her. That's all. All I want to do is talk to her." And this time he was stumbling along with greater determination.

Humming and whispering to himself: All you do, baby, is complain, all you do is complain, gon put yo ass out in the rain, gon put yo ass back on the train. Not the right song. Already gone.

A white-and-brown tomcat shot across his path and crossed the street.

Then Man fell, tripped on something. *"Shit!"* Going down, he landed first on his right knee, then the palm of his right hand, then his right shoulder, and he rolled over, and he heard the whiskey bottle hit the bricks of the sidewalk. Been down so long down don't worry me.

But don't have to stay down. "Goddamn sonofabitching sidewalk," he mumbled, feeling around for the lost bottle. His hand touched a large wet spot on the bricks, then the bottle. He picked it up and turned it up to his mouth and drained the last couple of drops from it. "Sonofabitch," he said. "Goddamn sonofabitch." And he threw the bottle over on a patch of grass in front of the nearest house. It hit with a dull thud. He laughed, mumbling to himself—

> That old jailer gave me whiskey,
> Yeah, that old jailer gave me tea.
> I say that old jailer gave me whiskey,
> Yeah, that old jailer gave me tea.
> But that dirty bastard wouldn't give me that key.

When he reached the church he stopped and looked at its front side. A glass door painted black and over the paint in white—seen double—letters these words: THE REVEREND DR. BAYARD SPALDING, HIS HOLINESS, SERVANT OF GOD, PASTOR. Beneath the pastor's name, he saw these words: BEHOLD, I MAKE ALL THINGS NEW.

On either side of the door were large grocery store–type plate glass–covered showcases. Same words in black—seen double—letters trimmed with red on the glass on both sides: NORTH STAR BAPTIST CHURCH.

And beneath the one on the left, Man slowly, silently, read: *"The ways of transgressors is hard."* And beneath that, he read: *"Wine is a mocker, strong drink is raging."* He stepped over to the other side and read: *"Man that is born of woman hath but a short time to live, and is full of misery."* Man said, "Shit."

Inside the showcase window was an open Bible and an assortment of pamphlets with one word titles—*Charity; Honor; Faith; Love; Sin*—spread out around the Bible.

Again, he said, "Shit."

He tried to see through the plate glass but all he saw was crepe paper behind the display and a looming darkness above it.

Man stumbled back and looked around, up and down the street. All was silent.

Walking to the left side of the building, he looked at the little walkway that ran to a gate about eight paces back. He staggered on to the gate and reached for the latch, tried to lift it, shook it, but it was locked.

Suddenly the last of the three side windows down at the end of the path bloomed with yellow-white light. Man heard a muffled scuffle and a bump, a thud. Somebody getting up. Ha! Caught her in the act. Man shook the gate again, this time reaching over the top trying to open it from inside. But it wouldn't open. Then he felt a padlock, cold and solid, at the tip of his fingers.

A heavy man's voice came from the back of the house: "Who's out there?"

Man, leaning on the gate, opened his mouth, as he gazed at the lighted window. He mouthed the name *Cleo* without making a sound. My wife, he thought.

> Like Jack the Bear,
> I ain't nowhere.

Now the window flew up and a man's head and shoulders came out, black and sharp against the yellow light. "I said who's there?"

"My wife in there?" said Man in a low, thick, husky voice. But Man was in shadows and knew the preacher—if this was the preacher—couldn't see him.

"Who? Who's there?"

"My wife," said Man. "Is—?" A helpless, pleading, pathetic tone overwhelmed his voice. Let me down slow. Oh, Mary, Mary, don't you weep.

"This is Reverend Spalding," the man said. "if you don't leave the premises immediately I'm calling the law. Whoever you are—"

> Turn out the light,
> Call the law.

"You got my wife in there," called Man over the gate. Oh, Mary, don't you weep, don't mourn for me.

"Your wife? Who *are* you?"

A light went on in the house next door to the church.

"I want my wife," said Man, with an almost-whimper.

"Are you *drunk*? I don't know anything about *your* wife. Get on away from my church, whoever you are."

Behind him, in the street, Man heard a car stop. He turned around and saw a young man getting out of a big black Buick, saw him and his car double. The car lights still on, beaming down the street. Man could see one side of the young man's face pretty well in the streetlight. He had a narrow black face and a thick upper lip, eyes sunk deep—like a gorilla's—beneath a protruding forehead. He was dressed in a raincoat and pajama pants and house slippers. The gorilla was coming toward

229

him, holding a huge black pistol. When he was about five paces from Man, he said, "Get away from that gate or I'll blow your head off."

Man wavered for a second then staggered toward the pistol. The whole moment seemed unreal, like a dream. He didn't feel any danger.

How long—?

The gorilla stepped back a couple of paces. "You drunk or something? Get the hell on away from my father's house, you drunk fool."

Man walked right on by the pistol, but still in shadows, headed toward the sidewalk. He kept his face down, not deliberately, but drunkenly.

The gorilla quickly skipped around Man, keeping his back to the wall of the church. You can dance, you can prance. I ain't scart of dying, if I'm lying I'm flying. You think you a bad fucker, shoot me sucker. Shoot me dead, right through the head.

On the sidewalk Man stopped and looked back.

Then the gorilla followed him out to the sidewalk. Said: "What you messing around my father's house for?"

Man kept his back to the gunman who was under a streetlight but Man was still in the shadows as he moved.

"He got my wife in there," said Man, without looking back. Low-down dirty shame. Shoulda listened to my second mind. Low-down dirty, dirty shame. Low-down.

"You out of your mind, nigger?"

"Don't call me nigger," whispered Man as he walked on, mumbling to himself like a crazy person. Musta done lost my mind sho as shit. Nothing left to lose.

"Well, get on away from here and stop *acting* like one. My father don't know anything about your wife. You're just drunk and out of your mind."

Man wavered on the sidewalk, still not looking back but knowing the pistol was still pointed at him. "You don't know nothing. You ain't nothing but a pimple on the ass of time."

"I'm telling you for your own good, get on away from here. I'll blow your ass away. I ain't scared of you."

Man thought this over and glanced for the first time back at the young man's house slippers. Then he started giggling, pointing at the slippers. "You something else, out here with your gun."

The gorilla looked down at his slippers.

Man looked around. Lights were now on in houses across the street. Faces peeking around edges of curtains and blinds.

Man threw up his hands and dashed them out at the gorilla in a gesture of dismissal. "Fuck it! I'm gon get me a drink." And he turned his back on the pistol and started off down Twenty-fourth.

My baby is sweet, sweet, sweet.
I may have the wrong house,
But I sho got the right street.

When he'd stumbled along only one block he stopped, realizing Solly's place was right across the street. Why hadn't he thought of it before? It made sense. Holly.

He sort of floated across. The night breeze picked up.

Holding onto the railing, he climbed the squeaky wooden steps to the porch, wrapped his fist around the doorknob, turned and pulled, but the door was locked. Leaning against the wall near the door was an old rusty red bike with a basket on the front.

From the porch, he looked back down the street. The big black Buick was still parked down there in front of the church but the lights were off.

Man shook the doorknob and the whole door rattled. He felt a sneeze coming on and covered his nose. Nice breeze make you sneeze. Miss Ernestine come out here and shoot me sure as shit. Bet that broad so mean she shoot her own shadow. He shook the door again.

Jack the Bear here—
Open the door, my dear.

Then he heard a car coming up Twenty-fourth. He leaned against the house, in the darkness of the porch, and watched it approach and pass. Police car. He watched it as it stopped behind the black Buick, watched the two white cops get out. He could see now: Two people— a short fat man, a woman with her hair in curlers—were standing in bathrobes with the gorilla in front of the church when the cops walked over.

Then Man remembered the fire escape up to Solly's apartment. He tiptoed off the porch, keeping in the shadows, and walked around the right side of the house, walking on the wet grass, and stopped when he came to the spot where the fire escape hung. But it was too high to reach. He jumped up, trying to grab it, hoping to pull himself up, but the tip of his longest finger never even touched it. Lost his balance and fell flat on his ass in the grass. The dampness soaked right away through the seat of his pants and underwear to his skin.

He looked around for a pebble, crawled till he found one close to the house, then stood up and backed away from the fire escape and gently threw it up and hit the window glass, hoping like hell he hadn't awakened Miss Ernestine. That old bat sure as shit would call the cops. He waited to see if Holly would come to the window. But he wondered now what he wanted to say to her. How would she know anything about

Cleo? They barely knew each other. Cleo would not have gone to Holly for help. Yet he felt that it was important to see Holly.

He found the pebble again and threw it up, hitting glass again, and this time Miss Ernestine's light came on. Man suddenly felt sober and he trotted back to the front, spotted the bike on the porch, and, instead of running toward the street, he staggered up on the porch, skipping most of the steps, almost falling, and grabbed the bike by the handlebars, and rolled it down the steps.

On the level walkway, miracle of miracles, he threw one leg over the other side, made foot contact with the pedal, and got himself firmly on the seat, balanced but wobbly for the first second or two, then rode down the walkway to the sidewalk, eased off the sidewalk into the street. Glancing back, he saw the cop car still down in front of North Star Baptist Church. He giggled as he moved—cutting a wavering path—toward the center of the street, unsteadily riding the white line, heading south.

> Up in the sky gon take me one long ride.
> Some day, mama, gon take me that long ride,
> Up in the sky gon take me one long ride . . .
> Mama, mama, sho hope you still be by my side.

A skunk ran across the street. He barked at it, laughing. After a couple of blocks he started calling, *"Cleo! Cleo! Cleo!"*

And he kept wheeling his drunk ass on down the main drag.

He counted six blocks and he was at Benney. Felt sick and dizzy but strangely free. Throat dry from shouting. At Benney a car was coming west and the sudden headlights shocked him. But it was a slow shock, like something in slow motion. The driver hit his horn and held it down, still coming right at Man, or so it seemed to him. And Man lost control of the bike, trying to turn too quickly to get out of the way. He went sideways in one direction, landing on his left shoulder, and the bike scooted in the other direction.

The car drove right around him and kept going on across Twenty-fourth. Man caught a glimpse of the driver and the passengers, a man with a beer bottle turned up to his mouth, a woman beside him, another man and another woman in the rear. They were all laughing and looking out the windows at him as he fell from the bike and lay in the street. The driver shouted, "Get the fuck outta the street, coon."

Man lay there for a minute, then lifted himself up on his good side and moved the hurt shoulder. He felt pain in the shoulder but it seemed to be somebody else's.

Back on the bike, he continued on down toward Lake Street. Could use a drink. Then he remembered Cleo. Yeah, *Chicago where she gone.*

232

Bet you any money. Then he saw headlights behind him as he approached Miami. Pulling to the side, riding close to parked cars, he hoped to let the car go on by, but it seemed to be slowing down, staying behind him. And when he glanced back he saw it was the police.

They pulled up alongside him. The one in the passenger seat said, "Hello, there, night rider."

"Hey," said Man, trying to grin.

"Don't you know you spose to have a light on that goddamned bike, fella?"

"Sorry, officer. I get it fixed."

"Make sure you do."

And the police car sped up and moved on far ahead of him and turned west on Lake.

When he stopped at the curb in front of Miss Etta's he couldn't figure out why all the lights—outside and inside—were off. He stood there holding the bike by the handlebars. Glancing over at the Palace, he saw that it too was closed. The liquor store on the north corner was also closed. What time is it?

He got on the bike and crossed the intersection to the liquor store. The lights were on inside. On the wall over the checkout counter the big clock said three-twenty. Then something happened to Man.

It was as though he woke suddenly from a nightmare. Feeling sober and clear, he felt the hardness of the bike handles, touched the wall of the liquor store, felt its hard grainy coldness, saw dimly his own distorted reflection in the plate glass, reflected against the rows of colorful, sturdy liquor bottles on the distant shelves. And he knew now sure as shit that his life was changing again and there wasn't a goddamned thing he could do about it but try to ride it out and not lose himself again in the process.

He got off the bike and gently let it rest against the liquor store.

Walking a block south, he turned at Grant and looked into the dark window of his sister's shop, at the empty chairs. The counter behind them crowded with bottles of shampoo, hair creams, and pomades.

He saw the chair where Cleo worked facing another chair with the little table between them across which she cut and polished fingernails. Well done run dry. He threw a kiss to the dark empty chair. You don't miss yo water. Threw another kiss. You don't miss yo water till yo well run dry.

Then he set out up Twenty-fourth and kept walking and didn't look back.

◉

When he opened the door, there was Cleo standing in the dimly lighted

233

hallway looking at him with those big pretty eyes, but they were eyes filled with fear.

Cleo?

He felt almost sober and the sickness had settled back like the river after a flood. "Cleo?" he said, straining to see her, not fully believing she was real. "Cleo," he said again.

Was she a ghost?

"Fred?" she whispered, stepping toward him, both hands reaching out to touch him. "You okay?"

He reached out and took her in his arms. "Yeah. You?"

"I'm fine. Why are you home? Are you sick? The bathroom—"

"Where you go?" He barely recognized his own voice.

"Debbie came down here out of the blue and insisted I come up and have dinner with them. Said she was feeling sorry for me being tied down all the time, with nobody to talk to but Karina and those women at work. She thinks I'm suffering because I don't have any friends here yet." Cleo laughed. "After dinner she did my hair and we watched television but I fell asleep. She drove us back home a little while ago. But why are you home so early? You got fired?"

"I love you," he said, still holding her close.

He felt her pull back to try to see his face then he heard her say, "I love you too, but tell me what's wrong."

And he still wasn't sure she was real.

◉

He feels the hard new rope resting loosely around his damp neck. A mob of about a hundred jeering dog-faced white men are gathered around the base of a pile of scrap metal on which he stands. He smells fern. He smells apple pie. Dandelions are dangling from his shirt pockets. Closing his eyes, he sees a little birdhouse, and looking through the little hole, inside he sees a little old man sitting in a rocking chair. The old man is himself, a self that will never be. His hands are tied behind his back with a rope made of afterbirth. Overhead high in the dome, birds—golden eagles, red-tailed hawks, snail kites, and white ibises—are flying around in a frantic pattern. The rope is tied to the chain hook suspended from the crane rollers. No one, yet, is up in the cab. Mad dogs on chains are far in the back behind the mob barking. He is sweating and trembling in mortal fear. His terror is so acute he can't speak. His voice is stuck in his throat. Out of the sides of his eyes he can now see somebody climbing the fire escape–like ladder to the cab. Man's feet suddenly feel cold and he strains to look down. The pile of scrap metal has turned to a pile of scrap wood. He smells kerosene. One of the men, walking around the base with a tilted bucket, is dousing the pile of wood with the stuff. He knows he's in the Lomax main bay but at the same time it seems like a hellish semi-open area steaming with smoke from a recent fire. Everything is charred black. One man spits a wad of garlic up at him and laughs, exposing a row of broken brown teeth. This is a jungle. Out beyond the men he can see black trees but they look like stacks of rebars and beams. Man opens his mouth, gasping for words and a nightingale flaps out and flies off above the heads of the men. Man's throat is dry. The sole of his left foot itches. The kerosene has soaked into his bare feet. He feels it on his pants legs. He smells a fire torch burning. The men are still shouting and shaking their fists up at him. One man to his left throws a bucket of bird and mice droppings onto the pile. A mop and a broom are thrown on. A mop bucket lands near his feet. Far in the distance he can hear the banging of sheers. He turns his head, looking for crazy old Ralph, and sees the backside of somebody, possibly Eliot, feeding the body of a child into the machine. As he realizes it's his daughter he notices a man below circling the woodpile sprinkling hay from a hayload that has been wheeled in from the yard. A skinny man with glassy red eyes and the face of a palomino climbs up to him, forces his mouth open by pushing at his jaws, and stuffs a bullfrog down his throat. He now feels the heat. Somebody is now in the crane cab shouting down to the crowd. They cheer him on. "This'll teach you!" they shout. He is standing on his own grave and he knows it. But he has stopped shaking. Terror has turned rotten, like loose shit, in his veins. It is as though he's already dead. Caterpillars are crawling from his ears. Somebody throws a chamber pot of piss into his face. A chimney sweep swoops down and sits on his head. A small cradle with no bottom is tossed onto the woodpile. He smells smoke, hears the crane start. Gabriel's horn is blowing. He'd drink silver water if he had some. His feet are so hot now he's lost touch with them. The mob is screaming joy. This is it and he knows it. How unlucky can he be. The flames are gaining power, lapping up at his pants legs, cutting into his crotch.

SUNLIGHT—AND SOMETHING ELSE, possibly somebody hammering on some- **CHAPTER** thing and the smell of bacon and eggs frying **THIRTY-** somewhere in a skillet—woke him and he lay **TWO** there blinking, trying to open his eyes fully, feeling something terrible had happened, but he couldn't put his finger on it. Felt like he'd been spit up out of the belly of a whale.

But he knew the taste of death was in his mouth. His heart was beating too fast. He felt like his whole body had been put through a ringer.

And where was he, anyway?

> Baby, baby, guess I just don't understand,
> Baby, baby, I just don't understand . . .
> Why you'd need another man.

Then he saw the things in the room, the chair by the door, the doorway. He was in his own apartment, upstairs over Sofia Sweeney's. If I blink I'll sink.

> One of these mornings gon rise up,
> Gon throw these dice out light.
> One of these mornings gon rise up . . .
> Gon take a walk up in the sky
> Just one time afore I die.

It hit him hard: Cleo gone. He was sure she was gone for good this time. And it was his own fault. Love that woman. Fucked up big this time. Really fucked up. Why was it he always destroyed what he wanted most? What happened last night? Only bits and pieces came back: Sick at work, sharing a joint with Percy in the locker room, the bus ride to North Omaha, looking out the bus window at midnight houses, some lighted, others not, seeing imaginary cat witches, Brother Rabbit, Mister Monkey Man, buzzard faces, two-headed grandmothers, possum eyes, Poppa Leon, Caledonia, winos, and John the Conqueror, gazing out with eyes big as baseballs. That sickness in the stomach covered up by the reefer high. Something about a police car. No memory of coming home, going to bed. But he did remember dreaming something about a bike, riding a bike and falling. He remembered talking with Cleo but that must have been in a dream. His shoulder felt sore. Strange, if that was a dream. Shit, who knows what happened. Didn't make any sense but he accepted the possibility that he was somehow on a bike last night, fell off and hurt his shoulder. Something like that had to have happened. And it worried him.

He heard Cleo in the kitchen. "Fred? You wake? You hungry, baby?"

Then he heard his daughter say something and bang a spoon on a plate.

Sitting up, he realized how weak and hungry he felt. He also felt an overwhelming sense of relief. She really was still here. He hadn't dreamed her. But last night? Last night something deep and ugly came out. Deep down inside, something, what is it. Got to be something strong enough to grind me down to sawdust. This thing inside, fear. Yeah, they say scared shitless. But of *what?* Must be scared shitless of something. Of being alone, lost and alone? Been alone before. Can that be it? Whatever it be got to face it, boy. If you scared of it look that fucker in the face and dare it to jump. Stand yo ground. Whatever shakes the soul, Mama useta say, fore the lighted day, in the black place, go up to that big bad fuckface and hug it. She didn't say fuckface. But stand up, boy. Face it, little Freddy boy, face it, you big enough to sleep in a dark room by yoself now. Face it Freddy, my boy. Live strong, boy, till you die. It's everything. Nothing else worth doing. Hug the darkness even if it brings tears to yo eyes.

Yeah. Something had happened. He'd hit bottom last night. And while down in the crisscrossed darkness of himself he'd come up hard against his own flesh, up against his limitations, had seen the watered-down end of himself. Yeah. What'd they call it in the Bible? A revelation. He had had himself a revelation. Saw his own naked fear and had himself a scared-shitless revelation. From the depths of his own self-disgust he'd looked up, somehow, if blindly, and sensed, with fear, what he was doing to himself.

And he suddenly now knew—even with death bells ringing in his ears—what he must do, had it come as a clear thought: I wants to live. And he knew this was at the center of that plan always in the back of his mind. May not be able to take the twist out of the grapevine but you sho can cultivate it.

Yeah. Got to start acting my age and not my shoe size. Don't wants to die, not even going down slow. And the way to do that is stop drinking. Killing myself with Dirty Bird. Gots to start treating myself right. Only way Cleo too gon get the best I can give her. Gots to be best for myself first. Gots to boogie fore you can woogie.

He heard Cleo again, "Fred, you hear me—you hungry?"

Weakly he called back, "Yeah, I'm hungry!"

She came into the room.

He held his arms out to her.

She sat on the side of the bed and he hugged her as she rested her head against his shoulder. He whispered to her: "Baby, I'm gon stop drinking. No mo for me. I *mean* it. Last night was the end of it."

She lifted her head and looked into his eyes and touched his cheek with her fingertips. "You do mean it, don't you?"

"You see."

Then the doorbell rang two, three times.

"Who could that be this early in the morning?" Cleo said.

"Probably Solly." He suddenly remembered the gut-wrenching effort, sitting on the floor in the bathroom. Hug the darkness. If you can hear me, demon in there, hear me talking to ya: I'm bigger and badder than you, motherfucker, and I can kick yo ass any day in the week. His stomach growled as though the demon was responding. It got a chuckle out of him.

> Nobody wants to shake yo hand,
> When you need a hand to shake.

The person was now knocking at the door. The blues came knocking at my front door. Worry me down to my last nerve.

Cleo left the room.

He heard her talking at the front door with Solly.

She came back to the doorway with Solly behind her.

> Some of these mornings,
> Yes, Lord, some of these mornings—

Cleo said, "How you doing, Solly?"

"Just trying to keep my eyes open," Solly said.

Cleo gave him a plain smile. Said: "I'm making Fred some breakfast, Solly. You hungry?"

"Smells mighty good, but no thanks, Cleo, I just et."

"Suit yourself," she said cheerfully, going back to the kitchen.

Standing by the bed, Solly said, "*Wooh-wee*, man, you looks bad, like something the cat spit up. Shouldn't you be in the hospital or some-where?"

Talking into the bed cover, Man said, "I be all right. Go kitchen tell Cleo send glass water."

"That all you want? I got a little taste in my pocket here. Yo favorite, Old Crow. See."

Man twisted his face just a bit and, straining, saw the half-pint bottle Solly was holding up to the bright sunlight coming at an angle through the window.

> All I want is a little bit.
> Don't want it all.
> Just a little bit.

Then Solly split and came back with the glass of water. "Hey," he said, standing there looking up into the living room. "I see you gots yoself a bad telephone now." The black telephone—which looked like a small version of the Cross—was on the nearest end-table alongside the couch. Damn! Last night. Phone there all the time. Plum forgot.

Man was sitting with his back to the headboard. "Yeah, we been had it for a few weeks now. Getting a television too pretty soon. We be cooking with gas. It just take time."

◉

A second later, Cleo came in and placed a tray of food on Man's lap. He looked down at it: two sunny-side ups, four thick slices of bacon with the skin still on, grits with a big chuck of butter in the center, three slices of toast on a saucer, a glass of tomato juice, a cup of steaming hot coffee. He thought he felt a wave of sickness coming over him but it turned out to be a deep surge of hunger and he picked up the fork and stuck it into the grits first. It was like he hadn't seen food in a week.

"This looks great, baby. Good, too!" he said, picking up a piece of bacon and, with a shaking hand, sticking half of it into his mouth.

Then he picked up the tomato juice and put it to his mouth. His teeth clicked against glass as he swilled the thick red cold stuff down, all the while painfully aware of his wife and Solly watching him.

> All I want, Lord—

Now Man wolfed down half a piece of toast then bit off another chunk and chewed it a couple of times before swallowing.

> Just a little bit—

Then again. Forkful after forkful of egg reached his mouth, and he chewed, closing his eyes, straining, and as he chewed he felt better and better, faster and faster. But his throat felt sore and raw.

Solly said, "You wants some of this in your coffee?" He held up the Old Crow bottle.

Cleo snapped, "He don't need that stuff. Let him eat."

Solly giggled. "Scuse me for breathing!" Then he turned the bottle up to his own mouth. "I'll drink his share too."

"You do just that, Solly," she said.

> Just a little walk, a little walk
> With a friend,
> A friend who will stay
> With me till the end.

Karina called, "Mama! Mama!"

And Cleo turned and shot to the kitchen.

Solly again held the bottle toward Man but Man shook his head no.

Solly's eyes stretched with surprise.

"I stopped drinking, Solly."

> Don't care where you bury my body,
> Gon be getting up in the morning.

Solly said, "Don't shit me, man."

"On the square," Man said as he took a slice of toast, raked up some egg with it, and stuck it in his mouth and chewed and chewed.

> Don't care where you bury my body,
> It gon rise like the sun.

Chewing bacon and egg, Man closed his eyes, half remembering his visit last night to Daffodil's apartment.

Solly whispered, "I was just next door."

"What happened?"

In the kitchen Cleo said, "Karina! Look at the mess you've made."

"She stopped me on my way here," Solly said.

"What happened?"

"She ast me to come in."

"No, you can't have any more bacon. No! I said no!" Cleo said.

Then Karina started crying.

"There you go again," Man said to Solly between sips of hot coffee.

"She squeezed my bad boy."

"I think I upset Daffy last night," Man said.

"She told me bout yo drunk ass stopping there. She ain't mad at you. She know you was drunk outta your mind, nigger. I guess you know you been fired."

Man was only mildly surprised. "I don't want to be no janitor the rest of my life no way."

"I hear ya. This morning I overheard Smith telling Percy you was fired far as he was concerned. That nightwatchman told em you was too drunk to work. And you know Smith: he don't even like people who smoke cigarettes. They probably have yo check waiting for you when you go back."

"I don't give a shit. Draw unemployment. This way I can gig Friday nights without ducking and dodging Percy."

"Where was Cleo last night anyway?"

"At my sister's." Keeping the cup of coffee, he put the tray on the bedside table and lay back against the headboard and closed his eyes. He held the cup and rested it on his thigh.

Solly drank from the bottle, then sat it down on the bedside table. "You need some music round this place."

Man watched Solly get up and walk around the bed and go over to the radio on the other bedside table and turn it on. KOIL. Somebody was giving the "Farm Report." Solly turned to WOW. A man said, "Did you know the Duke of Clarence was forced down into a barrel of wine and drowned?" And Solly laughed. Said: "Now, that got to be the way to go." Solly kept turning the dial. Then he left it on WAAW, country music.

Man said, "That sound good." His face sideways in the cover. Then he felt Solly touch his shoulder.

Whispering, Solly said, "I'm going back next door and talk to Daffy." And he bopped over to the doorway, stopped, turned around. "I'll be back."

Cleo called out, "You leaving, Solly?"

He called back to her, "I'll be back."

Man sipped the coffee and gazed at the wall in front of him. Got to get my act together. Hank Williams' voice now on the radio. Man closed his eyes. Thought for sho she was gone. Seemed so real. Didn't even check the closets. Coulda checked the closets. Sho thought she was gone, gone—

> Steal away, steal away,
> Steal away, steal away.
> Ain't gon never turn back,
> No, never turn back.

Man put the coffee cup down on the bedside table and stretched out on his stomach. He fell asleep instantly.

When he woke there was Solly, Solly grinning. Solly said: "Oh, man, I swear. Look likes I'm gon mess around here and fall in love for sho."

He figured he had slept no more than five or ten minutes.

"What happened?" Man turned over and pulled himself up against the headboard, resting his back, and looked fully at Solly.

"What *didn't* happen?" Solly was jumping around like he had ants in his pants. He came close to the bed and whispered like an excited child, "Fred, man, that woman laid that stuff on me so good, I swear I just might leave my happy home. I'd eat her shortening bread day and night. She shook my apple tree just right. She dug up my potato vines. She made it slow and good, man. She cut her cherry pie and gave me the biggest slice. I swear, Lord, Lord. She drained me dry. I'm happy as a man can be. She ast me to come back in the morning when I get off."

He could still hear Cleo in the kitchen running water, probably washing dishes. Karina was silent.

How long had Solly been gone? Man yawned. Where was Ajax when all this steam was rising? Man tried to laugh but only a grunt came out. "Solly, I swear," Man said, lowering his voice. "You get mo ass than any twelve mens got a right to. Yo wife jes come back to yo ass and you still cain't leave it alone." Man shook his head, thinking: Nigger when you gon grow up. Solly, Solly, Solly. Guitar man, guitar man. "Where was her kid?"

"Over some girlfriend house. Dig, man. I got to split. Cop some nods. Get ready for tonight. Anything you want me to bring you fore I go?"

"Naw."

"Okay. Dig you later," said Solly, backing out the room.

And Man heard Cleo turn off the radio and walk back to the bedroom doorway. She turned and said, "You going to be okay?"

"Yeah. Where you going?"

"Florence Market. We're out of coffee and a lot of other stuff. If you're not feeling well I can leave Karina next door until I get back."

Went to the river and got high.
Went back there, baby,
And the river she was dry . . .

"It's all right," he said. "Leave her here. Cleo?"

She'd turned to leave but she turned back. "Yes?"

"I love you."

She smiled and came back into the room, bent down and kissed him on the mouth. "I love you too."

He didn't know how to begin but he began anyway: "Solly just told me I been fired."

For a moment she reacted with something like surprise but he could see she really wasn't. With a faint smile, she said, "Just because you were sick?"

"Yeah. The nightwatchman told Smith I was drunk."

She kept looking at him but didn't say anything. Then: "What're you going to do now?"

"Draw unemployment whiles I look for something else."

She shrugged. "I guess we'll get by. Good thing I'm working too."

"Don't worry." He could tell she was concerned about the bills. But he had no doubt they'd be paid. Always been po but got holt of some bread when it was needed. Shake a money tree, swim the sea, get that bread like I said.

He could hear Karina in her room making sounds that passed for singing. He imagined she was holding one of her soft dolls, rocking and singing her to sleep.

AFTER CLEO LEFT, MAN GOT UP, weak-kneed, and he stood there breathing deeply for a few minutes. Then he took one step toward the living room, moving like an old man. Hear ya knocking. Didn't come here to stay.

CHAPTER THIRTY-THREE

When he reached the windows in the front he looked down at the street. Children were running along the sidewalk playing. One of them, a big boy, reminded him of himself at nine, towering over the other nine-year-olds, feeling big and stupid. He heard the screen door to Sofia Sweeney's place slam. August rent was just about due. Sure coulda swore Cleo had gone—

> Train whistle blowing,
> Hear that old train whistle blowing,
> And there it goes yonder down the track . . .

Crazy how real it seemed, thought Man, as he walked up to his daughter's room and looked in at her. She was talking to her doll, trying to make her eat imaginary food. Man smiled and decided not to break the spell.

Looking at his daughter, he felt life made some kind of sense. She was a kind of music. She was his music. And she made Cleo all the more important. She is a life growing out of my life. In her own time. She's mine and not mine. She belongs to herself. Cleo belongs to herself too. Jes passing through.

He made an about-face and walked into the toilet and put the stopper in the bathtub and turned the hot water knob. Just like a ship lost out at sea. He stripped down and stepped in and sat down. Just like a ship, baby—

He left the bathroom door ajar so he could hear Karina. When he heard her start for the kitchen he called out, "Karina, go back to your room and play till I finish my bath, baby!"

He heard her stop just outside the door.

"Go play in your room, honey," he said.

"Okay," she said and he heard her trot back.

Hurrying, he finished bathing and wrapped a towel around himself and looked in on Karina to make sure she was all right, then walked across the hall to the bedroom. He found clean cotton underwear in his drawer, put them on, put on a freshly pressed cotton work shirt and a pair of dark slacks. Getting his harmonica, he settled down in the living room. He blew a few warm-up notes and Karina came wandering in carrying her doll in one hand and with the thumb of the other hand in her mouth.

Man stopped playing and smiled at her.

"How is Daddy's baby?" he said and reached out for her.

"Baby," she said, holding out the doll.

She hesitated then walked slowly over to him and stood by his knee. He lifted her up and sat her on his knee, cradling her in his left arm. Then he started blowing *Old MacDonald Had a Farm*. It was her favorite. And the minute she heard it she started clapping her little hands together and trying to sing the words.

Old MacDonald Had a Farm suddenly brought back a sharp and painful memory. He hadn't thought of the incident since he was a kid.

◉

It happened when he was four or five. His father's older brother, Uncle Aloysius, and his wife, Aunt Effie, were visiting. They lived way over in Aiken, South Carolina. They had come before when Man's older brother Billy was maybe three or so. Billy was seven or eight now. This was the first time they'd come since Man was born.

The minute his Uncle Aloysius laid eyes on him he said, "My goodness, Quincy, that young'en there is justa about the ugliest, blackest little monkey I ever seed." A big gorilla of a man, he broke into a belly-rocking booming laugh.

Man didn't fully understand what was going on but he knew from the way his mother and father and Billy reacted that his Uncle Aloysius had said something mean about him. So he started crying.

The uncle went on—as family legend had it—to congratulate his wife and himself for having light-skinned kids. They had three: two girls and a boy—Nona, Netty, and Cyrus, who were standing there in the doorway with them. Aunt Effie was herself very light. A tambourine-beating, church-going little woman, she was often upset by the things her husband did and said, how he casually hurt people.

When Man cried his Aunt Effie picked him up and held him against her bosom. Trying to comfort him, she said something like, "Aloysius, you ought to be shame of yoself, hurting this child's feelings like that. Why, he a *nice*-looking boy." But even as she said this she too seemed to be laughing at him. She *was* laughing.

Wiggling and struggling against her, he wanted down from his aunt's arms. And when she finally set him down, wanting to hide his shame and pain, he ran out of the house, and down the back steps, and hid himself under the back porch, sobbing and holding his stomach, tears dropping in the dust at his naked feet.

A minute or two later, Billy came under there and crouched down beside him and told him what their uncle had said, but Billy also said, "Don't mind him. He stupid."

Man wasn't so sure though. Billy knew a few things but he didn't know as much as big people. Grown-up people knew all about God and the devil, about food, where to get it, how to cook it, knew about animals like chickens and pigs. They knew how to make dogs do things like sit or run. Big people surely knew who was ugly and black and who was not.

It was a long time before Billy convinced Man to come out from under the back porch. Even then his eyes were still wet and swollen from crying. He felt like there was a big hole in his chest.

Later, when Billy led him out, the two girls, over by the fence, were turning a rope and their little brother was trying to jump it each time it came low to the ground.

Nona was the oldest, Netty next, and Cyrus, the youngest.

Nona and Netty were singing:

> Juba up, juba down,
> Juba up, juba down,
> Juba all around the town.
> Juba beans and juba bread,
> Juba beans and juba bread,
> Juba all he ever said.

When Man and Billy came near they stopped turning the rope.

And Nona got right in Man's face and glared at him. Said: "You black, you black, you black, black, black, black."

"I'm not," said Man, tears still in his eyes. "I'm *not* black."

"You is too," she insisted. "Tell the truth snagger-tooth: You black as doo-doo."

Netty said, "Black is ugly. Daddy say you black. You a monkey."

"Not no monkey," whined Man.

"Ugly," said Cyrus. And Cyrus hit at Man.

Man pushed him down. The boy, Man's size, landed on his butt and sat there, shocked, trying to decide whether or not to cry.

"Don't you be pushing my baby brother," said Netty. And she pushed at Man but he didn't fall.

"Yall leave my brother lone," said Billy, placing a protective arm around him.

"You black and ugly too, you a ziggerboo, a coon," said Nona.

"I'm not," said Billy.

Cyrus climbed back to his feet, glaring at Man.

"Billy, you not as black as yo brother but you black an ugly. Freddy, you blacker'n coal," said Nona. "You ugly as a baboon."

"I'm not no baboon," Man insisted.

"Baboon," said Cyrus.

Nona said, "You is too a baboon."

"Not no—"

"Baboon, baboon, baboon, baboon," said Netty.

"You a baboon," said Nona.

"Not."

"Is."

"Not."

"Is too."

"Not no—"

"Not—"

"He's not a baboon," said Billy.

"Is too. And you too," said Nona.

"Baboon, baboon, baboon, baboon," sang Netty.

"I'm *not* no baboon," said Man. His bottom lip was poked out. A bumblebee suddenly sailed around his head, going around and around.

"You black as night," said Netty. "People cain't see you at night. You got big ugly lips."

The girls laughed and Man cried.

"*We* got pretty light skin," said Nona. "See—" and she held out her skinny light brown arm and made a snooty face.

Sneering, Billy said, "You think you so cute."

"I *am* cute," said Nona. "I *fine!*" And she threw her skinny little hip out toward him.

Cyrus squatted to the ground and scooped up dirt with both hands, stood, and awkwardly tossed it toward Man, but the little pile of dirt fell and scattered before it reached him.

The bee flew away above the dust.

Netty said, "You so ugly a bumblebee don't even want to sting you."

"You ugly yoself," said Man, choking on his tears.

"I pretty. My daddy always tell me I pretty," she said, stepping closer to Man. She reached out and touched his woolly hair. "You got this ole cuckle-burr hair too."

Billy knocked her hand away from Man's head.

But before he could regain his composure, she swung back quickly and socked Billy in the stomach. She was bigger and stronger than Man's brother. He fell back against the fence.

Netty giggled.

"Don't you put yo hands on me again, you ugly smokestack-nigger," Nona said. Her hands were on her hips and she was squaring him off. "I don't care how big you is I whip yo ass into next week." She was up in his face now.

He stepped back a couple of paces.

"I whip you and yo little brother ass. See these ten bones?" She held up her fists to his face. "I bloody yo nose you ever touch me again."

Billy seemed to get courage from somewhere because he swung at her with a sudden fist that landed on the left side of her head, stunning her. She stumbled.

Then something strange happened. Instead of rushing Billy, she turned to Man and kicked him in the stomach, and he fell on his ass and his head banged against the fence.

Dust hung in the air.

After that seemed like everybody was crying.

The next thing Man remembered he was sitting on his mother's lap on the front porch. Charity was rocking him and she started singing a song he'd never heard before. It was about somebody named MacDonald who had a farm and some chickens and cows. It was a happy song.

But that must have been the first time he had the blues. And now he thought, Maybe *Old MacDonald Had a Farm* was his first blues song.

◉

Cleo came back an hour later with a bag of groceries held against her stomach.

Man was still thinking about that long-ago incident and realizing how much, all these years, he had missed his brother, missed him something terrible. Korea—wherever in hell it was—was no place for Billy to have ended up.

◉

Later, Man and Cleo were in the living room together. Cleo was sitting in the armchair with the phone to her ear, talking to Shawn. First long-distance call on the new phone. Man was resting on the couch, looking at the ceiling. When Cleo hung up she said, "What'd you call Shawn for last night?"

Turning his head, he looked at her, and she was waiting for an answer, had that waiting-for-an-answer look. "I thought you'd gone back to Chicago."

She came to him, settled to her knees beside the couch, and hugged his leg. "Fred, you know I don't give up that easily."

THE PALACE WAS BEGINNING TO
hum with excitement. Man laughed as he **CHAPTER**
and Solly slapped hands. He knew Solly had **THIRTY-**
just left Daffodil's bed and was feeling he had **FOUR**
the whole world in his hands, like some Black Cat
Oil had just worked for him, like a lucky crapshooter, like the cardplayer
with the best hand. Man shook his head. "Percy gon fire yo ass. He
know why you ain't showing up Friday nights."

"Percy can't fire nothing but a fart outta his asshole. Don't start me
talking bout Percy." Solly was standing there looking around. "When we
go on?"

"Right now. You got your mojo working?"

"I got my mojo and my blacksnake too." Solly grinned.

The crowd seemed restless for some live entertainment. Everybody
wanted to boogie.

Sipping Coca-Cola, Man looked around. "We keep getting the peoples
this excited pretty soon you be able to quit slinging a mop and do just
this. I rather be toting the blues than a mop bucket. How bout you?"

"Damn right. Boogie all night every night far as I'm concerned," Solly
said, grinning. "Thing is, you get to love this life so much I heard it can
eat you up. It be like dying from too much pleasure." Then he drew
back, making a face. "But you put down the fun juice, so what would
you know about it."

Man, ignoring the last comment, said, "I wouldn't let it kill me. You
wouldn't have to overdo it, just a little bit at a time like you would anything else."

"You didn't useta say that bout liquor." Solly laughed.

"Yeah," Man said, rubbing his chin. "I useta overdo the liquor, I ain't
gon lie. Liquor had me staggering in my sleep. Liquor changed my mind
and I'm changing my mind about liquor."

"So you gon stay sober, huh?"

"Gon try. I was sober first fifteen years, don't see no reason why I can't
be sober again for fifteen mo years or mo."

"Cause you overdo everything, motherfucker," Solly said, laughing
harshly. "You overdo fucking and loving, you get a big pot of black-eyed
peas and ham hocks, you overdo that too."

"I just a charged-up person, that's all, gots me a lot of energy to burn, makes me want to do everything up full."

"That's the difference between me and you," Solly said. "I know how to cool it and you don't, maybe that's why we get along. I be cooling it and you on fire, going off and getting yo ass shot full of buckshots, stuff like that."

Man didn't say any more. His head was humming: Trying to save my wife, yes, yes, trying to save my wife, almost lost my life, near bout lost my life. Lord, Lord.

Solly had his guitar and it was time for them to go on.

They finished their drinks and put their glasses on the bar. When they started toward the stage, clapping, whistling, and foot-stamping started.

They stepped up on the stage and got situated, Solly on a stool, and Man standing at the microphone. Cheers and shouts went up, some more hand-clapping. Man said, "Evening, ladies and gents. Me and Solly here gon try to give you some entertainment for next hour or so. All right?"

The crowd shouted, *"All right!"*

Man said, "All right. Let's boogie a while." He took his harmonica out of his pants pocket and warmed up a little. Yo mama ain't got no hair and yo daddy don't care. Solly ran through some chords, warming up.

The crowd said, *"Boogie, then!"*

Man answered, "Now, when yo troubles done come down on you, all the moneyed peoples got they own and nobody care nothing bout you, this is what you say—" And he hit it:

> *Boogie everybody!*
> *Boogie, boogie—*
> Ain't no use in crying cause she split.
> Ain't no good in crying cause your woman,
> She done split.
> Go down by the river,
> Find you a ole stone and sit.
> Well, you might as well boogie,
> Boogie yo dirty blues hard.
> I say you might as well boogie,
> Boogie yo dirty blues hard.
> Boogie all night long,
> Boogie till your butt turns to lard.

Man gave them some stomping train-on-the-track fast-riding harmonica. Country boogie. Do the country boogie. Solly whipped in with

some twelve-string cow-cow Chicago-howling-hawk-winds strings behind Man's fast-stepping—

> *Boogie everybody!*
> *Boogie, boogie—*
> You can get into yo sweet ole rocking chair,
> Get into yo rocking, rocking chair,
> Try to rock yoself, baby,
> Till you ain't got no mo care.
> Might as well boogie your blues hard.
> Boogie till you play yo last card.

And Solly backed up and laid it on them again, staying with the same
song, stretching it out, playing with it, working it, this time with a long,
thick clear country-boogie sequence of Lightning-like intense talking-
strings—

> *Boogie everybody!*
> *Boogie, boogie—*
> Well, some folks, they got all the money,
> So I might as well boogie real, real hard.
> I say some folks, they got all the money.
> So I might as well boogie, boogie real hard.
> I say some folks, they got all the money,
> But my baby, she got all the honey.

And they rode through it again, the crowd roaring with them, clapping. Foot-stomping joy. The Palace was rocking—come rain or come
shine—and the liquor was pouring. Man looked out at the faces. Happy,
sweating, intense black, brown, yellow faces. Coffee grind, daddy, coffee
grind. Saw the insides of mouths, gold tooth–laughter. One old guy got
up and slow-boogied in a clearing between his table and the bar.
Everybody cheered him on. Come on baby. Have a good time. Then the
old guy got tired and sat back down. Other people at his table slapped
him on the back and stamped their feet and roared with laughter. This
was the way Man liked it. He was happy. Oh, baby, you make me feeeeel
so good. Could nearly forget his troubles, making other people happy.

Almost without stopping, they jumped bad into *My Baby Don't Stand
No Cheatin,* then did that old standby, *Mojo Hand.* Somehow he got
through *Cleo Blues,* then Solly did a solo of *Got No Money.* Old-time
Negro song about better days coming. Gots to boogie fore you can woogie. Somebody in the crowd called out for Man to sing his *Hey, Hannah*

song. So they got it going, riding it on in as the finishing number. Solly, worrying the hell out of his strings.

The crowd went crazy with excitement and applause.

◉

Later, Man and Solly walking in the night breeze up Twenty-fourth. As Solly drank from a half-pint bottle of Old Crow, he kept asking Man if he wanted a sip, jusa sip, tiny tiny sip, and Man kept refusing. Finally Solly said, "You ain't no fun no mo."

Man ignored him. Said: "Makes me feel real, real good to make peoples that happy like tonight," Man said.

"You sho you don't want a taste, just a taste?"

"Naw, man, I told you. Wasn't tonight great?"

"Yeah, but you know they don't be really appreciating it, half the time I think they just carrying on to be carrying on, making noise, just cause they drunk and shit."

"The music must got something to do with it. People get happy with it."

"I know it make me happy," said Solly. "I be playing and I feel happy. Matter fact, it almost good as fucking." He laughed.

"I knowed you was gon say that."

"Now you think you can read my mind, huh?"

"I *been* reading yo mind, Solly." He laughed and punched Solly playfully on the shoulder.

"If you can read my mind so good what I'm thinking bout right now?"

"Pussy."

Solly burst out laughing. "Yo sho right bout that. Okay. What I'm thinking now?"

"You thinking if the river was rye you jump in and drink it dry."

"Naw, nigger. I was thinking bout my mama. See, you ain't no mind-reader."

Man started singing:

> The jailer gave me whiskey,
> The jailer gave me tea,
> The jailer gave me everything
> But that doggone key.

"HEY, PERCY. HOW YA DOING?"

Man and Percy slapped palms.

"I'm okay. Say, come on up to the house. The guys up there drinking a little beer and playing cards. Your ace Solly up there. I just come out to get me some cigarettes and more beer."

"Sounds good." Let the good times roll. What I say?

CHAPTER THIRTY-FIVE

◉

Percy parked his blue sedan in the vacant lot beside his house and they walked up the narrow dark stairway to his second-floor apartment over a used-furniture store. Going up Man was humming to himself— Somebody been talking bout me. Way over town. Way, way over town.

"Solly say you put down the Dirty Bird." Percy was looking at him and grinning, waiting for a response.

"Yeah, I can't handle the shit no mo."

"Well, that's what I always say, if you can't handle it, you ain't got no business messing with that panther piss."

Percy opened the door and Man followed him in. Right away Man could hear loud talk and laughter coming from deep in the apartment. A radio was on somewhere and one of those fluffy singers was singing *If I Knew You Were Coming I'd've Baked a Cake*. He followed Percy's camel-like stride through the living room, the dining room, the kitchen, out onto the screened back porch where Man noticed right away a woman he'd never seen before sitting behind Orson looking over his shoulder at the cards in his hands. Around the table with Orson were Lorenzo, Solly, and Francine, Percy's woman, playing blackjack.

Solly looked up and said, "Hey, blood!"

Man grunted a greeting to Solly and everybody else.

Francine was dealing. She hadn't spoken. Concentrating so hard? She had a cigarette hanging from the left side of her mouth, squinting to avoid the smoke drifting up past her eyes. And in a grave and hoarse voice she said: "Ain't nobody close to taking this dealership from me. I'm *bad*." And her cackle was mean as a mistreated junkyard dog. With a buzzard-like head, she was flat-chested, lanky, and dried-up looking, with big bloodshot yellowish eyes. Now she looked up at Man. Said: "Oh, hey, Fred. Long time. How ya doing?"

He spoke and pulled up a chair behind her, watching the game. It must have been a hundred degrees that afternoon, and humid, at least eighty on the porch. Lord, Lord. Looked for me some shade, but that was one thing God hadn't made.

> Looked for me some tall grass,
> Looked all day long.
> Looked for me some tall, tall grass,
> Trying to keep that ole sun off my black ass.

Percy came out with opened bottles of beer and placed them on the edge of the cardtable. Francine reached for one and took it up to her lips.

Percy sat down behind Solly.

Francine said, "Nice and cold. That gal yonder, Fred, is my first cousin, my mama's sister's child, from Little Rock. Nora Jean. She just come up here."

"Hi, Nora Jean," he said, grinning at her. She was a plump, light brown–skinned young woman with nappy edges, big angry pretty eyes and a heart-shaped mouth painted red. The other thing Man noticed right away: she was drunk. He could tell by the sloppy way she held the glass of clear stuff, probably gin, and the messy focus of her eyes as she shot him a glance, frowned, and tried to refocus on the card game.

Solly said to Man, "Hey, Fred, where you been?"

"What you mean where I been?"

"Ain't seen you for a couple of days, man."

"Been around. I got a new song for Friday night."

Percy said, "Them songs feeding your black ass yet?"

Orson and Lorenzo laughed.

Man said, "They may not be feeding this here body but, shit, I gets mo nourishment outta my songs than yo ass gets outta a pot of neckbones and black-eyed peas. And anyway, me and Solly together done made the Palace mo popular than it ever been."

Francine said, "You can say that again."

Lorenzo giggled, wiggling in his seat. Threw a card down and said, "I thought songwriters suppose to make some *long* bread."

"Yeah," said Orson, "just like baseball players, Jim."

"World Series next month," said Percy in a dry voice. "What you wanna bet New York wins."

"Bullshit," said Lorenzo. "Philadelphia gon tear their asses up, man. American League can't touched the National League. Look how they been acting this season."

"Any money," said Percy.

Man said, "I'll bet you ten dollars, Percy, Philadelphia will whip the shit outta New York."

"Deal," said Percy. "Yall my witness. Just so I don't have to come looking for this nigger with my gun. You heard him."

Solly said, "I don't follow baseball much as football. I really dug the Rose Bowl this year, Ohio State whipping the snot outta California, seventeen to fourteen." He threw down a card and picked up another.

"It was closer than that," said Percy.

Francine said, "Fred there's a bottle of gin in there in the icebox, honey. Get yourself a glass."

Percy said, "He don't drink no more."

Francine looked at Man with big eyes. "You stopped drinking?"

Man nodded, feeling guilty like he'd let everybody down.

"A man don't drink make me feel nervous to be around," she said, pushing her lips out while looking at her cards.

"I know what you mean," said Solly.

Lorenzo said, "Nigger'll be drunk again by tonight." He giggled, squeezing his elbows to his ribs and lifting his feet off the floor.

Man, to Francine, said, "You got any Coca-Cola?"

"Some 7-Up in there in the icebox," Percy said.

> Went to the river and got high.
> Went back and that river, she was dry.

Man went in and started back with a bottle of 7-Up. On the kitchen radio some woman was singing *A Bushel and a Peck*. The soda was cold and tasted sweet and he liked the bubbles. Well, what the hell. He wondered if Old Crow was a jealous god.

Back on the porch he stood leaning against the banister, sipping the soda, watching the game and out of the sides of his eyes, looking at Nora Jean's heart-shaped red lips. He couldn't believe it but here he was, madly in love with his own wife and looking at another woman's lips. Was a man nothing but a dog, like the songs said? She drained her glass, stood up, almost fell sideways, and, holding onto the backs of chairs, stumbled to the kitchen, slamming the screen door behind her.

She came back with a half glass of gin. If I don't die from gin, sho gon die from sin.

Francine said, "Take it easy, Nora."

"Huh?" She sat down with a plop, tucked her left fist under her right arm, and brought the glass unsteadily to her mouth and drank a long time. Really hitting it hard. If I don't die from sin, sho gon boogie all I kin.

To anybody or everybody, Francine said, "Yall have to excuse my little cousin. She's heartbroke."

Nora Jean, in a heavy southern accent, said, "I'm all right. Shucks. Don't be spreading my business."

"Ain't nothing to be shamed of," said Francine, making big eyes.

Solly said, "Happens to the best of us." He winked at Man.

Nora Jean leaned over and kissed Solly on the cheek. "Thank you for understanding."

"Look out!" shouted Percy.

"Mercy me," said Lorenzo.

Solly's tongue was sticking out in a dry laugh, as he leaned back, holding his cards close to his chest. He looked over at Nora Jean. He touched his own cheek where she'd pecked the kiss. "Would you mind doing that one mo time, Miss?"

And she smiled and leaned over again to kiss him but he turned his head and caught the kiss on his lips. Nora Jean lost her balance, spilled some of her gin, and almost fell forward on the card table. But Solly caught her and held her.

Man watched her sit back in her chair and lift her glass to her face, closing her eyes as she drank. Solly got her in his pocket. Boy don't waste no time. Have mercy.

◉

An hour later Orson and Lorenzo had split and Francine had helped her cousin walk in the house and into the bedroom, saying, "She ain't but eighteen, yall. Don't know nothing bout no drinking." And Solly and Man were in the living room sitting around with Percy. Percy and Solly had to be ready to go down to Sears by eight-thirty. Percy always looked clear-eyed no matter how much bush he smoked or how much booze he drank. But then he never drank much. Into reefer mostly. He was sucking on one now. When he finished it he passed it over to Man who, without taking a hit, passed it on to Solly. Solly took a big hit.

They stood up.

Solly said, "I'm going in to say bye to Nora Jean."

Francine said, "She sleeping, Solly. Leave her lone."

Percy barked, "Ah, hell, let the boy go in an say bye to the girl."

Francine gave Percy a sheepish look, opened her mouth but said nothing. She looked at Solly and waved her hand toward the bedroom. The door was standing open and, from where he stood, Man could see the girl lying across the bed, her skirt halfway up her fat thighs. He watched Solly bop into the room and lean over the bed and kiss Sleeping Beauty on the cheek. The girl moved her head but she didn't wake up.

"HI STRANGER."

Turning, Man saw Beverly Frye standing right in front of him. He and Solly had just finished a set and were taking a break. Since Drusilla was slow with the table service, and Jorena didn't knock herself out like that, people tended to come up and buy their drinks at the bar. Bev had an empty glass in hand, no doubt working her way to the bar for a refill. Not many bothered to bring empty glasses back to the bar. Usually they let them pile up on the tables. Drusilla made a sweep of the room about once every hour. Man said, "Hey, Bev. When you get back from L. A.?"

She was giving him this hateful smile. "I been back almost two weeks now. How's your wife?"

"She's fine."

Reaching over and touching Solly's shoulder, Man introduced him to Bev.

Solly spoke but kept his eyes focused now on the stage where Greg and the cats were cutting loose on *Cherokee*. The crowd was cheering, stomping, and whistling.

Bev reached across somebody and handed her glass and two quarters to Jorena. Jorena handed Bev a fresh glass of tap. She shot another nasty smile at Man and said, "Maybe we can talk later. Huh?"

"Anytime."

◉

It was after midnight and Man had put his harmonica away for the night. Solly had bopped on up to Daffodil's.

Man was standing out front of the Palace smoking a good, pungent-smelling cigar, catching some fresh air.

Across the street in front of Miss Etta's, a little way away from the crowd packed at the entrance, a drunk woman was leaning against the building just under the black window on which Miss Etta's name was printed. She was shaking her finger at the sidewalk and cussing out somebody only she could see. Ghost always somebody's host. Ghost somebody's all-night host. Lord, Lord. Worry you down to yo last nerve. A police car was parked in front of the tavern, two white cops in the front seat listening to the radio and watching the niggers.

Hearing somebody call him Fred, he looked back and saw Bev coming out.

Gently sinking his teeth just slightly into the tip of the cigar, liking the taste, he watched her approach.

Ruffled up, Bev stopped beside him. He looked at her in her bright yellow sequined dress with chiffon pleats where it was stuck to her girdle and stockings. "You was just gonna *leave* just like that?"

He grinned, taking the cigar out of his mouth, confused. "I jes stepped outside to get some fresh air."

"Oh. You want to go for a walk?"

"Sho, let's walk."

They started off south down Twenty-fourth, staying in the bright lights of the storefronts, past the office of the *Messenger*, Webster's Tailor Shop, Carter's Cafe, on past other dark storefronts to the corner of Grant, and crossed. "How's your wife?"

"Fine, she just fine." Man wasn't sure he wanted this conversation. He stopped, took out a match, struck it and cupped his hands around his cigar's tip, and sucking in on it, lighted the thing, blew the bittersweet blue smoke away toward the gray street, and started walking, hitting a rhythm again. One hand in his pocket, the other holding the stogie just a ways from his pant leg.

Bev said, "So, is that the way you wanted it?"

He laughed. "Bev, what kind of question is that? Listen, how *you* been doing? Thas what I want to know."

He could tell she was hurt, put off. Said: "I'm doing all right. Never should have gone out there to Los Angeles."

"Why not?" The cool night air felt good. In the blues you could ride a pony in the night air but you were not really riding a pony, it was just another way of talking back to the wind. Lots of things happen better at night.

"That man showed his ass. I never seen such carrying on in my life. Too many crazy people out there in L.A. Don't like no big city like that."

Man remembered old folks saying: You can take the nigger outta the country but you cain't take the country outta the nigger. And he smiled.

Bev was still talking: "I mean, in the first place, he never should have asked me to go out there. He already had more women hanging around than he could handle. And I ain't never been one to play second fiddle. Not me. No, sir. Gon sit on somebody else's knee, gon kiss somebody else under the apple tree."

"So where is he now, still out there?"

"Yeah, and he better keep his ass out there too. Omaha ain't big enough for the two of us. I don't want him coming back here." She laughed her angry, harsh laugh.

A white car, long as a lumber truck, moving by slowly with dark blue, vibrant figures inside, stopped at the corner of Burdette for the bright splash of red that was the stoplight. Nat King Cole's cool, smooth voice on the car radio was singing *Mona Lisa.*

Man said, "How yo father?"

She didn't answer right away. She seemed in a trance.

He looked at her frowning pink face, now blue-brown tinted in the night lights. She was holding her breath, then she said, "My daddy died back in June. Didn't you know?"

"Now that you mention it, I think I did hear something like that." He blew cigar smoke toward the street.

"I'm sure Debbie musta told you. Me and her made up. She tell you? I like Debbie. I thought I'd ask her for my old job back but I'm working at Leona's now—right up the street there near the corner of Parker." Then suddenly he felt her eyes on him. "You ever think about me?" Her smile had a lot of fear in it.

Man laughed. "Sho I think about you." But he was thinking how little he ever thought of her. He thought of her only when something or somebody reminded him. He never went out of his way to remember her. But he had to admit she turned up in his dreams sometimes, turned up like some harmless bystander, a witness to the main action.

"You still consider yourself a free man?"

"I don't know what you mean."

"I mean, do you wanna come home with me tonight? For old-time's sake? Or are you *too* married?"

Looking away from her, he smiled, then shot a glance at her and said, "Listen, Bev—"

She cut him off: "Forget it." She was mad now. He saw the anger flash in her eyes like white lightning. "I wasn't serious anyway," she snapped.

And she abruptly turned around and without another word swished back up the sidewalk toward the Palace. Had no intention of hurting her. Tried to let her down easy. He remembered what old folks used to say: Ashes fly back in the face of the one who throw them. Better blink.

She went back into the smoke.

He kept on by, heading home, sweet home.

A couple of blocks up, a big, flamboyant, low-hung red Cadillac, with a big, very black sugar daddy at the wheel, cruised by going north. The driver brazenly took the cigar out of his mouth and held it out the window as he smirked, glancing over at Man hotfooting it, and, tapping the cigar with one finger, the sugar daddy knocked ashes into the street. If Champion Jack Dupree hadn't been tickling the ivory and groaning out the *Dupree Shake Dance* from the car radio Man would have sworn the sucker was a preacher. And Man thought: I may be booting it, but that's all right. I sho don't wanna be you. Go head on. Kitty on up the road, sucker. I got my own thing. It cost mo than that hog. And you wouldn't even know what to do with it if you could see it.

And he suddenly felt happy.

AS HE APPROACHED THE ENTRY-
way to the stairs he knew somebody was in
there in the darkness waiting for him.
His antenna for danger was standing tall as
it could get. Still on the sidewalk, he said, "Who
in there?"

CHAPTER THIRTY- SEVEN

He could smell a strange yet familiar presence.

And he heard a shuffling movement, then something like a whimper, then he saw Holly step out of the shadows into the streetlight. Who woulda thought! Holly of all people!

"Holly! What you doing here?"

She pushed her hair back from her face but didn't say anything as she stepped closer to him. He couldn't tell yet if she was herself or not. Not that he had ever seen Holly not herself. But seeing her here like this put him on guard. Anything was possible. Peoples can do some crazy things.

"Whas wrong, Holly?" He couldn't imagine why she was in the dark hallway. And he couldn't yet sense her rhythm, which key she was in, so to speak.

"Let's walk," she whispered. "I need to talk to you."

They started off down Wirt toward Florence.

Walking with her arms folded in front of her like somebody trying to hold herself in, she opened her mouth, and he looked at the way the streetlight fell on her tongue. She was trying to catch her breath like somebody who'd just choked on her own mucus. And in the streetlight he could see on her cheeks streaks where she'd been crying. Don't blink.

Again he said, "Holly?"

> You know the blues ain't nothing
> But you keeping on keeping on . . .

"Fred?" she whispered. "Oh, Fred." And she began to sob.

> I said, the blues ain't nothing . . .

Man placed an arm across her back. "Stop crying, Holly. It gon be all right. Come on now."

Ain't nothing but you staying alive,
You keeping on keeping on . . .

Sobbing louder, she seemed to be choking on her own snot. Her shoulders shook and he tried to hold her closer. Steal away, steal away, steal away. She let her body sag against him. Don't care where you bury my body, it gon rise like the sun. He held her as close as he could, surprised that tears were coming to his own eyes. Don't blink.

When you ain't got nothing left to lose.

"Come on now, Holly. It gon be all right, whatever it is."
She blew her nose in her handkerchief. "Yeah?"
As they walked under the giant black oaks, a dog in the distance started barking in dog rhythm.

When you hear them bedsprings popping,
Popping, popping all night long,
When you hear them bedsprings popping,
Popping, popping till the morning bell toll,
You know somebody copping, copping
Off yo jellyroll.

By the time they reached the end of the block, Holly was walking pretty much on her own. Man kept his arm around her as they stood on the curb ready to step down. Finally she said, "Fred, I can't stand it no more. I swear I can't stand it no more. I'm scared, Fred."
"It gon be all right, Holly. You see."
"No, Fred." They started across now, slowly. "No, it ain't. Nothing's going to change. I swear, tonight I started to go up there and kill both of them. I swear. If I had had a gun I would've done it."
He took in what she was saying and knew she meant it. Yeah, she had woman blues, which he sometimes thought had to be a lot harder to carry than man blues. A man, he tend to make tracks and don't look back, but a woman stick in there slipping and sliding in lard, fighting the blues hard, right down to playing her last card.
"What does he think I am? Some kinda *fool?*"
"Take it easy, Holly." And even as he tried to console her, he knew he had no good reason to ask her to not be upset. It was like Solly had hitched a wagon to her ass and was treating her like she was a mule. If she left him, Man thought, he'd feel worthless as a dog. When this good woman gets over him and leave, he gon be up shit creek with no good stuff and only a bluff. Dumb fucker. Man was mad. Mad!

"No, I'm not going to take it easy. I'm going to get the hell out of this town before I kill somebody."

"You don't want to—" Mad, yes, yet he was still trying to calm her, make her feel better.

"Oh, yes I do. I came to talk with you. You're his friend. You know him better than anybody, maybe even better than me. I don't know him. I *thought* I knew him."

He was thinking: You got to know ain't no one man got it all, little mama. How could he tell her she could learn to love another man when she loved Solly? Sepia baby with pretty thighs don't have to listen to a dirty man's lies. Thinking these things, yet he was still talking another way.

"Don't talk silly," he said. "You know Solly better than anybody on this earth. And he loves you. You know that, Holly."

"Then why he treat me like this?"

"Holly—"

"He ain't been in bed with me for two weeks now. At first he used this old night job as an excuse. But I knew from the beginning when he first started fucking that cow. I smelt her all over him. You can't fool no woman. You men have a hard time learning that."

"Yeah, we do." Man let his arm fall away from her.

"Anyway, Fred, I came to ask you a favor."

"Anything, Holly."

She stopped walking and turned to him. "Would you *talk* to him, tell him what he's doing to me and his child? This is just not right."

Man stopped too, feeling cornered and guilty. "I don't know what to say."

"Tell the fool he's losing his wife."

"Okay, Holly. Sho." He sighed.

She started walking again. "If you can't reach him, I don't know . . . I know one thing. I'm packing my things and getting out of this one-horse–ass town."

"I understand," he said, feeling like a fool.

"Then try to make Solly try to understand. I mean, I know he's going to regret it after I'm gone. I'm the best thing ever happened to him."

Man shook his head yes. It was what he too believed, but he knew Solly, knew Solly's need for other women, to be wanted by other women. For Solly that look in the eyes of women was almost as important as water and food. Don't blink. It made him happy, made him feel good about himself. Man didn't have much hope of reaching Solly on that score.

"I might be able to get on at Michael Reese, too, or Booker T. Washington Memorial. I called my sister tonight. You remember my sister?

Fern? No? I thought you'd met her. She said my brother, William, if he knew what Solly was doing to me he'd come out here and put a bullet through Solly's head. William would do it too. That's why I don't want him to know about it. But if Solly don't straighten up, I'm going back to Chicago sure as hell. My mother already told me she'll help me get back on my feet. But I just don't want to have to deal with her. Once she do you a favor she makes you feel like you owe her your life. You remember my mother, Hattie? So if I go back I'm going to probably stay with Fern."

Man laughed. He did remember Hattie, falling-down-drunk woman in a baggy dress, always carrying a shopping bag around. Folks said she owned buildings but ate out of garbage cans.

"What's so funny?"

"Nothing. Life, I guess."

"You can say that again."

He couldn't think of anything else to say.

"Why is it yall can't act right, Fred?"

He laughed. "We jes trying to live. Thas all, Holly. I think Solly want to do the right thing, you know. But he gots to live too, you know. Be himself. Do things." He stopped himself, feeling odd about defending Solly, the one clearly in the wrong.

"Do things? He got to *do* other women? Is that what you mean?"

"I don't know what I mean, Holly. All I'm trying to say is I know Solly love you."

"That's what I thought too for a long time. But I'm not so sure anymore. Maybe he's the way he is because of his family. They're not close. I mean, his sister, Billy Jean, she's back with her mama and daddy, Elizabeth and Russell, but it's not because she wants to be, she just don't have nowhere else to go. That girl been out on her own since she was thirteen and so has Solly." Holly stopped again. "I left Annie by herself. I better get back."

"What was you doing in the hallway?"

She sighed and blew her nose again. "Like I said, if I had had a gun, I was going to go right up them steps and kill them both. I called the Palace and Jorena told me he'd left. And when he didn't come home I knew where he was. I knew Solly wasn't working down at Sears tonight. So, I'd expected him home. Then when he didn't show, the time kept going by. I walked down to that cow's place, looked up at the window. I started to go up there, but then I just sat on the steps in the dark trying to make up my mind what to do. Then you came. I hadn't been there but a few minutes. I'm telling you, if I had a gun I would have gone up there."

"You wouldn't want to do that, Holly."

"I know. That's what I told myself. I got to be here for Annie. Why should I go to the penitentiary and leave my child out here in this mess of a world by herself?"

"Why didn't you ring the doorbell and talk with Cleo?"

"I don't know Cleo. Funny, isn't it? I'd *like* to know her but I don't think she wants to know me." Holly rubbed her neck slowly. "Got a stiff neck from this night air." She went on rubbing her neck and turned her head slowly from side to side. "I've got to go back. Annie might be awake. Thanks for talking with me, Fred."

"Wait," he said. "I'll walk you home."

TUESDAY MORNING MAN GOT UP and walked in the kitchen, poured himself a cup of coffee, took it out on the back porch. He'd gone downtown after being fired and picked up his last check from Jack Smith and applied for unemployment at the unemployment station three blocks west of Sears. Today he was expecting his second unemployment compensation check. Cleo was working mornings now at Debbie's shop.

CHAPTER THIRTY-EIGHT

Karina was up at North Star Baptist. Luck was with him. So far nobody up there had made a connection between him and the crazy man who'd menaced the church that night. Too ashamed of that night, he'd never given Cleo the details.

The radio in the kitchen was on and he sat there on the back porch listening to country singing and waiting for the news and weather. The telephone up in the living room rang the minute he settled down with the coffee. Carefully placing his cup on the railing, he got up and walked stiffly up the hallway and got it on the fourth ring but it was somebody who wanted to speak to Magdalene Schmaleberger.

Back on the back porch, he propped his feet up on the banister and looked up at the big clear cold blue sky, then down the line of Wirt at the oaks with their brown, yellow, and red leaves along both sides of the street. Leaves some pretty things, like notes of music, some falling, some staying on the tree, and there was a kind of pattern, a rhythm, you know, to it all. Some country guy on the radio in the house was singing *Good Night, Irene.* When he finished, the news came on. Man could hear it all pretty well out here, hear it through the screen door. Newsman said two Puerto Rican nationalists tried to kill the president, but they'd caught both of them. Then something about an earthquake way on the other side of the earth, an earth too big to imagine. And General MacArthur saying something about the Thirty-eighth Parallel in South Korea. Four hundred million children in the world hungry this morning, said the man. Lots of other stuff Man only half listened to. Senator Joseph McCarthy saying lots of secret communists in the government, among high-ranking officers in the army. Alger Hiss. Trials. Questions. Threats. Black folks in South Africa rising up against oppression. Then the sports news. World Series coming up and it looked like it was going to be New York and Philadelphia, after all. Man watched a tan-yellowish leaf fall slowly to the ground, and he sipped at the hot coffee. Music, music, music. Everything was music.

The morning smelled of burning leaves.

He heard a car or a small truck stop out front on Twenty-fourth. Probably one of Sofia Sweeney's delivery men. They usually came mornings.

At that moment he looked up, hearing Solly's voice. He was coming off the sidewalk, opening the gate, entering the yard, and looking up. "*Thought* you'd be out here on the back porch. I know you like the palm of my hand," Solly said, coming up the steps at a trot.

"Solly," Man said.

Solly stepped onto the landing saying, "Look at you, nigger, living the life, sitting on the porch drinking coffee and I just got off work, slaving all night." And he haw-hawed a couple of times as he leaned against the railing.

"Hey," said Man, remembering Holly, Sunday morning, remembering his promise to her. But had he really promised? Seeing Solly now jammed up something in Man and he avoided looking into Solly's eyes. Guitar man, guitar man, whatcha gon do without a plan?

Solly sat down on the top step, looking toward the street. Then suddenly he looked back over his shoulder at Man. "Spected you down at Miss Etta's. But that's right, you stopped drinking."

"Naw. Just hanging out, drinking some coffee." He took a sip. "I was gon come try to find you. I gotta talk to you, Solly."

He could see Solly caught his tone. "Yeah? What bout?"

"Bout, uh, well, Holly."

Solly frowned. "What bout Holly?" His bottom lip was hanging and he was frowning, waiting.

Man told Solly the whole story of how he'd come home early Sunday morning and found Holly sitting on the steps while he and Daffy were up there in her apartment doing—to put it one way—what came naturally. Man said, "She was right up there in the hallway."

"No *shit?*" Solly's eyes stretched. "What the *fuck* was she doing here? Where was Annie?" He stood up like ants were attacking his ass.

"She was by herself. Look, man. You my friend. I don't like to be telling you this, but, shit, Holly put me on the spot. I ain't got no choice. She axed me to talk to you."

Solly leaned against the railing. "Just wait," said Solly. "I know what this bout. Holly been here telling you some shit on me. Right?"

"It not like that, man. I'm telling you."

Solly suddenly stood away from the railing and glared at Man. He'd never seen such a glare in Solly's eyes.

"She jes concerned about you, Solly." Man could tell Solly wasn't himself. Probably been smoking weed with Percy. And on top of that a few drinks already at Miss Etta's. He could tell when Solly had weed in him. His eyes flamed. He acted crazy, hotheaded, ready to go off the handle.

Solly's eyes blazed. "What you got to do with me and my woman? Huh? You spose to be my friend!"

"Nothing," said Man, concerned. He and Solly had had scraps but nothing serious. "I *am* yo friend."

"Then why you in my business?"

"Hey, Solly, you got it all wrong. Holly come down here. She was upset, Jack. Real upset. She thinking bout leaving yo ass."

"What she down here telling you that kinda shit for?" Solly threw his arms out in a violent gesture, ready to fight.

"Solly, cool it—"

Solly began moving about the porch in a nervous pattern. "Don't tell me to cool it, I'll—"

"Hey, Jack! What wrong with you? All I'm trying to do is tell you—"

Solly was twitching with anger. "You can't tell me nothing bout my marriage. You spose to be my friend. Not somebody meddling in my marriage. I really thought you was my friend."

"I *am* your friend. All Holly was doing was—"

"Had no business up here. And the bitch didn't tell me nothing bout coming here. Secrets!" Solly was moving about the porch now in a very agitated way.

"Wont no secrets, Solly. She—" Man took his feet down from the banister.

"She my wife, Fred. You ain't got no business—"

"I'm not in your business."

"Yes you *is,* man," Solly shouted, turning away.

"Hey, Solly! This is—"

One second Solly's back was to him. In the next Man saw a blur, felt pain spread throughout his face as he lost his balance, sailing backward, the chair beneath him flying out from under him sideways and scudding across the floor as his big butt hit the planks of the porch, shaking the house. The coffee cup flew out of his hand across the porch, coffee spilling in a dark wet jigsaw pattern on the dusty floor.

Solly, with more strength than Man ever knew he had, had socked him between the eyes, just above the nose. Instantly, he tasted his own salty blood draining down from his nose to the back of his tongue. He wiped his nose and there was the bright red stuff spreading all over the back of his hand. And right away he felt blood running down his face from his nose to the corners of his mouth and he tasted the blood again this way and it was saltier. He tried to say something, but the feeling in him was too thick, as he braced himself to get up, pushing his hands against the floor. Lord, Lord. Some of these days gon take a ride, hope you still by my side.

Then he felt Solly's hands on his shirt, trying to pull him up, and Solly was saying, "Fred, Fred, Fred, I sorry, man, I sorry, I swear, Fred, I sorry. I don't know what—"

And Man, halfway up, without thinking about it, out of pure anger, swung at Solly, landing a weak blow against the side of his head, which anyway sent Solly sailing against the banister, shaking it. Solly came close to falling over.

Then Solly shouted, "*Hey!* What the fuck?"

Fully on his feet again, Man raced at him—still choked with anger, mainly at the sight of his own blood—before Solly could recover and drew back his knotted right fist and blindly drove it into Solly's loose, wet mouth. Instantly, at the speed of a fast-time boogie-woogie, Solly went rolling down the steps, upside-down, over and over, and landed—grunting and hissing—on his head in the yard, screaming, "Motherfucker! Motherfucker! I'll *kill* you, motherfucker!"

And Man felt more concern and fear now than anger, watching Solly tumble down the steps and watching him lying there trying to get up, stumbling and falling back from dizziness or drunkenness or both. Was he hurt?

But when he got up so quickly, Man felt instant relief. Solly's mouth was bleeding but he seemed otherwise all right.

And Man shot down the steps as Solly was climbing to his feet, rubbing his knee where the flesh showed through his torn pants. Blood was dripping from Solly's mouth to his shirt front. He saw his own blood and, wiping it on his sleeve, said, "Motherfucker! You think you sober *now!* Get you for this!" and he rushed at Man with both fists ready.

Man backed up and ducked to the left as Solly swung for his head again. Man grabbed Solly's right arm and swung him away, then in almost the same motion drove another fist into Solly's face, this one landing higher on the bridge of the nose. Solly lost his balance again, staggering out into the yard under the big oak tree, and turning around, he started looking frantically around on the ground. "You gon get it now, motherfucker," he said thickly, with a mouth full of blood, blood pouring from his nose.

You can drink till you sink,

Man was dimly aware that Sofia Sweeney was watching from her back window. He caught a glimpse of her alarmed face. She likely to call the cops. He was also vaguely aware that other neighbors—across the street, down the street—had come out and were grimly watching from yards and porches. One old man was on the porch across the street leaning on his cane watching like it was a cockfight.

You can truck till you drop,

But Man was mainly watching Solly who had wandered out to the edge of the yard and picked up a brick from the line of loose dusty red bricks between the sidewalk and the yard.

Now Solly came charging up the walkway with the brick raised, ready to strike Man. But Man was watching for his chance. It was like trying to deal with somebody holding a gun or a switchblade. Man called, *"Solly!"*

But one day you gots to stop.

And at that point Solly released the brick, throwing it straight at Man's face, but Man ducked, scudding on the scruffy, acrid-smelling grass to the right of the cracked walkway, and the brick crashed into the stairway landing about halfway up.

Solly leaped on Man while he was down and started beating him with his fist across his head and neck, beating his back. Man had an arm raised, trying to protect himself. But soon he got his balance and used his weight to throw Solly off. And Solly went over, landing on his back on the grass.

Man got up on his knees then to his feet and rushed over to Solly before he could get up, grabbed him with both hands by the upper arms, and yanked him up. He shook Solly back and forth like he was a big rag doll. He shouted into Solly's face, "Solly! Solly! What you doing?"

"Son-a-bitch," spat Solly, trying to free himself.

Man held him, shaking him. "You may as well calm down, nigger, you can't whip my ass. I'm bigger'n you."

"Son-a-bitch."

"Ain't got nothing to be fighting about, Solly."

"Son-a-bitching lie! In my *bid-ness!* Son-a-bitch!"

Man slowly relaxed his hold on Solly.

For a second Solly looked confused. Maybe embarrassed. Suddenly he turned around and stumbled over toward the street. At the gate, he turned back, shouting, "This ain't the end of it, son-a-bitch. Motherfucker! I'm gon get yo ass! You wait and see!"

Man stood there, bloody, watching his friend Solly run toward Twenty-fourth, with Sofia Sweeney and the other curious people still watching. He saw two women, who had come out on the sidewalk across the street, shake their heads in disgust. One old woman called across to the old man: "Mister Simon did you ever see anything like it?" and Mister Simon in his weak voice called back: "This here used to be a *good* neighborhood." And women on both sides of the street chorused: "Ain't it the truth."

Man turned around and walked slowly back up the steps, picked up the brick and tossed it down into the yard, and walked on up to the porch, picked up his coffee cup, turned around and opened the screen door and stepped into the house.

When he finished washing his face and hands, he stumbled into the bedroom and sat on the side of the bed. Holding his face in his hands, he bent his face down to his knees. He was in shock. How could this have happened? How could he and Solly have come to blows? This was the last thing he would ever have guessed. Never should have said anything about Holly being here. Lipped off one time too many. Shoulda stayed outta it. He suddenly sat up straight, making fists, leaving them on his thighs. Then he smashed his right fist against the bed. But that wasn't enough. He almost had a taste for a sip of hush-mouth he was so pissed.

He got up and walked over to the mirror on the back of the closet door and just stood looking at himself in the half-light, watching the grays, the browns, the soft blues of himself, and around him, behind him, the lighted windows through the glass. Then before he knew it he felt his fist smash into the glass, breaking it, causing dark cracks to crawl out in two directions from the point of impact. One line moved up right at about a forty-five-degree angle and the other went off left and down at about a sixty. Then he looked at his fist. Not a scratch.

CLEO WAS AT WORK AND HIS KID was up at North Star. It was a little past ten in the morning when Man walked down to Twenty-fourth, out of habit, but not for a drink. He was about to enter the Palace for a Coca-Cola when he saw Percy standing across the street in front of Miss Etta's. Percy motioned for him to come over.

CHAPTER THIRTY-NINE

When Man got over there, Percy was grinning and his eyes had their usual glazed look. "Where you been hanging out, nigger? I don't see much of you anymore now that you don't drink no more and you a bigshot at the Palace. Folks tell me you packing em in like never before. Don't you hang out anymore?"

Man grinned and said, "I been around. Whas up?"

"You *know* what's up. New York's winning. That's what." Percy kept an unchanging grin that seemed to have glued his mouth open.

"Oh. Yeah," Man said. He remembered the bet. He'd bet Percy ten dollars Philly would beat the shit out of New York in the World Series. The games had started. He knew that but hadn't been paying much attention. "Who winning?"

"Ain't you something? Who's winning? *New York* is winning, punk. That's who. You might as well hand over the ten dollars right now."

"They ain't won it yet."

Percy's expression changed suddenly. "I'm hungry. I wants me some sausage and eggs. I can't drink no more liquor on this empty stomach of mine. You had breakfast?"

"Naw. I guess I could eat something too."

No car was coming so they walked across the street on the red light.

On the other side Percy said, "Too bad about your boy."

Man looked at Percy. "What?"

"Solly. You know, don't you?"

"Know what?"

They kept walking past the Palace, past Webster's Tailor Shop where, just inside the shabby doorway, Mister Webster, frail and bent, was pinning the hem of a blue wool dress on a stout lady who seemed to be holding her breath as she gazed piously at the ceiling. On the far wall was a picture-calendar of Jesus with raised hand and raised eyes, just like the lady's.

"Solly lost his mind. Went crazy on me. I had to fire him." Percy shook his head. "Solly ain't yet figured out that the price of his hat ain't the measure of his brain."

"What happened?" Man felt a tightness in his chest.

They walked past the office of the *Messenger*. Through the opened door, Man saw the reception desk and a pretty young woman at it painting her fingernails red. Red, his color for life, for sex, the color that screams. Behind her the door to the publisher's office stood open. The publisher, heavy and middle-aged, with jowls, in a striped but badly worn suit, a fellow Man knew on sight but whose name he didn't know, sat at his desk looking important. The publisher sometimes came into the Palace trying to get Jorena to buy ad space.

Percy was still talking. "Came down there too drunk to work. Scared the living shit outta that old white man Oscar. Talking all that loud nigger talk. Oscar came close to shooting em. Would have too, if I hadn't stepped in. Told Oscar that the boy's wife left him and he was upset. Oscar put his gun away."

Man opened the greasy door of Carter's Cafe and let Percy go in first. The strong smell of red pepper–spiced sausage hit Man in the face. The air was thick with stale and fresh cigarette smoke, harsh stove smoke, and rancid grease. The tables were full but three of the six seats at the counter were empty.

Man was thinking, Holy shit, holy shit. Miss Viola Blossom, the owner, another woman so heavy she could barely walk, said good morning to them as they sat down. She was standing behind the counter down at the end. They returned the greeting, Percy greeting her the loudest, saying something about the weather, about winter coming. And she started walking up the counter and squeezed past the two waitresses—one of them, Dora, her daughter—and waddled on up to the cash register at the front. Grunting and huffing, she sat down in her high chair—a huge old baby—and looked back down the counter.

Dora, a nice-looking dark brown young woman with hair curled under all the way around, stood in front of them smiling, waiting, yellow pencil poised over small white pad. Over her shoulder Man could see the cook, Floyd Love, with gold teeth all across the top front, back there at the big black hot stove, cooking up a smelly storm, lard popping and the sound of Floyd's scraper scratching in the big skillet.

While Man read the menu—handwritten on a hard piece of gray cardboard—checking out things he could order, Percy was eyeing the other waitress, Carla. She was pretty, with long curly brown hair tinted red. And *very* married. Man knew that because Solly had tried once to hit on her and got told off.

Now Percy ordered eggs, sausage, grits, and coffee. At Carter's, free biscuits came with breakfast.

Then Man said, "I'll have the same." And handed Dora the menu back. Then when Dora walked away, Man said, "So you fired Solly."

Percy shook his head. "Too bad too, cause I like Solly. Solly a good old boy. He just got to get himself straightened out. Got to grow up some. Got to learn that pussy and fine clothes ain't everything. Got to get this idea outta his head the world owe him something. Ain't no nigger in his right mind got no business walking round thinking like that." Percy laughed.

Dora brought two glasses filled with ice water then went back and brought steaming hot coffee.

"So what happened? What he do to get fired?"

Percy looked at Man. "Just like you, coming to work drunk. Cept he was worser: starting all that loud talking at Oscar. That mighta been enough to get his ass booted outta there. But I was trying to be good-hearted, thinking maybe he could push a broom a little bit and sober up some. I seen boys come in there drunk before and once they start swinging a mop they get sober real fast, sweat all that poison outta they bodies. So I was gonna be Mister Nice and not send Solly home, you see. You member Solly worked the fifth floor—luggage, gifts, and shit?"

"Yeah. Other side over from the kitchen stuff and the snack bar."

"That's right. Well, I figured, cause he was drunk, I'm gonna keep him close by me where I can watch his ass. So I put Orson up there and kept Solly down there with me on the first floor in men's clothing. He was spose to do both, men's then children's on second. I was on the mezzanine part of the time. You know, I'm always down on first and the mezzanine."

"Don't tell me he went to sleep on the job?"

Percy laughed. "I wish it was that simple. That ain't nothing compared to what he did."

"Yeah?"

"After about a hour I goes up to check on Solly, and I find him messing around. He ain't swept nothing yet. Broom lying gainst one of them counters. I said, Look, Solly, you gon get to work or I'm sending your ass home. I'm trying to give you a break."

"Yeah?"

"Went back a hour later and there was the nigger all dressed up in one of them suits off the rack standing in front of the mirror drinking straight from a bottle of liquor. Just standing there *admiring* himself."

"What'd you do?" Man could see Solly. The image brought a slight smile to his face. But his heart also beat faster for Solly. It was like seeing part of one's self tossed out into the ocean unable to swim.

274

Percy laughed. "I made him take off the suit and he spilled whiskey all over the damned suit trying to take it off."

Dora brought both hot plates and sat them down. Looking at the food, Man suddenly knew how hungry he was. He picked up his fork and forced it into the sausage. At the same time, he picked up one of the two biscuits and bit into it. Then put the sausage piece into his mouth and chewed both together. He managed this without taking his eyes off Percy for more than a second or two. Said: "Then what'd he do?"

Percy started eating, making Man wait for an answer. Then he said, "He didn't have to do *nothing*. That was when Oscar came. Walked right down the aisle and stood there beside me, looking at Solly with the whiskey bottle in one hand, the suit on the floor, his clothes on the floor, standing there in his underwear. Well, that was it. Nothing I could do from that point on to save his ass. Oscar saw everything."

"What you say to Solly?"

"I told the nigger he had to go home."

Man said, "What Oscar do?"

"Ready to call the cops but I stopped him, said give the boy a chance. Solly didn't mean no harm. Wont stealing nothing, just acting silly, trying on a suit. So, me and Oscar marched him to the mezzanine door and put him out."

"You didn't fire him on the spot?"

"Naw. I got a policy. I never fire a drunk man. I wait until they sober up. Smith fired him the next day. Called that landlady—what's her name, Miss Ernestine?—where he lives and left the message."

Man thought: Just like he fired me, calling my sister's house and leaving a message. Man and Percy ate for a while in silence. Feel like dice thrown in gambling, just like dice. Blues ain't nothing but staying alive. Then Percy said, "What's this I hear about you and Solly falling out?"

"Long story."

They paid and left tips.

Outside, they stood in front of the cafe, Percy picking his teeth with a toothpick, gazing sleepily up the street in the direction of Lake. "So how come you and Solly ain't talking no more? Yall was like blood brothers."

Man didn't want to talk about it. Said: "Yeah." He suspected Solly would soon return to Chicago if he hadn't already gone. Point me to the Chicago track, point me, brother, to the Chicago track, gon keep right on going, never come back. Train whistle blowing, taking me back where it's snowing.

"You ain't gon tell me?"

Then Man simply told Percy the story right down to the detail of the fistfight that almost ended with a brick to the head. He felt horrible about the loss of Solly's friendship, about lost Solly. As if whiskey and hard times weren't enough, he had to lose his best friend. Oh crap-shooter, oh crapshooter, where you gon throw yo dice? When you done already lost twice?

Percy whistled. "That cat's losing his cool, blowing his stack. *You* the best friend he had. Now his wife put his ass down. What the fuck is he trying to do to hisself?"

Man felt bad. "And he was, uh, the best friend I had. Friends for a long time."

"So you want to come back to work? Tired of loafing?" Percy was grinning.

Man wasn't ready for that. "Uh, I don't think so, Percy."

"That unemployment shit don't last forever. You must be close to running out?"

"Got one mo check coming." Man grinned, holding up one finger.

"It's gon get cold out here." Percy looked around. "If you wanna come back you got to let me know soon. I can get Smith to take you back. You was a good worker. And you ain't drinking no mo. But I gots to hire somebody quick."

"I'll think about it." But he didn't mean it. All he could think about was his growing success at the Palace. The last couple of times Jorena had given him seventy-five dollars and his total weekend tip take had been over a hundred. When people were drinking and having a good time they were generous.

Man walked with Percy up to where his car was parked on Lake around the corner from Miss Etta's. "You need a lift?"

"Naw. Thanks. Catch you later, Percy."

◉

Booting it up Twenty-fourth, Man smiled to himself. Life was funny. It was hard to imagine not being friends with Solly any longer. And yet here he was friendless, sober, west of the wide Missouri, jobless, saxophone-less, but strangely with a lot still to feel good about. If he only could. Got Cleo. She ain't gone nowhere. Got things going nice at the Palace. No craving. Ain't raving. Doing mo than hanging on. Any day now something. Don't know what but *something* could give. Time. Just gots to take yo time. Own sweet time. He could hear the rhythm of his footfalls, a music: slap do blap, slap do blap, slap do blap, slap do blap. Time. All it takes is time. Something could give. Something big. Something real. Things be changing all the time. Never can tell what gon come round the corner and step on yo toes, or kiss you between the eyes, shake yo hand, and lead you on.

MAN DECIDED HE'D GO AND TRY
to talk with Solly, to apologize, if neces- **CHAPTER**
sary, though he still felt it was Solly's place to **FORTY**
do that. Walking the short distance, he got into
a nice rhythm. George Washington cut down trees.
Little George cut down some trees. Elephants got four knees. Lord
knows elephants got four knees. Santa Claus got his bags. I'm out here
freezing in my rags. Had to laugh at himself. Sometimes he felt like he
was still a kid. Maybe always would be.

Miss Ernestine came to the door and opened it, glaring at him.
"What'd *you* want?" she snapped, and before he could respond, said,
"You listen to me. Your old no-good friend don't live here anymore. Left
here without paying me my last month's rent too. If I find him I'm going
to get the police on him. You can just tell him that for me." And more to
herself than to Man, she said, "No-good niggers make me sick."

"He didn't say where he was moving to?"

"I know the cabdriver who picked him up. Decent church-boy named
Roy. Roy says he drove him downtown to the Union Bus Station on
Sixteenth. The Chicago and North Western goes out from there to
Chicago. He would have gone to the Douglas Street Station for the
Burlington or the Arrow or to Fifteenth Street for the Missouri or Pacific
bus. So he probably took his old no-good ass back to Chicago to try to
get his wife back. She's a fool if she takes him back. She left him, you
know, and I don't blame her. No-good drinking niggers never meant nobody any good, not even themselves. I've learned my lesson, I tell you.
My father was a minister. My folks been in this town for generations. My
grandparents helped rebuild this community after the tornado of 1913. I
was among the first to invest in the North Side Bank of Florence eleven
years ago. I helped rebuild businesses out here seven years ago, after the
flood. I'm a respected person out here. I come from *fine* stock, respec-
table people. And you can *believe* me, from now on, I'm renting rooms to
only folks that belong to churches—Methodists and Baptists people, voting people, NAACP people, people in the Urban League. No more
riffraff. Only decent family folks. Why, I could have rented that place up
there a dozen times to *good* people stopping in here asking for rooms.
One lady sent over here by her lady's fraternity, but, no, I was too good-
hearted—"

"Thank you, thank you, Miss Ernestine, thank you," he said, backing away and waving to her.

⊙

Friday afternoon. Man knocked on Percy's door. Francine opened it, grinning in his face. "Come on in, Fred. He just woke up."

"Thanks, Francine." Man walked out onto the back porch and waited for Percy.

Percy came out, rubbing his chin, sleepy-looking, and sat down beside Man. He yawned and stretched his arms above his head. Said: "What you into today?"

"Just come to give you yo money."

"What money?"

"Yo ten dollars. The ten dollars you won off the bet."

"*Oooh!*" Percy flashed a grin, showing his long, cigarette-stained upper row. "Yeah. How bout that? Give me my money. New York beat the shit outta Philadelphia. National League ain't never been able to touch the American League no way. Give me my money." He kept grinning, and now holding out his hand.

> You gots to give yo mama some,
> You gots to give yo daddy some.

Soon after this, late one afternoon, he had picked up Karina and was resting on the couch, waiting for Cleo to get home. Karina was sitting on the floor playing nearby.

He has to be somewhere and time is running out. He is in a hazy world, walking on eggshells. Catcalls in the background. His skin feels like eelskin but he's dressed in a suit, and Cleo is with him. She's in her Sunday best. And he has Cleo's hand and they're running through a dark cold building big as Sears, maybe it's Sears, but a gutted Sears, with no lights. Birds—glossy ibises, cedar waxwings, ospreys—are flying overhead, screaming. Pipes are clicking and water is running in the background. He steps on a hagfish and slips, almost falls. But keeps going. Cleo's palm is sweating in his own. They're into a buzzard lope. Man has an appointment somewhere in this black building, and he's already late, but there are no names on doors, no doors, and though there is the sense that there is a floor, possibly two, three, or more floors above them, there is no way to get up there, no stairway, no elevators. They run past a door that stands

*alone with nothing around it. It's painted green. Is it Good
Friday? One of Cleo's fake-gold earrings drops to the muddy
floor. They keep going, searching. A gut-curling sound echoes
through the place. Maybe somebody cutting a goat's throat. I
may be crazy but I sho ain't lazy, he thinks, as they slow
down. Cleo says, "Maybe we have the wrong building." But
he knows this is the right one as they wade through a puddle
of black water, going farther back into the structure. Back
here there is a symphony of babbling voices: hag-hollering,
mad dogs yelping, thousands of crickets chirping, the sound
of a guinea fowl captured. At the rear of the building they
come upon an oak door, only the second door in the whole
place, and it's brightly lighted and has a gold nameplate
at eye level:* MANFRED BANKS. *Has to be a coincidence
because Man knows this is not his office. Man lightly knocks
at the door and it opens onto a giant open space, an office
without walls. A greenish white sky is behind the elderly
businessman sitting at a long desk. He waves them over and
gestures toward the two plush chairs facing his desk. Man
and Cleo are suddenly sitting facing this older fellow in a
business suit. Man can't tell if the guy is black or white: he's
gray with green light around him. His face is that of a paso
fino horse. "My uncle and I own this company," the horse-
faced man says. "After my parents died in a car accident in
Camden I went into business with my uncle. Back then he
used to go all around the South with one of those big old
two-ton crank-up recording machines. He had to go out in
cotton fields where the real blues singers, like Son House and
Charlie Patton, were, out where they had no electricity to
record those great singers. Now, we are proud to add your
name." Man feels his chest swell as he says, "Well, shoot
me lightly and let me die politely. I must be dancing on my
good foot!"*

⊙

The sound of Karina running through the bedroom woke him from his
happy dream. He shook his head and slowly sat up, going through the
dream again, step by step, wondering at the clearness of it.

Now he heard Cleo out in the hallway greeting Karina. He heard the
door close, heard her coming down the hall, through the bedroom.

And there she was, smiling, and carrying Karina against her bosom,
coming toward the living room.

He got up and met his wife and daughter.